PENGUIN BOOKS

BREATHLESS

D0718888

30131 05722723 0

LONDON BOROUGH OF BARNET

ALSO BY JENNIFER NIVEN

All the Bright Places

Holding Up the Universe

BREATHLESS

Jennifer Niven

PENGUIN BOOKS

PENGUIN BOOKS

UK | USA | Canada | Ireland | Australia
India | New Zealand | South Africa

Penguin Books is part of the Penguin Random House group of companies
whose addresses can be found at global.penguinrandomhouse.com.

www.penguin.co.uk
www.puffin.co.uk
www.ladybird.co.uk

First published in the USA by Alfred A. Knopf,
a division of Penguin Random House LLC,
and in Great Britain by Penguin Books 2020

001

Text copyright © Jennifer Niven, 2020

The moral right of the author has been asserted

Printed and bound in Great Britain by Clays Ltd, Elcograf S.p.A.

A CIP catalogue record for this book is available from the British Library

ISBN: 978-0-241-37192-3
International paperback ISBN: 978-0-241-50220-4

All correspondence to:
Penguin Books
Penguin Random House Children's
One Embassy Gardens, 8 Viaduct Gardens, London SW11 7BW

MIX
Paper from
responsible sources
FSC® C018179
www.fsc.org

Penguin Random House is committed to a
sustainable future for our business, our readers
and our planet. This book is made from Forest
Stewardship Council® certified paper.

For Justin,
the real Jeremiah Crew.
I love you more than words.

Nobody has ever measured,

not even poets,

how much the heart can hold.

—Zelda Fitzgerald

You were my first. Not just sex, although that was part of it, but the first to look past everything else into me.

Some of the names and places have been changed, but the story is true. It's all here because one day this will be the past, and I don't want to forget what I went through, what I thought, what I felt, who I was. I don't want to forget you.

But most of all, I don't want to forget me.

MARY GROVE, OHIO

8 DAYS TILL GRADUATION

I open my eyes and I am tangled in the sheets, books upside down on the floor. I know without looking at the time that I'm late. I leap out of bed, one foot still wrapped in the sheet, and land flat on my face. I lie there a minute. Close my eyes. Wonder if I can pretend I've fainted and convince Mom to let me blow off today and stay home.

It's peaceful on the floor.

But it also smells a bit. I open an eye and there's something ground into the rug. One of Dandelion's cat treats, maybe. I turn my head to the other side and it's better over here, but then from outside I hear a horn blast, and this is my dad.

So now I'm up and on my feet because he will just keep honking and honking the stupid horn until I'm in the car. I can't find one of my books and one of my shoes, and my hair is wrong and my outfit is wrong, and basically *I* am wrong in my own skin. I should have been born French. If I were French, everything would be right. I would be chic and cool and ride a bike to school, one with a basket. I would be able to ride a bike in the first place. If I were living in Paris instead of Mary Grove, Ohio, these flats would look better with this skirt, my hair would be less orange red—the color of an heirloom tomato—and I would somehow make more sense.

I scramble into my parents' room dressed in my skirt and bikini

3

top, the black one I bought with Saz last month, the one I plan to live in this summer. All my bras are in the wash. My mom's closet is neat and tidy, but lacking the order of my dad's, which is all black, gray, navy, everything organized by color because he's colorblind and this way he doesn't have to ask all the time, "Is this green or brown?" I rummage through the shelf above and then his dresser drawers, searching for the shirt I want: vintage 1993 Nirvana. I am always stealing this shirt and he is always stealing it back, but now it's nowhere.

I stand in the doorway and shout down the hall, toward the stairs, toward my mom. "Where's Dad's Nirvana shirt?" I've decided that this and only this is the thing I want to wear today.

I wait two, three, four, five seconds, and my only answer is another blast of the horn. I run to my room and grab the first shirt I see and throw it on, even though I haven't worn it to school since freshman year. Miss Piggy with sparkles.

At the front door, my mom says, "I'll come get you if Saz can't bring you home." My mom is a busy, well-known writer—historical novels, nonfiction, anything to do with history—but she always has time for me. When we moved into this house, we turned the guest room into her office and my dad spent two days building floor-to-ceiling bookcases to hold her hundreds of research books.

Something must show on my face because she rests her hands on my shoulders and goes, "Hey. It's going to be okay." And she means my best friend, Suzanne Bakshi (better known as Saz), and me, that we'll always be friends in spite of graduation and college and all the life to come. I feel some of her calm, bright energy settling itself, like a bird in a tree, onto my shoulders, melting down

4

my arms, into my limbs, into my blood. This is one of the many things my mom does best. She makes everyone feel better.

In the car, my dad is wearing his Radiohead T-shirt under a suit jacket, which means the Nirvana shirt is in the wash. I make a mental note to snag it when I get home so I can wear it to the party tonight.

For the first three or four minutes, we don't talk, but this is also normal. Unlike my mom, my dad and I are not morning people, and on the drive to school we like to maintain what he calls "companionable silence," something Saz refuses to respect, which is why I don't ride with her.

I stare out the window at the low black clouds that are gathering like mourners in the direction of the college, where my dad works as an administrator. It's not supposed to rain, but it looks like rain, and it makes me worry for Trent Dugan's party. My weekends are usually spent with Saz, driving around town, searching for something to do, but this one is going to be different. Last official party of senior year and all.

My dad sails past the high school, over Main Street Bridge, into downtown Mary Grove, which is approximately ten blocks of stores lining the brick-paved streets, better known as the Promenade. He roars to a stop at the westernmost corner, where the street gives way to cobbled brick and fountains. He gets out and jogs into the Joy Ann Cake Shop while I text Saz a photo of the sign over the door. Who's your favorite person?

In a second she replies: You are.

Two minutes later my dad is jogging back to the car, arms raised overhead in some sort of ridiculous victory dance, white paper bag in one hand. He gets in, slams the door, and tosses me the bag filled with our usual—one chocolate cupcake for Saz and a pound of thumbprint cookies for Dad and me, which we devour

5

on the way to the high school. Our secret morning ritual since I was twelve.

As I eat, I stare at the cloudy, cloudy sky. "It might rain."

My dad says, "It won't rain," like he once said, "He won't hit you," about Damian Green, who threatened to punch me in the mouth in third grade because I wouldn't let him cheat off me. *He won't hit you,* which implied that if necessary my dad would come over to the school and punch Damian himself, because no one was going to mess with his daughter, not even an eight-year-old boy.

"It might," I say, just so I can hear it again, the protectiveness in his voice. It's a protectiveness that reminds me of being five, six, seven, back when I rode everywhere on his shoulders.

He says, "It won't."

In first-period creative writing, my teacher, Mr. Russo, keeps me after class to say, "If you really want to write, and I believe you do, you're going to have to put it all out there so that we can feel what you feel. You always seem to be holding back, Claudine."

He says some good things too, but this will be what I remember—that he doesn't think I can feel. It's funny how the bad things stay with you and the good things sometimes get lost. I leave his classroom and tell myself he doesn't begin to know me or what I can do. He doesn't know that I'm already working on my first novel and that I'm going to be a famous writer one day, that my mom has let me help her with research projects since I was ten, the same year I started writing stories. He doesn't know that I actually do put myself out there.

On my way to third period, Shane Waller, the boy I've been seeing for almost two months, corners me at my locker and says, "Should I pick you up for Trent's party?"

Shane smells good and can be funny when he puts his mind to it, which—along with my raging hormones—are the main reasons I'm with him. I say, "I'm going with Saz. But I'll see you there." Which is fine with Shane, because ever since I was fifteen, my dad has notoriously made all my dates wait outside, even in the dead of Ohio winter. This is because he was once a teenage boy and knows what they're thinking. And because he likes to make sure *they* know *he* knows exactly what they're thinking.

Shane says, "See you there, babe." And then, to prove to myself and Mr. Russo and everyone else at Mary Grove High that I am an actual living, feeling person, I do something I never do—I kiss him, right there in the school hallway.

When we break apart, he leans in and I feel his breath in my ear. "I can't wait." And I know he thinks—hopes—we're going to have sex. The same way he's been hoping for the past two months that I'll finally decide my days of being a virgin are over and "give it up to him." (His words, not mine. As if somehow my virginity belongs to him.)

I say this to Saz at lunch, and she laughs this booming, maniacal laugh, head thrown back, dark hair swinging, and raises her water bottle in a mock toast. "Good luck to you, Shane!" Because we both know there's only one boy in Mary Grove, Ohio, I want my first time to be with, and it isn't Shane Waller. Even though I tell myself maybe one day he'll say something so exceptionally funny and I'll get so lost in the smell of his neck that I'll change my mind and sleep with him after all. Just because I don't think Shane's the one doesn't mean I don't *want* him to be.

I say a version of this out loud. "You never know. He can be really funny."

Saz says, "He can be kind of funny." She gathers her hair—heavy and straight and the bane of her existence—up on her head

7

and holds it there. She is always cutting it off and growing it back, cutting it off and growing it back.

"Would it be so bad for Shane to be my first?"

Our friend Alannis Vega-Torres drops into the seat next to me. "Yes." She digs a soda and protein bar out of her bag and tosses Saz a couple of hair ties. "By the way, it doesn't count as losing your virginity if your hymen doesn't break. I bled buckets my first time."

"That's not true," I say. "Hymens don't actually break. That's a big, fat, ignorant myth. Not everyone bleeds, and besides, not everyone has a hymen. Don't be so heteronormative. Virginity is a bullshit social construct created by the patriarchy." Saz holds up her hand and I high-five her. As much as I completely, one hundred percent believe this, I'm still desperate to have sex. Like, *right now.*

Our other friend, Mara Choi, throws herself down across from Alannis, cardigan buttoned up wrong, tampons and lip gloss spilling out of her backpack because—except when she's in the presence of her traditional Korean grandmother—she lives in a constant state of chaos. She disappears under the table, gathering the things that fell. She says from under it, "Fun fact: Did you know you can order hymens on the internet? There's this place called the Hymen Shop that claims they can restore your virginity in five minutes." She pops back up, picks up her phone, and immediately starts googling.

"The hell?" Saz rolls her eyes at me like, *These two.*

I look at her like, *I know,* as Mara starts reading from the Hymen Shop website. "Says here they use medical-grade red dye that looks just like human blood. Oh, and they are the 'original and most trusted brand of artificial hymens.'"

Saz says, "What a thing to be known for."

Alannis says, "That's nothing. I read somewhere that girls in China pay seven hundred dollars to have their hymens surgically rebuilt."

I stop eating because, sex-obsessed as I am, the idea that you could place a price on virginity is, to put it mildly, insane. I say, "This whole concept is so antiquated. As if all that matters is penis-plus-vagina sex. Something like twenty percent of Americans identify as something *other* than completely straight, so why are we still so focused on a *woman's* first time with a *man*? And why is a girl's virginity such a big deal anyway? People don't get excited about a straight guy having sex. It's all high fives and 'Now you're a man.' They don't sit around wringing their hands and searching the internet for replacement parts."

Saz snorts. I'm on a roll.

"And another thing. Have you ever thought about the way people talk about virginity? As if it's owned by *other* people? Someone 'takes it,' and suddenly it becomes theirs. Like it's something we give away, something that doesn't belong to us. She *lost* it. She *gave it up. Popping* her cherry. *Taking* her virginity. *Deflowering*—"

"*Deflowering?*" Mara stares at me over her phone. "Who says *deflowering*?"

"Virgins." Alannis raises her perfectly groomed eyebrows at me. Alannis Gyalene Catalina Vega-Torres has been having sex since ninth grade.

"Why do you always single me out?" I wave pointedly at Saz, my partner in virtue. When we were ten, Saz and I promised to celebrate every one of life's milestones at the same time, including falling in love and having our first real relationship—which would, of course, include sex—so that we would never leave each other behind. It was our way of making sure we always put each other first and never let anyone come between us. Alannis pats my arm like I'm a poor, confused child.

Mara's face is back in her phone. "It's only thirty bucks to 'turn back the clock and bring the va-va-voom back to the bedroom.' " And that's it. We fall apart at this.

Saz sings out, "To va-va-voom in the bedroom!" The four of us clink cans and bottles.

And then we forget all about artificial hymens and virginity and stare as Kristin McNish walks through the cafeteria like a perfectly timed public-service announcement, with her chin jutting out and an unmistakable bump around her middle.

At home, I dig through the laundry pile, but the Nirvana shirt is still nowhere to be found. I find a black minidress lying on my floor and settle for my dad's Ramones shirt, which I throw on over it. For dinner, Mom and I order from Pizza King because Dad has a work thing and he's the cook in the family, his specialty being elaborate meals paired with theme music and wine. Saz loves eating at my house because it's almost always an event, but I love eating at hers. The Bakshis eat at the bar in the kitchen or in front of the TV—takeout, fast food, or Kraft macaroni and cheese, best thing on earth, something I never get at home unless I make it myself. My dad refuses to cook any food that requires you to add orange powder to it.

When I open the door to the delivery boy now, the one Saz calls Mean Jake, even though his name is Matthew and he isn't mean at all, I'm like, "Well, hey, you," as seductively as possible.

He goes, "We were out of ginger ale, so I brought you Sprite instead."

* * *

Later that night, I lie in Trent Dugan's hayloft, underneath Shane Waller, my senses in overdrive, lost in the heat of his skin and the smell of his neck. I'm thinking, *Maybe this will be it. Maybe I'll lose it right here, right now.*

It's what I love about making out with someone. The possibility that this could be the one. Cue the lights. Cue the music. Love raining down on us all. Not that I'm all that experienced, especially compared to Alannis. I've officially given a few hand jobs and three or four unsuccessful blow jobs, had five and a half orgasms—not including the ones I've given myself—and made out with three boys, counting this one.

Shane is kissing me, and his hands are everywhere—*Oh yeah,* I think, *there. That's good.* The kissing is strictly for my benefit because Shane, like a lot of other guys at Mary Grove High, is more about all the things that aren't kissing. His goal, always, is to get in my pants. I know this and he knows this, and he will kiss me for a while just to get there. And I'll let him because he's actually good at it, and hey, I love kissing.

And then all he's doing is grabbing me, but it's working because he's so obviously into me that I'm starting to feel a bit into me too.

I think, *Don't let it get too far,* even as I'm helping him unzip his jeans. And then we're kissing again, harder and harder until I half expect him to inhale my tongue and my mouth and my entire face, and in the moment I want him to because of the way my body is pressing into his, wanting to feel more. I feel swept away and powerful at the same time. *What are you waiting for?*

Shane has his tongue in my ear, but I can still hear the music outside. Laughter. Someone yelling something. At first I'm like, *Oh God, yes,* but then his tongue is a little too wet and he's giving

11

me swimmer's ear. I want to push him away and shake the saliva out, but then he says, "God, you're so hot."

Being hot is not what I'm known for, so I kiss him a while longer. But then I can't get over the fact that we're making out in a barn. At first I think, *Okay, this is kind of sexy* and *Oh, look at me,* but now I'm not sure I believe it. I imagine losing it to Shane Waller here in this hayloft, but of all the ways I've pictured my first time, it's never once been in a barn.

Then he gives my underwear a tug, chasing the thoughts away. Leaving just Shane and me, nearly naked on top of all this straw, which is jabbing into my flesh like sharp little pencils. It's funny that I haven't really noticed the straw before this moment because I've been so swept up in the feeling of my flesh against Shane's flesh, the little fireworks that are springing up between body parts, threatening to set the hayloft on fire. This isn't the first time I've been nearly naked with Shane Waller, but it's the first time in a barn. I feel drunk, even though I'm not, and some far-flung part of me worries that if I can get turned on under these circumstances—sharp, jabbing straw, drunken classmates yelling outside—I will probably sleep with too many boys in college. Because making out is that much fun, even when you aren't in love. Sometimes it's just about his mouth or his eyes or his hands or the way they work all together. Sometimes that's enough.

Shane's hands are snaking their way down, and the thinking, responsible part of me—the one that's saving herself for a boy named Wyatt Jones—mentally pulls back into the hay, just enough to separate from him, even as the physical part of me keeps right on going. I try to lose myself in him again, but the only thing I can feel is a million straw pencils digging into my back and the fireworks fizzling to an end so that all that's left is the after-haze and a distant burning smell.

12

Suddenly there's something hard and damp against my thigh, and I shift a little so he can't slide it in.

"Claude . . ."

His voice is blurred, like he's out of focus, and my name sounds like *Clod,* which I hate. I feel momentarily bad because I was never going to have sex with him. It always ends the same way—him coming into the air or into his shirt or onto himself or against my leg.

Saz says I feel safe in my virginity, like Rapunzel in her tower. That I let down my hair just enough, enjoying the shine of it in the sun and the way it temporarily blinds the poor bastard waiting on the ground, before I yank it back up out of reach. And maybe I do feel safe in it, not just because I'm saving it for Wyatt Jones, but because my life is safe and Saz and I are best friends and I actually like my parents and I don't have anything to prove to anyone. It's my body and I can do what I want.

Shane is staring at me and his eyes are rolling and his breath is coming faster and faster, and he's humping my leg like a dog. His face is half lit from the sliver of moon that shines through the crack in the door. I'll give him this: he's pretty good-looking and he smells nice. And for whatever reason he seems to like me. From what he can tell right now, I'm still in it. I haven't told him to stop or pushed him away. Until he strays a little too far from my leg and I go, "Slow it down, cowboy."

He's going to tell his friends either that I'm a tease or that we did it. I wish I could explain that it's not about teasing or doing it; it's about the *possibility.* It's the almost. It's the *Maybe this time,* the *Maybe he's the one.* I want to say, *For a few minutes I make you greater than yourself, and I'm greater than myself, and we're greater than this barn because we are all this possibility and almostness and maybe.*

But you can't explain things like almostness to a guy like Shane, so I maneuver my lower half away from him, and that's when he groans and explodes. All over my inner thigh. And this is where I freak out a little, because I swear I can feel some of it dripping into me, and I roll over fast, pushing him away.

He groans again and falls back onto the hay. I use his shirt to wipe myself off and then I untangle my dress from around my shoulders and smooth everything into place, and I can already hear what I'm going to say to Saz, the funny little spin I'll put on it just for her: *Unlike so many of our classmates here in farm country, I guess I'm just not a person destined for barn sex.*

I stand up, and to make conversation, I say, "Did you know the Germans used to have a specific word for a male virgin? A *Jüngling*. Doesn't it sound like it means the exact opposite?" I'm an almanac of virgin trivia, especially in awkward situations when I don't know what else to say.

Shane says from the hay, "You know, you're like this series of boxes, and every time I open one, there's another one inside. It's like box after fucking box, and I don't think anyone will ever be able to open all of them." He gets up, pulls on his jeans, pulls on his wet, crumpled shirt.

He stares down at the stain and I say, "Sorry."

"It's my fucking Snoop Dogg shirt. Jesus, Claude." *Clod.*

I say, "I think we should just be friends." *Better to have too many boxes than not enough.*

He says, "No shit," and leaves me there.

I find Saz at an old weathered-looking picnic table, talking to a group of people that includes Alannis and Mara, as well as Yvonne Brittain-Muir, musician and gamer, and her girlfriend of three hundred years, Leah Basco. For the past few weeks, Saz and I have envisioned every possible scenario in which Yvonne dumps Leah and professes her undying love for Saz. Or at least agrees to have sex with her.

One of the guys passes around a joint, and another is telling this long story about the college party he went to last weekend. Leah holds out her hand to Yvonne—pale as a ghost in the moonlight, long yellow hair dyed blue at the ends—and they go rambling off toward the barn of iniquity, Saz staring after them like they just ran over her dog.

I say to her, "Do you want to leave?" Even though it's not even eleven o'clock.

"More than anything on earth."

I throw my arm around her and we walk across the field toward the house and the long gravel driveway where we parked. As we go, I sing Saz the cheer-up song we made up when we were ten: "Ice cream, ice cream, freezy, freezy. You can get over her easy, easy."

A lone figure comes toward us, and Saz is jabbing at my ribs, going, "Stop it, maniac, before someone hears you," which makes me sing louder, and then the figure steps into the moonlight and of course it's Wyatt Jones. Like that, I forget about Saz and Yvonne and Shane and boxes and everything else that came before this moment.

Wyatt is going away soon, across the country, across the world, to California and girls with long, swinging hair and sundresses. A fact that makes him seem taller and separate from the rest of us. Saz and I were supposed to go to California too, where I would find him and get to know him, strangers in a strange land, initially bonded by our unfortunate Midwestern roots, and then— gradually—as two worldly adults who discover they are destined to be together.

Wyatt catches my eye, and my bones turn to liquid. There's a rumor that he likes me. That he wanted to ask me to prom but was too shy to do it. That the reason he and three of his friends toilet-papered my house two months ago was because somehow I was special. Until my dad the marathon runner interrupted them and *chased them around the neighborhood on foot.* I break our gaze now and stare at my own feet because the memory is still mortifying.

"Hey," he says.

"Hey," I say back.

I make myself look at him again. Deep brown eyes, light brown skin, broad shoulders, smiling mouth. Even though my lips are still throbbing from all the kissing I was doing *minutes ago,* I want his hands on me.

"You leaving?"

"Yeah."

"Too bad." He breaks into a full-on smile, as blinding as the sun, and everything fades away except for the two of us. His dad is black, his mom is white, and she died when he was a baby. He doesn't remember her, but he always says she gave him his smile.

He's saying something else right now, but it's drowned out by music and laughter and someone screaming. We turn at the same exact moment, and it's Kayla Rosenthal, who always screams at parties. She's standing on the picnic table, waving her drink around like a human sprinkler.

He nods in her direction. "And she got a scholarship to Notre Dame." I laugh a little too hard. "Did you come with Waller?" he asks me.

"No, but he's here somewhere." I wave my hand like, *Whatever,* and hope these five words imply everything he needs to know: *I don't care where he is because he's nothing to me. It's you, Wyatt. It's always been you.*

He nods again, like he's thinking this over. "Hey, congrats on salutatorian."

"Thanks."

"Does that mean you give one of the graduation speeches?"

"A shorter one, but yeah." Jasmine Ramundo gets to speak for ten minutes, but I only get to speak for five.

"Can't wait to hear it." He grins and then does this thing that always makes my stomach flip—contemplates the ground like there's something profound and important there. He looks up at me. "Are you here for the summer?"

"I am."

"Me too."

We are staring at each other, my face getting hotter and hotter, and all I can think is, *I want you to be my first, Wyatt Jones. If you ask me to go into that barn right now, I will race you there and be naked by the time I reach the door.*

He coughs. Looks away. Glances up. Smiles. "See you around, then."

"See you."

He sails past, and it's just an ordinary party filled with ordinary people, and I am one of them.

"We can stay."

I turn and blink at Saz. *Where did you come from?* But even though I want to stay, I see her face. "No way." Friends first. Always. I sing the rest of the way to the car.

An hour or so later, I lie in my bed and think of Wyatt Jones. Of every dirty thing I want him to do to me. My room is heavy with night, except for the moon, which is making everything glow.

I close my eyes, and I am still me, lying here in these yellow

17

daisy sheets and the navy blue pajama shorts and top I got for my last birthday, books everywhere because ever since I was six years old I've liked to bury myself in a pile of them.

So I am me, but right now I am me with Wyatt on top of me. Wyatt Jones, with his soccer legs and swimmer's shoulders and hair that smells like chlorine and the sun. Wyatt Jones, with eyes that burn when they look at you. He is above me. Under me. His skin on mine. My mouth on his.

My body is warm against the sheet, and my hand is where I'd like his to be. I kick the books away and they go crashing to the floor. My nose starts to itch and I scratch it. A hair tickles my forehead and I blow it away. *Holy hell.*

Breathe.

Concentrate.

Wyatt.

Wyatt.

And there he is again in all his naked glory.

Wyatt.

After a minute, a thousand little needles start prickling my skin.

He says, *Are you sure?*

For all his beauty, Wyatt Jones is famously shy. When he does speak, it's in this soft, scratchy voice that implies great thoughtfulness. I've built an entire inner life for him in my head, one where he is kind and empathetic and sensitive, yet strong enough to pick up a girl—me, specifically—and throw her onto a bed.

Yes, I say. *YES.*

It's you, Claude. It's always been you.

Stop talking, Wyatt. Stop talking right now.

The needle pricks are spreading throughout my body, and Wyatt morphs into the boy I saw on a plane once, the one who stared right at me as he walked down the aisle. Now I am on that plane, dressed as a flight attendant—a stylish one, the kind on overseas flights. Red lipstick, red uniform. Or maybe navy because it goes better with my clown hair. I follow him to the bathroom and he pulls me in after him and locks the door, and picks me up in his big, strong hands and sets me on that little counter, the one with the sink, and I wrap my legs around him.

Just as he kisses me, hands in my hair, he fades into Mean Jake, the delivery boy. We're in his vintage Trans Am, and it smells like pizza and cigarettes, but I don't care because we're tearing off each other's clothes, and suddenly he blurs into Mr. Darcy.

No. Mr. Rochester. Only I'm not Jane Eyre, I'm me in some sort of riding costume, and he's kissing me by candlelight. We're in front of the fireplace, and suddenly there's a bear rug, only I'm not sure why there's a bear rug. *Is there one in the book?* I'm staring at the bear, and the bear is staring back like, *You murderer,* and it's just so depressing, so I get rid of the rug, and now we're lying on the floor, Rochester and me, but it's *freezing* because Thornfield Hall is, after all, a castle in the English countryside. Rochester produces a blanket, but it's too late; I send him away.

And now it's Wyatt again, sauntering toward me like he does in the halls at school, and his eyes are on me, and they are so intense and serious that I know *this is it.* And we're in his room and his parents aren't home, and things slow down so much that I can hear my own breathing, short and fast, and I can almost hear his as he looks me in the eye and I can see everything—him, me, us— reflected there.

He says, *Claude.*

Claudine?

Claudine.

And then I can feel him. All of him. And I don't worry if I'm too small or too big anywhere because he doesn't even have to say, *You're beautiful.* He's already telling me.

And it's Wyatt and me, closer than I've ever been to anyone, and I'm wrapped around him and into him, and all at once I breathe, *Yes!* as my entire body lifts off the bed. It just rockets right off and hovers there in midair, shooting off fireworks of every color. I am an explosion of color and fire, and my room spins with light. A million fireflies of light swirling and sparkling around me, holding me in the air.

I want to live up here, circled by this flickering light storm. I want it to last forever, but one by one the fireflies start to ghost out and die away. I try to catch them and keep them, but gently, gently, I feel myself floating back down to the bed.

Gradually, the bed absorbs me, head to toe, and I go limp and still.

I open my eyes and the only light is coming from the moon. My body is heavy now, so heavy, and I feel myself drifting away in these daisy sheets, thinking I should have studied more for Mr. Callum's class and I never did find my left sneaker and I can't forget to bring Alannis her green sweater on Monday. And then my mind drifts to Shane and the barn and my wet, wet thigh, and what if some of it got in me and I get pregnant and have to have a baby and marry Shane Waller and live in Ohio forever?

The last thing I remember as I drift off to sleep, underneath daisy sheets, in navy blue pajamas, is Wyatt saying, *See you around, then,* which could mean anything because as of today the entire world is still possible.

7 DAYS TILL GRADUATION

It is almost eleven a.m. and I am in my room, talking to Saz on the phone. We are talking specifically about our summer plans. First and foremost, our road trip, which will be the two of us exploring the entire state of Ohio before we bid it goodbye forever, or at least for the next four years. We've bought matching bikinis (black for me, red for her) and Kånken backpacks (sky blue for me, yellow for her), and Saz is getting permission to borrow the car for a week or two. She wants to start north and I want to start south, and we're both talking and laughing at once, which is why I don't hear the knock on the door.

Suddenly it opens and my dad is standing there, and there is this look on his face as he takes in the posters on the walls and the T-shirts and jeans and dresses all over my floor and the books everywhere and me standing on a mountain of clothes like I'm on the peak of Kilimanjaro, and I'm still laughing but also trying to remember when in the hell he was last in my room, if ever.

I should suspect something then, but I don't. Instead I say, "I'm on the phone."

He says, "I need to talk to you."

And now I'm not laughing and neither is Saz, who goes, "Is that your *dad*?"

She sounds every bit as surprised as I am.

He perches on the corner of the bed, feet on the floor, looking like he might spring up and away at any moment. At first I think something horrible has happened to my mom. Or that he's going to tell me the dog is dead or the cat is dead or my grandparents are dead. I rummage through my memories, trying to unearth the last time he sat down like this to talk to me, and I can't remember anything prior to age thirteen, when he looked at my mom and said, "I didn't speak teenager even when I was one. She's in your hands now."

I sit down next to him, several inches between us. I am wondering where my mom is and if she knows he's here, and then he says, "Your mom asked me to talk to you. . . ."

For some reason my mind goes immediately to Shane and the hayloft. *Please don't let them know.* It is the worst thing I can imagine, because my life so far has been reasonably quiet and reasonably uneventful, which is apparently why I can't write with any sort of feeling. I've never even had a cavity.

And then my dad clears his throat and begins talking in this low, serious voice, which is not at all like his usual voice. And as he talks, he starts to cry, something I've never seen him do before.

I'm thinking, *Stop this. Don't cry. Not you. Dads don't cry.* Which is stupid, really, but there you go.

I think I say, "Don't cry."

Or maybe I say nothing.

Because he is telling me that he doesn't love us anymore, my mom and me.

That the past eighteen years of my life—

the eighteen years that make up my entire life—

have been a really horrible joke and that he never actually loved us at all, not once, or that maybe he did for a tiny while but love dies when the objects of that love are as unlovable as my mom and I are,

and unfortunately, it's our fault that we can't be his family anymore.

That he needs us to go far away so he never has to look at us again because our mere presence makes him ill. He's still talking, but I'm not listening. I'm too focused on the way the tears are rolling into the stubbly beard on his chin and disappearing. *Where are they going?*

"Clew," he says. My nickname. The one that only he calls me. Our special name, the one just for us and secret bakery runs before school and secret ice creams before dinner and driving too fast and watching scary movies. All the things my mom is too momish to allow. Even though all my life it's always been Claudine and Lauren, Lauren and Claudine, the Llewelyn women, because Mom never actually took Dad's name, and we've always been more Llewelyn than Henry. Which basically means we believe in possibility and magic instead of always looking at the practical (i.e., darkly realistic) side of things.

Meanwhile, my dad has stood on the perimeter, not as much like us, watching and applauding and joining in as much as he can. All my life, everyone loves us, the two Llewelyns. Everyone, apparently, but him.

"Clew," he says again. "It's not because I don't care about you." Even now, at this moment, as the floor of my room is disappearing, as I'm staring down, past my feet, wondering how I'll ever stand again, he can't bring himself to say *love.* As in *It's not because I don't love you.*

And then he says, "I just can't have a family right now."

And maybe he says none of this, really, but it's what I hear. And at that moment I stop looking at his tears and his beard and I am staring at the place where the floor used to be. All I can think is how one minute the floor was there and now it's not. How you could go through an entire day, every day, not thinking about the floor or the ground because you just assume it will always be there. Until it isn't.

The real conversation goes more like this:

Dad: "I need to talk to you."

Me: "Okay."

"I don't want you to think there's anyone else. It's important that you know that. But your mom and I are separating, and she asked me to tell you because it's not her idea; it's my idea." He looks away when he says this. And then: "I just can't do this right now. I can't do it." Followed by: "It isn't you and it isn't your mom. It's me. We wanted to stay together for your senior year. We didn't want to uproot you. For the next two weeks, we'll stay here together in this house, and then we'll separate."

When he says *separate,* I think of a heart being cut open, of limbs being sawn off.

"But yesterday you drove me to school." What I mean to say is, *Yesterday we were normal. We ate thumbprint cookies and rode in companionable silence and drove faster than anyone on the road.*

"It's something that's been building for a while," he says. "We've just been trying to figure out what's best for you and your mom and me."

So he knew about this as we drove across Main Street Bridge. As we drove downtown. As we ate cookies outside Joy Ann.

I suddenly feel left out. Like all these years, even when it was Claudine and Lauren, Lauren and Claudine, I believed it was the

24

three of us married to each other, and I'm only just realizing it was the two of them all along.

"I don't want you to talk to anyone about this, Clew, not even Saz. Not until we get everything sorted out. I know you love Saz and her parents, but they're our good friends and we're not ready for them to know. We're not ready for anyone to know. Not yet."

This is how numb I am: I don't get angry; I don't even ask why. I don't say, *You can't tell me who I can or can't talk to about this. You don't get to tell me the world is ending and then ask me not to share it.* Instead I just sit there, hollowing out, hands withering in my lap, heart withering in my chest, feet dangling over the bed into space because the floor is nowhere to be found.

He says from very far away, "This town's so goddamn small—the last thing we need is people discussing your mom and me because they have nothing better to do. And I don't want them making this harder on you than it has to be."

I don't hear anything else after that.

After he leaves, my mom comes in and puts her arms around me. She tells me we can talk if I want to, that it's important to talk and get things out. "You have to let the tears come," she always says. "Because if you don't, they'll come out eventually—maybe not as tears, but as anger or something worse."

"So this is real," I say.

"This is real."

And, all at once, there is this rush of feeling in my hands, in my heart, in every part of my body that just went hollow and dead, and I nearly double over from the pain of it. I feel as if a bomb has dropped from the sky directly into my room, directly onto my head.

"I know it's sudden. And it's a lot. And I'm sorry. So sorry." She pulls me in tighter.

"Dad says I'm not allowed to talk about it." For a minute I wonder if she can hear me, because my voice is so far away, as if it's locked in a dark, empty room with no windows or doors.

"Not outside the house, just while we try to figure this out." I attempt to strangle the hope that bubbles up over *while we try to figure this out,* as if this whole thing is something fixable and undecided.

"How are Saz and I supposed to go on a road trip without me saying anything?"

"I'm not sure the road trip is going to happen, Claude. At least not right away."

"But we've been planning it."

"I know, and I'm sorry." And I can see that she's as lost as I am. "Honestly, I'm trying to understand all of this myself." She goes quiet, and I can almost hear her choosing her words so, so carefully. "But what you need to remember is that it has nothing to do with you. Your dad and I love you more than anything."

After she leaves, I lie in bed. No pile of books. No dreams of Wyatt or plans for a road trip. Just me, wondering where the floor disappeared to.

I lie there for a very long time.

The house is so still, except for when I hear the whirring of the garage door and the roar of my dad's car driving away. And then, a little later, when there is a banging at my door, which is my cat, Dandelion, wanting to get in. But I can't move. So I lie there.

And lie there.

When Vesuvius erupted, the citizens of Pompeii were caught

completely unprepared, but we know from the letters of a survivor that there were warnings. Plumes of smoke. Earth tremors. *How could I not have seen the signs? How could I not have known?*

I think of all the people in the history of the world whose lives have changed in an instant, like the woman I was named for. Claudine Blackwood, my mom's great-aunt, was only five years old when her mother shot herself in the bedroom of their Georgia island home. It was after breakfast on a Thursday, and Claudine's father had left the house moments earlier. Claudine was the one who heard the gunshot, who found her mom lying in a pool of her own blood. It was one of those tragedies that my mom the writer refers to as a *defining moment:* that moment when life suddenly changes and you're left picking up the pieces. She says it's actually *how* you pick up the pieces that defines you.

Aunt Claudine and her father remained in the house, even after that. She spent a few years in Connecticut at Miss Porter's School for Girls, but returned to the island for good when she was nineteen. When her father died, she inherited the house. I often wondered what that must have been like, to grow up in the same space where your mother killed herself, to walk by that bedroom thousands of times over the years.

Aunt Claudine was my mother's favorite relative. When Mom was ten, she went to visit her and found the bullet hole in the closet door. She said she could fit her finger inside it. From the pictures I've seen of Claudine, she looked like a neat and tidy woman with a short blond bob and three fat dachshunds that supposedly followed her everywhere. She dressed in button-down shirts and khakis, but according to my mom, she carried herself like royalty.

I wish I could ask Aunt Claudine if, looking back, there were signs leading up to what her mother did, but Claudine died before I was born. And maybe she noticed signs, maybe she didn't. After all,

Aunt Claudine was only five when it happened. Whatever memories of her mom, and the girl Claudine might have been if that gun had never gone off, went with her. She didn't leave a husband or children behind, or anyone who could tell us why she stayed her whole life in that house on some island off the coast of Georgia.

It makes me wonder, *Is this a defining moment for me? And if so, what will I do with all these pieces?*

At some point I realize that I should keep moving. That lying here is only making it worse. So I pick up my phone. Saz has sent fifteen texts and left three messages. Instead of going downstairs to eat what my dad calls "breakfast for lunch," like I have every Saturday morning for the past eighteen years, I turn the phone off and reach for the notebook and pen I keep on my bedside table. All my life, I've given stories to everything because I've felt that everything deserved to have a history. Even if it was just an old marble lodged into the basement wall. *Where did it come from? Who put it there? And why?*

The thing no one knows—I am writing a novel. A bad, overly long novel that I am in love with even though it has no plot and about seven hundred characters and I'll probably never finish it. So far it fills three notebooks, and I am still going. One day I will either throw the notebooks away or type all these words into my laptop.

I open the notebook. Uncap the pen.

I stare at the page.

It stares back.

"Stop staring at me," I tell it.

I write my name on it, just to show it who's in charge here. *Claude.*

I circle it. Circle it again and again until my name looks like it's trapped inside an angry cloud.

I write my full name. *Claudine Llewelyn Henry.* Llewelyn, as in my mom's maiden name. I cross out the *Henry* and write: *Claudine Llewelyn.* Maybe this is who I'll be from now on.

I reach for my phone, turn it back on, and call Saz.

"What did your dad want?"

"What?"

"Your dad," she says. "What did he want?"

"Nothing. Just to talk to me about graduation. My grandparents are coming to visit us so they can hear my speech." And I think, *Oh, I'm really doing this. I am really not telling her.* I look down at the inside of my arm, where I am pinching the skin so hard it's turning blue.

"You sound weird. Are you sure you're okay?"

"I'm good. Just tired. I didn't sleep much." I think about telling her then, even though my dad said not to, even though my mom agreed I shouldn't, about the bomb he just dropped onto my head and onto my heart. But that would make it real, and right now it doesn't feel real. Instead I say, "What are you doing later?" Just to see what happens, I poke my skin with the tip of my pen, again and again, until the skin is blue all over from the ink, or maybe from bruises.

"Nothing. Right now I'm kind of half watching a movie and making a Leah Basco voodoo doll."

"Can you get the car?"

"Probably. You can always come over here." Saz lives three blocks away.

"Okay."

"Or we can go to Dayton instead."

I think of driving fast and turning the music up loud, loud, loud. "That sounds better."

"Are you sure you're okay?"

I look down at the notebook, where I've filled the page with my name. *Claude* three hundred times. At the little spots of blue on my arm.

"I'm sure."

We hang up, and I prepare to wait in my room for the next five or six hours so I don't have to sit downstairs and talk to my mom.

Saz drives. Her car is a five-year-old Honda that she shares with her brother Byron. We drive fast with the music up and the windows down, and we don't talk about Yvonne or Wyatt or Shane. We let ourselves become part of the air and the night and the song, and we sing until we're hoarse.

This is part of Saz and Claude, of two best friends growing up in a town that is too small. She was the first person who made me feel at home in Mary Grove. We bonded over the fact that neither of us was born here, and we became outsiders together. At ten, as soon as we discovered that we were both planning to be writers, we decided we were going to leave Mary Grove and be Big Deals out in the world someday. Leaving this town and Ohio behind was something we agreed was necessary to our survival. That's when the list started—a list of everything we would do and accomplish once we were free. In fifth grade we formed an all-girl band so that we could leave sooner. We weren't very good at playing music, but we were great at listening to it, and our love for all decades and genres brought us to Françoise Hardy and the yé-yé girls of the 1960s. These were women we learned about in seventh-grade French class who—in all their amazing, exotic Frenchness—transported us out of ourselves and away from our small Midwestern town and inspired an obsession with all things old and French.

In Dayton, we climb the steps of the Art Institute, which is closed tight but lit up on the outside. We sit huddled against the wind and the cold, even though it's nearly summer. We watch the sky change from gray to gold to pink to navy. The moon appears, followed by the stars, which are too bright. There is something unfair about them.

At age eleven, when Saz concluded she was adopted because her small, quiet brothers and small, quiet parents didn't begin to understand her, we decided she was a foundling instead. And even though I love my parents and I am exactly like them, split down the middle, I decided I might be a foundling too. In spite of Saz's Lilliputian size and my too-long limbs, her brown skin and my freckles, her dark, straight hair and my electric orange mop, we told ourselves we were separated at birth, and the only explanation had to be that we were stolen from our real family. We created an entire written history for ourselves of our original parents, our original siblings, and the people who had stolen us. At thirteen, we made a plan—when high school was over, we would go to California and share an apartment and earn our living as writers. Over the years, as we became better and better friends, it was hard to tell where Saz began and I ended.

Yet somehow, this fall, we are going to different schools. Me to Columbia in New York City. Saz to Northwestern in Chicago. We've agreed not to talk about it until the end of summer because the thought of being separated is unbearable.

Saz pulls a bottle of vodka out of her bag. She passes it to me and I drink, hating the taste. What I do like is the warm, burning feeling I get in my chest as soon as I swallow. Like there's a little furnace deep inside. We sit, staring out over the city. Since sophomore year, this is where we come when we don't want to talk but need to feel better. We think of it as *our* Art Institute, the way we think of I-70 as *our* highway, and Mary Grove as *our* town, even if we don't fit in.

I pass the bottle back to Saz, but she shakes her head. "Driving."

I take a drink for her.

"Hen," she says, "I have something to tell you." She's been calling me Hen, short for Henry, short for Claudine Henry, since we were ten years old. *Lew,* I want to say. *Call me Lew instead. I'm Claudine Llewelyn now.*

I have something to tell you, too.

She breathes out as if she's been holding her breath for a long time. "I slept with Yvonne." Before I can say, *But we just saw her with Leah last night—or was it days ago?* she says, "I'm sorry I didn't tell you when it happened."

I say the first thing that comes to mind: "But she's got a girl-friend."

"They've been off and on for a while."

"When did you sleep with her?"

"Three weeks ago. Remember when Mara and I went to Adam Katz's? That weekend you were hanging out with Shane? It happened then."

I say, "Oh."

Three weeks ago.

"I know we were supposed to wait to fall in love and have sex so we could do it at the same time, but we were ten when we made that pledge, Hen. You know I've dated. Maybe not a lot. Not as much as Alannis."

"No one dates as much as Alannis."

"Right? But, I don't know, no one's ever really mattered before. Like this. I mean, they mattered, but they didn't get in there. As in right here." She rubs at the area over her heart and then thumps it twice. "I didn't see it coming. I didn't see her coming. I guess

32

you're not supposed to." And she smiles, lost in the memory of Yvonne.

For some reason, this news hits me almost as hard as the news about my parents, because here is another secret someone was keeping from me. *I am a person other people feel the need to keep things from, and all the things I thought were truths aren't actually truths.* I can feel my lungs give out. I stare down at the concrete steps, but they're no longer there. There's only all this air between my feet and the ground.

I clear my throat, which has suddenly gone completely dry. "Why didn't you say anything?"

"I don't know. I should have told you. I just wasn't sure what it was, what we were, Yvonne and me. I guess I wanted to figure that out first."

"And did you? Figure it out?"

"Not completely, not yet. But I didn't want to *not* tell you about it any longer."

"You mean you didn't want to keep it a secret any longer."

"Yeah."

Even as I sit there guarding my own secret, hers stings like an open wound. I want her to take it all back and rebuild the stairs so we can sit on them together, side by side, just like always.

"Did Yvonne make you swear you wouldn't say anything? Because she was still with Leah?"

"No. The fact that I didn't tell you, that's on me. Besides, virginity is so fucking subjective, Hen. It's like something made up by the old, straight, white men who run this country, or whoever their equivalent was back in ancient times, to make you feel left out and less than and somehow incomplete. It doesn't actually mean anything, not to me."

"But your first time with Yvonne meant something."

"Yeah. It meant everything." And her voice cracks—like, actually cracks, as if it can't begin to hold all the emotion she's carrying.

I should put my hurt and anger aside and ask Saz what it was like, how she's feeling, what this means for her and Yvonne. I should ask her something about her because this is momentous and big and, like it or not, Yvonne is happening. But when I open my mouth, the only thing I'm capable of saying is that I might be pregnant with Shane Waller's baby.

"You know it's not the 1950s, right? Like, you have other options if you somehow *are* pregnant, which by the way you aren't."

"He thinks I'm a series of boxes, and every time he opens one, there's another one inside." I look down, past the place where the steps used to be, and the ground has disappeared too.

She says, "I think we both know there's only one box he wants to get into."

It's thirty-five miles to Mary Grove. Instead of talking, we blast the music so loud that I can feel it entering my bloodstream, taking root in my bones. Saz drives with one arm out the window. She takes a corner too fast and we're yelling along with the song, and I pull my hair back because it's blowing and blowing and if I don't hold it back I'll swallow it whole. With my free hand I grab the vodka bottle and drink, and the burning and the bone-vibrating music make me feel alive. We reach Mary Grove in twenty minutes because Saz drives faster than anyone I know, even my dad.

In the glow of the dashboard, I study the inside of my arm, where the bruises are. The little bruises from the little pinches I gave myself sometime between this morning and right now, just to make sure I wasn't dreaming this.

We turn into my neighborhood, following the curve and slope of the road.

I can still tell her.

We go down one hill.

I can tell her now.

Round a bend. Another.

I can open my mouth and let the words come out, and then she will know and she can help me make sense of this and I won't be alone, and then it will all be real.

The car rolls to a stop in front of my house. We sit there a moment, the music still playing. I don't want to go inside. I don't want to see my parents.

But I can't sit here forever, because Saz will want to know what's going on, so I start to get out of the car. She leans over the seat and lays a hand on my arm, stopping me. "You realize this isn't the end of us, right? Not just you going to New York and me to Chicago, but Yvonne and me? Falling in love wasn't about you, Hen, or all the plans we had. It's about this girl I really like and the right, I don't know, moment. But there'll never be an end of us."

"I know." But there's an uneasy flickering in my heart. Saz broke a promise. Maybe it was a silly promise. An eight-year-old promise given by ten-year-olds. But more than the promise, it's that Saz kept Yvonne a secret from me. We haven't even graduated and left home yet. How many more secrets will there be once Saz is at Northwestern and I'm at Columbia and we're not here, together, in Mary Grove? *Sometimes things end, even if you don't want them to.*

Maybe none of it would bother me so much if I didn't have a secret of my own, a secret belonging to my parents that they've now handed to me. A secret I don't want.

I force myself to take her hand. I say, "I wish we were going to California."

"Me too."

Her eyes meet mine, dark and flashing. Saz usually looks as if she's thinking a million exciting thoughts at once. But right now her eyes are quiet, and behind the happiness that's there over Yvonne, I can see the worry and the sadness and maybe the fear that I'm upset with her.

I say, "I could never be mad at you. Especially not for following your heart." *Especially not when I'm keeping secrets too.*

"Promise?" she says.

"Promise."

I can see the relief in her face. She squeezes my hand. With the other hand she scoops up the vodka bottle. Takes a drink now that she's so close to home.

She says, very low, "I really like her."

And it feels almost like a death, like Old Saz and Old Claude are suddenly gone. I squeeze her hand this time, because if I don't, I might burst into tears and lose it right here, right now. Then I hug her hard and long before climbing out of the car.

"Hey," she says, leaning over the seat, eyes shining. "I love you more than Tootsie Rolls and Ariana Grande and summer."

We've done *I love you more than* since we were ten, because we love each other beyond three words and needed to find a way to say it.

"I love you more than Kraft mac and cheese and Zelda Fitzgerald and spring." But the words fall flat onto the ground around me. She holds up her hand and waves her pinkie, and I hook it with my own. Then I slam the door and run for the house.

6 DAYS TILL GRADUATION

When I wake up the next day, the world is different. It's a different I can feel more than see, as if something in the gravity of the earth has shifted.

There's a short story by Ray Bradbury about a man who pays a company named Time Safari to go back in time for the privilege of shooting a dinosaur. He can only kill this specific dinosaur, which has been carefully marked, because it's old and diseased and going to die no matter what. In killing it, the man won't upset the balance of nature. He's warned to stay on the path Time Safari has built. Never venture off the trails. If he kills anything else, no matter how small, it could throw off the future of the world.

And of course he goes off the path, and they almost leave him there, and when they get back to the present, it all looks just as it did when they left it. *But not the same as they left it.* And then—*dun-dun-dun*—the man finds a dead butterfly on the sole of his boot. And he knows he has changed everything.

What sort of world it was now, there was no telling.

That is how it feels in my room, in my house, in my life. Mom, Dad, Saz, sun, earth. Atmosphere. Stars. Floor. All gone.

THE WEEK OF GRADUATION

The days that follow are strange, like the aftermath of a natural disaster, when the world goes too still. My parents and I move carefully around each other, glass figures in a glass house, and when we are outside, we move even more carefully, so as not to give anything away to anyone we see.

My dad and I are rarely alone together. I tell Saz he needs to be at work early this week and ask if I can ride to school with her. She talks the entire way, but I like how the words fill the silence and the air and the hollows that have grown up inside of me.

At home, if my dad walks into a room and finds me by myself, I make up some excuse to walk out. I don't know what to say to him right now: *Please bring my dad back because I don't recognize you, this person who's decided to leave my mother and me. I don't even know you anymore. I don't want to know you anymore.* He seems to get this—or maybe he doesn't know what to say to me, either—because he doesn't push it. My mom, on the other hand, hovers. But the strange thing is that they are also acting weirdly normal. They run errands and we do our usual chores and we watch Netflix together and eat dinner together except for a night or two when Dad works late. But this is normal too.

As we ease into our everyday roles, I feel this tiny, delicate bud of hope growing in my chest. *Maybe it won't happen after all. Maybe this is some sort of midlife crisis that all dads go through.*

Maybe Mom will talk him out of it. Maybe it was all a mistake. I stare at the floor of my room until I tell myself that I can see it again and that it won't break like thin ice if I walk on it.

Meanwhile, life goes on, and I try not to be shocked that it does. I go to school on Monday—my last Monday of high school—and wait for everyone to see that I'm Claude, but not Claude. The old Claude has been replaced by Robot Claude, who sits in class and walks through the halls and eats lunch and listens to her friends talk about sex and college or complain about their bodies. I've never realized how hard we are on our bodies. I think, *Why are we so mean to ourselves? Why aren't we happy with what we have?* And then I say it aloud, and Alannis and Mara stare at me like I just told them they were monsters.

I get my period during lunch hour, which means I'm not pregnant with Shane Waller's baby, but I barely feel it—the relief. I see Shane afterward, in calculus, and we don't talk. He doesn't even look at me, and it's as if we're strangers who didn't go out for two months. It's so fucking bizarre to me that one minute you can be naked with someone and the next it's as if you never met, yet I'm so strangely okay with this that I wonder if I ever really cared about him. Maybe Mr. Russo is right and I'm incapable of feeling.

Except that later that day I'm in the hallway outside the library when I see Wyatt Jones and Lisa Yu making out against her locker, and as I watch it happen, I can feel myself unraveling. Lisa is cooler than anyone has ever been on this earth. She is cooler than I can ever dream of being. And now she has her mouth suctioned to his. *Not you, too, Wyatt Jones,* I want to say. *I need you to stay still, to remain the Wyatt you've always been. No changing. No leaving like everyone else.*

Saz says, "Control your face, Hen. Look away! Look away!"

I blink at her because until this moment I didn't know she was there. I say, "When did that happen?" And I mean Wyatt and Lisa. "Wyatt doesn't like Lisa Yu. He likes me. Since when is she someone who gets to kiss him? That should be me making out with him, not her." On and on. Even to my own ears, I sound like a complete and total baby.

Saz starts to sing the ice cream song, and I think, *What is my normal reaction to Saz singing the ice cream song?* I access my memory banks and make a face at her. She makes a face back, and I feel relieved because she thinks I'm being regular everyday Claude.

"Men suck," she says. "That's why I'm thankful I like women."

That night my phone buzzes and it's Shane. I stupidly think maybe he's going to apologize for—what? Wanting to have sex with me? Not being the boy I wanted him to be? He's sent a photo, and at first I'm not sure what exactly I'm looking at, but then I recognize it. Shane naked from the waist down, and the caption This is what you're missing. Let me know if you change your mind.

There are a thousand things I could write back—*Your dick is the last thing on my mind,* for starters—but instead I just delete the whole thread. *Goodbye, Shane Waller. I can't remember what I ever saw in you.*

The next morning before school, I sit on the rug in my room thinking back on the first year we lived here. My old bedroom in Rhode Island is now a hazy, fuzzy blur, but this room, even more than this house, is my home, my very first own space that I filled with me. My safe haven from everything—exams, teachers, breakups, fights with friends, the stress of the outside world. Until the day my dad walked in and took away the floor.

A knock on the door and my mom appears. She comes in and

sits down next to me. Without thinking, we tilt our heads, letting them touch. We've been doing this since I was little.

I say, "When did you know? That you and Dad weren't working?"

"It's hard to explain."

"Like, for a while? Or did you just find out?"

"Yes and no. I knew but didn't know."

My mom, who is never cryptic with me, is being cryptic for the first time in my life, and I feel my heart slow and quiet and grow very, very still because somehow this is worse than my dad sitting on my bed crying.

"Is this what you want or what he wants?"

She sighs. "Claude."

"Mom."

My mother never lies to me, and I'm hoping she's not going to start now, even though, right or wrong, I already feel lied to.

"Is it what you want?" I say again.

"No," she says, and I can tell this is the truth.

I've been waiting for them to change their minds and tell me they've decided to work it out. Instead she tells me about an island in Georgia where they send wives and children who are no longer loved, where there are no cars and no phone service, and where alligators and wild horses roam free. She tells me that we are being banished there. That as soon as I graduate, the two of us will be leaving this house, where we've lived for the past eight years, because my dad is sending us away.

What she really says is that we are spending the summer in Georgia on the island where my great-great-aunt Claudine Blackwood lived and died. Mom and I usually visit her family in Atlanta this time of year, so we've already got the perfect alibi for our friends in Mary Grove. We'll stop in Atlanta like always and then head for the island.

41

I say, "Why should we be the ones to leave when he's the one who wants out?"

"Because I need to get away from Mary Grove and your father and this house. Just to clear my head for a while."

"Well, Saz and I are going on our road trip. So I don't need to go to an island to get out of his way because I'll be gone."

"Claude."

"Mom." And I know what she's going to say.

"The road trip will unfortunately have to wait. I promise you can do it at some point, but right now . . . just for a few weeks . . ." She shakes her head and her eyes are suddenly wet. "Honey, right now I need you to come with me."

Divorce Island is a national seashore or a state park or something. In addition to alligators and wild horses, it is filled with ruins and family history. For almost five weeks—exactly thirty-five days—we will be staying in a house belonging to Mom's cousin Addy. Mom was there for Addy when she got divorced and when her son drowned in a rip current the summer he was twelve. Now it's Addy's turn to be there for us.

The cat will go with us and the dog will stay with my dad. Even our pets are separating.

On Friday afternoon, my dad's parents arrive from Pennsylvania. I wait for him to tell them about his fractured marriage and the fact that he's sending their daughter-in-law and their only grandchild away as soon as I have my diploma, but instead no one says anything and my dad spends all day in the kitchen creating one of his meals—tournedos of beef with braised asparagus and a four-cheese mac and cheese he makes from scratch.

42

While he does this, my grandparents take turns standing in the kitchen doorway, where Mom marks their heights. This is a tradition my mom started when we first moved in—measuring everyone, kids and adults, writing names and dates beside each mark. Even Dandelion the cat and Bradbury the dog are on there.

The entire time all this is happening, I can feel the words forming, sitting there on the tip of my tongue. *He doesn't want us anymore.* But my dad has told me not to talk about it, and besides, he is home for dinner, so we all eat together, a happy family.

"I'm sorry your folks couldn't come," my grandmother says to my mom at the table.

"Me too." Apparently Mom has told her parents and sister enough about the separation that they're angry with my father and don't want to see him. They're so angry they're skipping my graduation, and frankly I don't blame them. I'd skip it myself if I could.

"Neil tells us you're working in Georgia this summer."

"That's right. I have the chance to organize the papers of the Blackwood heirs, some of my ancestors."

"The Blackwoods, as in *the* Samuel Blackwood?"

Mom nods. "In the 1920s, he built a home off the coast for his only son. I'm thinking there might be a novel there." Her voice is cool and calm.

Gran's eyes are dancing. "How exciting." My grandmother is Mom's most avid reader and biggest fan. "Can you say anything or is it too soon? You know what? Don't tell me." She holds up a hand. "I don't want you to give anything away, but just know if you need an early reader, I'm here."

"Thanks, Maggie."

Gran looks at me. "And you're going to help her?"

I stop picking at my food and set my fork down. And then I

realize I have nothing to say. Mom answers for me, no doubt so I don't have to lie to my own grandmother. "She's my best research assistant."

Gran turns to my father. "What on earth are you going to do without them, Neil? I hope you'll at least go down there for a little while."

I wait for him to tell her this was his idea, that he can't wait to have us gone, but instead he glances at Mom, at me, and says, "I'll have to get along somehow." He glances at us again and I can see the guilt in his eyes. *You can still stop this. You can change your mind and we will stay and none of this needs to happen.* He looks away, down at his food.

I almost say something right then. I feel like a person being held against her will, like a hostage or a kidnap victim, and all I want to do is yell at the innocent bystander, *Please help me,* and run for freedom.

But the conversation moves to my grandfather's work and his golf game and the church they go to and their neighbor, poor thing, who is in the midst of a terrible divorce.

GRADUATION

On Saturday, at graduation, I stand on the stage behind the microphone, behind the lectern, and look out at the sea of blue caps and gowns. The faces of my classmates swim into focus. There is Saz, my best friend, and Wyatt, the boy I love, who was supposed to love me but now apparently loves someone else. There is Shane Waller, who has seen me naked, and Matteo Dimas, who has seen me almost naked, and my friends Alannis and Mara, phones up and pointed at me. There is Lisa Yu, the girl who stole Wyatt Jones from me without knowing it, and there is Yvonne Brittain-Muir, who is stealing Saz. All of them waiting for me to share some words of inspiration. Beyond them I see my parents, sitting side by side with my grandparents, eyes on me.

I open my mouth and out comes my speech about dreams and wonder and all the things I used to believe in before my world imploded. " 'Stuff your eyes with wonder. . . . Live as if you'd drop dead in ten seconds. See the world. It's more fantastic than any dream.' Ray Bradbury, *Fahrenheit 451*."

I hear myself but I can't feel myself, as if the actual Claude is far, far away from here, and the one up on this stage is just filling in. I want to say, *Don't believe a word of this garbage. Get ready for divorce and heartache and betrayal and feeling like you're completely, utterly alone no matter how big a crowd you are in.*

As I somehow finish and wait for the applause, I smile out at everyone and think, *Isn't it funny that they can't see I dropped dead a week ago?*

I walk across the stage in my cap and gown, and afterward Saz and I pose for photos. I'm so hollowed out I'm practically invisible and I wonder if I'll even show up on camera.

Saz says, "I love you more than freedom and vodka and skinny-dipping."

I say, "I love you more than libraries and sunshine and boys with guitars."

Suddenly the breath goes out of me and the room is spinning. The whole world kind of tilts, and for one peaceful, terrifying second, everything goes black.

And then I come to on a bench outside the gym, and Wyatt's face is the first thing I see. For a minute, I think it's all been a dream—the past seven days. But he is checking my pulse and Alannis is fanning me and Mara says something about locking my knees up on that stage and how her sister made that same mistake at a wedding. Saz is telling the onlookers, "It's okay, nothing to see here, she's fine," and I want to yell, *I am not fine at all.*

But then I look up at Wyatt and he looks down at me and I say, "Wyatt?" I reach for him.

And now Saz is next to me, holding my hand and patting me. "You fainted, Hen. Jesus." She shakes her head and her cap comes loose. She yanks it off and tucks her hair behind her ears so that it's not hanging in her face and she can see me clearly. She leans in and studies me. "Are we sure you're not pregnant?" She says it under her breath, and she is joking, and the normalcy of this is so comforting and familiar that suddenly I feel the tears coming.

"Sazzy," I say.

But then everyone is crying—Saz and Mara and Alannis—as

they pile on top of me and hug me tight, and Alannis shouts, "Mary Grove High forever!"

That night Saz and I drive, just the two of us, with the music up and the windows down. We are driving just to drive, and somehow, in a town we know inside and out, we find ourselves on a street and in a neighborhood I don't recognize.

Stretching ahead, as far as the eye can see, are all these little houses, small and neat and identical. Saz turns off the music and rolls to a stop. Each house faces away from the road, with the entrance on the side, and a single orange streetlight marks the entrance of every driveway. Little mailboxes. Little porches. All a perfect distance from one another. Not a light on in any of them. A concrete rabbit sits in a garden.

"Where are we?" I say.

"The loneliest place in the world."

No, I think. *The loneliest place in the world is my house.*

We pass cul-de-sacs and side streets. It's like a maze, everything identical. I almost tell her then, in spite of my dad and in spite of my mom, but suddenly Saz says, "I know where we are. We're in purgatory. All of these unseen, sleeping people are waiting, just waiting, for proper deaths. Here in Nowhere."

I shiver, and this is part of the fun. Trying to spook each other. And I think these are the kinds of moments I'll miss most when I'm gone this summer and when I'm at college. I tell myself, *Be here while you can.*

Saz turns the headlights off and we creep up and down the streets, a great, rolling shadow. In a dead end, she turns the car around. My head buzzes. I hang out the window, and the air is cool on my face. The moon is bright and close.

We see it at the same time, up near the left. This house is as neat and tidy as the others, but there's a light flickering inside, and I can see the blue of the television. At the edge of the driveway, trash waits to be picked up. A FOR SALE sign stands on the lawn.

Saz stops in the middle of the road, engine humming. "Look, Hen. They're moving out of purgatory." We sit, taking it in, letting the quiet settle around us, watching the flame of blue flicker and waver inside the house.

I say, "I bet they're going as far away from here as they possibly can and never coming back." And I feel a little blue flame of my own—hope, maybe—dancing in my chest. "We should do that. Start driving west."

"Don't I wish."

"Why not?"

"Because we can't. Where would we stay? How would we pay for it? And what about Wyatt?"

What she really means is, *What about Yvonne?*

She's still talking. "It's not that I don't want to but . . . Hey, hello? Earth to Hen. Where'd you go?"

"What? I'm here."

"Uh-uh. You're here but not here. What's up with you lately? And then today—passing out like that."

"I'm good. It's just a lot of change." And then I tell her that my mom and I are leaving for Atlanta soon. Like, *soon* soon.

"What about our road trip?"

"I'll be back in a few weeks."

"*A few weeks?* It's our last summer, Hen."

"I know."

"The hell?"

"Sorry."

"Why don't you stay here with your dad? Or you could stay with me?"

"Because I can't." And I could say it nicer but she won't let it go, and I can't tell her why, and now there's Yvonne, which means that if I stay with Saz and her family, I will eventually be in the way.

I don't know how long we sit there looking at each other, my heart beating so loud I can't hear anything else. Finally her eyes go back to the road and she steers us away from the house. I stare into the side mirror at the blue light, at the FOR SALE sign, and feel the little flame in my chest flicker out.

4 DAYS BEFORE WE LEAVE

On Thursday, I walk a mile to the college where my dad works. Past Roosevelt Hall, with his office on the fourth floor and an executive assistant named Pamela and the window overlooking National Road and the patch of sunflowers—little spots of yellow—hugging the building. I walk through the student union out into the warm early-summer air and across the parking lot onto the grass that will lead me to the soccer field, where I see a blur of legs—long, strong legs attached to long, strong boys.

I walk until I can see the faces attached to these boys attached to these legs. I stand on the field, feet planted in the grass, and it's hotter out here than I thought, but I'm too mad and numb to feel it, really feel it, so I stand there and stand there, and eventually one of the boys with long, strong legs yells "Hey!" at me. I don't say anything. I keep standing there until he runs over, shirt wet through. He is blocking the sun so that all I see of him is this outline that is like a glow.

"Claude."

"Wyatt."

I knew he would be here because the first time I ever saw him was on this field, back when I thought he was a college student, before I saw him in the hallways at school. But the moment he says my name, I know why I've come here today. No more waiting. Nothing to lose.

"You okay?"

"I'm good."

"You sure?"

"I'm sure." I smile, and it's easy. Without telling them to, my lips automatically curve up at the corners. My teeth flash. My mouth spreads open wider and wider until my face may crack in half. And then he reaches out and takes two of my fingers in two of his, and I feel the jolt of his skin on mine, even this little bit of it. And it's more than the jolt—it's the sudden closeness of another person, touching me, that makes me say: "Actually, I'm not good. My parents are separating. I'm not supposed to say anything. Saz doesn't know. But if I don't tell someone, I might disappear. Please don't repeat this to anyone."

"I won't."

"I mean it."

"I promise."

I take a breath. I shouldn't have said anything, but he doesn't know my parents, and his parents don't know my parents, and he doesn't really know me, and I don't really know him, which is *why* I told him. Somehow I feel my secret will be safe here.

"In case I never see you again, I just want you to know that I like you. I've liked you since sophomore year." I should feel bad about Lisa Yu, but I don't. She is the furthest thing from my mind. Because after suffering a loss, you become a ghost in your own body. You observe yourself doing things and saying things that you might not normally do or say. You need something to ground you and prove to you that you're still here. As a way of feeling something. Anything.

Which is why I say, "I want to kiss you now. I hope that's okay."

I wait for this to register. It only takes a second or two, and then he gets this smile on his face, and says, "That's definitely okay with me."

I lean in and kiss him. His mouth is warm. I can taste the sweat and salt. *I am kissing Wyatt Jones.* I tell myself this to make myself feel it and believe it and know it as much as I can. I keep my mouth pressed to his as long as possible.

When I pull away, I lick my lips, drinking in this little bit of him. He moves his head and suddenly the sun blinds me. I close my eyes for a second and he's still there, a silhouette.

I open my eyes again and he is looking at me with a mix of confusion and concern, and his friends are yelling at him, and now I can see his eyes, which are brown and deep-set.

Just in time, I scratch at the tear that goes running down my cheek, pretending it's an itch. And then, before he can say anything, I walk away.

THE NIGHT BEFORE WE LEAVE

On our last night as a family, my parents and I sit at the dining room table and eat dinner together and pretend the world isn't ending. They talk in these courteous, matter-of-fact voices that make me pinch my arms. Upstairs, my bags are packed and waiting.

"If we leave by ten, we can beat the traffic around Cincinnati and make it to Atlanta by dinner," my mom says.

"You should leave by nine to be safe." My dad sounds worried. "Earlier if you can."

Both of them are speaking so *politely,* as if they're just meeting for the first time.

My mom sets down her fork. "Why?"

The word sits in the air between them.

"Why, Neil? Why do I need to leave by nine?"

I look back and forth at Mom, Dad, Mom, Dad. She is hurt and she's not hiding it anymore, and this throws me. And for the first time I see it—the divide, as if a crack in the earth has suddenly opened up. I feel stupid for not having seen it before now. So incredibly stupid and blind and naïve. Sitting there, I make a promise to myself: *I will never be surprised again.*

I say, "The chicken is good." Even though I can't taste it. Because suddenly I don't want to see any of this—the hurt, the divide. For the next few minutes, or as long as this dinner lasts, I just want them to be the parents I've always known.

They look at me, remembering I'm here. I see them remembering and this is when it hits me. It will not be the three of us anymore. It will never be the three of us anymore. From now on, it will be:

Claude.

Lauren.

Neil.

Every person for themselves.

Afterward Dad finds me in the bathroom brushing my teeth. Before I can run away, he says, "I love you, Clew. No matter what. I need you to know that."

He hugs me. And then, like that, he lets me go. The door closes behind him. I spit. Rinse. Dry my mouth. And then I hold on to the sink and get ready to cry all the tears I've been carrying around since May 30, enough to fill that crack in the earth. My mom is right that tears come out eventually, but that doesn't mean I want anyone to see them.

I hold on and I wait but nothing happens. I stare at my face in the mirror, and my eyes are burning and tired, a little red, but completely dry.

I can't sleep, so at two a.m. I sneak out. The neighborhood is quiet, the houses dark, the streets empty. I walk three blocks, turn right, and I'm at Saz's place. Her room is in the basement and she always sleeps with the windows open, even in the dead of winter, because she's a human furnace and also because she wants me to be able to get in at night if I need to. It's the same reason I leave our living room window unlocked for her.

I squeeze through the opening and land on the rug. I can hear her snoring. I give my eyes a minute to adjust, and then I tiptoe over to the bed and climb in next to her. She stirs. "Hen?"

I whisper, "Sorry."

"Are you okay?"

"I don't want to go away."

"I know." We lie on our sides and she throws an arm around me. "I don't want you to go either."

There's this part of me that's angry at her for falling for Yvonne and for sleeping with Yvonne and, more than that, for not telling me about it. But mostly I'm angry with her for not knowing that something's wrong with me. She should be able to read my mind and figure out what I'm going through without me telling her. She should force it out of me so that I have no choice but to tell her, which means my parents won't be able to get upset. *If we're really best friends, she should just know.* But then, I didn't know about Yvonne until she told me, did I? And there's this other part of me that's mad at myself for being able to hide things so well.

"Sazzy?"

"What?"

"Are you scared about college?"

"A little. I wish we were going to the same place."

"Me too."

"I wish you and your mom didn't have to leave so soon."

"I know."

"When are you coming back from Atlanta?"

My throat is aching, right at the swallowing point, and all I can do is shrug. *I'm not going to Atlanta the entire time. I'm going to an island, and I won't be back from there until the end of July, maybe even early August.* Ever since I chose Columbia and she chose Northwestern, I knew it would be hard to say goodbye to her, but I didn't expect to have to do it so soon.

She says, "I'll miss you more than the stars and Dairy Queen Blizzards and Françoise Hardy."

I say, "I'll miss you more than my room with the green walls and my daisy sheets and my bookshelves stuffed with books."

And my dog and my dad and my house and even this town. And you, Saz, most of all. You.

THE ISLAND

——

ONE

DAY 1

I stand at the rail of the ferry, my hair blowing like a kite, wearing the oversize sunglasses I found at my grandparents' house in Atlanta, where, for the two weeks we were there, we completely avoided the subject of my dad. In this moment, I hate the wind and I hate the salt water that is stinging my face and I hate my hair. My dress is sticking to me because the air is as heavy and humid as a hot, wet towel, and I've never felt this kind of heat before. Dandelion's carrier is wedged between my ankles so he doesn't go sliding away. To get here we have driven nearly eight hours from Mary Grove to Atlanta, and then another five hours from Atlanta to the coast on the southern tip of Georgia, where we boarded this boat. It is another forty-five minutes to the island, and this is what it feels like to be exiled.

There are just nine of us on the ferry, including the captain and a young white guy, maybe college age, who loaded the bags onto the boat in a bright red wheelbarrow. The captain looks like he's been in the sun for a hundred years, and the young guy has bleached hair, the color of an Ohio winter, that pokes out from underneath his baseball cap. They speak in these languid, drawling voices, which make me know I'm in a completely foreign place. A couple of the passengers sit under the little covered area and the rest of us sit—or, in my case, stand—in the blazing sun.

We pass paper mills, hulking on the banks of the mainland, and the hot, heavy air smells like sulfur. The factories are ugly and I'm happy they're there. They keep this place from being too beautiful. Then suddenly we are turning and the mainland is at our back.

I stare down at my phone, and there is one little bar. And a text from Wyatt Jones.

Let me know when you're home. I've been thinking about that kiss.

Normally I wouldn't type back *right* away, but this is an emergency—who knows how long that one little bar will last? I write:

I've been thinking about it too.

As I hit send, I feel a pang of guilt over Lisa Yu, but it's over-shadowed by the enormous panic I'm feeling over that bar disappearing.

Another text appears from him:

I should've asked you out last year. I want to kiss you again.

Me: I want to kiss you too.

Him: Get home soon, Claud Henry.

He spells my name wrong, but I don't care. After all, he's the only one who knows my secret, which in some cheesy-movie kind of way means we're bonded.

Me: I can't wait to see you.

And then a photo. Him without a shirt, lying on his bed. My heart nearly stops because he is that beautiful. I want to lick the screen, but instead I scroll through my photos and try to send him one of me from spring break in my bikini to remind him what I look like and to show him that I have curves—such as they are—and legs and skin that would feel good against his own. I press send and wait. And the phone is trying and trying, but of course my picture doesn't go through because now there are no bars, which means no service, which means no Wyatt.

I want to shout all my frustration and anger into the wind and the warm salt air. I want to fling my phone into the water and have a full-on kindergarten tantrum. Instead I grab onto the railing so tight, it's a wonder my fingers don't snap.

I'm glaring over my shoulder at the paper mills when I feel a thump on my foot. A giant bear of a red dog sits there, one paw on my shoe.

"That's Archie." The guy with the baseball cap leans on the rail beside me. He smells like weed and incense and wears too many skull rings. "Island dog." Archie looks up at me, panting, and then trundles off into the covered area and the shade.

All these little boats are going by us, and the people aboard wave at our captain and us, I guess, because this is what people on boats do. Except for me. I am still gripping the railing with both hands, because if I don't I might pitch myself over the side.

"That's Palmetto Island," the boy says. He nods at the one we're passing. "That was where they quarantined smallpox victims, like, two hundred years ago. Now there's nothing on it but wild hogs and gators." I can't tell if he's trying to impress me or if he's just doing his job by passing along information.

"Grady!" The boy turns to look at the captain and then ducks back into the covered area, leaving me to think about how I am no better than a smallpox victim from the 1800s or whenever it was they had smallpox. The island is scrubby and desolate, no signs of life anywhere. No wild hogs in sight. No gators. We are getting farther and farther away from the mainland.

There are islands on either side of us, but we keep going.

And going.

And going.

Until I half expect to see the coast of Ireland on the horizon. We are sailing through the world's largest moat. Not only do we have to move to a different state to give my dad the room he needs, but we apparently have to put an ocean between us.

"Look," Mom says, coming up next to me, and there is another island rising up to the right of us. We stand side by side as the ferry follows the shoreline, cruising through dark blue water, cutting through the marsh. There is something grand about this island, which makes it seem more important than the others. For one thing, it's bigger than I expected. According to Mom, it's twenty miles long and three miles wide, a third larger than Manhattan. It has a full-time population of thirty-one. The only vehicles allowed are those belonging to residents or the Parks Department. There is a general store that supposedly has Wi-Fi. There are no paved roads. There is no cell service.

My immediate impression is that it's very green. Uninterrupted green from one end to the other. This is more nature than I have ever seen in my entire life, and it's hard to take it all in. The island looks wild and untouched. I don't see a single house or structure.

"It's beautiful," Mom says, and I can hear the surprise. She's been here before, growing up, so the surprise is for something else—maybe the fact that she can feel something like awe after all that's happened. "You can't see it from the shore, but through there is what remains of Rosecroft, the Blackwood family home. It was the gathering place, not just for the family but for everyone who lived on the island. It's where your aunt Claudine lived. Two months before she died, the mansion burned down, and all that's left is ruins."

She knows my love for ruins and ghosts and haunted places, for finding the story in everything. Not a love she had to teach me, but one I was apparently born with, inherited from her. And even though I want to ask her all the questions that are now buzzing

62

around in my head—*How did the fire start? Is this the same house where Claudine's mother shot herself? Why did Claudine stay here on the island?*—I don't take the bait. After all, my mom is in this too. It wasn't just my dad saying, *Don't talk about it.* She's also been keeping secrets. So I stand there, mute, hands on the railing, staring blankly at all that green.

Mom is still talking when one of the other passengers lets out a yell, and everyone comes flocking to the rail to take pictures of the lone gray horse that is galloping on the beach. She has already told me about the wild horses that live here, descendants of the Spanish and English horses that were brought over centuries ago, but seeing one for myself makes my heart—so recently laid to rest—jump. The horse is running, paying no attention to us, just doing what horses are meant to do, and suddenly I think, *You can be anyone here.*

I feel the butterflies stir somewhere deep and distant.

I imagine myself as free as that horse, and for a minute I'm nowhere and everywhere. Floating. I imagine an entire summer of becoming the person I want to be, whoever that is. Doing the things I want to do, whatever those are. Not thinking about anyone else because no one is thinking of me. I see flashes of myself as the girl I think I used to be—happy, secure, a floor beneath my feet. *Fuck everyone,* I think. *Fuck them all.*

Then, just like that, the butterflies go still and my mouth goes dry. And this is what happens when someone takes away your voice. *Don't say a word. Don't talk about it. Don't let your feelings out. Keep quiet. Keep it inside. Silence.* You just smile and smile until your mouth goes dry.

All at once the sky is too bright. The water too choppy. The forest too dense. The trees feel like they are gathering, ready to march toward the ferry, toward me. *What sort of world is this?* I look down at my arm and I have goose bumps. I look at my mom's arm and she has them too.

There is a dock ahead and the boat slows and a smiling boy wearing glasses and a bright yellow shirt stands waiting for us. He is slight and wiry, tan skin, light brown hair, and looks all of sixteen. I feel this relief and surprise that there's at least one other person around my age here. Our luggage is tucked under benches amidst all the duffel bags and backpacks. As I grab my suitcase, I think, *This should be even heavier.* After all, my entire life is in here.

"I'm Jared," the boy says. He has an earnest, friendly face. "Leave that there and we'll take it up to the inn for you. You can wait for me up under the trees at the end of the dock if you want and I'll show you where we're going."

"We're not staying at the inn," I say.

"We're at the Birches'," Mom adds, her hand on my shoulder. I shrug it off.

"I've got it, Jared." The voice belongs to a boy who's my age, or maybe older, and who has what I call resting wiseass face. He's suntanned and barefoot, baggy shorts hanging off his hips, black T-shirt, dirty blond hair. He's taller than Wyatt, and his voice is a lazy Southern drawl.

I step off the ferry and my eyes meet his. And, for a fraction of a moment, less than a millisecond, I freeze and he seems to freeze too.

Then he looks me up and down and flashes this big old grin, dimples, the whole nine yards, and goes, "Here comes trouble."

I roll my eyes and make a point to look away. The air is a hot, wet blanket and I've just traveled five hundred years to get here. My hair is matted to the back of my neck, my dress is plastered to

64

my skin, and my makeup has completely melted off my face. Even my elbows are dripping. But this boy isn't sweating like the rest of us. He looks like he just rolled out of bed and landed here from somewhere cool and shady.

I turn to look at him and he stares back. And then Archie the dog goes running past and nearly knocks me over.

"You okay there, sunshine?" The boy says it like I'm just so, so amusing.

"Amazing." I give him my fiercest smile, one that tells him, *Your charms don't work on me. Take them somewhere else.* Because I don't plan on getting to know anyone here. I will stay in Addy's house until it's time to go back to Ohio.

He arches an eyebrow and then collects all our bags and leads us up a white sand path littered with crushed shells. He is talking to my mom but looking at me out of the corner of his eye. I put on my headphones and walk behind them, looking at everything but him, listening to the same Françoise Hardy song I've been listening to since we left Mary Grove: "Tous les garçons et les filles." Which roughly translates into "All the boys and girls in the world are happy but me. I, Claudine Llewelyn Henry, will be alone forever."

Suddenly we are under this canopy of trees, and it's like nothing I've seen before. They're live oaks, right out of *Grimm's Fairy Tales,* grotesque, knotted, twisted creatures that look as if they could come alive at night. An ancient wood from a fairyland, a strange, haunted-looking place. Spanish moss hangs off them like spiderwebs, like ghosts, and it is impossible to see the sky.

The inn sits majestically in the midst of this, like a genteel and elegant old lady, all polite good manners. Wide porch, white columns, red roof. As I told Jared, we're not actually staying in the inn itself, but in a house across the way, the one belonging to Addy.

I follow the boy and my mom down a path that leads past a handful of shotgun shacks painted bright green, yellow, and pink, and past a barnlike building with an old gas-station pump in front and kayaks stacked inside and outside. There are wild horses grazing underneath the live oaks. When we get to the two white columns that sit on either side of the main path—the one that continues round in a circle past two more shotgun shacks and back to the inn—we are there. At a coral-colored one-story house with a broad porch, blue shutters, and a red tin roof that looks like a squashed hat. It sits, surrounded by blooming flowers, on the edge of the tree line, forest on two sides.

I cut through the grass, ahead of my mom and the boy. He yells something, and I pull off one of my headphones and turn.

"What?"

"I said you don't want to cut through there because of cactus spurs."

"What's a cactus spur?"

"You'll see."

He and my mom head up the path, but I keep going just to show this boy that I don't care about cactus spurs or snakes or anything else that might live in the grass. I step up onto the porch, which creaks like an omen, and look down at my shoes, now covered in tiny green balls. I reach down to pluck one off, and it pricks my finger, drawing blood. I take off my shoes and leave them there. There is a single animal skull sitting by the front door.

Inside, I'm hit with a blast of air-conditioning, which I wish I could drink. The house is divided in two, a bedroom and bathroom on each side. A note from Addy welcomes us. *Make yourselves at home. I love you. See you soon.* The kitchen and dining room and living room kind of blur into each other, and there's a fireplace opposite the couch. The ceilings are high. There's a cramped office off the kitchen. And the best thing of all: a reading nook with built-in bookshelves on either side of a window seat and a large dormer window looking out toward the inn.

I take the bedroom on the left, closer to the inn, so that my mom can have the larger one facing the woods. I go into the room and shut the door and stare out at the wall of trees and at the horse that stands outside my window. I suddenly feel this punch of homesickness, right in the throat. The floor is bare and dark. The bed is too large. There are two windows, not three, and they are in the wrong place. The walls are pale yellow, not bright green, and covered in someone else's art. It's too quiet here, and I miss my mom, even though I can hear her in the next room talking to the boy.

I check my phone, and there's no signal. I text Saz anyway and hope by some miracle it goes through. When there's a knock on my door, I don't bother looking up. "Come in."

It swings open and the boy is there with my bag. He comes right in, lifts the bag up onto the trunk at the end of the bed, and says, "Holy shit."

"Thanks. Bye."

"What's in there?"

"Bricks, books, maybe a body or two." I turn my back on him, hoping he'll get the hint.

"I've found when carrying bricks or bodies or—for example— an attitude, a backpack works better. Easier on the shoulders. It's all about weight distribution."

I set the phone down because apparently it's useless and frown at him. "Is there anything to do here? On this island? In hell?"

"So you're glad you came."

"It's a dream."

He gives me a look and it's hard to read, a little less *I'm so charming,* a little more real.

67

"What?"

"You just remind me of someone. Anything else I can do for you, my lady?" Just like that, the *I'm so charming* is back.

"I'm good, thanks."

In the doorway he turns. Beyond him I can see my mom in the kitchen, putting things away. He says, "There's everything to do here. Depending on your attitude, of course." He walks out, and I sit watching as he helps my mom, as they talk and laugh, as he scratches Dandelion under the chin. I get up and close my door.

In an hour, everything is put away in the closet, which is too narrow, and the dresser, the one that wobbles when you open it. There is a framed photo hanging on the wall above the dresser of a freckled and grinning twelve-year-old boy. He is shirtless and barefoot, standing on a beach, dunes rising up behind him, and this is Addy's son, Danny, the one who drowned.

I sink onto the bed and write Saz a real message: So my mom and I took off and I didn't tell you. We're living on a remote island now because my dad is having some sort of emotional midlife crisis and can't have a family anymore. You're in love and I'm still a virgin and probably always will be because Wyatt is 10,000 miles away. And we're not going to the same school in the fall, so I don't know what that means for you and me.

I write more. Pause. Reread it. And then I delete it. Up on the wall Danny grins back at me, and in spite of my broken heart and the lump that now lives in my throat, I feel bad for complaining about anything. I say, "I'm sorry you drowned. I'm so sorry you died so young."

* * *

The refrigerator and cabinets are stocked with juice and milk and cereal and fruit, and every other food we could possibly want, courtesy of Addy. The clock above the stove says it's 6:34. I grab a pear and walk around that lofty, open room, looking at every photograph, every souvenir. Addy is everywhere, and as nice as it is to see a familiar face, it's clear that we are in someone else's home, someone else's life.

My mom appears, Dandelion in her arms. "It seems nice."

"It does."

"There are a lot of boys running around."

I ignore this because the only boy I'm interested in is back in Ohio.

I say, "So the Blackwoods are family and we're like the poor, down-on-our-luck relations?"

"Something like that. Your great-grandmother Eva was Sam Jr.'s oldest child, Claudine's big sister. Eva was already off at boarding school when Claudine was born. After their mother died, she never lived on the island again. . . ." She rattles off names and dates.

Even though I want to know more, I'm not about to let on. I interrupt her. "I'll just take your word for it."

It turns out that Samuel Blackwood Sr., my great-something-grandfather, was a famous railroad tycoon. One of *the* railroad tycoons. As in American royalty, which feels like one more secret I never knew.

"So basically all those years I was babysitting and working at the bookstore and Dad was buying all his shirts on eBay and you were driving your ten-year-old Volkswagen, we could have been living the high life?"

"The Blackwood fortune disappeared years ago."

Too bad, I think. *I could use that money right now to get myself home, or, even better, to New York or Los Angeles, somewhere I can start over, where there aren't people I love who will keep letting me down.*

"Did you let Dad know we got here?" *Not that he cares.*

"I did."

"Was he like, 'Oh, thank God. I'm so glad you all are far, far away'?"

"No, Claude. He misses you."

I stare at the floor.

She says, "I was thinking we could explore a little. Maybe go to the inn for dinner."

"I don't care. Whatever." I wonder what my dad is doing back home, if he's lying around eating thumbprint cookies or running miles and miles. If he's making an elaborate meal for himself and Bradbury, or maybe wishing he hadn't sent us away.

Mom sets Dandelion down, and he slinks off, running here and there and all around, sniffing everything, ducking under chairs and tables.

"Addy once told me, 'Don't lose today.' As in don't hide behind yesterday or hold back from tomorrow. We're going to make this an adventure, Claude. If any two people can, it's us."

And then she hugs me and I breathe her in, my mom who smells like roses—only she doesn't smell like roses anymore, she smells like honeysuckle, and for a second my world tilts. It was my dad who gave her the rose perfume every Christmas, and from now on she will smell like honeysuckle instead.

Even though I don't want to, I say, "Fine. Let's go explore."

And when she pulls away, she gives me a smile that says, *I know this is hard for you, and I appreciate your meeting me halfway, or at least partway.* My smile in return says, *I'm trying,* and as usual we're talking without words, a conversation my dad has never been able to join in.

The live oaks on the left side of the path and the live oaks on the right side of the path reach for each other, limbs entwining overhead, creating a tunnel. The path rises and we follow, climbing over a row of dunes, long grass toothpicking out of them like feathers. After this is a meadow, and then dunes again. The sand is as thick and deep as a plush carpet. It suction-cups to my feet, which sink with each step so that it's like walking through mud. And then, suddenly, the sky opens up.

Even behind my sunglasses, I'm blinded by white and blue. The white is the beach, stretching as far as the eye can see. The blue is the water, lapping against the sand. Mom grabs my arm for balance, pulling off one shoe and then the other. She gathers her hair, blowing wild in the wind, and ties it back into a messy knot. She is beautiful—as bright and vivid as a field of daisies—but she doesn't know it. This is because all her life, everyone has been telling her how smart she is, but the first time someone other than my dad told her she was pretty, she was, like, thirty.

I say, "You look beautiful." It's now my job to say these things, and to buy her honeysuckle perfume. And in that moment I want to tell her I've decided not to go to Columbia, that instead I'm going to stay with her forever so I can make sure no one ever hurts her again.

She throws an arm around me and stares out at the sea. "Your dad once told me I was the second-prettiest girl in the room, and I was so flattered because I knew he was being honest. But now I'm thinking that was a really shit thing to say."

She looks at me. I look at her. And maybe it's the fact that we're finally here, in this place I've been dreading, and it doesn't look like a prison at all, or maybe it's the fact that we are two emotionally shattered people in desperate need of sleep, but we sit right down on the sand and start to laugh. It's a laugh I need, and I hold on to it longer than I would normally because it feels so good. As it dies away, we both make this winding-down noise, like a sigh, at the exact same moment, and that gets us started again.

Finally, she wipes her eyes and says to me, "Promise you'll let me know what you need this summer. I'm still your mom, and I want to be here for you."

"I promise." But even as I say it, the laughter is already fading and I can feel myself closing up. We're here together, but there is still the sense of separation, of every woman for herself.

DAY 1

(STILL)

By the time we get to the inn, the sky is turning a soft pinkish gold. In spite of its grandness, the inn also feels welcoming, maybe because this was once a family home, and I wish we were staying here instead of at Addy's, which feels too personal. Here, at least, I might trick myself into believing we're just on vacation. We join the other guests, who are gathered on the wide front porch, drinks in hand, for cocktail hour. They smile. I smile.

"I'm Lauren Llewelyn and this is my daughter, Claudine."

"Claudine," someone says.

"Claude," I say.

"Claude."

They introduce themselves, and I will never remember their names, but I smile and chat and laugh politely, wearing my green sundress, the one with the ballerina skirt, because at the inn you dress for dinner. We walk past the rocking chairs and porch swings and go inside, which is cool and dark and from a different era.

By now most of the guests have moved down the hall to the living room, which looks more like a rambling old library. There are two portraits on opposite walls, one of an African American woman in a white dress, around forty years old, arms crossed, dark eyes fixed on some faraway object, the other of a white woman in red, about the same age, with a sleek blond bob, pistol at her waist. She stares out of the frame as if she's daring you to cross her.

Mom says, "That's Claudine." We stand in front of her and she half smiles, half glares down from the frame as if she's making up her mind about us. This is not the Claudine I imagined. All this time, I'd been picturing someone frail and hollow-eyed, worn down by tragedy, but this woman sits ramrod straight, as if her spine is made of steel.

I can't help myself. "Why did her mother kill herself?" I ask without looking away from her, because for some reason I can't look away from her. I don't want to.

"I don't think anyone knows the real story. She didn't leave a note, and there was speculation that she was depressed. I'm hoping my work here will help me find out."

In spite of her mother's suicide and the fact that she never left this island for long, even after she was grown, Claudine looks fierce and fearless—as if she could take on the world—and I want to be her.

Mom says, "Claudine was not only the grandmother I wish I'd had, but the woman who turned this estate into an inn. Before that it was a kind of guesthouse, meant to go to my grandmother after she married, but of course she didn't want it, so it became a home away from home for family and friends, a place for everyone to gather. Claudine saw its potential. She was a woman outside her time. And that"—she nods at the woman in white—"is Clovis Samms. She built the island's first hotel, up at the north end, and was the first and only female root doctor here, some said the best in all the South. She used herbs, roots, and ointments to heal people. Also a woman outside her time. I don't know enough about her, but I want to learn more."

She puts her arm around my shoulders, and we tilt our heads, letting them touch. Then we separate and, carrying our drinks, mingle with the guests. I imagine myself through their eyes. Lanky. Freckled. My mom's younger twin.

Maybe that's why. Because we're too much alike. He feels out-numbered.

After a few minutes, I tell my mom I need the bathroom and wander down the hall to the bar, which is empty. I give it a minute, and when no one comes in, I slip behind the bar itself, double-check that the coast is clear, and grab a beer from the fridge. I twist it open and take a drink.

"I'd say you're about five years too early for that."

The boy who carried our luggage moseys over to me, takes the bottle out of my hand, and empties it into the sink. He's wearing the same shorts and black shirt from earlier, his feet still bare. He looks totally out of place here in this genteel old inn with everyone else dressed in their finest.

"Actually, now that I look at you, maybe *six* years too early."

"I'm eighteen."

He studies me for a second. "Huh." Then he picks up a pen and flips open the notepad that sits on the corner of the bar. "Drinks work on the honor system, Lady Blackwood, so you'll want to write down everything you take, which I'm guessing is going to be a lot. I'll let this one slide." He walks around to the fridge, where I'm still standing, for some reason, and reaches past me, so close I can smell him—like fresh sheets and the great outdoors. He hands me a soda. "Go ahead, you try." He nods at the pad of paper. Gives me an encouraging smile.

I set the soda down unopened.

I say, "My mom is waiting for me."

"Don't let me keep you."

I reach past him this time, grab two minibar-size Absoluts, and drop them into my pocket.

I say, "You can write them on my tab." And walk out. A second later, I come back in. He's watching the door like he's expecting

75

me. "By the way? I'm older than my years. And if there's really 'everything to do here,' why don't you show me?" I cross back to the bar, pick up the pen, and write my phone number on the notepad.

Heart thumping, I walk out again and into the first room I come to, which is a cozier version of the living room. It is floor-to-ceiling books and smells like leather. I meant to find the living room instead, but the boy is still out there, so I pretend this is where I want to be. I choose a book at random—*The Secret Garden*—and take a seat on the couch. I fish the vodka bottles out of my pocket, swallow the contents of both, and place the empties side by side on the end table.

My head buzzes a little and my blood feels warm. I flip through the book for a minute and then lay it down and scroll through my phone, rereading the text chain from Wyatt. I pull up the shirtless picture and stare at it, imagining lying beside him, on top of him, underneath him, just so many naked limbs intertwined.

The universe is clearly playing a funny, funny joke on me. Because now he asks. *Now.*

I write: I'd love to hang out. In Georgia right now with my mom but will be home soon. But there's nowhere for it to go, so it sits there, unsent.

I sink back, disappearing into the couch, and chew on my finger, thinking of ways to get to him. I could catch the ferry tomorrow and go to the mainland and ask Saz to pick me up. I could call my mom's sister, Katie-May, who lives in Savannah. Or hack into my dad's Uber account and order myself a car to take me to Ohio.

At some point, I hear the ringing of a bell. The rise and fall of voices. The creaking and clacking of footsteps on stairs. My mom appears in the doorway. "That's dinner." She's expecting movement—close book, stand up, walk out of room. Her eyes go to the Absolut bottles, then back to me.

"Claude."

"Mom."

She frowns at the bottles, so I pick them up, place the book back on the shelf, and brush past her. I return the bottles to the bar, which is now empty. I don't look to see if the boy took my number. I just walk right out and keep going, Mom on my heels, down the stairs to the dining room.

We sit at a large table with three sisters, a photographer from Nashville, and a family of four. Jared from the dock, with the glasses and friendly face, is one of the servers. He waves at me from across the room. I wave back.

And then I look around at each person and think, *How many floors have you pulled out from under people?* This photographer, this mother of two, these sisters—somewhere in this world there is probably someone who's missing a floor right now thanks to them.

The conversations are the same: *What brought you to the island? Where are you from? What do you do back in the real world? How long are you here?*

I tell them: "We're in hiding."

"Witness protection."

"We witnessed a murder."

"My father was a serial killer."

"We're here indefinitely."

"Probably for the rest of my life."

With every comment, Mom comes along behind me, cleaning up my mess, assuring everyone that I'm a writer, too imaginative for my own good. She gives me a look and I ignore it.

After dessert we all begin to trickle out, and as I walk past Jared, he says, "There's a group of us that works here. If you get bored, come to the kitchen. You can find us there till around midnight, sometimes later."

"Is this your summer job?"

"I'm year-round. Most of us are."

"How old are you, anyway?" I'm not sure what makes me ask this, maybe because he looks too young to be here full time.

"Twenty-one."

"You look sixteen."

"I know." He laughs like, *Oh well,* like this is something he's used to hearing. "People usually don't take me seriously till they get to know me. I'm everyone's little brother. How old are you?"

"Eighteen."

"You look sixteen too."

"I know. It's annoying."

"Yeah." And I think maybe, just maybe—if I were planning to get to know anyone here, which I'm not—we could be friends. I glance over at my mom, standing by the stairs, talking to the photographer and the sisters. I say, "So where's the kitchen?"

"This way." I follow him into this little room with baseball caps and photos and books for sale, and beyond it is the kitchen, which is enormous and homey, and bustling with cooks and staffers my age or a little older, laughing and talking and joking around as they work. I want to be a part of it—of them—and suddenly I feel left out of everything everywhere. I picture Saz and Wyatt back in Ohio at some huge, raging party.

"There's really no phone service here?"

"Only for inn guests and emergencies."

"And no Wi-Fi?"

"Just at the general store, but the hours are weird. The good thing is, you get used to it after a while, being offline. It helps you be here, as in here"—he waves his hands at the room—"and not out there." He waves them broader, as if encompassing the whole world. "You'll see. Time moves a little differently. People move differently. Here you can just be, well, you. It's one reason we stay. Or if we do leave, we end up coming back."

"Is there a map of the island?"

He hands me a map from one of the gift-shop shelves and says, "You can have it."

"Thanks. Jared, right?"

He grins. "Yeah. Claude?"

"Yeah."

Outside, the hot, heavy air is humming—Mom says the sound is cicadas, but they're ten times louder than any cicadas I've heard before, a rattling, pulsating sound you feel in your skin and your bones. As we walk through the dark to our house, she doesn't mention the vodka, but she does tell me to curb the witness-protection, serial-killer talk.

"Just making conversation." And the meanest part of me, the part that is furious and hurt and wants her to make things right with my dad so we can go home, the part that thinks maybe some of this is her fault as well as his, likes the feeling of pushing her away.

It's after eleven when I crawl into bed. Dandelion curls up next to me and starts to purr, and I stretch out on this new mattress and these new sheets. I've pulled the curtains and left a light on in the kitchen and also in the bathroom so that I don't get lost if I get up in the night.

I lie there staring up at the photo of Danny, frozen in time with a sprinkling of freckles and a sunburned nose. For the rest of my life, he will always look like this. I wonder if he's a ghost. They say that can happen with a violent death—imprints and energies left behind.

I don't bother reading. Instead I write Saz the world's longest text. I want to know why she didn't tell me about Yvonne. I want to know her reasons for keeping this secret from me. Did someone order her not to say a word? Did Yvonne say, *You can't tell anyone, not even Claude, because Mary Grove is too small a town and we don't want this getting out*?

I write until my eyes grow heavy, and then I delete the text and turn out the light and lie there in the dark, sinking into the bed under the weight of my chest, no longer hollowed out but filled with—something. A feeling of homesickness. Of not being wanted. Of being all alone in the world. On earth. In the universe. And everyone has someone, but I am just me. And at night they all go inside and lock the doors and turn on the lights and pull the curtains, but I can still see the light shining out of the windows. And I am outside, in the dark, alone.

I have lived through this day. This first day. Only thirty-four more of them to come.

DAY 2

The next morning, I feel it before I open my eyes: I am somewhere else. The air is not Ohio air, but Georgia air, warm and sultry. There is something old and seductive about it. And the summer has a sound here—the constant hum of cicadas.

There is more to it than geography, though. I am somewhere else in other ways. And this, I know, is part of growing up. The part they don't tell you. That you can find yourself suddenly in another room, one that looks nothing like the one you're used to, and there's no getting back—no matter how much you want to—because from now on there is only here, and the only thing to do is settle in and try to make sense of it and tell yourself that this is your life now. This is what it looks like. And you're going to be okay. You can do this. Because you don't have a choice.

I eat breakfast in the reading nook while my mom gets ready to go to the island museum, where some of Aunt Claudine's papers are apparently stored. She was up early for a run on the beach, and this is another thing that is different. My dad is the runner, not my mom. For years he's tried to get her to go running with him, but she would never do it.

She says now, "Why don't you come with me to the museum? I'm not exactly sure what I'm walking into, research-wise, and I'd be shocked if anything's been documented or cataloged. I could use your help."

"Thanks, I'm good." I'm not budging from my window seat. I am going to sit here reading until August.

"Humor me. If you don't feel like helping me with work, at least pretend you're going to explore. Bicycles are on the back porch."

"Okay." She is distracted this morning. She knows that I never learned to ride a bike.

"There's plenty of lunch stuff in the fridge, but we can meet for dinner at the inn, although we should really be using some of this food Addy left for us. I've told her I'm paying her back—for all of this."

"If anyone should be paying her, it's Dad."

"Well."

And she goes quiet as she gathers her things and opens the door.

Mom, I want to say, *I hope the museum is everything you want it to be. I hope you find a story there or something to lose yourself in so you won't be sad or lonely.* Because our exile here isn't just about me. But for some reason I don't say it. Maybe because my parents have asked me to be mute, and now I am.

Instead I say, "I think I should go home sooner than August. Like, in a week or two."

Her smile wavers. "No."

"Mom."

"Claude."

I stare at her and she stares back.

I say, "If the separation was his idea, he should have been the one to go."

"My work is flexible. His isn't." She sighs, and suddenly she doesn't look sad or tired or like she's trying to make the best of things. She looks angry. "And I'm protecting him again." She shakes her head at the ceiling and then turns her eyes back on me. "I never want to disparage your dad to you, but I've got to learn to stop doing that."

"Probably."

"Here's the truth. I didn't want to leave home either, not after we decided to separate. He didn't tell me we had to leave, but I couldn't stay, not in that house, and not in Mary Grove. I hope you can understand that."

But August might be too late. Yvonne will replace me as Saz's best friend, a best friend she can also sleep with, so guess what? Yvonne wins. And Wyatt will marry Lisa Yu and I will die here on Virginity Island.

Instead of saying any of this, I get up from the window seat and hug her. I whisper into her hair, "I hope the museum is everything you want it to be."

Ten minutes later I'm alone except for Dandelion, warming himself in the sun that hits the dining room floor. It's been nineteen hours since I've talked to Saz, and this is the longest we've ever gone, our whole lives, without hearing each other's voices. I try to imagine what she's doing. If she's with Yvonne. I tell myself not to feel jealous, but I do, even though Yvonne isn't me and I'm not Yvonne and we mean different things to her. I think of my dad in our house all alone except for our dog. I say to Dandelion, "You may not miss Bradbury, but I do."

So it's just me.

And my thoughts.

And so much silence.

I pick up a book, the latest Celeste Ng, a novel I've been saving for summer days just like this one. But the problem with reading is that it's too easy to get distracted. I read the same words over and over, and it's like reading air or clouds or something else intangible. I set the book down and look out the window. The trees are the kind that come alive when they think you're not watching. I sit waiting for them to move, to give themselves away. They stay perfectly, unnervingly still except for the Spanish moss swaying in the breeze.

I get up and wander the living room, looking at the framed pictures, the shelves. Addy's books are mostly beach reads, dog-eared with bent spines, spanning the past twenty years. I pull out *The Joy of Sex* by Dr. Alex Comfort, which looks as if it hasn't been opened since the 1970s, and flip through the pages. The illustrations make me think of police sketches, and there is hair *everywhere*. I'm so mesmerized I don't even sit down. I just stand there reading.

> *Never blow into the vagina. This trick can cause air embolism and has caused sudden death.*

"Oh my God," I say to Dandelion. "You won't believe this." I keep flipping and reading. Each entry is funnier and more outdated than the next.

> *Vibrators are no substitute for a penis.*

> cassolette: *French for perfume box. The natural perfume of a clean woman: her greatest sexual asset after her beauty.*

I say to the book, "How about her brain?" But the book seems uninterested in this. Instead it advises women to protect and cherish that natural perfume as carefully as they do their looks. Two chapters later, the author sings the praises of the "well-gagged woman."

And that's it. I'm done with Dr. Alex Comfort. I slide the book back onto the shelf and hunt for the TV. There are famously no televisions on the island, and it takes me a minute to find where Addy has hidden hers. I study the DVD collection stacked beside it. I pull them out, one by one, and even though I'm a sucker for music and books and films from olden times, there's nothing I want to watch, except maybe the last one, a movie Saz has mentioned to me more than once. It's French, black-and-white.

I study the picture on the DVD cover. The girl looks cool. So cool. Like someone so strong and fearless, her heart could never be broken. Someone who would pour a drink over Dr. Alex Comfort's misogynistic head. Or give her number to a handsome, barefoot stranger on an island. Or do whatever the hell she wants.

I hold it up so Dandelion can see. "What do you think?" He yawns and rolls onto his back, paws curled, blinking at me.

I turn on the television, slide the movie in. I watch, studying Jean Seberg as if I'm going to be tested. Hair. Clothes. Smile. Walk. Every gesture. Dandelion curls up next to me and kneads my leg. I pet him without thinking, and he stays until it's over.

As the end credits are rolling, I shiver. I'm not sure if I loved the movie or hated it, but I know this: I've never seen anything like it. Boy falls for girl, girl falls for boy, boy has a gun, girl wants to be a writer, boy steals cars, girl betrays boy, boy refuses to leave girl. All of this happens in beautiful, photogenic Paris, and I sit there feeling like I need to see the Eiffel Tower and the Champs-Élysées *right now*.

But there's something else. In the pit of my stomach, a slightly ominous burning feeling is growing, which means, against all better judgment, I'm about to do something inevitable I'll probably regret. I rummage through the kitchen drawers till I find a pair of scissors, tuck the DVD case under my arm, and march into the bathroom.

Twenty minutes later, I have chopped off my hair, giving myself a pixie cut. I don't know what makes me do it except that Jean Seberg looks so completely secure and happy and comfortable in her skin, like nothing bad or upsetting will ever happen to her because she's just too together, too sure of who she is. Besides, short hair is more practical. It's too warm on this island to have long hair, and it's just hair, after all.

I hold up the DVD case and compare. Unlike Jean Seberg, I am a cross between an elf and a fairy, and it is not a good look for me.

I throw on my bikini, a T-shirt, and black pants, the tightest I own, which is the closest I can come to Jean's iconic outfit. I decide from here on out to go braless when I'm not wearing a bathing suit. Let's face it, I don't really need one anyway. I rummage through my mom's makeup until I find what I'm looking for—a red lipstick. I draw it on. Make a pout. Draw it on more.

I grab my map. Grab my notebook and a pen and throw them into my bag. There's liquor in the house, but it's locked in a cabinet. I scrounge through drawers for the key, but the only thing I come up with is an old pack of Virginia Slims. I throw these into my bag too, along with a lighter. On my way out, I grab a navy blue Greek fisherman's cap that hangs in the hall—the kind my dad and Addy's ex-husband, Ray, used to wear sailing when we lived in Rhode Island—and put it on, making my hair disappear entirely.

I walk outside. As I'm standing in the sun, a deer trots away, across the dirt road that curves past the house. "I'm not going to hurt you," I yell, which of course makes it run. I adjust the hat, tugging at my hair. At where it used to be.

DAY 2

(PART TWO)

Following my map, I start down Main Road, which connects one end of the island to the other. In all that emerald green of forest, it's a slash of white—sand, solid as concrete, crushed with shells, and rumble strips in a washboard pattern. I head south now, the only person on earth.

At some point I see it up ahead—Rosecroft. The drive curves toward the remains of the house, which rise up through the trees. This was where Samuel Blackwood Jr. first settled with his young wife. Where my great-grandmother was raised until she left the island, never to return. This was the homestead where my great-great-grandmother, Aunt Claudine's mother, died—where the gun went off, where they found her body, where the bullet carved a perfect hole in the closet door—and where Claudine lived out her life until the house burned in 1993 and she died two months later.

Rosecroft itself is enormous and vast, a watercolor against the blue, blue sky. Most of the roof is gone, and the remaining walls follow a jagged line. Except for one intact section of the second story, there is grass instead of floors. Instead of a ceiling, there is sky. Vines twine in and out of doorways and windows, which are like eye sockets, blank and staring. A sign warns AREA CLOSED, NO TRESPASSING. I walk past this, up the steps, and onto the grass.

I climb in and out of windows and doors, trying to imagine

what each room was used for. *Here is the kitchen. Here is the library. Here is the nursery. Here we laughed. Here we fought. Here we loved and dreamed. Here is where the fire started. Here is where the first brick fell. Here is where we died.*

I wander to the back of the mansion and stand on what must have been the veranda. Directly in front of me, several yards away, a fountain sits silent and empty.

I drop onto the top of the steps that lead down and away from the house and dig through my bag for my notebook and pen. The sun burns my arms and shoulders. I pull out the cigarettes, light one up, and inhale. This is my very first cigarette, and it feels momentous. The taste immediately makes me want to hurl, and I cough for a full five minutes. I finally wind to a stop, eyes tearing, and turn to a blank page.

Dear Saz.

I stare at these two words. There is so much to say to her, but how do I say it?

It's probably time I told you why this letter is coming from the coast of Georgia, not Atlanta, and why I won't be home this summer.

She is going to be surprised and probably angry that I didn't tell her. But I have to tell her.

I write six pages, front and back, and then I sit there a while longer, smoking the cigarette down to a nub. I light up another one, and another, inhaling them all, until I see some of the guests I recognize from the inn, walking sticks, cameras, heading for the ruins. I take one last drag and then throw up in the bushes and head for the beach.

* * *

The sky is electric from the sun, and I've forgotten my sunglasses, so I'm holding my hand over my eyes and squinting. I take off my hat and I feel naked without my hair, like I might burn up and melt away. I slip off my shoes and the sand is soft and cooler than I expected. I see a truck way, way down the beach, which is strange because I thought this island was no cars allowed. But right here there is no one. It's just me and this ocean, stretching for miles.

I pull off my clothes, stripping down to my bikini, the black one I bought with Saz back in April, when we were making plans for our last epic summer before college. I leave the clothes on the sand in a crumpled, wilted heap beside the shoes and the fisherman's cap, as if this beach is my bedroom floor. I wade in, and the water is warm. I pause when it reaches my shins.

My earliest memory is of my parents and me standing on a beach, feet in the water, holding hands. I remember the waves rushing in, rushing out, and the way the sand clung to my ankles as the ocean tried to drag it away. I remember my mom laughing and shouting "Don't let it take you!" to the sand or maybe to Dad and me. I remember breaking free and grabbing at the sand, trying to help it stay.

I wade deeper.

To my knees.

To my thighs.

To my hips.

I catch my breath. My heart is going *thrum thrum thrum*.

To my waist.

To my chest.

I wait for the drop-off, but the thing about the drop-off is that it happens all of a sudden, without warning. I think, *Not this time.* And I go under. My decision. *This is the drop-off because I say it is.* I close my eyes and swim into the ocean. In Rhode Island, we lived on the Atlantic. I know the danger of currents and swells and whirlpools. I know how to swim in calm water and wild water and what to do if I start to panic. I've been swimming as long as I've been walking, first in the ocean and then at the Municipool in Mary Grove, Ohio.

Underwater, there is no more bottom, no more floor. I open my eyes and imagine what it would be like to live here, in the sea. I swim, and it feels good to move like this. The waves grow choppier, but I keep going. When I get tired, I float on my back, letting the current carry me. Part of me is terrified and part of me is thrilled and part of me doesn't care at all. I pretend I'm dead and let my body go limp. The water holds me up, and this is always surprising because I feel so heavy, I should sink like a stone.

I tread water, looking all around me, and there is nothing but open ocean.

Which is why I open my mouth and scream. I scream and yell and shout, throwing everything I can—everything I've been holding in since that day my dad came into my room, every bit of the anger and fury I'm feeling at both my parents—at the ocean and the sky. I hurl words and sound as far as I can, until they disappear into all that blue.

A wave hits me in the face like a slap. I sputter, snorting in water, snorting it out, and when I catch my breath again, I am quiet. I float on my stomach and open my eyes, staring downward into nothing because it is too deep and dark. My body drifts. I am being tossed back and forth like a ball.

I come up for air, and the current is strong here and the island seems far away. *How did it get so far away?* I picture myself drifting over the waves, all the way to Africa, where I will wash up on shore and begin again. New name. New continent. Maybe my dad will worry. Maybe he'll realize he made a mistake and that he actually does want a family.

I go facedown again and float.

I am thinking I should turn back soon because I've lost track of how long I've been out here. My stomach growls and I feel the hollow ache of hunger.

Suddenly, something grabs me around the middle, and my head jerks up and I am breathing and coughing because I've just inhaled half the ocean. My first thought is, *Shark*. But there are arms around me, carrying me through the water, and the arms are attached to a boy.

I manage to cough out, "Let me go."

"No."

"I don't need saving. I grew up on the ocean."

"I don't care if you're part dolphin."

It's the boy from the bar, the boy from our luggage, and now, I guess, he will also be the boy from the beach. I start pummeling him, and he just tightens his grip and drags me toward shore.

"I need you to chill the fuck out, Ariel." He is gold from the sun. "You know this is the largest breeding ground for sharks on the East Coast."

And all at once I'm thinking about my cousin Danny, Addy's son, and the rip current, and I see how far out we are, and I don't know anything about these particular waters here, off the coast of Georgia, or what lives in them. I don't know the currents, and I don't know anything. And what if something happened to me? My mom would be completely alone.

I put my arm around his neck and now I'm holding on, and there's a tattoo there on his shoulder blade. A compass. Of course. So beautifully, stupidly, perfectly ironic. I'm facing him, my back to the island, and I'm watching all that ocean. I turn my head and there's the island growing steadily closer and closer, but it's still a long way away. I keep an eye out for fins.

In the time it takes us to reach the shallows, I think about how stupid I am, how I can't afford to be reckless, even as part of me is picturing my dad's face when he gets the call. *Neil Henry? There's been an accident. If only you hadn't sent them away.*

We're close to shore when I let go and break away from him, and now I'm swimming harder and faster than I ever have. I am racing him because I suddenly have to get back to land and feel it underneath me, and because I won't be outdone by a boy, and no man is going to save me, and he needs to see what he is dealing with. I pull ahead, and then he's beside me and we're pushing as hard as we can. I win by a hair, and we collapse onto the beach.

My body sinks into the sand. Warmth all around me, reaching into my flesh and bone. It's the first time I've felt warm all the way through since May 29. I am tucked away behind my eyelids, as if my head is a room and they are the doors that close me in. The sun is so bright that it's impossible to shut it all out. One day, someone will walk down this beach and they'll see an imprint of my body, like a chalk outline, buried deep beneath the sand.

"What the hell is wrong with you?"

I open my eyes and he is standing over me.

"Listen, Calamity Jane, is that it for today or should I stick around? You know what, I'll help you out. The marsh is that way." He points in the direction of the trees. "Through there and across Main Road and keep going west till you run out of land. You can't miss it. Take a swim while you're there. You'll love it. There are alligators and poisonous snakes just waiting for you." He leans over, grabs the shirt lying on the sand, and starts to go. No mention of our interaction at the bar or the fact that I left him my number.

"Claude," I say. "My name's Claude."

He turns, walking backward away from me. He holds out his arms. "I don't fucking care." And disappears through the dunes.

I go back through the dunes, back through the live oaks, back onto the dirt road. I look for the boy, but I don't see anyone.

I pull off my cap, shake out what's left of my hair. If I could collect all my hair and stick it back onto my head, I would. As I was chopping it off, it never occurred to me to remember that this island is only temporary and I am only temporary and I will need hair when I go to college in the fall. Now I will start freshman year being mistaken for a boy. I dig for my lipstick buried deep in the pocket of my pants. Rub it over my lips. Just in case I see him again. Then I hear a rustling in the brush and I start to run.

DAY 2

(PART THREE)

My heart is still pounding by the time I get to Addy's. The screen door slams behind me and I call out for my mom. No answer. I call out for Dandelion. No answer. For one terrible second, I wonder if they've left me too. I make a beeline for my mom's room, and there are her things, spread across the dresser and the chair and the bed. There are her clothes in the closet. I breathe. Dandelion appears from nowhere, stretching, yawning. I pick him up and kiss him all over his face.

In the bathroom, I shed my wet pants and shirt and hat and stand there in my bikini, legs and arms eaten up with bug bites. I scratch at them until they turn into welts, and then I peel off my suit and take the world's longest shower.

An hour later, I am parked in the window seat, fisherman's cap hiding what's left of my butchered hair. My notebooks—the ones holding my bad, overly long novel—lie beside me. I have too much to say and nothing to say and I'm staring at this towering pile that is my book as if it's a long-forgotten loved one hooked to a ventilator. I think, *It's time to pull the plug on you.*

Someone or something bangs the front door, and I nearly jump out of my skin. There's no one here I want to talk to, so I ignore it. They bang again, and I keep right on reading. But then there's a rap on the window and the someone is standing there. The boy from the beach.

I stare at him, unblinking, and wonder if somehow I can make myself invisible. Through the glass he says, "I see you."

I set the notebook down, get up, open the door.

"What do you want?"

"You're alive."

"I am."

"I figured odds were pretty good you were lying somewhere out in the marsh half eaten by a gator, so I thought I'd better check. Just because this place looks like a version of paradise doesn't mean it can't also be deadly." He turns away, jogs down the steps, comes right back up. "You know, it's probably a good time to warn you about the snakes. Rattlesnakes, copperheads, water moccasins. Oh yeah, and never get between a wild hog and her piglets. That'll also ruin your day. Watch where you're walking and swimming and you'll be fine. Especially at night, because some of the creatures here are nocturnal. The beach is okay, but you know what, I'm thinking you shouldn't do that by yourself either. The last thing any of us needs is to have to call a medevac to come get you."

And like that, he's down the steps again and heading for the road.

I move out onto the porch. "Do you give everyone this little pep talk when they arrive?"

He turns around to face me. "Only the reckless ones."

"Well, sorry you had to waste a trip. I'm planning to stay inside the rest of the time I'm here."

"And how long is that?"

"Thirty-four more days, if you count today. Which unfortunately I do."

"I'll be sure to warn the Park Service. You know. In case you change your mind." He saunters away without a single look back. I stand watching the way the sun lights his hair and the way his shoulders move under his shirt as he swings himself up into the dusty black truck that waits in the road.

That evening, my mom and I sit in rockers on the front porch of the inn, drinking lemonade. We are wearing nearly matching blue dresses. An accident that leaves me feeling irritated.

Mom is overflowing with facts she picked up at the museum. "Did you know the history of the island is rife with strong women who had to rebuild after tragedy? Claudine and your great-grandmother Eva were descended from a line of them. Before the Blackwoods ever came here, women were running this place."

"Rife?"

"Yes."

"So you're saying we've come to Amazon Island."

"Pretty much. This is where we are right now. Here on Amazon Island, surrounded by the ghosts of strong women. Maybe there's something we can learn from them. Maybe we can both find something to write about."

She lets these words linger, and when I don't ask about the work—how long she thinks it will take her, what kinds of materials the Blackwoods left behind, what the most fascinating thing was she learned today about the people who once lived here—she tells me about Doña Grecia Reyes, a Timucua Native American who married a Spanish soldier and fought with the Spanish for possession of the island. How she wrote a letter to the king of Spain demanding the money she needed to oversee the entire coast of Florida and Georgia. How he not only wrote her back but also sent the money to her, and how ever after they called her Princess of the Island.

Behind her sadness, there is a brightness in my mom's voice, a purpose. She is on the brink of a project again, and the research is giving her something to do.

I don't say anything, but some small part of me that is still me thinks, *I need something to do other than wander around the island like rotten old Miss Havisham.* And the part of me that is angry at her doesn't want to tell her that these stories are interesting or that I care about them in the least.

"It suits you," she says, touching the ends of my hair. "It's sophisticated."

"It's too short."

"Why'd you do it?"

"I needed a change."

"I'd cut mine off if I thought it would look good."

"It would look better on you." Everyone knows I'm the Ron to her Harry.

"The last thing you need is your mom trying to be your twin. I need my own thing. Maybe I'll get a tattoo."

As she talks, I think about roles. How we all have them. How we all play them, whether we want to or not. Mine is the Good Daughter of Two Exceptional People She Will Never Be Able to Surpass. The girl who took an IQ test when she was six years old that said she was a genius, even though she's never felt like one. She is a less glittering version of her mom, whose role is Famous Award-Winning Author and Everyone's Favorite Person.

My dad's role is the One Not Like Us. Except that he's creative too. He can play any musical instrument he picks up, even though he never had a lesson before he went off to Juilliard, back when he was twenty. He can pick out a tune on the piano or guitar after hearing it once, and he can paint, but he doesn't. Mom says he's a frustrated artist and that he belongs in a different era.

My role on this island can't just be Shunned Daughter of Father Who Can't Have a Family Anymore. Or Lauren Junior/Lauren's Shadow. It has to be more than that. And I think again about how Old Claude is dead and New Claude has taken her place, even though I don't know the first thing about New Claude.

A minute later, I tell my mom I need the bathroom. I go inside, where it is immediately five hundred degrees cooler, down the stairs, and straight to the gift shop, which is empty. I fiddle around with the books and the baseball caps and the cards and pretend this is all I want.

Jared appears from somewhere. He's dressed in a white button-down shirt and black pants, the uniform for kitchen staff. His sleeves are rolled up, and for the first time I notice the tattoo on his right forearm. He says, "Hey."

And I have to remind myself that this is an island and there are only, like, thirty-one people here.

"Hey. I'm trying to find the guy who carried our luggage up to the house."

"You mean Miah."

"Maya?"

"Jeremiah Crew. But we call him Miah. *M-I-A-H*. Some of the Park Service guys, back when he first came here, called him J.Crew, but he put a stop to that pretty quick."

"Can you tell me where to find him?"

"Here, there, everywhere. Miah kind of goes where he wants and does what he wants."

"He seems like he's in charge, or like he *thinks* he is."

Jared shrugs. "He's been coming to the island awhile."

"What does he do, anyway? Like, why is he here? Does he work at the inn with you guys?"

"He works for the Baileys—they live on the north end—clearing trails with Outward Bound groups. He runs errands. He goes to the mainland when people need supplies. He builds things."

"But why *here*?"

"Maybe you should ask him." Then he gives me this look like he knows the real reason for all my questions. "He doesn't have a girlfriend. At least not as far as I know." He grins, and I can tell he definitely knows why I'm asking but he's not judging me for it, and in that moment I think, *Maybe Jared and I actually can be friends.*

"That's not why I'm asking. But thanks, Jared."

"You're welcome, Claude."

I start to walk away and then I turn back. "What does your tattoo say?"

He holds out his arm so that I can read it. *August 12.*

"Your birthday?"

"I got it in honor of a friend of mine who died."

And I can tell by the way he says it that he knows what it's like to have the floor disappear suddenly.

"I'm sorry about your friend."

"Thanks." He blinks down at the tattoo, just for a second, then looks back up at me. "Hey, we're hanging out tomorrow night, if you want to join us."

"Where?"

"The Dip."

"What's the Dip?"

"Serendipity. It's where the staff lives."

"Maybe. Thanks. I'll see."

* * *

I sit at dinner listening to the rise and fall of voices, deep in conversation—the same conversations over and over again, so that I have both questions and answers memorized—and I am thinking about Jeremiah Crew. This is what I know about him:

People call him Miah.

He doesn't like being called J.Crew.

He's been coming here awhile.

Everyone relies on him.

He probably doesn't have a girlfriend.

We're walking back to the house when my phone buzzes. "Is that you?" Mom says, her face to the sky.

I pull my phone out of my pocket.

I love you more than Black Widow and peanut butter and "Umbrella." When are you coming home?

Rihanna's "Umbrella" has been our song since we were little.

I type the lyrics back to her as fast as I can, but my phone is now searching, searching, and it's trying to send the message, and then, like that, Saz is gone.

DAY 3

I wake up early. Sometime during the night I've shed my pajama bottoms and I lie there in my top and underwear. I try to conjure Wyatt's face. His mouth. But instead of Wyatt, I see Jeremiah Crew. Wise-ass expression. Compass tattoo on his shoulder. Hands, broad and strong. I push his image away, but he comes right back.

Claudine, it says, that mouth of his, *I want you. Don't you know how I feel about you? Don't you know how much I want you?*

Yes, I breathe. *Take me.*

Something buzzes around my head and near my ear. With one hand, I swat at the mosquito even though I can't see it. *Buzz buzz buzz.* I smack at the air with both hands and then I sit up, shaking my hair—damp from all that Georgia heat—in case it's decided to nest there. The buzzing continues and, *poof,* Jeremiah is gone.

I slump back against the headboard. *You win, mosquito. Have at it. I hope I die of malaria here in this Georgia wilderness. It will serve my parents right.* Jeremiah Crew will come to my funeral, and my ghostly vessel will stand beside him as he cries over my casket or urn, whichever. He will be forever haunted by me and the thought of what might have been.

It's raining by the time I emerge from my room. My mom is in the kitchen, rinsing dishes and stacking them in the wooden rack on the counter. She's dressed in jeans and a bright summer blouse, hair pulled back in a ponytail.

"Morning," I say, reaching for the coffee.

"Afternoon." She brushes a loose strand off her face and nods at the window seat, where there is a large brown box. "From your father."

He's no longer *Dad*. He's *your father*.

"What is it?"

"I don't know."

In the distance, lightning flashes. I count—*one, two, three, four*—and there comes the thunder. I lean against the counter, eating cereal, staring at the box as if it's a bomb set to explode. Mom is talking, but I'm not hearing her because all I'm thinking about is that box. She says something about the museum and dinner, and then she is collecting her bag and an umbrella and heading out the door.

I'm still leaning against the counter when she comes right back in.

"Is this yours?"

"What?"

She stands in the doorway, staring down at something. I walk over to her and follow her gaze to the tube of cortisone cream and can of Off! that sit there. There's a note taped to the bug spray: *For Her Ladyship. It's worse if you scratch them.*

I say, "Actually, I think that is mine."

I glance past her, but there's no sign of him anywhere.

She looks down at the note and then up at me, unable to hide her smile. "Do you want to tell me who it's from?"

"Not really." I give her a smile of my own and go back into the kitchen, where I make a show of pouring myself more cereal. In a moment she calls out a goodbye, and the door clicks behind her.

I wait three minutes before picking up the cortisone cream and bug spray and bringing them into the house. I examine the familiar-looking note, which was clearly torn from a certain notepad. I flip the paper over and there is my phone number, exactly as I wrote it. And below it: *Phones don't work here. If I want to find you, I'll find you.*

My dad has sent me Edna, my favorite childhood doll, a journal of song lyrics that Saz and I wrote over the years, my vintage Nancy Drew books, and a clay cat I made when I was in fourth grade. All of it wrapped in Avengers birthday paper. And the following message:

> Dear Clew,
>
> Just a few things you left behind that I thought you might be missing. I hope you're having fun on the island and that it's not too bloody hot. Bradbury and I are plugging along here. It's a busy time at the college, but we're looking forward to seeing you in August when you're home. We miss you.
>
> > Love,
> > Dad

I flip through the journal, stack the books in a neat pile, set the clay cat on top. I pick up Edna and study her face—the whiskers that were meant to be stitches, which I drew on her cheeks after I got stitches of my own following an accident on the school playground; the bald spot where I cut her hair; the eye shadow I gave her with purple permanent marker.

"Why are you here?" I say to her. "Why did he send me these

104

things when I'm going back home in a few weeks?" *Unless you're not going home,* a voice whispers deep inside of me. *Unless he never wants you to come home again.*

I leave everything on the window seat. Edna lies on her back, one foot propped against the wall. Dandelion hops up beside her and starts bathing what's left of her hair.

I grab the fisherman's cap and my shoes. I leave so fast that I forget to bring an umbrella, and in minutes I'm soaked through. The cap has the smell of wet dog.

As I walk, I am thinking about the fact that my parents loved each other until my dad decided he didn't anymore, that he wanted a family and then he didn't. What makes someone stop loving you? One day there's love; the next day there's not. Where does it go? Something that lived and breathed like that—how can it just vanish as if it never really existed? I imagine a room or maybe an entire planet where all the love goes to live once we're done with it. Like a kind of junkyard. Little remnants of love scattered everywhere. People picking through, collecting the strongest, biggest pieces, and trying to make something of them again. Isn't this what we do every time we meet someone new or fall for someone new or start loving someone new? Pick up the old battered bits of ourselves and try again?

Eventually, I see a house just off the road. A bright blue shotgun shack underneath an enormous live oak. Bright blue rocking chairs on the front porch. Lights in the windows. It looks like a storybook house, cozy and inviting, and I want to go in and make myself at home.

I keep walking, because if I don't, I might stay here forever. Just down the road there is another shack, this one a sunflower yellow. The next house is a soft green, the one after that a kind of rose color. From the outside they all look warm and welcoming, as if nothing bad could ever happen to the people living there.

The general store is just two short aisles packed with candy and cereal and junk food and calamine lotion. There is an ice cream freezer and a refrigerator with cold drinks. There are postcards of the island that look like they're from the 1970s and a small counter where a woman with a round, scrubbed face sits reading a magazine. Her name tag says TERRI.

I clear my throat. "How often does the ferry run?"

She glances up at me, magazine still open. *People.* "Three times a day to the mainland and back, but if you've got money, you can charter a boat."

"If only," I say. "What are your hours here?"

"Whenever I feel like showing up." She looks down at her magazine and continues reading.

Past the counter, over in one corner, there are a couple of round tables with chairs. I sit, dig out my phone, and call Saz. It rings once before she picks up.

"Sazzy?"

"Hen! Are you still in Atlanta? When're you coming home?"

And all the pieces of me that I've been holding together for the past few weeks start talking at once, fractured and separate, but united in their ache. In the pain that comes with saying, "I'm not coming back for a while because my mom and I are literally on an island and this is where I have to be. Because my dad doesn't want us and my mom is trying to figure out what comes next, so we came here. And I still can't make sense of it. If he wanted out so badly, why didn't *he* go away instead? Why did my mom and I have to be the ones to leave everything, like fugitives, like convicts on the run who've done something so horrible that no one can speak of it and who don't even deserve to say goodbye?"

I don't say *home* because Mary Grove isn't my home any more than the island is. It's just a place where I used to live. I'm not sure where home is. Maybe living in the junkyard with all the ruins of love.

Saz listens and listens, even when I tell her about my hair and how I cut it all off, and when I start to cry, she says, "Motherfucker." And keeps listening. I can hear her sitting very still, not breathing, so that I can say everything I need to say, and after a while I'm not even sure what I'm saying because it's not me saying it; it's the pieces of me. And even as I'm crying, I can feel them slowly, slowly stitching themselves together again. Very loose. But together.

When I'm finished and there are no more words and the pieces of me are breathing hard and holding on to each other, Saz says, "First, I love you."

"I love you too."

"Always. I mean it. I don't want you to ever think for a minute that my love is going away. Second, fuck him. I'm not surprised, but fuck him."

What does she mean, "I'm not surprised"? The part of me that loves my dad because he's my dad wants to tell her to fuck off, but I can't go around protecting him forever. So I echo: "Fuck him." And a fraction of my heart chips off and falls away as I say it, because the words feel like a betrayal.

"Third, we need to get you out of there."

And the idea of this makes me sit up a little straighter, and then I'm brushing the tears away because I want them off my face so I can concentrate on what she's saying.

"What's halfway between here and there? If I can get to . . . Hold on. . . ." She goes quiet for a few seconds. "If I can get my ass to maybe Greenville, can you meet me? Can you, I don't know, steal a car or get on a plane or something? I can be there tomorrow."

I pull up the map on my phone, and it keeps glitching because the service is shit, but finally I'm studying the route, and my heart is skipping faster and faster, just imagining running away, far from here.

"I don't want to go back there," I say. Even though I miss my room with its green walls and my dog and my house and my friends. Things I've taken for granted all my life.

"Of course not. We could hit the road. Just us. Thelma and Louise. A couple of outlaws. One last trip before college. You and me, wild and free. Maybe Asheville. We can find that sanitarium where Zelda Fitzgerald burned to death."

And I can see it, the two of us. Claude and Saz. Saz and Claude. The way it's always been and always will be. Stopping at every tacky tourist site between North or South Carolina and California. Because that's where we'll go. The West Coast. Los Angeles. No more winter. No more cold. Just sunshine and bright skies and city as far as the eye can see. We'll lose ourselves and find ourselves.

Then Saz says, "Hold on." And I can hear her talking to someone. And then laughing. And then saying something else. And then, to me, into the phone: "I'm back. Sorry. Yvonne's ordering pizza and we can't ever agree on what to get. I'm like, *Pepperoni, extra peppers,* and she's all, *Ham and pineapple.* Which is so completely disgusting." She practically shouts this, and I know it's for Yvonne's benefit, not mine.

"Am I on speaker?"

"What?"

"Am. I. On. Speaker?"

"Yes. . . ."

"Take me off it now."

Because I wasn't calling Saz and Yvonne, I was calling Saz.

"Okay. It's off. Sorry. It's just you and me. Yvonne can't hear you."

It's the way she says *Yvonne,* like they have secrets between them. Ordering pizza and having sex and falling in love, while I'm on the outside, 843 miles away.

"So let's meet in Asheville," she says.

"Is it serious? You and Yvonne?"

"She broke up with Leah." And waits for me to say something. When I don't, she goes, "Hen?"

"Sorry. I wasn't sure if you were talking to me or her." And it's there in my voice, the hurt I'm feeling. "Did she do it for you?"

"She says she didn't, but this was, like, last Thursday, and we've been together ever since. She deflowered me again. And again." And she laughs and laughs. "Oh, wait, hold on. . . ." And she is gone again, and then back, gone and then back, over and over.

Each time she comes back, she apologizes, but I can feel myself shrinking. The island and its ruins and humidity and horses and wild hogs are closing in on me until I'm the size of an ant. For as long as I've known her, Saz has never felt like her parents really *get* her. They don't begin to understand her sexuality or her sense of humor, but they are sweet and well meaning, and they try. Her dad goes to marches with her and wears Pride shirts and lets her decorate his car with rainbow bumper stickers, and every night he tells her he loves her, no matter what. Which is why she can't possibly understand what I'm going through. Also, she's being really fucking rude.

I suddenly want to hang up. I want to say, *In the past four weeks, my entire world has fallen apart, and you're arguing about pizza?*

109

She goes, "So sorry, Hen." And they're talking again. And I'm sitting there waiting. And my palms have gone sweaty and my face has gone hot, and it isn't the Georgia humidity that's doing it. It's the two of them. And it hits me right then—no matter how much I want it to, nothing will stay the same.

When she comes back on, I say, "I gotta go. My whole world is upside down, and you're too busy with Yvonne to even listen."

"I've been listening this whole time. Look, I'm sorry if I'm being an asshole. I didn't know you were going to call, and I'm so glad you did, because I miss you like hell, Hen, I do. It's just that she's here, and I don't know what I'm doing. This is all new territory for me—you gone, me in a relationship."

We fall quiet. And in that quiet I feel the chasm between us growing so big and deep that I wonder if we'll ever be able to fill it again. *We were never supposed to have secrets. We were supposed to always be Claude and Saz. Saz and Claude.*

She says, "I'm serious about meeting you somewhere. Wyatt's been asking about you."

"He texted me." And then, for some reason, I add, "I told him."

"You told him what?"

"About my parents."

"You told Wyatt?"

"Yes."

"When?"

"Before I left Ohio."

"But you didn't tell me."

I start to say something about Yvonne, but instead I say, "No. You're too close. It would have made it real." It feels foreign to edit the things I say to her. Instead of rebuilding the floor, I'm building walls.

She goes silent.

I say, "Are you still there?"

"Yeah." Her voice has gone inward, as if she's swallowed it. For a minute, neither of us say anything.

Finally, she sighs, "So let's do it. Let's meet somewhere and then get you back to Mary Grove." But the way she says it, it sounds like the last thing she ever wants to do.

And even though I'm furious with her for going on with her life while I'm here, frozen and paralyzed, and even though she's furious with me for telling Wyatt before telling her, there's a part of me that wants to. I almost say, *Yes. Let's do it. Let's just go.* For a few seconds, I can see it again—Thelma and Louise on the open road. Wyatt and me, together at last.

But then I look around me at this store and, out there, beyond it, the live oaks and palm trees and marsh, and suddenly I'm right back here on this island, and on this island is my mother, elbow-deep in letters and papers and God knows what else. Trying to keep herself distracted and busy and filled with purpose so that she doesn't crack in half.

"I can't." And saying it makes me feel as if *I'm* going to crack in half. And this will be the start of it. The point where I don't look back but vow forever to be allied with my mom. In that moment I make this lifelong choice. Her over him. Her over everyone, including me.

"Hey. We're going to figure this out. You're not alone, Hen. No matter how much you feel like you are. You're never alone. Not as long as I'm on this earth."

"Okay," I say. But the thing is, I am alone. And the chasm is still there. And Yvonne is there, taking my place. "What did you mean you weren't surprised, when I told you about my dad?"

"I mean, your parents never argue. And they both work all the time, and I've never seen them hold hands."

"They hold hands." But even as I say it, I'm trying to remember a time when I've seen them hold hands or kiss or show any real physical affection toward each other the way Saz's parents do. "Just because you've had *one* relationship—if you can even call it that—doesn't mean you know everything about love."

"The hell? I just *said* I don't know what the fuck I'm doing. I know things are shit right now, Hen, but you don't have to take it out on me."

"You have no idea what I'm going through."

"No, I don't, because you only told me ten minutes ago. Unlike Wyatt Jones, who has apparently known for a while."

We sit in silence. I can hear her breathing fast and sharp on the other end. I almost end the call, but then she sighs loudly and says, "Listen. I don't like you very much right now, but I love you more than *Riverdale* and bookshops and sunflowers."

What about Yvonne? Do you love me more than her?

The door to the store opens and the photographer from the inn walks in.

I say, "I have to go."

And then I hang up on her.

I stare down at my phone, where Saz just was, and my heart is pounding and my blood is boiling and my pulse is racing and my head feels like it's going to burst. I pull up the texts from Wyatt and try again to send the photo of me in the bikini. This time it goes through. I write: Wishing you were here.

I don't pay attention to direction. I just walk. I walk until I look around and I don't see the bright blue shotgun house or the wild horses, only trees and marsh and sky. I turn back toward where I think the general store is, but the underbrush soon grows wilder and the trees thicker and the sky disappears.

If I could, I'd call my dad right now and tell him: *It's your fault I'm lost. You figure it out. If I don't make curfew, you find a way to get in touch with Mom and tell her I'm okay and where I am, and then you get me back to where we're staying. You fix this.*

I search my phone for some sort of GPS, but it comes up blank. So I try walking in another direction and another until I'm completely turned around. At some point, I feel drops of water on my face. I look up at the sky, and a storm cloud the size of Texas has gathered overhead.

"Shit."

And in that moment the sky opens and the thunder booms, and once again I am soaked through, but I keep walking because this storm isn't going to stop me. I *am* the storm. I walk and walk until I hear voices and see a building through the slanting rain, and then I run for it. This is not the house I saw earlier. This one is two stories, yellow paint chipping, set against a backdrop of live oaks and Spanish moss that have a haunted, murderous look. There are people on the porch.

Jared says, "Claude?"

DAY 3

(PART TWO)

Jared is sitting on the top step, beer bottle in hand. A girl with thick black braids and large, dark eyes is next to him, along with another boy, African American, round face, round body, who gives me a wave and a smile, even though I've never seen him before.

I climb the steps and join them, and Jared passes me a beer. I drink it down, and it's cool and bitter, and I like the taste of it. Something in it reminds me of Ohio and Trent Dugan's party. I take off the fisherman's cap and run a hand through my wet hair, trying to smooth it down and give it some sort of shape.

"Welcome to Serendipity," Jared says, opening his arms. "Better known as the Dip."

Several beers later, I know that the girl is Wednesday, another inn staffer, originally from Alabama, and the boy is Emory, a junior nature guide who grew up in South Carolina. He takes inn guests for tours of the island in the Park Service trucks. Today is their day off. The rain rattles against the roof of the porch as the sky turns into night, and I feel my bones start to settle. *You're safe. Not lost. It's okay. You're here. They're here. You're not alone.*

The three of them start telling ghost stories and I'm half listening, half thinking about Saz and my dad and Wyatt, who is probably, right this minute, having sex with Lisa Yu.

Wednesday says to me, "Have you ever seen a ghost?" Her voice is velvety, and something about it and the beer and the rain act like a lullaby. I feel warm and content, eyes heavy, body heavy.

I answer, "No."

"You will here." My skin prickles.

Emory shakes his head. "Man, Behavior Cemetery has some scary vibes, but nothing like Rosecroft or the Dip."

I say, "Why does the inn staff live all the way out here anyway?"

Emory stretches his legs out, crossing ankle over ankle. "You're not allowed to build on the island because it's protected, and this is the only place big enough to house us all."

I glance around at the woods. No other houses, no other lights. The Dip feels like the most remote place on earth.

"Have you heard of the baby man?" Jared is looking at me.

Emory starts shaking his head and going "Dude, dude" under his breath.

Wednesday says, "Don't tell that one, Jared. That one freaks me out. Like, seriously freaks me out. It's worse than, I don't know, the guy with the hook or whatever that stupid urban legend is."

Jared leans forward, his voice low and measured. "The baby man is this kind of humanoid thing, with, like, a baby face and old-man hair. He says *mama* a lot. And if you say it back, he'll come closer and try to get you."

And then of course we fall into silence, and I am listening for *mama* over the sound of the rain. Except for the rattling on the roof and the music coming from inside the house, it's amazing how still the night is. As if the island is holding its breath, the trees frozen in mid-reach.

And then I hear it: "Mama," so quiet and high-pitched that for a second I think it's the actual baby man. Wednesday and I jump, and she knocks Jared right off the porch.

He gets up, straightens his glasses, brushes himself off, and sits back down as if nothing happened.

"Shit," Emory says. Nervous laughter all around.

We gradually fall quiet, and then Wednesday turns to me. "Is that your real hair color?"

"Yes."

"What's your astrological sign?"

"Aries."

"Do you have any pets?"

"A cat and a dog." I don't mention that Bradbury is back in Ohio.

"If you had the choice between this island and Patagonia, which would you choose? Don't think, just pick one."

"Neither. I'd choose California."

She says, "What's your favorite breakup song?"

"Currently? Or all-time?"

"All-time."

I say the first song that comes into my head. " 'Irreplaceable' by Beyoncé."

She nods a kind of grudging approval. "So what's your story?"

I think, *I don't have one fucking clue what my story is, thank you very much.*

I say, "I don't have one." Not yet, at least, unless you count being the girl whose entire world blew up days before she graduated from high school.

Wednesday smiles at me like she knows better.

I smile at her. "Do you always ask so many questions?"

"I'm a very curious person."

"Who doesn't have a filter," adds Emory.

I say, "I'm here because my mom's working on a project. What's your story?"

"I love Greek mythology, zodiac signs, and makeup. I'm learning Japanese. I have a Chihuahua named Teddy who's the love of my life. I've been playing guitar since I was twelve." She sighs. "More than anything, I want to sing. Professionally. But my family, they think that's something you do in the car or in the shower. They don't get it." She takes a drink. Sets her bottle down. "We couldn't afford college, so two years ago I ran away from home." She says it matter-of-factly. I study her in the light of the porch, and even though she apparently loves makeup, she's no-makeup pretty. She looks like she was born outdoors, probably in the branches of one of these fairy-tale oaks, or like she came out of the sea and now here she is, some sort of land mermaid, a little damp but not sweating down her face like I am. "I'm here year-round like Jared."

"Is Wednesday your real name?"

"When I left home, I renamed myself. After Wednesday Addams." She tugs at a braid. She doesn't offer her real name.

I say, "Does your family know where you are?"

"They do now." But I'm not sure I believe her.

I look at Jared. "Why did you come here?"

"I grew up nearby, a little town outside of Jacksonville. Summer before college, I was planning on going to the Philippines to visit my dad's family. You know, learn about that part of my culture, but then . . ." He holds up his arm, the one with the tattoo. "My friend died. Suicide. He was my person. Honestly, the only one who's ever really known me. And it pretty much turned the world upside down."

This immediately gets me thinking about Saz. Even though she's still here on this earth, it feels like she's somewhere else, somewhere much farther away than Ohio.

Jared says, "It's been almost three years, but I still miss him. You have to make the most of it, you know. Life lessons. I always thought I'd go to, I don't know, Atlanta or New York or some-where bigger. But then I heard about the job here and it seemed more manageable, more what I wanted. Not so far away. Not so big and loud and in your face."

"Life lessons," I echo.

"It's something I tell myself."

"Does it help?" I want him to say, *Yes, it helps. The mere act of saying it chases all the sadness and anger away forever.*

"Not really." He seems to think this over. "Maybe sometimes. A little."

Wednesday hooks her arm around Jared and lets it rest there for a minute.

"What about you?" I say to Emory. "What made you come here?"

He stares out into the night as if he's looking for the answer. "I could tell you it's because I always dreamed of being a nature guide, that I've always been fascinated by this island. Both true." He shrugs and looks back at me. "But mostly? It's just far enough away from home."

We sit. We drink. I wonder if they also feel the night closing in.

After a minute, Jared says, very low, "It can get kind of nerve-racking when you realize how isolated you are from the actual world here. But all the scary stuff doesn't really compare to getting lost in your own mind."

And somehow this, more than anything else, chills me.

Another beer later, the rain has stopped, and I'm dry and cozy and tucked into the couch of the living room of the dorm-type house that they share with the other staffers. There is music playing and there are about a dozen people of various ages, most around twenty-one or twenty-two. Wednesday is dancing and singing, and she sounds just like Adele. She pulls me up so I'm dancing too. I don't know the song, but it feels good to move. There's a line that says something about feeling homeless or hopeless, or maybe both. And I love this line. I love it more than any lyric I've ever heard in my life.

"That's me," I say to no one and everyone. "That's exactly how I feel."

Someone hands me another beer, and I drink it fast. And I feel lighter and freer, like I'm shedding the past four weeks—as if it was a skin—right onto the floor. I'm singing along with Wednesday and the music, and she and Jared and Emory and I are jumping and dancing and spinning, and I'm completely, utterly free.

When the song ends, I fall back into the couch and there's this boy with a messy shock of white hair and too many skull rings. The boy from the ferry.

He points to himself. "Grady."

I point to myself. "Claude."

"Claude." He nods like he approves. "What's that short for?"

"Claudette." It isn't, of course, but I like the sound of it.

He rests his arm on the back of the couch, and he smells intoxicating. Not like weed and incense but something else. Hair wax, maybe. Pine needles. Something Christmasy. He's talking, but the music's too loud and I don't hear him. And then Wednesday is pulling me to my feet again and someone cranks the music up louder.

At some point Jeremiah Crew walks in. At first I think it's a mirage, but no, it's him, arms folded, leaning against the counter in the kitchen, talking to Jared and some of the others who live here. He's wearing jeans. A dark V-neck T-shirt. No shoes. He catches me staring at him and keeps right on talking the whole time he's looking at me.

"Oh shit, your face," Wednesday yells over the song.

"What?"

"You like Miah." She looks at me through cat eyes.

"I don't even know him."

"Hmm," she says.

The song changes and it's some country tune I don't know, slow and croony. I watch Miah as he stands there. As he talks to people. As he takes a handful of chips and eats them. As he walks away from everyone. As he walks right past Wednesday, who's practically burning a hole in him with her eyes. As he offers me his hand and does this kind of exaggerated bow like I'm royalty.

"Dance?"

I pretend to think this over. I look around the room like I'm weighing my options.

Finally, I shrug. "I guess."

He pulls me close and wraps his other arm around my waist. We dance for a few beats like this, and then I look up and he's staring down at me.

"Your hair is shorter. Like, really short. Is that why you tried to drown yourself?"

"I wasn't trying to drown myself. And it was like this when you interrupted my swim."

"I was too busy saving your life to notice."

"You didn't save my life. . . ."

"I mean, it isn't horrible." He stares at my head. "It'll grow back. Eventually."

"Okay."

"I may actually like it better."

"Great. Thanks. And thanks for the bug spray."

"You were beginning to look like a plague victim."

"Well."

"I also heard you were asking about me."

"Only because I felt like I needed to clear something up about yesterday."

"The fact that you gave me your phone number?"

"No."

"And then I returned it?"

"No. I just wanted you to know that I wasn't drowning and I wasn't trying to drown. I'm sorry it seemed that way and that you felt you had to save me."

He says, "You looked like you were drowning."

"Well, I wasn't."

"Okay. Good for you. And you're welcome."

"For what?"

"Saving your life."

"You didn't save my life."

"I kinda did."

"Anyway. That's all I wanted to say."

Over his shoulder, Wednesday gives me this arch, smirky look and walks away. And maybe I should walk away too, but I don't. I don't want to. It's good to feel hands on me. It cuts the loneliness in half.

Then he goes, "Yeah, this makes sense."

"What?"

"You like to lead."

"No I don't."

"You do. It's okay. I'll learn ya."

"That is so incredibly sexist."

"No it's not. I'm not talking a man-woman thing here. Sometimes you got to let go and let other people lead for a while. I'm guessing that's a problem for you."

A flash of dimples and my stomach goes quivery. I tell it, *Don't*

121

get so worked up. They're literally dents in his face, just little hollow pits at the corners of his mouth that mean nothing.

I say, "Can we just dance without talking?"

"Of course."

He pulls me in and my head brushes his cheek, and for a few seconds it's just the music and his hands on my back. Then I feel his breath in my ear and he says into it, "Why so mad at the island? Or is it the entire world that's pissing you off?"

I pull back and look at him. His mouth is serious, but his eyes are grinning down at me like I'm the funniest thing he's ever seen.

"I'm not pissed off. I'm great. I love it here. It's amazing."

"Okay."

"I'm serious." To prove it, I smile at him. My best smile, the one I've been perfecting for the past few weeks.

"I don't believe you."

"No, it's true. I can't think of another place I'd rather be. Even if this isn't where I'm supposed to be right now. Even if I was never supposed to be here. Even if I was supposed to be in Ohio. At Kayla Rosenthal's party, as a matter of fact. Drinking vodka with Saz and my other friends and making out with Wyatt Jones and getting ready for the road trip of a lifetime and going home and sleeping in the bed I've slept in since I was ten. Even though I never wanted a canopy bed, but my dad thought it must be something little girls like, and so he surprised me, which was really sweet. But that was back when he wanted us. And even though I'm now sleeping in a bed that doesn't belong to me, staring at a photograph of a dead boy who will always be twelve years old. No matter what. So if I put you out yesterday because I was upset, well, I'm sorry. But I wasn't drowning. Not literally. I didn't ask you to save me. Because I can save myself. Not that I need saving. But you know what I mean."

"Yeah, I actually don't know what any of that means."

My chest is tight and I'm wishing I had another beer to drown out the noise in my head. The song bleeds into another and he doesn't let go, so I stay there. And when that song ends, before he can pull away, I say, "Do you want to get out of here?"

DAY 3

(PART THREE)

We ride through the night in his old black truck with the windows down. There's a collection of sand dollars and other shells on the dash. A camera propped on the center console. A pocketknife and some coins and a can of Off! in one of the cup holders. A bottle of water in the other, which he offers me now.

I drink and then hand it back to him.

"You should probably have some more."

"I'm not drunk."

But I drink it anyway, spilling some down my shirt as the truck bumps over the road.

He says, "So tell me. If you weren't trying to drown yourself and you weren't drowning, what were you doing out there?"

"I don't want to talk about it."

"I don't believe that for a second. You've been yelling and talking every time I've seen you."

I almost say nothing. But the thing is, I do want to talk about it. And he's here. And he's asking. And he's not about to run off, at least not while he's driving. Besides, I don't have to say much. He doesn't know my family or me, so it's not as if I'm giving our secrets away.

"It's my parents. My dad, actually."

His smile flickers out like a candle flame just extinguished. You can still see the trace of it, but it's turned to smoke. "Dads." And in that moment, I see it—he's got his own dad story.

"They're separated. Like, just separated."

"Sorry."

"Thanks." And then, like an idiot, I start to cry.

Under his breath he goes, "Shit."

In a minute I feel the truck roll to a stop, and he's reaching for me across the seat and wrapping me in his arms. He doesn't say anything, just lets me cry. At first I let myself go, mostly because I can't stop. My face is pressed into his shirt, and one of his arms is around me and the other is stroking my hair, and this makes me cry harder, so hard that I'm worried I won't ever be able to quit. Into his shirt I say, "I'm so sorry. I'm so sorry." But it comes out muffled and garbled because I'm crying so hard. And then I think, *Oh my God, what if I never stop? What if we're still sitting here in August?* Because that's how many tears I have inside me.

But I have to stop because I don't know this person and he doesn't know me, and people don't like you to cry or talk about things that are hard or upsetting. They like you to smile and say everything's fine, which is why I gather all the pieces of me and put them back together enough that I can sit there, hiccupping and shaking, and say, "I'm okay. Just being stupid. Sorry. Maybe I had more to drink than I thought." And wipe my face dry and sit straight as a board, not touching him, all on my own like a big girl.

"You sure?"

"I'm sure."

"Because I haven't seen a flood like that since the last hurricane."

"Nope. I'm good."

He kind of pats the side of my head, and then he drives on, one hand on the wheel, the other on the window, eyes on the road.

In a minute he goes, "How you doing over there?"

"I'm okay."

I manage to keep my head up, even though it weighs a hundred pounds, and smile at him so he can see it's true.

I say, "I thought you weren't allowed to have vehicles on the island."

"Park Service, the inn, and residents. I bought the truck off my friends Bram and Shirley."

"Do you live here?"

"Only during summer, but I've been coming here since I was thirteen."

"Because even if you do leave, you end up coming back?"

He glances at me, eyebrows raised. "Actually, yeah."

"Jared told me that."

He nods. "I thought maybe we'd won you over."

"Yeah, no. So why here?"

"It was either this or juvie. I haven't always been the clean, upstanding citizen you see before you."

I glance at his bare feet on the pedals. At the way his elbow is draped on the open window, his hand resting there, perfectly at home.

"Are you ever serious?" It comes out before I can stop myself.

"Sometimes."

He shoots me a smile, which flashes in the dark of the cab like a firefly.

I say, "I don't want to go back to the house yet."

"What about your mom? Won't you be missed?"

I lie. "No. She's asleep by now."

He leads me toward a place called Little Blackwood Beach. Just past the dunes, he sits down and gestures for me to do the same.

"What are we doing?" I whisper because there's something stealthy and secretive about it all.

"We're waiting." Out here in the night, under the moon, his own voice is soft and blurred.

I want to ask him what we're waiting for, but his energy is like my mom's. Calming and soothing and warm like a campfire. My head spins a bit from the beer and the night and him.

We sit and wait.

And wait.

I've stopped crying, but I can still feel it in my eyes and my nose and my entire body, as if the tears were blood, and now that they're gone, I'm empty.

Finally I say, "What are we waiting for?"

"Loggerhead turtles. They swim hundreds of miles to give birth here. Most years—between May and August, sometimes September—they return to nest on the same beaches where they were born. They've been around since the dinosaurs." He falls quiet and then speaks again, his voice coming and going like the waves of the ocean. In and out. In and out. "A female can lay as many as two hundred eggs. Two months later, if the nest survives, the hatchlings will claw their way out and head for the ocean. Most of them won't make it."

And now I'm picturing these baby turtles, no mother there to help them.

"Isn't there anything we can do?"

"We help how we can—we mark and date the nests, cover them with netting to protect from coyotes and raccoons—but at some point you have to let nature do its thing."

I think about the effort—the mother fighting to get back to the beach where she was born, to make a nest for her babies, and then leaving them there to fend for themselves.

"Why doesn't she stay?"

"She does what she can for them and then she has to go. I don't know why, exactly."

Then he rests his hand on my arm, and suddenly it's the only thing I can think about. His hand on my flesh. My whole arm has gone warm and now the warmth is spreading to my other arm and out into the rest of me.

Then he takes the hand that was on my arm and runs it through his hair. I look at him and he looks at me and for the first time in weeks I feel almost okay. I remember something I learned in science class—about the weight of water. How one gallon weighs 8.34 pounds. I probably cried at least three gallons in Miah's truck, which has left me feeling lighter, as if I could float away over the earth and up into the sky.

He says, "So what happened with your parents?"

And maybe it's this strange, magical night or the way his voice has gone soft or the flash of his smile in the dark or his bare feet, but for whatever reason, I do something I haven't done in weeks. I open my mouth and talk.

I tell him without editing.

And he listens.

And listens. And as he listens, he glances at me from time to time, and then back at the ocean. Back at me, back at the ocean. After I'm finished, I immediately want to gather all the words I've just spoken and stuff them back inside me. *It's the alcohol,* I tell myself. *Don't drink so much next time.*

Finally he says, "So just like that? I mean, that's all he said— *I love you, but I gotta go?*"

"Just like that."

"Huh."

"I knew I was going to have to say goodbye this summer, but

128

not like this. Not this kind of goodbye. I just . . . I don't know. I was supposed to have more time."

"We're always supposed to have more time. Look, if it makes you feel any better, it could be worse. You could have one parent who can barely function and sometimes can't get out of bed. And then you have to make your own birthday cake, and let's face it, you suck in the kitchen. So then you're like, *Maybe if I steal a birth-day cake from the store* . . . But stores don't like that."

"Did that really happen?"

"There's a pretty good chance."

"I just keep thinking I should have seen it coming. And I could have been a better daughter."

"I don't know your dad, but I do know something about dads who leave, and I'm pretty sure this doesn't have anything to do with you."

"I'm kind of torn between hating him—really hating him—and missing him. I want him to fix this and make it better and make it so it never happened. I'm angry at my mom for not doing some-thing to stop it, and I'm angry at myself. Basically I'm angry." It's the first time I've said any of this out loud.

I feel his arm brush mine, and the feel of it reminds me that I'm not actually the only person left on earth. I take a breath. Let it out. I tell myself, *You've talked enough for one night.*

"I get that," he says. "Remember when I said you remind me of someone? I was talking about me. I was angry for a long time. I used to get into fights. I hated anyone who was different from me. I thought I was better than everyone else. I was a real asshole. I got caught smoking weed on school property, and maybe I sold an ounce or two, but never to kids. Always over at the college, and the money went to my mom and groceries for the family. In my mind, I was a kind of drug-dealing Robin Hood. The first time I came here, it was because the judge gave me a choice: spend a summer camping with a bunch of aspiring criminals or spend a summer on a juvenile-detention work farm with a bunch of aspiring criminals. Camping sounded better, so I came here through this group called Outward Bound—heard of it?" I nod. "And I cleaned up the beaches and cleared trails, all the shit nobody else wanted to do. Man, I hated it. I fucking hated it."

"So what changed?"

"My dad left for good right after I got home. I woke up one morning and he was gone. No explanation, at least nothing Mom would ever tell us. She's always been good at making excuses for him while telling me what an asshole he is. I haven't seen him since, which is honestly no great loss, but it's made things harder for my sisters. My brother was serving his first tour in Afghanistan by then, but they were so young when it happened. Mackenzie and Lila were ten and nine, Ally was seven, and Channy was only five."

I sit there beside him, thinking about fathers, his and mine.

"Did you know he was going to leave?"

He shakes his head and kind of grins at me. "See, the thing about my dad is that he doesn't like to talk much. That includes not telling your wife when you're going on a bender for a night or two, and not saying goodbye to your family when you plan to leave them forever."

"So just like that?"

"Just like that."

"No more floor," I say. "It was yanked out from under you."

He squints up at the moon, considering this. "Yeah. Except in my case, I don't think there ever really was a floor." He shifts, his arm brushing mine again, and I suddenly have a bird's-eye view of the two of us, side by side on this vast beach, looking out over this vast ocean. "You know, all my life I knew my parents were shitty.

130

I can't imagine what it must be like to have the perfect family and then have it obliterated."

I look at him and he looks at me, and in that moment I feel like he knows me better than anyone.

"Moonlight suits you, Captain."

" 'Captain'?"

His eyes go to my hat.

I say, "It's a fisherman's cap."

" 'Fisherman' doesn't have the same ring to it."

"What happened to 'Lady Blackwood'?"

" 'Captain' is better."

Our eyes stay locked. I say, "What do you do here? On the island?"

"I save reckless girls from drowning."

He smiles.

I smile.

And then this red-lipped, short-haired island Claude takes a breath and, without overthinking or thinking at all, reaches out and traces the freckles on his arms—a faint sprinkling, faint remnants from another summer or maybe brand-new from this one.

He watches my face as I do, and then he takes my hand and slowly twines his fingers through mine. There's another tattoo on the inside of one wrist: an anchor. And on the other: *Joy*. I feel this pang because Joy might be a girl he loves, but then I tell myself, *Don't think.*

I say, "I want to kiss you now. I hope that's okay." The exact words I said to Wyatt before leaving Ohio.

His eyes start dancing and a smile lingers on his lips. "Okay."

"Okay?"

He shrugs. "I mean, yeah. Why not?" He sounds all whatever, but his eyes are laughing.

I lean over and kiss him.

For a second I'm worried he's not going to kiss me back.

But then his lips are on mine just as much as mine are on his, soft and searching, little sparks everywhere. There is a pinch on my ankle—the tiniest bug—but I barely feel it. I lean into him.

And then his hand is on my face and I like the feeling of it there, strong and warm and pulling me in, not pushing me away. I open my mouth and his tongue finds mine, and I'm tasting him and he tastes sweet and also dangerous, and I move in closer and he pulls me closer and I'm kissing him and he's kissing me, and this isn't any Claude I know. This is some girl with short hair who makes out with strange boys on strange beaches. And she likes it, this girl. She likes him. She's not thinking about what comes next or what could happen. She's not making him someone he's not or wishing he would be the one. She's not overthinking him or herself. She's just here with him, mouth to mouth, tongue to tongue. Let him think I'm a girl who makes out on beaches or anywhere else she wants to. As far as he knows, this is exactly who I am. And then my hands are all over him and his hands are on my waist, and I want this moment to last forever because in it I don't have to think or be the me I used to know, the one who was sent away without a choice.

But suddenly he pulls away, and it takes me a minute to come down to earth, back to this beach. And he's smiling at me like I'm a kid and not the woman who's just been kissing him senseless for the past couple of minutes.

"Wow," he says.

And I think, *Yeah. Wow.*

"You really want me."

I push him away.

He laughs. "How old are you again?"

"Eighteen."

"Just being sure."

"How old are you?"

"Eighteen. I'll be nineteen in November."

And then I'm Claude Henry again, making out with some strange boy on a strange beach in my jeans and light blue hoodie, the one with the grape-juice stain on the hem, covered in sand, skin freckled and burned a bright, painful pink from the Georgia sun, and being bitten everywhere by unseen Georgia bugs.

He says, "The sand gnats are out. You're getting eaten alive."

Jeremiah Crew parks the truck in the drive and walks me to the house. There's only the sound of us cutting through the grass and, somewhere in the distance, cicadas doing this rise and fall, loud and then soft, like a chorus.

We climb onto the porch and come to a stop in front of the door. The lights are on inside, and moths bat at the windows, trying to get in.

He stands, hands in pockets, looking down at me.

"How did you get all the way out to the Dip anyway?"

"I walked."

"You know you can borrow the island bikes, right?"

"I actually don't know how to ride one."

I expect him to make some big exclamation like everyone else when I tell them this, but instead he says, "I guess I'll have to teach you then."

"We'll see."

He nods his head a little, mouth hitched up, one dimple just starting to appear. Then he glances at the moths fluttering against the windows, at the porch ceiling. "So Addy's your cousin?"

"That's right."

"Which means you're a Blackwood."

I jut out my chin. Bat my eyes. "So you were asking about me?"

The other dimple appears. "Your mom may have mentioned it the day you got here."

"I'm named for Claudine Blackwood. Of Rosecroft. But I'm not a Blackwood. Not 'Her Ladyship.' More like whatever the opposite of that is."

"It fits, though."

"What?"

"Strong woman. I mean, from what I hear, the Blackwoods had their issues, but weak women wasn't one of them."

"That's what my mom says." I think of Claudine's portrait, fierce and fearless. "All I know is, I don't feel so strong right now."

For a few seconds, our eyes stay locked. In that moment, I wonder if he's going to kiss me again, and for some reason this makes my stomach flip and my throat go dry. I cough. "Do you own any shoes?"

His face goes blank and then he laughs. "Not really." He gives me a little salute. "Good night, Captain."

"Good night."

The cicadas are no longer humming. They are buzzing—so full and loud that the air is heavy and warm. A sultry summer night. The porch light casts a glow onto the grass in front of the house, but beyond it is nothing but blackness, as if the whole world just ends. He doesn't kiss me again, even though I want him to, maybe because I want him to. He just walks down the steps and down the path, and I watch as he's swallowed by the dark.

DAY 3

(PART FOUR)

I slip off my shoes and close the front door so, so carefully, pretending I'm a burglar and my life depends on not getting caught. I creep past the kitchen, even though I'm dying of thirst, and past Dandelion, who hops down from the window seat to rub on my legs. "Shoo, Dandy," I whisper. I walk on actual tiptoe to the bathroom, and that's when a voice from my mom's room says, "It's after one."

I freeze.

"Claude." She appears, dressed in pajamas, holding a book, her finger marking the page.

"Mom."

"I was worried."

"Sorry."

"Where were you?"

"It's not like I could call or text, and I was kind of far away."

"I know you're eighteen, but as long as we're sharing a roof, you need to let me know where you're going and when you'll be back. You can stay out all night when you're at Columbia, though please don't tell me if you do. But I'm not exactly thrilled about you doing that here."

"Because there's so much trouble I can get into?"

"Actually, yes. I'm thinking specifically of poisonous snakes and alligators."

"I just lost track of time."

"So let's set some ground rules. Back by one a.m., no later. And you let me know what you're doing."

"Fine."

"Thank you."

We stand in the hallway looking at each other. This is the most I've ever talked back to my mother in my life, and my heart is beating fast and loud.

She says in this quiet voice, "I worry about you."

"I worry about you, too."

"You know I'm here and you can talk to me. I'm still your mom. I found a therapist on the mainland who seems good. I thought we could go over once a week and get you started with him. You need to talk to someone."

Right now she sounds like a therapist, or like an adult trying to reason with an angry child. Her quiet, quiet voice is making my skin crawl. I stand perfectly still, but I can feel the storm brewing inside me, gathering fast and dark. I fold my arms to keep it there, in my chest, in my lungs, but I know she can see it in my eyes and feel it in the air around us. "Now you're telling me I need to talk about it?"

"Yes."

"Because one minute you say I can't talk to anyone, so I don't. I left my best friend without saying a word. So I'm here, cast away on this island where there's zero cell service, and now you're telling me that I need to talk about it, now that I'm finally used to not talking. You need to make up your mind."

All at once, everything collapses—her shoulders, her face. She shakes her head. "I know. And I'm sorry. So incredibly sorry. I should never have gone along with that."

There's more I could say, but I don't. Because as angry as I am, I love her. And she feels bad enough. The two of us stand there, and the only sound is the *tick-tick-tick* of the old-fashioned clock on the wall in the living room.

A minute later, she says, "You know, Aunt Claudine never had children, but when her niece, your grandmother, was old enough to visit, Claudine traveled to the mainland to pick her up and then traveled back again to see her off on the train. Claudine was hard of hearing, so she couldn't hear the train until it was close by, but she could feel its vibrations from miles away. Apparently she stood there for a long time after the train had left until she couldn't feel it anymore."

"How does that relate to me?"

She smiles. "I'm always here, no matter what I'm going through, even when you're not in front of me or when I'm off in my own head or over at the museum or trying to sleep. You can talk to me."

And she hugs me and I hug her back, but I can feel it there— the divide between us.

I shut my bedroom door.

Lean against it.

Him, I think.

Not Wyatt Jones.

Jeremiah Crew.

There's something about this person who knows nothing about me other than that I'm here right now, that my name is Claude and I have red lips and I kiss boys on beaches. Him. Jeremiah. I kissed *him* on the beach.

This person who, after one night, actually knows more about

me than anyone right now, more than Shane Waller ever knew about me after two months. There's nothing to lose and I don't have anything to prove and there is no expectation of me, of him, of us ever being an us. There's no expectation at all.

I won't be losing anything. Or giving anything up. Or letting anyone take something from me.

I've already done all that, been through all that. There's too much of that happening already. No more *Claude, go here. Claude, go there; goodbye, Claude, I never want to see you again.* This will be me taking charge of my life again and deciding what I do and where I go when and where and how.

DAY 4

The general store is crowded with campers filling up the space with too-loud voices and sunburned bodies. I find a chair in the corner and wait for them to go, flipping through texts and social media. Wyatt, tanned and laughing, waterskiing at Whitewater State Park, swimming at the Municipool, drinking shots at Trent Dugan's. He looks sun-kissed and happy, like someone in a movie. I think, *He'll be right at home in California.*

Here's a diatribe from Mara about the hymen company. Here's Alannis with a hot lifeguard. Here's Saz, who never puts her whole self in a picture. Instead she photographs different parts of her— hair, ear, chin, shoulder, elbow—depending on her mood. Her photos are almost always solo, just all the little pieces of Saz. But here's a recent post of two foreheads, one dark, one fair, tilted together against a backdrop of sky as if they're sharing secrets. The caption is one of my favorite quotes: *And everything, absolutely everything, was there.* Ray Bradbury, *Dandelion Wine.*

My heart moves into my throat and settles in as if this is its new home. I was the one who forced her to read *Dandelion Wine.* I was the one who wrote that quote in her last birthday card and told her it made me think of us when we first met, back when we were outsiders who hadn't found our place.

I look up and the campers are gone. It's just Terri and me.

I call Saz.

The phone rings and rings and rings. Just when it's about to go to voice mail, she answers.

"Hey."

"Hey."

A long time ago, after our first fight, we agreed we would always talk to each other, no matter how angry we were. No silent treatment, no ghosting.

She says, "I can't really talk right now. Yvonne is here." And then I hear Yvonne's voice in the background.

I say, "That's okay. I can't talk either. A crowd of people just walked in and I can barely hear you." I say it louder than I need to. Terri looks up from her book and frowns at me.

"I'll talk to you later, then. Or maybe you should call Wyatt and talk to him."

She hangs up on me. No *I love you more than,* no goodbye.

I sit staring at the phone. I'm still staring at it when a text comes through from—speak of the devil—Wyatt. Hey, beautiful, my family is going whitewater rafting in NC and I hope I can see you before then.

I think about writing him back. I start to, but I'm not sure what to say.

I'm pretty sure I won't be home before your trip because I'm entombed on Godforsaken Island.

I wish I could kiss you. Although right now all I can think about is kissing Jeremiah Crew.

Sometimes at night I close my eyes and imagine you're in my bed. When I'm not imagining Jeremiah Crew instead.

I delete every text because what's the point? I'm trapped here for the summer and Wyatt Jones will probably be on his way to California by the time I'm back.

But there's something else—there's last night and Jeremiah

Crew. There are all the things I told him and he told me. I've never done that with anyone other than Saz—essentially walked up to them and said, *Here is me. All the messy, unattractive things that I keep locked up inside. Every last ugly, broken, complicated piece.* And he didn't bat an eye. He just opened his mouth and showed me some of his own messy pieces. And instead of running away, he kissed me.

In its 288 pages, *The Joy of Sex* contains a single page on virginity, which tells us that girls are less likely than boys to enjoy their first time and only a third of us will actually have a good experience. Which means that most of us are going to be extremely disappointed. But don't worry, the book says—your literal first time doesn't have to be the important one. Think of it more as a practice session, a technicality.

As much as I disagree with Dr. Alex Comfort on most things, I like the way he's not putting a lot of expectation on a girl's first time. When it happens, it can just be about checking off a milestone. Like getting your license or voting. It doesn't have to be about anything more than that.

I walk back to Addy's, pop on my headphones, and try to imagine it. For starters, there will definitely not be a barn. There will be music, of course, maybe something French. I scroll through my library and by some miracle I find a band called Cœur de Pirate, which is typical Saz. She's always adding music to my phone that she wants me to hear. I press play and lose myself in the day and the melody. I close my eyes for a few seconds and just walk, feeling the sun on my face.

When a horn blasts behind me, I nearly fall off the road. A dusty black truck rolls up, engine idling. Jeremiah Crew sits behind the wheel, one arm resting on the open window. I take off my headphones.

He says, "Here's the thing. I don't want you getting too crazy about me, because I'm only here for the next few weeks."

"I'll do my best."

"I'm serious. Four weeks. Twenty-eight days. More than enough time."

I say, "I'm only here for thirty-five days, and three of those are already gone. I'll be fine."

"So I don't have to worry about you falling in love with me and getting your heart crushed?"

"I'm pretty sure I'm good."

"I need you to be, like, one hundred and fifty percent sure. I mean . . ." He smiles, dimples and all, the whole nine yards. He points to himself like, *See what you're up against?*

"I'd say I'm at least *two* hundred and fifty percent sure I'm not going to fall in love with you."

"In that case, get in."

We drive past Rosecroft, past the remaining outbuildings. Miah stops the truck in a grassy patch on the edge of the trees. He gathers a few things—bug spray, a flashlight, a pretty serious-looking camera with a faded brown strap, which he slings over one shoulder. He gets out, door slamming, so I get out, door slamming. Then he's standing in front of me and this is the closest we've been since last night, but instead of kissing me, he aims the bug spray at my legs and arms and starts spraying.

"Seriously, Captain. They do have nature where you're from, don't they?"

"Not like this."

142

He sprays until the can gives out. Then he tosses it into the truck and says, "Let's go see more."

I follow him deep into the woods. Sensible Claude, the one raised by two sensible parents, is going: *You don't even know this boy. Don't go into the woods with him.* This is the exact way horror movies start. A girl alone in the woods with a stranger. Never to be seen again.

But the Claude who sat on the beach last night with Jeremiah Crew, who spilled her soul *and* twelve gallons of tears, keeps walking.

I expect him to bring up the talking, the making out, but he doesn't. Instead we wade through undergrowth and brush and I try not to think about ticks and snakes and all the other things that live here.

I swat at tree limbs and spiderwebs and horseflies. I step over poison ivy and duck under vines. Like a kid on a car ride, I want to ask, *How much farther?* But I don't. He's not talking, so I don't either.

We're a good ten minutes into our hike when we suddenly emerge from the woods. I blink like a mole under the glare of sun and sky. There are horses grazing, and beyond them, Rosecroft. Just down the road from the ruins, I can see the truck.

"Did we get lost?"

"No."

"Then what was that?" I point to the woods. To the truck. To the woods again. "We went in a circle."

"I said let's go see more nature."

"Are you fucking kidding me?"

And then his hands are on my waist, on my hips, his fingers widespread and strong, so warm against my shirt that the warmth reaches into my skin. He pulls me to him and says, "I'm going to kiss you right now because I've been thinking about kissing you all morning. I'm telling you this because it's going to be a fucking incredible kiss, so I want you to brace yourself. I know you promised me you wouldn't fall in love, but I completely understand if that changes after this. I will now await your blessing."

Before I can tell him exactly how full of himself he is, I say, "I'm not worried."

"Is that a yes?"

"That's a yes. But nothing's going to change."

"We'll see."

And then he kisses me. His lips are soft but firm, and I fall into them. There, underneath the sun, my brain goes light, my skin goes light, I go light. I am weightless. And then I slide my hands under his shirt, up his back, across the fine, taut muscles, and gently, so gently, run my nails up and down his skin. He's not the only one in control here. I can feel him bend into me, and then I let him go.

He smiles down at me. I smile up at him.

"Still two hundred and fifty percent sure, Captain?" His voice is husky.

"Let's make it three hundred."

I walk off toward the NO TRESPASSING sign, pretending I'm not a little dizzy, a little breathless. I walk up the steps and then he passes me, leading us around the side of what used to be the house. He aims the camera at the ruins and takes a couple of shots. He studies the screen. Takes another shot. Studies the screen again. I catch up with him but I can't help feeling as if I'm intruding on something—a dialogue between him and the camera.

I pretend to look around, but I'm really looking at him. He's so different from Wyatt. He looks like he was born in the outdoors, maybe on the beach, wherever the sun is brightest. But, more than that, he's direct, honest, and completely himself. My lips are burning, wanting more.

"We can get in there," he says, hand shading his eyes. Before I can ask, *Get in where?* he's picking his way through the overgrown grass to a set of stone steps that lead down into the ground. At the bottom is a crooked door that swings right open, and now we're in the basement of Rosecroft, whole and standing, cooler than outside and lit only by the light coming through these narrow windows up at ground level.

I follow him, doing my best to see in the dark, trying to pick my way through this pitch-black maze, while he leads the way, bare feet and all, not caring what he steps on.

He says, "So, since you're a Blackwood, I thought you might appreciate seeing the ancestral palace."

"I'm not a Blackwood. This"—I wave my hands all around me—"isn't me. I live in Mary Grove, Ohio, farm and factory town. My dad works at the college and my mom writes books and I babysit to earn enough money to buy lip balm."

"Well, then consider it a crumbling memorial to dysfunctional family."

"That's more relatable."

And he tells me how the only Blackwood son, Samuel Jr., oldest child of the great railroad magnate, moved with his wife, Tillie, from the family home in Virginia to the house his father built him, Rosecroft. How they had two daughters, my great-grandmother and Claudine. How Tillie was a midwife who delivered most of the babies on the island. How she got pregnant again, but there was a flu epidemic, and she became bedridden and lost the baby.

Tillie, I think. *That was her name. Tillie Blackwood.* I imagine her traveling this island delivering babies, and my image of Tillie Blackwood—just like my original image of her daughter—shifts

145

a little. No more fainting couch and smelling salts, but someone with backbone.

There is something low-ceilinged and muffled about the acoustics down here that give his voice an end-of-the-world quality. "One morning, not long after, she shot herself through the heart in her bedroom closet."

"Where did she get the gun?"

"It belonged to her husband. He felt so guilty over not being there when she died that he buried her in the front yard so he could see her grave from the house."

Miah stops walking and we're in what must be the middle of the basement, no windows, no light except what's coming from his flashlight, but I can see that we are surrounded by relics of a life, spanning the decades. A steamer trunk, a rocking chair, an old umbrella, slats of wood, a stack of bricks, a lopsided hat rack. There's a story for each one, probably long forgotten, and suddenly I want to know everything. Whose trunk was this, and how far did it travel? Who carried this umbrella? Who sat in this rocking chair? My mind is racing, cluttered with images and scenes.

"They say one night he dug up her grave and cut off a braid of her hair and then reburied her. Supposedly he carried the braid with him the rest of his life." In the dim light, he studies me. "Obviously she had more hair than you do, Captain." Miah reaches out and fingers the ends of it, and like that, I forget about Tillie and Claudine.

Kiss me again, I think.

For a second I believe he's going to. Then his hand is gone and he's leading us past another trunk, an old wardrobe, two little chairs, child-size. The light of his flashlight is bouncing ahead of us, illuminating dark corners and more buried treasure. All these things just abandoned here, as if the people who owned them fled in a hurry.

"Years later your great-great-aunt had her mother moved to the family cemetery so she could be laid to rest next to Sam."

And now we've reached the end of the basement, and there's light coming in again from narrow ground-level windows. And there, sitting by the chimney, is a rickety, old-fashioned baby carriage. The hood is intact except for a small tear in the fabric, but the basket part is missing, hollowed out, so that it's really just a skeleton.

He's telling me about Tillie's ghost, that she loves jewelry, that he thought all ghost stories were bullshit until the second summer he lived here and the doorbell rang at his house over and over again between two and three a.m., no one there. "If you haven't already, you'll hear it—the screen doors here. I call it the island slam. They are *loud*. I go back to bed, and just as I start to drift off—*slam*."

I'm trying to concentrate on the words, but as soon as he says them, they change into *touch kiss feel skin naked*.

He's telling me about this bracelet thing his sisters made for him. He's raising his hand so I can see it, a black braided cord looped a couple of times around his wrist. The words morph into *See these hands? I want to touch you all over with them.*

He's telling me how, when he got up the morning after the doorbell, the bracelet was gone. How he discovered it on the other nightstand, the one on the opposite side of the bed. I'm only half listening, and then he says, "Now, here's something you don't know about me, Captain—I don't ever move in my sleep. Like, the other side of the bed is still made because I don't go over there."

I completely miss the next thing he says because I'm now

147

thinking of him lying in bed, probably naked, alone on his side, the other side still made. *What is he trying to tell me? That he doesn't have a girlfriend? That he's not sleeping with anyone right now? Is this something he wants me to know?*

I tell myself, *Control your face, Claudine.* And I stand there listening and nodding my head and hoping to God he can't read minds.

"So there's my bracelet on the other nightstand. Where I didn't put it." *The other nightstand on the other side of the bed where no one is sleeping.* "Two months later, I'm having dinner with Bram and Shirley up on the north end, and Bram says something about a ghost and a screen door slamming, and I'm like, wait a minute."

And then he looks up, so I look up. There, propped against the wall, is a faded portrait of a young woman in a large oval frame. The woman is blond and lovely, dressed in blue, smiling brightly. She's not wearing a single piece of jewelry. Her only adornment is a crown of flowers in her hair. Just over her heart, there is a small tear in the canvas.

And suddenly I'm wholly and completely here in this basement.

"What's your full name, Captain?"

It's an effort to drag my eyes away from her. "Claudine Llewelyn Henry."

His eyes are smiling and he's looking into me. "Claudine Llewelyn Henry." The way he says it. My name on his lips. And then he turns away and says to the portrait, "Claudine Llewelyn Henry, meet Tillie Donaldson Blackwood."

Tillie beams down at me.

"They found the painting like that, with the rip in the canvas. Because supposedly it wasn't the gunshot that killed her. It was a broken heart."

"Over losing her baby?"

"Probably. Combined with losing her brother in a car accident and her mother to the flu, all in the same month."

"How do you know all this?"

"My friend Shirley. Her grandmother Beatrice was the island storyteller."

We are there for what feels like a long time. There's something in me that wants to stay here, because there's something in me that relates to the ruins and the ghosts, to Claudine, who haunted this place until her death, and to Tillie and her broken heart. Especially to Tillie and her broken heart, and the way her life changed in an instant—not once but three times—before she decided to end hers.

I turn at the sound of scratching and watch as Miah etches our initials into the brick. Not *JC loves CH* or vice versa, but there, side by side. I like the semi-permanence of it—the fact that our names will be there for as long as that brick exists. Like a time capsule. No matter where I go and what happens, we were here.

We're back at the basement door, where we came in, and he pulls on the latch but it doesn't give. I say, "Wouldn't it be funny if Tillie locked us in here?"

"Hilarious."

He's running his fingers along the frame of the door and pulling, and it's not budging. I'm watching him tug at it, and it's dawning on me that, *Oh hell, maybe we really are locked in here, way down deep in the bowels of Rosecroft. With a ghost.* A shiver runs through me.

And then Miah turns to look at me and goes, "We're locked in."

"You're not just doing this for dramatic effect? Or to, you know, make a move on me?"

"I'm not that smooth."

And part of me thinks, *Too bad*.

"It's locked from the outside. Try for yourself."

I give the door a tug and it doesn't budge.

"Welcome to the island, Captain," he says, and in that moment I think, *Maybe there are worse places to be*.

I wait for him to take me right then and there, but no, he starts digging around in all the relics that surround us, clearly hunting for something.

"What are you doing?"

"Trying to find a crowbar or knife or anything we can use to pry the door open."

I help him search, and as I search, I'm thinking that all these discarded, forgotten things—this umbrella, this comb, this empty bottle of perfume, this bowler hat—were once picked out and purchased and brought to this house and used by the people who lived here.

Suddenly we hear a voice from upstairs. "Hello?"

I jump as if it's Tillie herself, back from the dead.

Miah lays a hand on my arm like, *There, there, it's okay*. Only the heat from his palm has the opposite effect on my skin.

"Jeremiah? That better not be you."

He calls out, "It's me. We're in the basement."

"What are you doing in the basement?"

"Making out with this hot girl I found down here. But now you've locked us in." And he lets go of me so that he can walk toward her voice.

"You should have found me and told me you were coming."

"I was too busy making out."

"I can't hear you."

"Where are you?"

"I'm up here."

And on like this until he says, "Where'd that come from?"

We go up a narrow, dark staircase—not the outside staircase that we took to get in here, but one that leads into the house itself. Cobwebs are brushing me on the cheeks and the shoulders, and I'm batting them off. At the top of the stairs stands a tall, broad African American woman who must be Shirley. Behind her, the sky is a brilliant blue and the house is once again in ruins. We come up and out onto the first floor, into a hallway with walls and no roof.

"Jeremiah Crew." The woman's hands are on her hips and she is shaking her head.

But you can tell she loves him.

Shirley and her husband, Bram, are originally from the island, but now they split their time between here and out west, leading Outward Bound groups. They were Miah's guides when he was in Outward Bound and they're the parents he wishes he had, the ones who refused to give up on him when everyone else did.

We stand in the hot sun. A white Park Service truck comes rolling up the drive, loaded with inn guests. Shirley says to me, "I've known this boy since he was thirteen years old. Be glad you didn't know him then. I can blame him for every gray hair on this head of mine." But she laughs.

He give me this sheepish look, holding up his hands like, *It's true.*

"Can I trust you with these ruins?" she says to him.

"Probably not."

"You two come up to the house for dinner one night. I know Bram would love to see you."

151

As they talk, there's this tiny, rattled feeling in my chest that makes me want to run away until I'm on the other side of the wall I've been forging since the beginning of summer. Like the fact that these people love him somehow makes me more alone in the world, as if their loving him has anything to do with me.

He drives me to Addy's and once again walks me to my door. I say, "I hope you're not going to get too crazy about me. I'm leaving in a few weeks and I'd hate to break your heart."

He stares down at me, eyebrows raised. "I'm pretty sure I'm willing to risk it."

I wait for him to kiss me. When he doesn't, I move in close to him, so close we're almost touching, and I can feel his breath on my cheek. The heat is coming off us as he takes my face in his hands, as he looks into my eyes. As a strange look comes over him. As he whispers, "Stay still."

With one hand, he turns my head so that I'm staring away from him, and then I feel a sharp and terrible pinch on the side of my neck.

I jump back and my hands are checking for blood. "What the hell?"

"That was me saving your life again." And he holds something up so I can see it in the light—a tick. "Shoe, please."

"What?"

"Give me your shoe."

I slip one off, hand it to him.

He sets the tick on the porch and crushes it with my sandal. "I'd check yourself all over when you get inside, just to make sure that's it."

And then he goes sauntering down the path, no kiss goodbye, no mention of other adventures or when he might see me again.

I take the world's longest shower and scour my entire body for ticks. Even though I don't find any others, I can feel them crawling on me.

Back in my room, I open one of the notebooks that hold my novel. I flip through, reading random passages and pages. Some of it's good and some of it's bad, and most of it is somewhere in between, but it all seems overwrought and overwritten, and none of it rings true. Mostly it just feels long ago, as if it was written by another person in another lifetime. Someone who thought she knew about life and love and clearly didn't.

I slam it closed and bury the novel in a drawer where I won't have to look at it. And then I search the house for an empty notebook. I find an old blank one in the office, on a shelf: yellowed pages, battered blue cover. I sit down at the desk and write—not about Claudine, but about Tillie Blackwood, who died too soon, and the man who loved her. How she was here, and then she wasn't.

Sometime later, I hear the front door open and close and my mom's voice calling me. The screen door slams behind her, and this is the island slam, and I know this because maybe I'm not feeling like such a stranger here after all.

DAY 5

The next morning, I am up earlier than usual. After my mom leaves for the museum, I do my best to style my hair so it's more Jean Seberg than Christmas elf, and I paint my lips red. Outside, the day is blindingly bright, a few puffs of clouds hugging the horizon. I wander the sandy roads, the ruins, and then the beach, but there is no sign of Jeremiah Crew. I spend the day swimming and sunning myself and reading my book, and trying not to be disappointed.

After changing for dinner, I tell my mom how pretty she looks and walk with her to the inn. She glances down at our linked arms and raises an eyebrow, and then she tells me about Blackbeard Point, at the northeast tip of the island, where the notorious pirate Edward Teach—better known as Blackbeard—supposedly buried his treasure. I listen and ask questions, and as we climb the steps to the broad front porch, she says, "Thank you," and gives my arm a squeeze.

"For what?"

"You know what. Thank you for trying."

I bend down and pull a cactus spur off my shoe, hating that she feels the need to call attention to it because *this is how self-absorbed I've been*. "You're welcome," I mumble to the wood of the porch.

During cocktails, when she gets into a discussion with the

Nashville photographer, I excuse myself and wander into the library, where I find an old volume on loggerhead turtles. I sit reading till dinner, doing my best to concentrate on the words rather than the memory of Miah's lips on mine as we stood on the beach two nights ago. This is what I learn:

- The largest turtles can weigh as much as 375 pounds.
- Every two to three years, they return to nest on the same beaches where they were born.
- Just one in four thousand baby turtles will live to adulthood.
- Turtles are air breathers, although they can stay underwater for hours. But too often they become entangled in fishing nets, and when they struggle to break free, they can quickly use up their oxygen and lose the fight.
- There is something called a *false crawl,* when a turtle comes ashore to nest but for whatever reason doesn't lay her eggs before returning to the sea.
- A turtle produces numerous offspring, which she leaves alone to fend for themselves—unlike, say, a horse, which has only a single foal and stays around to protect it until it's grown and ready to be on its own or until she is pregnant again. But it's turtles—not horses—that have been around since the days of dinosaurs.

So clearly there's something in having to fend for yourself. *Like me,* I think. And in some strange way this gives me hope.

After the meal, Mom and I sit on the porch. I lean back in my chair and stare at the moon, my eyes heavy.

"You've gone quiet since we've been here." And at first I think she means since we've been here on this porch, but no, she means here on this island.

"So have you."

She leans forward, crossing her legs, one foot swinging. "So I'll tell you something and you tell me something."

"You go first."

"Okay." She takes a breath. Lets it out. "You know, I didn't expect there to be much firsthand material from Aunt Claudine, but she actually left a journal and boxes of letters. As far as I can see, she documented everything. It's her mother who seems to be the enigma."

"What do you mean?"

"So far I haven't found a single thing from Tillie Blackwood. No diary, no letters, not even a grocery list. But there's a lot of other material from other Blackwoods. I mean *a lot*. And I'm thinking there's a book here. Claudine. Her mother. All the women who've lived and loved and died on this island."

"Is it a historical novel or nonfiction? Do you know what the story is?"

"Not yet. But I'll find it. After all, the writing can save you. And I could use some saving right now." Her voice is bright and strong, the voice of Wonder Mom, but something wavers in her eyes. She's said this for years—how, when life is upside down, the writing can save you.

"You'll find it," I echo, and that's so much of what I do with her these days—echo things she says because it's easier than saying how I really feel.

She asks, "How's your own writing? Are you working on anything?"

"Not really." I've written a few things down about Tillie and Claudine, but they're just interesting stories, things I want to remember.

"Okay." She shifts a little. "What else can I tell you?" She thinks this over. "The photographer asked me to join him for a drink."

"The one you were talking to?"

"That one."

Asshole. "What did you say?"

"Thank you, but no thank you. It's way too soon. I'm not ready. I may never be ready. But it was lovely to be asked."

There are moments, and this is one of them, when I can actually see her heartache. She carries it not just in her heart but in her arms and on her shoulders and in her face. I think about Tillie's husband burying her in the front yard and cutting off a lock of her hair and wonder if my parents ever loved each other like that or thought they did. *Why do some love stories have a shelf life and others last forever?* And suddenly I feel bad for being just an echo and talking to my mom from behind the wall in my chest.

She says, "Now you. Tell me something I don't know."

I try to push away the image of my mom with the photographer, this strange younger man who is not my dad. I want to ask if she and my dad are talking. If they're trying to work on their marriage or if this is it, the way it will be from now on.

But instead I say, "I'm not sure Saz and I will be friends forever. I always thought we would be, but we're moving away from each other. I can feel it. It's not just me coming here. She's moving on too."

"You're having a season," Mom says. "Moving on can suck, but it's normal. Growing pains. When you get through this, you'll find each other again, stronger than ever. And if you're worried about it, let her know you miss her."

I can feel what she's not saying: *Like I miss you.*

* * *

157

At some point I feel a bump on my arm and Jared is standing over me. He hands me a note. My first thought is, *Why is Jared writing me a note?* But then he gives me the biggest grin and a wink so obvious you can see it from Mars.

"Thanks," I tell him.

"Oh, you're welcome." He goes grinning away. I turn the note over in my hand.

"Who's that from?" Mom says, her voice sleepy from the food and the day.

"I don't know." But I do know. I hope I know.

Meet me outside your house at 10:30 p.m.

"Is there a boy?"

Yes, I think.

"Maybe," I say.

DAY 5

_____

(PART TWO)

The truck bumps down the lane and around past the inn, and once we're under the sprawling oaks, he switches off the headlights and keeps driving.

I reach for my seat belt.

"When you get in the truck and don't go for your seat belt, Captain, that's when you know you're an islander."

"Maybe I don't want to be an islander." But I let the seat belt go. "You could turn the lights back on so we don't go crashing to our deaths."

"The first summer I was here, Shirley wouldn't let me have a flashlight. She told me I could see in the dark. I just had to have patience and let my eyes adjust. Think you can do that, Captain? Have patience?" He glances at me, giving me this half smile that tells me he's not just talking about seeing in the dark.

My stomach flips. The butterflies stir. I half smile back at him. "Maybe."

The air sparks around us. Like that, we vanish into the island. Anyone watching us would think we were ghosts. Now we're here; now we're gone. At first I can barely make out the white of the road. It appears in front of us a foot at a time. The trees are walls of black on either side, and I want to tell him to turn on the lights before we run over something or someone. I think, *I don't care what Shirley says. My eyes will never adjust.*

But gradually the road grows a little whiter, the trees a little more three-dimensional. Pinpricks of light flash across the path and in the forest.

"Lightning bugs," he says.

And suddenly our way is lit by them. They are in the trees and on the path and in the canopy. Little blinking stars brightening the way for us. I catch my breath. I know in my bones that this is one of those deathbed moments, one I will always remember. I look down at his hand, broad and tanned, over the steering wheel, at his bare foot on the gas pedal.

It's a wild ride through the darkness, the fireflies twinkling like fairy lanterns. I try to hold on to the moment because I don't want it to end. I want to spend forever driving through the night with Jeremiah Crew.

I don't have any idea if we're heading north or south, but it doesn't matter. I don't need to know. I close my eyes and feel the warm breeze on my face and arms. I want to throw my arms up into the air like I'm on a roller coaster because this is how free I feel. Instead I hang an arm out the window, as if I can catch the night, which is humming and twinkling and whooshing by, and we are part of it.

And then we are slowing a little and I open my eyes. Miah pulls to a stop and we get out, doors banging shut one after the other, a sound that seems to carry for miles. As he rummages for something in the truck bed, I wait, completely here on this road, the trees behind me, the beach in front of me. *Whatever happens, I'm here right now.* There is a glow in the sky behind the dunes that must be the moon.

Miah comes around to where I'm standing, with a backpack and a blanket, as if he's planning to be gone a long time. I try not to concentrate on the blanket and the image I have of Miah laying me down on it. Then I look at him more closely and he's wearing these super-short shorts, the kind my mom and dad wore in gym class back in the 1980s.

"What in the world?"

He shines his flashlight on them and now I can see they're a dark camouflage green. "Official shorts of the US Army Rangers. Military grade. Basically, only badasses wear them."

"And you." I smile.

"Including me." He smiles. "My work shorts. Better to climb trees with. Better to clear trails with, especially in this heat. Easier to pull off when skinny-dipping." And then he drops his eyes and lets them linger on my mouth, which causes my heart to do an extra *thump-thump*. His eyes meet mine again. "Let's go."

Yes, let's go. Let's go right now. Let's go back inside this truck so you can kiss me all over my body or let's go to the beach and lay that blanket down on the sand. . . . But now he's walking, and what do you know, the shorts are starting to grow on me.

We pick our way across the dunes in darkness. When we come to a pool of water that floods our path, reaching up into the long grass on either side, Miah says, "Just a little water left over from the storm. Jump on." He turns around.

"What?"

"Come on, Captain. Jump on."

"I'll break your back."

"No you won't."

So I hitch up my dress to mid-thigh and climb on. We almost tip over because one of my legs is flailing around and the other is hanging on to him, and I'm practically strangling him with my left arm while the right one is grabbing at the air. I send up a silent prayer: *Please don't let me break his back. Please don't let him wonder what the hell I've been eating to make me weigh this much.*

I'm finally secure, and he's got his arms hooked under my legs. And he's wading right through the water, which barely brushes my toes. I lean into him. Too soon we come out onto a great, wide expanse of beach.

He throws down the bundle he's been carrying and I pull off my shoes. He does a handstand while he waits. Hangs out for a couple of seconds, legs in the air. And then he's right side up again and we start walking.

I wait for him to take my hand. To kiss me. To try to get it on with me right here under this moon on the blanket he brought.

Instead he says, "Want to walk?"

"Yes."

So we do. The waves catch us sometimes and the water is warm. There is no one awake but us, and we are the only ones in all the world. Jeremiah Crew and Claude Henry. Just the two of us. We bump into each other, arms brushing, close together, but we don't hold hands.

After a while he says, "We don't have to talk about your parents, but if you need to, this is a good place to do it. I've had a lot of conversations with myself at night on this beach."

And, like that, I can feel it all wanting to flood out—the same things I've already told him and more. But I also want to preserve this night, protect it from anything sad or painful, which is why I tell him about my parents Before, how they never fought, how they always got along. How it was always the three of us, all of my life, which is why I never noticed the plumes of smoke or the earth tremors.

He says, "People can be really good at only showing us what they want us to see."

"I think I'm learning that the hard way."

Then he tells me about his mom, who has to go to bed for days, sometimes weeks, at a time, and about the way he's had to take care of her for the past five years and raise his four sisters. When he talks about his mother, I can hear the heaviness in his voice— burden, love, responsibility, resentment, protectiveness. All these things weighing it down. And then he tells me about his sisters, one by one, and his voice goes light as a balloon floating up into the sky. I learn that Kenzie and Lila love to read. That Kenzie is already winning awards for her photography, and Lila has seen Harry Styles in concert three times. I learn that, at twelve, Ally already has a serious boyfriend, and Channy, the youngest, is the star of her soccer team. I ask him about his brother, and he tells me he served two tours in Afghanistan.

"That's enough about me," he says. "You know, for now. There's, of course, so much more you'll want to know, but I promise it's worth the wait."

I roll my eyes.

He laughs. "So tell me about your friends back home."

I tell him about Saz and Yvonne and our nightmare phone call. When I'm finished, he says, "It sounds like Saz is on her own island right now. You just have to give her time."

This is so similar to what my mom said that it catches me off guard.

"What?" he says.

"Nothing. That just sounded pretty wise."

"Because I am." He runs a hand through his hair and I stare at the anchor on his wrist.

"What's up with the tattoos?"

"This one"—he holds up the anchor—"is to remind me where I come from. The compass on my shoulder reminds me that I'll always find my way. And this one here . . ." He turns his other wrist over. *Joy.* "Because it's what I'm looking for."

Not a girl after all.

I say, "My mom is joyful. She makes things brighter just by being her. My dad hasn't always gotten that. He can be funny and fun, but also moody."

"Some people just aren't built that way. My mom, for one. Or maybe they are but something gets in the way. Like depression or loss. I work hard for joy, if that makes sense. Because I'm built for it but not built for it." He rubs at the tattoo.

"With my dad it's more than that. It's like sometimes he, I don't know, almost doesn't want to let himself be happy. It's hard to explain."

And even though I've always known that my mom and I are a lot alike, this is something I can see more and more, the farther I get from Ohio—Claudine and Lauren, Lauren and Claudine, the Llewelyn women. My dad, more like a guest star, making an appearance now and then.

Miah goes, "I don't know the guy, but I kind of feel sorry for him."

"You shouldn't. It's his choice, right? Not just ending their marriage but kind of, I don't know, removing himself when we were still there."

"Yeah, but he's missing out. He's missing out on you."

"I don't think he feels that way."

We walk, not talking, his arm brushing mine again, my arm brushing his, and my heart flutters under the moon. Suddenly I'm sorry I said anything about my dad. I don't want him on this beach with us.

I change the subject. "Where do you think you'll end up?"

"In the world?"

"Yeah."

"Like, ultimately?"

"Sure."

"Well, the odds say prison or rehab. But I don't know. For now, here's where I'm supposed to be. Shirley says the island has this way of giving you what you need."

"All it's given me is a bad haircut and bug bites that look like leprosy." *And this night, and maybe you.*

"Maybe that's exactly what you need." He bumps my arm with his and I bump his back.

"What about the end of summer? Where are you going in four weeks?"

"To join the CIA." He grins down at me. "What about you?"

"Ever since I was little, I always knew I wanted to go to California. It was so big and so far away and seemed full of, well, promise. Saz and I planned to go there together and be writers. But I decided to go to Columbia and she's going to Northwestern."

"Doesn't mean it can't happen someday. And it doesn't mean you can't go there on your own. I don't see the future as this road that's all laid out neat and organized: school, work, relationship. I think the future's kind of like the ocean—more, I don't know, fluid."

"Wow. That's pretty deep."

"Is it making you want me?"

"Not really."

"Just wait. I tend to have a delayed effect on women. It's part of my charm."

We turn around and start walking back the way we came, every single inch of me focused on this beach, the water washing over my feet, the night air, the moon, this boy.

Next to me Miah pulls off his shirt. "This spot right here. This is the one." And then he's pulling off the army shorts, and his clothes are lying on the beach, and he's fully naked. He walks away from me, straight into the ocean.

I stand there realizing I have a choice. I can sit down here on the sand and wait. Or I can take off my dress and go in. It feels like a pivotal moment in my life. *Stop thinking so much, Claudine.*

I wait till his head disappears under the water and pull off my dress. I drop it on top of his clothes, and now I'm in panties, no bra. I leave my bottoms on, cover up my chest with my hands, and half skip, half walk to the water before I can change my mind. I wade in until I'm up to my waist and then crouch down so that the ocean covers me.

Miah is a dark shadow in the distance, diving in and out of the waves like a dolphin. I crouch-walk a little farther and then remember Danny and the rip current and the fact that this is apparently a breeding ground for sharks. I stop and wait, heart pounding louder than the surf. A minute or two later Miah swims toward me. I crouch lower, trying to gather the water over me and around me. He comes up for air two feet away. In the light of the moon, he is glowing.

"See?" He grins. "Delayed effect."

We tread water, eyes locked. For some reason, it feels momentous.

He says, "Jesus, you're beautiful." And kisses me.

And then he's under the water again, and I swim after him until my feet can barely touch the bottom. The water is warm and gentle. The surface of it catches and holds the moon.

I think about the future being fluid like this ocean, and then I imagine myself part dolphin, part mermaid. I swim to Miah and wrap my legs around him, and even though I'm not naked, he is, and somehow this feels like the closest I've ever been to a boy. His arms are around me and we bob and float like this, my cheek to his, my chest to his, my heart to his, for a long time.

He walks naked all the way back to the pile we've left in the sand, and I can't help but sneak peeks at him, lean and gold, wet skin glimmering in the moonlight. When we reach our things, I pull my dress back on, and it sticks to me like seaweed. He grabs a towel and offers it to me, and then grabs one for himself. And that's when I let myself really look at him—all of him. And it's very, *very* clear that our time together in the water has affected him.

So now I'm trying to look everywhere but at him.

"What's going on, Captain?"

"Nothing. The moon is just so beautiful."

He laughs and finally he pulls on his shorts. We sit down on the blanket he's brought and drink the sodas he's brought, and I don't want the night to end. I think, *I could stay here. I could live right here.* And then for some reason I'm thinking about the Claude I was before this summer, the girl who didn't know that people go away and love can change its mind. This is how I feel in this moment on this beach under the moon with this boy—like me again.

We sit side by side, arms touching, and we don't say a word. We watch the water and wait. The waves are rolling in and out, and in the dark, in the black of the night, they sound ominous, like thunder. I shiver, and without a word he hands me his shirt. I pull it on, even though the night is so warm that my skin is damp from the air, not just the water, and my hair is sticking to my forehead.

We sit there for maybe an hour or longer. I lose track of time, and I like the fact that it could be midnight or it could be two a.m. Time doesn't really matter here, no matter what my mom says.

We sit like this, both of us staring out at the ocean. My arms wrapped around my knees, his propping him up as he leans back, long legs stretched out in front of him. I'm filled with this feeling of apart but together. We are the only two people in the world sitting here in this spot on this island waiting for the turtles to emerge from the sea.

At some point, I think I see one down along the beach. I lean forward, and I know he sees it too because he sits up. Together we hold our collective breath, but it turns out to be some other sort of creature, a raccoon, maybe, something low to the ground that scuttles along out of sight. Miah settles in and we wait and watch some more. I'm aware of everything, my body on alert, my skin at attention. The night air, the soft but scratchy feel of his shirt on my skin, the way the shirt envelops me and smells like him. The sand under my legs, the sand surrounding my feet as I bury them in the beach. The smell of salt water and the sound of the waves reaching for us, pulling back, reaching for us, pulling back. The bright of the moon and the stars and the fact that there are more of them here than I've ever seen, even in Ohio farm country. I am memorizing all of it, taking it into me, where I will keep it forever and be able to bring it out again someday, long from now, when I am far, far away from this island. *That summer boy, what was his name?* I might not remember, but I won't ever forget waiting with him on the sand for the turtles to come.

Suddenly, he stands and extends a hand. And I don't want to go, but I let him pull me up because it had to happen sometime. I follow him around the dunes and down the path, away from the beach. I want to go back and sit there till dawn, not talking, not touching, but together.

At the tree line, he turns and looks at me, traces the line of my jaw and chin with a single finger. It happens swiftly. His mouth is on mine, and he's pulling me in or maybe I'm pulling him in. Whichever way it happens, we kiss and kiss. When we finally break apart, he says, "Wow." Just like before, only not like before.

"Wow," I repeat.

"Wow," he says again.

DAY 6

The next day, I sit inside the general store and make my weekly phone call to my dad. The last time I talked to him was in the guest room at my grandparents' house in Atlanta. I asked to go home early, back to Mary Grove, and he said no. I imagine all the things I want to say to him now. *Mom isn't sleeping. I hear her at night because I'm not sleeping either. We're just in Addy's house not sleeping, waiting for you to change your mind and tell us to come home.*

But our conversation goes like this:

"How's the island?"

"Fine."

"Is it hot?"

"Yes."

"How's Dandelion adapting?"

"Okay."

(Many awkward pauses in here.)

"Bradbury wants to say hi."

And then I hear Bradbury panting into the phone, and all of a sudden I need to hang up or I will splinter into a thousand pieces. But first I say, "Bradbury, I want you to listen to me. I'll come back for you. I promise. Don't think we left because we don't love you."

Now Dad is on again and we talk about nothing of consequence for a minute or two more—he mentions some movie he just went to see and tells me about the marathon he's training for, and finally he says, "I love you, Clew."

It takes everything I have to say, "I love you too." And I do. It would be so much easier if I didn't.

That evening, everyone on the island descends on the inn for what they call a low-country boil, which is potatoes, corn, sausage, and shrimp boiled up in this giant outdoor cooker. While my mom mingles with the adults, I find Jared serving food. As he fills my plate, he says, "So the note I delivered. Did it live up to all your hopes and dreams?"

"Some of them."

He grins, and I can't help it: I grin too. And even though I'm younger than he is, I feel older-sisterish. I say, "What about you? Are you dating anyone?"

"I wish."

"What about Wednesday?"

"I'm not really her type." For some reason this sounds weighted, but then Wednesday appears, as if we conjured her, and says to me, "Hey, Mainlander."

I tell them I'll see them later for the fireworks, and find a spot on the grass near my mom. I eat silently while she talks with a trio of older women, all with sweet Southern accents. The photographer stands nearby, his back to us, and I think, *I dare you to come over here*. He doesn't. Afterward I meet Jared, Wednesday, Emory, and the other staffers on the beach. I look for Miah but he isn't there.

We huddle at the edge of the dunes and watch fireworks over the neighboring islands. There is something comforting about the crackle and pop and hiss as the air explodes with stars—blue, red, green, gold. I think of all my Fourth of Julys, and my parents are in every one. The three of us in Rhode Island, watching from the dock with a hundred other people. The three of us in Atlanta, eating a picnic in Piedmont Park under a sky of sparkling color. The three of us in Ohio, drinking fizzy lemonade with Saz and her family.

There is a sonic boom and gold rockets shoot into the sky.

Wednesday says, "Would you rather have penises for arms or tree trunks for legs?"

I say, "What kind of trees?"

"Live oaks. No—palm trees. The really tall ones."

Jared goes, "Penises for arms." And then he does his best impersonation of arm penises, which sends us laughing uncontrollably.

After we wind down, Emory sighs. "I need to get laid. There aren't a lot of options on an island."

"Thanks," says Wednesday.

"You know what I mean."

"What about our neighbors across the water?" I nod in the direction of the fireworks.

"He'll never leave here." Wednesday turns her face up to the sky.

Emory says, "I might have to. I'm not cut out to be a monk."

"I'd like to be in love." Jared says it in his upbeat Jared way, but a sigh escapes at the end of it. "Like, I wonder if sex is really different when you're in love with someone."

And even though I'm a virgin, I want to say sex is just sex. It doesn't matter who you do it with, as long as you have their consent and they have yours, and as long as you like their hands on

172

you and their mouth on yours. As long as they are all sorts of possibility and almostness and maybe.

But other than the consent part, I'm not sure I believe this anymore.

"I don't know." Wednesday stretches her arms out, like she's trying to grab the fireworks. "I want to see what it's like with different people. See what I'm like with different people. People of all genders. To have the chance to love who I love, and if I actually do *fall* in love, great. If not, at least I'll have some fun. The thing I know is that I don't want to get hung up on any one person right now." For some reason she's looking at me. "Because it always ends the same, right? You have a good time and they have a good time and everyone's having fun, and then once the chase is over, suddenly they start chasing after someone else like you never existed. Besides, I like being me too much."

I think, *Maybe it does always end the same, but I want to believe it doesn't.* I want to believe it's a lot more than just the chasing and the catching.

I say, "Don't you think it's possible to be you with someone else?"

She lets out this cynical-sounding laugh. "No, Mainlander. I don't. My friends, my mom—they all become versions of themselves. Like, fun-house versions. No thanks."

And in spite of my broken home and all I'm going through, I feel sorry for her. She doesn't seem to believe in anything, and maybe—just maybe—I still do.

Wednesday tugs at one long braid and then fixes her eyes on me again. "What about you? You ever been laid before?"

Jared shakes his head. "Don't feel like you have to answer her."

I watch Grady as he chats up one of the inn guests, a lady in

173

her thirties. I watch as the fireworks explode and then die over the water. I think about making up a story, something elaborate and erotic. Possibly even breaking out Shane Waller and my near sex in a barn.

But everyone else is being honest, including New Claude, which is why I say, "Almost. There's a boy back in Ohio." I don't mention that I barely think about Wyatt Jones now.

Wednesday says, "My sister believes it doesn't technically count as sex unless it's a penis and a vagina. Like, if she does anal, she's still a virgin."

Emory stares at her. "So then, according to her, nothing counts except hetero sex?"

"I'm just telling you what she believes. Don't get pissed at me."

"Man, that is some bullshit. Bull. Shit."

I say, "My best friend is a lesbian, and she's in love. And I don't think she'd agree that the sex she's having with her girlfriend doesn't count." I suddenly feel protective. Like, lift-the-car-off-the-baby protective. Not just of Saz, but of Yvonne. Of both of them. "I don't think there's any such thing as *technically*. It's about who you're with and how you feel. Sex is sex. Love is love. I don't need some stupid 1950s construct to tell me what it is or isn't. However it happens, whatever it looks like, I think you know in here"—I tap the space over my heart—"if you're still a virgin or not."

Wednesday sits forward. "It's like crossing this invisible threshold that only you see. You decide it. I decide it. We decide it."

"Uh. Yeah."

She says, "I agree."

"What?"

"I agree with you."

We sit blinking at each other, stunned into silence because *we feel the same way.*

174

Jared clinks my bottle with his. "I'll drink to that."

And I think, *I'm glad they're here.* It makes me miss Saz a little less and also more. I suddenly want to call her and apologize for not asking more about Yvonne, and more about how Saz is feeling, how it's going. She hasn't been the greatest friend lately, but I haven't either.

Emory and Wednesday tap their bottles to ours. She says, "God, we're profound."

Mom finds me then to tell me she's heading back to the house. When I offer to go with her, she says, "No, stay with your friends. It's good to see you having fun. Just be home by one o'clock at the latest."

The conversation turns from sex to the SDS, or Secret Drawer Society.

"Have you been in the Blackwood Suite at the inn?" Emory asks me.

"No."

"There's this ancient monster of a desk that takes up most of the room, and it has a kind of hidden compartment. People have been leaving notes in there since forever. Like, as far back as the start of the inn. There's love notes, stories about their stay, the island turtles, hurricanes. Things like that."

Jared takes a drink, wipes his mouth. "The love ones are pretty cool. There's a guest staying in that room now, but we can show you when the room turns over. I've written a couple letters. To my grandfather. To my friend Rashid, the one who died. But I've also written some to me. Like: 'Dear Jared, you need to remember that life is short, so make the most of every second.'"

Wednesday draws circles in the sand with a shell. "We all have. 'Dear Wednesday, don't be so hard on yourself. If you don't love you, no one else will.' When I first got here, I wrote one to my family because I couldn't tell them where I was or why I left."

175

Their voices rise and fall, reminding me of road trips with my parents when I was little, sitting in the back seat, staring out the window or reading, listening but not listening to them as they talked, close but far away. I stare across the blackness of the ocean toward the lights in the distance from some unknown island, thinking about what I would write to myself or maybe to Miah.

What if I just found his house tonight and slipped into his bed and surprised him? I imagine it. His skin. My skin. Naked. Hot. *Him. Him. Him.* This boy who knows me so well already and likes me anyway, in spite of myself. I touch my arm and it's on fire at the thought of him.

Five minutes later, he appears, a dark figure walking across the sand. I don't need to see his face to know it's him. I already know his walk and the way he moves. Without a word, he holds out a hand to me, and my blood starts pumping and my heart starts racing just like I'm waking up from a long sleep. Wednesday leans over to say something in Jared's ear, and then they're both watching us. Emory offers Miah a beer.

"Nah, I'm good, man," he says. Then, to me: "Want to get out of here, Captain?"

"Yes."

DAY 6

(PART TWO)

We drive north to a quiet strand of beach, where we walk and talk and watch for turtles. I wait for him to take my hand or kiss me, but he doesn't. I tell myself it's okay, we can just be friends. There's no time for anything else, anyway, with both of us leaving. We're two ships passing on a long summer night, and I'm the one deciding that, not him. As we head over the dunes and back to the truck, I actually slug him in the arm like we're old buddies.

"You okay there, Captain?"

"Grand." *Grand?*

On the way back south again, we approach the bright blue shotgun house, the one with the rocking chairs on the porch. Miah slows, one hand on the gearshift, the other on the wheel. It's the way his hand hangs there, so casual, so languid. Or maybe it's just him.

"Do you want to come in for a minute?" The truck engine idles.

"Is that yours?"

"No, I thought we'd break in."

"In that case, sure." *Yes yes yes.*

Like that, my entire body is on alert. If I go in, anything might happen. I try not to think beyond right now. I concentrate on getting out of the truck, on walking up to the house, on going up the steps, on waiting for him to push open the door, on following him inside.

The house itself is small. A single light is on, sitting on a table opposite the fireplace. As I look around, I decide it's like the inside of his truck—filled with treasures. Animal skulls of various sizes, bones and shells. Black-and-white photographs of more bones and shells, the Rosecroft ruins, the dunes, turtle tracks, the ocean. If I were designing a place for Jeremiah Crew to live, it would look just like this. A bright blue house. A cabinet of curiosities. Shelves overflowing with books. Maps and old cameras and relics everywhere. Everything a skeleton of some sort.

"Was all this here when you moved in?"

"Some of it. I've added a few things. Made it my own."

I pick up an animal skull. "It's a lot of nature."

He laughs. I set the skull down and perch on the edge of the sofa, forcing my mind to focus, to not get ahead of itself, to not picture the two of us naked in his bed, which is exactly what it wants to do. I watch as he pulls two sodas out of the fridge.

I look up at the walls, at the framed pictures. My eyes rest on a shot of the ruins, stark against a brooding sky. "Did you take the photos?"

He glances up at the walls. "It depends on whether you like them or not."

"They're haunting." They are a mix of raw and beautiful, dark and light.

"Then, yes, I did."

"You could sell them."

"I don't know. Maybe. Bram was the one who got me into it. He gave me the camera and said, I swear to God, 'Maybe this will help you see things other than yourself.'" Miah sets our sodas down in front of me. "He also gave me this house. Well, he and Shirley let me stay here during summers. I'd been through Outward Bound so many times, they eventually offered me a job. Living here is one of the perks." He's across the room again, sorting through a collection of records that are stacked beside a turntable. "Part of what I do is lead Outward Bound groups that come to the island, clearing trails, marking turtle nests, anything that gets people outside and working. Same kind of shit I did when I first came here."

"What happens when summer's over?"

"I join the space program."

"I thought it was the CIA."

"It's actually both." He sets a stack of records on the turntable. "NASA and the CIA were like, 'We need you. Name your price.' " He sinks onto the couch next to me as the first record drops. But there's something heavy in his voice. "Let's not talk about that while I've got you here. In my house."

He leans in. Kisses me. Before I can get lost in him, I pull back. "You okay, Captain?"

"Do you have anything stronger than water?" It's not about needing a drink to feel braver; it's about wanting to stop time—or at least slow it down—so that I can savor every moment.

He arches an eyebrow. "There's vodka in the freezer that's about a hundred years old. Courtesy of Bram and Shirley, but I keep it around for guests."

"Thanks."

I start to get up, but he says, "I'll get it for you. I'm not completely unchivalrous."

I watch as he goes into the kitchen, opens the freezer, pulls out the vodka, pours me two fingers' worth. I want to tell him to fill it up—maybe I need to feel a little braver after all—but I don't want to seem like a lush.

When he's back, I say, "Aren't you having some?"

"I've done enough drinking in my life. I stopped at fourteen. I stopped everything at fourteen." He hands me the glass, drapes his arm on the back of the couch, and looks me straight in the eye. "Well, not everything."

Our eyes stay locked as I set the glass down without taking a drink. At the same exact moment, we reach for each other.

He kisses me.

I kiss him.

My blood and my heart are pumping again, so strong and hard that I wonder if my body can hold them. He touches my face, and then his hand wanders south. And that's it. *Yes yes yes.* Suddenly I'm the bravest person in the world.

I climb on top of him so that I'm straddling his lap, and I can feel him through his shorts as we kiss harder and harder. And now we're lying down, me on top of him, and I have to pull away for a moment because it's too much and my heart is going to burst. We're both making these heavy breathing sounds as we try to fill our lungs, and I can hear my heart slamming against my chest as if it's trying to break out of there.

He throws the pillows on the floor to make more room for us. Kisses me again. Wraps his arms around me tight. Rolls me over so that I'm under him, and we somehow manage to stay on the couch. We lock eyes, and then he moves in, and everything is blurred, and his lips are on mine, and the only thing that exists is his mouth and his skin and the fine, tight muscles of his back under my hands.

I kiss him until we go boomeranging into the danger zone, the one barricaded and police-taped and littered with smoke bombs and alarm bells and CAUTION signs. The one that makes my brain go numb and keeps me from thinking about anything else. I ignore the voice in my head that's shouting, *This is actually going to happen.* I can feel myself close to the edge, and now the couch is on

180

fire and the entire back of me, head to toe, is burning, but I don't care. He senses it and I can feel him shift a little, but I won't let him go. So now we're both burning up right here on this sofa.

But this time I don't stop. Not even as he's telling me he's STD-free, only safe sex practiced here. Not even as he says, "Are you sure? Remember—four weeks. That's it. Less than that now."

"Yes," I say. "Yes."

"I'm kidding, but not, Captain. I won't go any further without your consent."

This throws me because I don't remember Shane ever asking me for my blessing. *I can say no, and we can stop right here.*

"Yes," I say again. "You have it. As long as I have your consent too."

And I can tell by the look on his face that this throws him. "Yes," he says, very low. "God, yes."

To prove to myself and him that I'm sure, that this is one thousand percent what I want, I pull his shirt off, kiss his neck, his shoulder, his chest. He groans a little and then he's pulling off my dress, the red-and-white one I bought last July 4. I'm braless, in underwear, and he's still in his shorts. I reach for these next, and when I can't get them off him, he helps, and he's not wearing underwear at all, so he's completely naked, and now I can really look at him because I think maybe it's expected or maybe I finally want to know, and there's this little trail of gold hair on his chest that leads all the way down.

I fight the urge to cover myself with my hands. Instead I let him kiss my breasts, and while I've technically gone this far with a boy, right now it feels so much further.

Next my panties come off, all at once, both legs at the same time, and he's looking at my body, and I resist the urge to grab the blanket on the back of the couch and cover up. I let him look at me, but not for long, because I'm kissing him, and his hands are in what's left of my hair, and then he's rolling on his side and fishing around in the pocket of his shorts for something.

He's getting a condom.

When he rolls back toward me, condom in hand, I go, "Wow. You're confident."

"Not confident. Hopeful. Although, *hello.*" He waves at his body and gives me this cheesy grin. And then his face shifts into a genuine smile, and I can't help it, I kiss the dimples on either side of his mouth, and then he's kissing my throat, and just when I think my body might explode like a firework, it happens.

I'm in my body and out of it at the same time. Even as it's happening, there's a part of me narrating everything for myself: *Now he's opening the condom packet. Now he's putting the condom on.*

My head is taking over, and I just want it to shut the hell up and let my body be in charge.

Now you can feel him. Now he's putting the condom in.

There's the surprise of him inside me, even though I'm expecting it. It's like my fifth-grade birthday party, when everyone hid in my bedroom, and I knew they were going to surprise me because Saz told me ahead of time, but I still freaked out when they started screaming and running at me.

He goes, "Are you okay, Captain?"

"Yeah. Of course."

My mind tells my body to stop thinking about my fifth-grade birthday party and move, for God's sake, so I move. But I feel like the Tin Man in *The Wizard of Oz,* all jerky and stiff. And suddenly I'm thinking about *The Wizard of Oz,* a movie I don't even like, and now I'm thinking about *thinking* about *The Wizard of Oz* so much that I almost forget to narrate what's happening.

Now you can feel him—all of him. And there's the surprise

again. Not pain, necessarily, but the surprise of my body register-ing something entirely new. I actually suck in air. A loud, gasping, hiccupping sound that makes him stop what he's doing and look at me funny. Before he can ask what the hell that was or change his mind about ever wanting to have sex with me, I kiss him. I wonder if I'm bleeding all over his couch, if my mythical hymen has actually broken. Even if it hasn't, and even if it's the most awk-ward, terrible sex that has ever been had on this planet, I know that technically this counts. This *counts*. Even though virginity is a heteronormative, patriarchal construct . . .

Now he's moving on top of you.

And you are moving with him even though you don't know how.

Please, please, please shut up, brain.

And then, by some miracle . . . my mind goes quiet. And my body takes over. It's as if it knows something I don't, as if my body and his know each other and understand each other, as if they're meant to move together like this.

But then, suddenly, we're done. Which means he's done. And this is another surprising thing—the fact that the ending seems to depend on him. I almost tell him, *Hey, I need more. I'm not done.* But I don't say anything.

And just like that, in a single moment, all those years of waiting are over.

Afterward, he rolls off me and we lie, me on my back, him on his side, squished onto this couch, which suddenly seems much smaller than it was moments ago, staring up at the mobile of skulls, which teeters and sways a little, the hollowed-out sounds of bone hitting bone.

He takes my hand. "When did that get there?" And somehow

I know he is talking about the ceiling, which until fifteen seconds ago was shrouded in smoke from the fire we created, and beyond that a sky of stars. The brightest stars.

"I don't know."

I lie there, the sofa cooling beneath me, feeling my heart settle back into place like a good little organ. I think about how six days ago I didn't know he could do a handstand and kiss me like no one else, and tonight I know everything about him.

I lost my virginity, and yet I tell myself I didn't *lose* anything. This is my body. I'm the only one in it; I got to choose what happened. I knew what I was doing. I decided where and when to have sex. Just like I will decide my life. No more waiting for other people to decide things for me. I'm writing it right now.

DAY 6

(PART THREE)

My name is Claude Henry, and I just had sex for the first time.

It happened five minutes ago. Jeremiah Crew is in the bathroom, and I am sitting here on the steps of his blue house, dress and underwear back on, staring out into the night because it's a million degrees inside and I needed air.

I should feel electrified and awake. Grown-up. Worldly. Maybe even the slightest bit French? But all I know is how I don't feel. Not like a woman. Or a girl. Or anything. It's as if I've been emptied out of who I am.

The door opens behind me and it's Miah, still naked. Instinctively, I look away, which is silly because minutes ago he was literally *inside me.* He steps out and sits down next to me. "Jesus, Captain. You ran out of there like you were on fire."

"Sorry."

"Everything okay?"

"Everything's great."

This isn't true, or maybe it is. But even if it isn't, I'm not about to sit here and talk about feelings with him. No crying or *Please hold me* or *I love you, baby* or *You make my world go round* or *Love me forever please please please.* Just Miah on top of me, heavier than I expected him to be, and a band called the Zombies playing in the background.

He says, "You look cold."

185

"I am cold."

And suddenly I am, down in my bones. I shiver and he hooks his arm around me and rubs my elbow, trying to warm me up. I lay my head on his shoulder, because if I don't rest it somewhere, it might fall off my body and go thudding down the path.

He says, "Do you want me to take you home?"

And for a minute I'm like, *Yes, please take me to Ohio.* But I realize he means the house where we're living now, my mom and me, this summer.

"Yes," I say to him. "I'd like to go home."

I follow him to the truck and climb in, and I'm not Robot Claude, exactly, more like Empty Claude. It's a wonder I can move my limbs. Miah turns the headlights on and it's like a little death. No more moon, no more fireflies.

I think about how amazing it is that you can have someone that close to you, that for the first time you literally aren't alone in your body anymore. Yet somehow you can still feel lonely.

Mom is lying on the sofa, television volume on low, book open on top of her, Dandelion napping against her leg. When I walk in, she opens her eyes.

"I'm sorry I'm late," I say. "Miah and Jared and I stayed at the beach to watch for turtles."

Maybe New Claude isn't always truthful after all.

"That's okay. What time is it?" She's still half asleep, but she clicks off the TV and closes her book and stands up like it's morning and she's ready to go.

"Ten after one."

"I think we can let that ten minutes slide." She hugs me then, and now she's looking at my face. "Everything okay?"

186

"Just tired. It was a good day, though."

And this is enough for her, my mom, the one person who's always been able to see through me and into me. One thing they don't tell you—sex can be a wall, and your mom is on one side and you're on the other. Actually, everyone is on one side, and you're on the other side all by yourself.

Even though it's two hundred degrees outside, I burrow under the covers in my bed, tucking myself up and in as tight as I can.

"Saz, if you can hear me, is this how it felt? Is this how you felt?" I whisper it to the night. *Why didn't I ask her how she felt after she slept with Yvonne?* More than anything right now, I want to talk to her. She may have been a little late in telling me about Yvonne, but she was trying to let me in. And, okay, I didn't let her in, but did that mean I had to stop being a good friend?

DAY 7

At ten-thirty the next morning, I'm still in bed. Mom knocks on the door and then pokes her head in. "I'm heading out, first to the museum and then to meet with some local storytellers to interview them. You okay?"

I give her a thumbs-up. "Just feeling lazy."

At noon I'm still in bed, eating crackers under the covers. I don't want to see anyone, not even my mom. I just want to lie here and think.

Dr. Alex Comfort writes in *The Joy of Sex* about something called *la petite mort,* "the little death." Apparently some women and the occasional man can pass out cold after orgasm. As an example of this, he mentions some poor man who experienced this with the first woman he slept with. By the time she regained consciousness, he had called the police and an ambulance.

An hour later I'm writing in the blank notebook I found in Addy's office, the one with the blue cover.

The little death.

Three words that could also refer to losing your virginity. Not in a morbid, tragic way. Not in a sad way. But in a this-is-the-end-of-your-childhood kind of way. Even though I still feel stupidly young.

I set down every feeling, no matter how dark, and every thought, even the ones that make me want to go back under the covers. Because whatever happens, I want to remember all of them.

By two forty-five p.m. I've stopped writing and am lying there once again. If I had any energy at all, I would walk to the general store, which may or may not be closed, depending on Terri, and sit at my corner table and call Saz. Because even though she didn't tell me about Yvonne right away, and even though I didn't listen when she *did* try to tell me, I want, more than anything, to talk to her and have her tell me she still loves me and I'm still me and everything's okay.

DAY 8

I am walking down Main Road and I'm not a virgin anymore.

I take my lunch to Rosecroft and eat on the steps and I'm not a virgin anymore.

Everywhere I go and everything I do, it's all I can think: *I'm not a virgin anymore.*

I study everyone's faces, my mom's especially, to see if they can register this fact.

I run my hands over my body, the way Miah did. I try to see myself with his eyes. I study my own face in the mirror—not that I expect to look any different, but I am looking for signs of virginity loss.

The thing is, I don't look any different from my regular old self. Honestly, it's a bit like the day after Christmas. A little bit of *Huh* and *Now what?* This is what it's like on the other side of something you've been anticipating for a long time. My parents are still getting divorced. Saz and I are still going to different colleges. I somehow thought it was going to be bigger and more monumental than it was. Instead, it just is.

Inside the general store's Wi-Fi zone, a voice mail pops up from Saz.

190

Claude, it's me. I'm sorry I didn't listen as well as I should have. It's just that Yvonne is here and you're not, and I didn't know you were calling and I didn't know you were going to tell me something earth-shattering or I would have sent her home. Friends first. Always.

Yeah, you shouldn't have told Wyatt before telling me, but I guess I get why you did. And yeah, you shouldn't have hung up on me, but I shouldn't have said that about your parents. What I should have said is that I'm surprised but not surprised. I'm surprised because this seems like a thing that can't happen in life.

You, your mom, your dad—you're like this weird unit where everyone does everything together and gets along. I can't imagine the three of you without each other. But I'm *not* surprised for all the reasons I said. I just should have listened better all the way around. Just know I'm here. And I'm serious about meeting you halfway. If it gets too bad out there on that island, let me know. I love you more than Katniss and thumbprint cookies and all the freckles on your face.

I lay my head down on the table and cry. It's not just Saz; it's everything. Something goes *clunk* next to me, and there is a box of Kleenex. Terri sets one hand on my head and then walks back to her seat behind the counter. I try to rein myself in, but the tears keep coming, even when I hear the door to the store open and close and the sound of someone's footsteps. There is talking between this person and Terri, and then the door opens and closes again. I lift my head and squint with one eye at Terri, who somehow isn't staring at me.

I wipe my eyes and nose and then I call Saz back. When it goes to voice mail, I tell her I'm sorry too, and that I'm not a virgin anymore and that I like this boy, really like this boy, but that I don't know how to feel. That I want to understand how she felt after her first time with Yvonne because I have no idea what I'm feeling.

When I hang up, I have a new notification. Wyatt has sent me a text. Hey. You home yet? Been thinking about you. After all the time I spent creating a deep and thoughtful inner life for him, after making him greater than himself and greater than Mary Grove, Ohio, and greater than all boys everywhere, after all the possibility and almostness and maybe, I feel nothing.

I start to text him back, but I don't have anything to say because I'm not interested in him anymore. I'm interested in someone else.

Before I leave, I set the Kleenex box on the counter in front of Terri.

"Sorry about that little scene. I miss my friend and I'm also getting my period. . . ."

She lays her book facedown. "You've been hanging out with Jeremiah Crew." And it sounds like an accusation. If she'd said, *I know you used to masturbate to Wyatt Jones,* I couldn't be more surprised. "Look here, it's none of my business, but you should be careful."

"Careful how?"

"Experience tells me that boys who get in trouble stay in trouble. And he might be on a bit of a clean streak lately, but trust me, it won't last."

I always wonder about people who feel compelled to give advice, as if they know you, as if you're someone who can't find her way in the world on her own. I want to say, *It's none of your business who I hang out with or what kind of fun we have,* but Terri means well.

I thank her for looking out for me, and then I get out of there as fast as I can.

I walk to the beach and I can see a group of tourists coming up from the ferry. Checking in like it's a normal day. If this were a movie, there would be some sort of heart-tugging song playing as I mooned around, but there's no soundtrack unless you count the cicadas.

Boys who get in trouble stay in trouble.

I try to push Terri's words out of my head. On the outside, the day is passing like any other. Miah is at work. My mom is at work. Jared and Wednesday and Emory and the rest of the island staff are at work. Guests are walking or biking to the beach or Rosecroft. The Park Service trucks are toting visitors up to the north end.

I wish I could go back to the night before last. I wish it was still ahead of me, that it was happening tonight. I want the chance to try to hold on to all of it—Jeremiah and me, naked together for the first time—longer. No one told the night before last that it was a historic occasion. It just passed in regular time, like any other.

Did I like it? Yes and no. Was it like I imagined when I closed my eyes and pictured Wyatt or Miah or Mr. Rochester? Yes and no. I didn't have multiple orgasms like in the movies. I actually didn't even have one, although I was right there on the edge, or at least in the general neighborhood. But there were fireflies and the room spinning. Do I feel closer to him because we had sex? Did it make me like him more? I don't know. It's complicated. I definitely feel more tangled with him.

You should be careful.

You should be careful.

You should be careful.

I walk for miles on the beach because I can't sit still and I have all this energy to burn. The thing is, much as I try, I can't get him off my mind.

I wonder if he's thinking about me now.

And now.

And now.

In the afternoon I'm walking back to Addy's and I see him—Miah. He is standing on the broad white porch of the inn, and my heart starts doing these wild Cirque du Soleil leaps, but then I see he's standing with a girl. He's leaning against one of the white columns and she's got her hand on his arm and he's laughing, and he leans in and says something in her ear, and now she's laughing. So much leaning and laughing.

And then she turns and I see it's Wednesday, and in that instant I feel so stupid. Hot boy on remote island equals he can have anyone he wants. This kind of thing must happen to him all the time, and I'm just another girl passing through.

I walk away, hoping he won't see me. I keep walking even as he's yelling my name, but I pretend I don't hear him. He catches up with me, breathing like he's run for miles.

"Jesus, Captain. It's a little late to play hard to get, don't you think?"

"Sorry."

"What's up?"

" 'What's up'?"

"Yeah. What's up?" He says it louder and slower. "We can keep repeating it or I can ask it another way. *What are you doing? How is your day?*"

"It's super, thanks." I keep walking.

"Hey."

"What?"

He falls in step beside me. "What. Is. Up?"

"Nothing," I say, and I sound like a child who isn't getting her way. "I just thought you were working today." To make it worse, I can see the aerial view of this—the way I keep walking, the way I won't look at him, even though he's done nothing wrong. I wish I had a Claude-size eraser so that I could make myself disappear. But instead I look up at the inn and at Wednesday.

His gaze follows mine and then he sighs. "I was afraid this would happen. I told you not to fall in love with me."

"I'm not in love with you." And the way I say it makes it sound like I absolutely am, even though I'm absolutely not because I literally met him eight days ago.

"First, Captain, you're jealous. Second, that ended last summer."

"What ended?"

"Wednesday and me."

"Oh."

And he might as well slap me across the face because of course there was a Wednesday and him. I mean, of course. *What did you think? You were the only girl he'd ever been with on this island? The only girl he'd ever been with anywhere?*

I suddenly feel cornered. And incredibly stupid. And like maybe Terri was right and I should be careful. If I don't start walking, I won't be able to breathe, and I know if I stay, I'll only make it worse by saying something I'll instantly want to take back, and I won't be able to take it back because it will be said and out there forever.

"I'm supposed to meet my mom at the museum."

"I'll drive you."

"That's okay. I like walking." *I like walking? Shut up, Claude.*

"What's going on with you?"

"Nothing."

Our eyes lock, neither of us blinking, neither of us looking away.

Finally he holds up his hands. "Okay."

He doesn't stop me as I walk away, and it's now and only now that I can think about what it is I'm feeling.

Afraid, for one. *Afraid. Afraid. Afraid.*

Unsettled.

Mad at myself for starting to open up to this person I barely know.

Mad at him for making me think I could open up.

Stupid for believing I was different and he was different and this was different in any way.

Trapped behind the wall I've built around myself, unable to move or breathe or do anything but keep building it up around me, brick by brick, fast as I can.

Guilty because I should have told him I was a virgin. And now if I tell him, he'll think it means more to me than it did, and that I'm asking him to love me or tell me there's only me or something, on and on, blah blah blah.

But here's the thing—maybe it was a bigger deal to me than I expected. Maybe it actually did matter.

*　*　*

One hour later, I manage to find my way to his house. I ring the bell and wait, scratching my bug bites, fanning myself in the heat. Even as I'm standing there, I'm telling myself, *Walk away. Don't make things worse. This doesn't need to be serious. This doesn't need to be anything.*

The door opens to reveal Jeremiah Crew, shirtless, barefoot, gripping a snake in one hand, and I don't mean a sexual-euphemism kind of snake, I mean an actual one.

"Hey," he says.

"Uh. Hey."

He holds the door so that I can come in. I bump into the doorframe, giving the snake the widest berth I can. The screen slams behind us. I follow him into the living room, and my eyes go right to the couch.

He says, "I thought you were going to the museum."

"I was. I am. Why are you holding a snake?"

"Stowaway."

"Is it poisonous?"

"Not this one." He holds the snake as far away from me as his arm will allow. "Make yourself at home." And then he walks out, screen door slamming again. Instead of sitting, I stand. I don't look at the record player or the couch because these are clearly instruments of seduction and I am not falling for them again.

The door bangs once more and he's back inside. I wait for him to say something about the night before last but instead he says, "So I'm on a ladder cleaning the gutters and I hear this thud from inside the house and the sound of something falling over. I figure it's Archie, the island dog, but something tells me to check, so I

197

go inside and there's this bird flying around. And the dog is happy as shit because all he wants is the bird, and I get him out of there so he won't be able to catch it. And I'm looking for something—a broom, a towel—and I'm gone for, like, thirty seconds when I hear a scream that sounds like a human sacrifice. I figure the dog's gotten back in, but no, I can see him on the porch, so I run in and that's when I see the snake. Which is now eating the bird."

"Do things like this happen a lot here?"

"Be more specific."

"Bird plus dog plus snake in house equals Jeremiah Crew, wild-animal wrangler."

"Wild-animal wrangler." He looks up toward the ceiling, giving this some thought. "I like it." He drops onto the couch—*the* couch—and says, "What's up, Captain?"

"Can I talk to you?"

"Let me guess, you want to know if I'm your boyfriend."

"Don't flatter yourself."

"I mean, sure, if you want me to be." He waggles his eyebrows and pats the sofa. "I get it. You want another round."

"No."

"Ouch."

"I mean, it wasn't horrible."

"Great."

"I just have something to tell you."

It's no big deal. He won't even care. He'll probably even be like, "So what?" But I keep standing there, not sitting, shifting from one leg to the other, scratching bug bites, running a hand over my hair, tucking it behind my ear even though there's nothing to tuck.

"Are you planning on telling me today?"

"I'm a virgin. Was a virgin."

"When?"

"Two nights ago. Before we had sex."

"You're serious?"

Part of me breathes this sigh of relief: *Oh, thank God I didn't bleed on his couch.*

I say, "No. Which is one reason I think I got a little weird earlier. I saw you with Wednesday and suddenly I'm like, *What am I doing?* I barely know you, and right now I barely know myself—"

"So let me get this straight. I ask if you're sure and you're like, '*Oh yeah,* I'm sure, just give me some vodka—'"

"I didn't say it like that, and I didn't drink the—"

"And suddenly we're doing it, and I ask you *again* if you're sure, and now you're telling me that was your first time?"

"Yeah."

"Shit." And he's not smiling anymore. He rubs his head, rakes his hands through his hair, stares at the floor like he's trying to memorize the Magna Carta.

"Say something." Coming clean makes me feel immediately lighter. At the same time, I feel the tears forming behind my eyes because I can see he's upset.

"Shit." He looks at me. Looks away. "That's all I got. Shit shit shit."

"I'm okay. You don't need to worry about me."

"Thanks, that's comforting."

"I'm serious. I knew what I was doing."

He looks at me again, and the way he's looking at me makes me wish he wouldn't. "Did you ever think that maybe I should know too? Like, maybe I'd want to know that bit of info?"

"I thought guys got off on virgins."

"Jesus, Captain."

"What?"

"We're not all douchebags."

199

"I didn't say that—"

"So now I'm the asshole. Hooking up with a girl I find both interesting and hot, and I'm not sure I would've done that if I'd known. It was your first time. It should have been, I don't know, special. I could have made it special."

"See, that's why I didn't tell you. I didn't want special. I wanted normal. I don't want to call attention to it like I'm some freak. And it's not like I needed you to tell me you love me, and I didn't want you to feel obligated to say you're my boyfriend." I'm starting to get a little mad.

"Wow. Okay. So why me? You just thought, *Hey, he's fun. I'll get my rocks off and I can tell all my friends back home that I scored with the island boy?*"

"Isn't that what you did with me? Scoring with the summer girl?" *Isn't that what you did last summer with Wednesday?*

"I don't know. Maybe. That's not the point."

"I've just been waiting all this time, and I was finally like, *What am I waiting for?*"

"So why not get it over with."

"Exactly. Kind of."

He looks up at me and this time he keeps looking at me. "Thanks."

"I mean, I'm glad it was you—"

"Don't."

I can tell he's hurt, and for the first time it occurs to me that he has feelings too. I stand there, not sure what to say, wanting to go back in time and fix this so that whatever we do, we don't have to be here in this moment.

Finally he sighs.

"You know, you seem really young right now. And you've got

a lot going on." He stands, walks past me, opens the door. "You should probably go."

"Seriously?"

We stare at each other, him holding the door, me rooted to the living room floor, neither of us budging.

I start walking. I stop in front of him. "I didn't have to tell you it was my first time and I don't owe you an explanation, but I came here because I like you and I wanted to be honest with you. I know you like to 'lead' and all, but you don't get to lead in this. We both made a choice, and if you can get your ass off your shoulders, we might even make that choice again. But it's a choice for both of us to make. And if we *do* decide to do it again, here's a word to the wise—it doesn't just automatically end when *you* come."

I stalk out and slam the screen door behind me. Then I go right back in. He is still standing where I left him.

I say, "And maybe, Jeremiah Crew, you should treat *every* time like it's the first time."

I slam back out and take off toward home.

DAY 8

(PART TWO)

That night after dinner, I don't run to the beach, but I walk as fast as I can in my ballet flats. I don't take time to change my shoes because that would mean going back to the house with my mom and more conversation. The hum of the cicadas is so loud, it feels as if they've taken root in my eardrums.

At some point I switch the flashlight from white to red because I've been told the red doesn't disrupt the turtles, and the beam of it bounces as I walk. Part of me hopes he's not there, and the other part of me hopes he is.

I come out of the dunes and onto the beach.

Which is empty.

I sit in our spot and I wait. And I wait.

But he doesn't come.

I try not to let my mind go where it wants to go.

You shouldn't have blown up at him. He has a right to his feelings. Besides, you don't know his history or who might be waiting for him back home. You don't know what Wednesday meant to him, or maybe what she still means to him. You don't know anything about him. You literally met him eight days ago. What did you think would happen? That he would spend his entire summer meeting you at the beach so you could sit here and watch for turtles? Jesus, Claudine.

No one can bring me to tears faster than myself. I sit there blinking into the night, refusing to cry. I dig my feet into the sand and shiver as a cloud passes over the moon.

Leave the boy alone. If he wants to see you, he'll find you. He knew you'd be here. If he'd wanted to see you, he would have come.

But then another part of me is like, *Just take it for what it is. You had sex for the first time. And to a guy who likes you and was— how did he say it?—interesting and hot. And it wasn't in a barn and it wasn't with Shane, who never really got you, and it wasn't with Wyatt, who—let's face it—you barely even know. And it wasn't two months from now in college when you've had too much to drink at a party and you wake up the next day and can't even remember his name, like the way it happened for Mara's sister. Life lessons, as Jared says. A false crawl. It doesn't need to be anything more than that.*

I am thinking about leaving when something dark and enormous emerges from the sea. And I know what it is without Miah here to tell me. The monster moves into the moonlight, and it's not a monster at all but a turtle. Encrusted with barnacles. Dragging herself through the sand as if each step is a struggle. I sit rooted, barely breathing, and silently cheer her on. Willing her to make it to wherever it is she's going.

She is enormous. I watch as the turtle lumbers to a halt several feet away and begins to scoop out the sand with her hind flippers. The work is laborious and slow, and I want to help her. But she's the only one who can do it. She's the only one who knows exactly how it needs to be done.

I can hear Miah's voice in my head: *A female can lay as many as two hundred eggs. Two months later, if the nest survives, the hatchlings will claw their way out and head for the ocean. Most of them won't make it.*

I am still as a stone and barely breathing, but my thoughts are racing and I wish I had my notebook to capture them, to capture this. I watch as the loggerhead burrows into the sand and sometime later—minutes, hours—covers the nest and drags herself back toward the water. I think about the effort. About how strong she is to swim hundreds of miles, fighting to get back to the beach where she was born, to make a nest for her babies. And now I'm picturing these baby turtles, no mother there to help them, and suddenly I feel like crying.

Isn't there anything we can do?

We help how we can, but at some point you have to let nature do its thing.

As I watch her lumber into the ocean, I want to yell at her to come back. I want to grab her and drag her to the nest and make her stay there. But instead I watch her swim away.

After a few minutes, I get up, brush the sand off, and tiptoe to the nest. I take the only thing I have—the flashlight—and bury it nearby, marking the spot. I shrug off my sweater and drape it across the sand. It's not wire netting, but it will at least offer some protection from the raccoons and coyotes and mark the nest until we can come back.

THE ISLAND

———

TWO

DAY 9

I know this about the general store: Terri is a volunteer from the mainland. She has three grandkids and a dog named Banjo. The campers buy more junk food than anyone. The most popular item in the store is—surprise, surprise—bug spray. Before it was a store, it was a schoolhouse, but it shut down in 1972 because there weren't enough children on the island. On days when it isn't busy, usually in winter, Terri goes home early because why sit around when no one shows up? Except for her lecturing me about Miah, Terri and I have become fast friends.

I sit in my usual corner, writing in my notebook—which I now carry everywhere with me—because it is less lonely here than it is at Addy's in the window seat. My notes are scribbles across the pages and in the margins and upside down and in word bubbles. It would take a code breaker to decipher them. I am being as honest with myself as possible, which is harder than it sounds. Who wouldn't rather write down pretty things and pretend they are the truth? But these notes are how I feel—an unedited, wild, messy jumble of emotions and thoughts without order, everything spilling out at once. Welcome to the chaos of my brain.

My phone buzzes and it's Saz. We've been going back and forth all morning. Topic: sex. Specifically: our first times.

Here's the thing, she says. No matter what they tell you, no matter what they show you online or in movies, it looks different in real life. Not worse or better, just different. It's different than doing it yourself because there's this other person there and maybe they don't know how to touch you like you know how to touch you, but there's a lot to say for you wanting them and them wanting you. Having sex with Yvonne makes me feel like I'm invincible, and it also makes me feel totally, I don't know, human. Does that make sense? I don't think that makes sense. But you'll be able to figure out what I mean, Hen. You always do. That's why I know we'll always be okay. Because you're my interpreter in this world.

I text back: It makes sense. Somehow him touching me and me *not* coming was bigger than me touching myself and coming. I've never felt more human in my life. Like every part of me is open and exposed, but also completely awake, and like I can feel everything in the world, good and bad. Like I'm able to feel *more* somehow. But how do you protect yourself?

Saz texts: Yvonne and I used a dental dam. Because guess what? Lesbians can get STDs too, folks. I'd never even heard of such a thing, but Yvonne's had more partners than I have, including Robbie Ziffren, and she's super careful. (Remember Ziff? He was a senior when we were sophomores.)

I text: I sort of remember Ziff. (He hung out with the Lawler brothers, right?) But I'm not talking dental dams or condoms or birth control because I know all about that (thanks, Mom). I'm talking how do you make sure you don't get hurt? Heart, mind, soul, etc.

I sit staring at the phone, at the little typing dots. I wait and I wait and I wait.

Behind the counter, Terri stands, stretches, and starts her routine of closing down the store for the day. She says, "Five minutes, Claude."

"Okay." I make a show of gathering my stuff, dragging it out as much as I can. Notebook in the bag. Pen in the bag. Hat on my head. Stand up. Push the chair in. Double-check that notebook is in the bag. Double-check that pen is in the bag. Dust off table. Pretend to look for keys when I haven't used keys since Ohio because everyone on the island leaves their doors unlocked.

When I can't delay any longer, I start walking toward the door. My hand is on the doorknob when the phone buzzes. I look down at the screen. After all these minutes, Saz has written just two words: You don't.

I find Wednesday at the inn, changing the sheets in one of the downstairs guest rooms, the one off the library. I knock on the open door and she looks up at me over the bed, black braids swinging as she works. "Hey, Mainlander." She doesn't seem surprised to see me.

I walk into the room and she wrestles with the fitted sheet, so I grab a side and together we cover the mattress and smooth the wrinkles with our palms, and then we add the flat sheet and the comforter. All the while I'm trying not to picture her laughing with Miah on the front porch, which is exactly what my brain wants to do.

We arrange the pillows and the two of us stand back, shoulder to shoulder. I reach for a corner of the comforter and give it a tug so that it's all perfectly even.

She says, "What do you want?"

"To ask you about Miah."

"Did he tell you about us?"

"Only that you had something last summer." I hate saying the words aloud because I hate that they're true. It's stupid, but I don't want to think about Miah and Wednesday. I only want to think about Miah and me.

209

"So did you do it? Did you sleep with him?"

"We've been hanging out—"

"So you are sleeping with him."

"I wanted to talk to you before we hang out again."

"Why?"

"Because friends come first."

"I wouldn't really call us friends, Mainlander."

"I just felt like I should ask you. It seemed like the right thing to do. So if you and Miah have something going on, I won't hang out with him anymore."

She sits on the corner of the bed. The whole time she's looking at me, she rubs at the comforter, smoothing the wrinkles she's created. "We were together for two or three weeks last summer, and that was it. But no, we don't have anything going on now. Not since then."

"Do you like him?"

"I barely know him." She stands, gathering the old sheets off the floor. "You'll see. By the end of the summer, you probably won't know anything about him either. So you're not going to bother me. But just be careful. Miah pretty much only cares about Miah."

Again: *Just be careful.*

"What do you mean?"

"Just that he's got this whole other life on the mainland that he never talks about, and when he's done with you, he's done. No 'Hey, that was fun, thanks for the memories.' So yeah, you can have him."

I wait for a minute, in case she changes her mind. She bunches the sheets under one arm and then walks past me to the bathroom, where she dumps the sheets into a laundry basket and starts collecting towels.

I don't know what to do or say, so I walk out of the guest room. I'm wishing I'd never gone in there at all when I hear, "Hey, Claude?"

"Yeah?" I move back to the doorway, half expecting to be yelled at.

Wednesday flips a braid over her shoulder and picks up the laundry basket, balancing it on one hip. "Thanks. It was nice of you to ask."

DAY 10

Another care package arrives from Neil Henry, 720 Capri Lane, Mary Grove, Ohio. In this one: a stack of my books, some photos of Bradbury and Dandelion and of me as a kid, my red Converse, two pairs of earrings, and my Miss Piggy shirt. I pull on the shirt, which suddenly seems too small, as if it belongs to someone much younger. I take it off and drop it in the trash.

His note reads:

> Dear Clew,
>
> Some more treasures from the depths of your room.
> Let me know if there's anything else you want or need.
> Bradbury and I miss you, and your things miss you too,
> which is why I thought I'd send more of them. Hope
> you're taking care of yourself, kiddo. Looking forward
> to August.
>
> Love,
> Dad

All these years my dad stopped setting foot in my room, and suddenly—now that I'm gone—he's in there all the time.

I pick up my phone and write him a text: Please stop sending me things. I'll be home in August and this is just more for me to pack up and carry back there. Unless you don't want my stuff around because it reminds you of me, in which case DON'T GO IN MY ROOM.

Every angry thought pours out of me. How dare he go into my room and take it apart, removing my things like he's conducting surgery, separating my things from each other, invading my home.

I leave the text unsent, undeleted. Mom says sometimes you need to write out your feelings but you don't necessarily need to share them—like maybe the person you're mad at just won't get it or won't care, so sending them a big long text or email will only make it worse. As long as you get the feelings out of you.

I add: In case you were wondering, Mom and I are doing fine. She's busy with work, and I've met someone and slept with him, which means—according to Dr. Alex Comfort—that I'm a woman now. No more Clew. I'm not your little girl anymore.

And what I mean is, *I'm still your daughter but it's different now. That's not because of Jeremiah, though. That's because of you.*

And then I sit there, the words out of me and on the screen. I let them stay there for a good long while before I delete them.

I almost don't go to the beach but something leads me there. A sense of obligation, maybe, to the turtles and to myself. There's something about the routine of it that I need. Seven-thirty p.m.: cocktails. Eight-thirty p.m.: dinner. Ten p.m.: ocean. There's this comfort in knowing what I'm doing when.

I walk to Little Blackwood Beach, the air buzzing, the heat settling into my skin. There is this moment that makes me catch my breath—when I emerge from the canopy of trees onto the sand, and the moon is in the sky and also in the water, and it's all I see, this enormous red moon that looks like it's on fire.

I go past the dunes, searching for the turtle nest I marked with the flashlight and covered with my sweater. The flashlight has been replaced with a wooden stake, and netting covers the sand. There's no sign of my sweater.

I walk a little farther and then sink onto the ground, and suddenly I'm not alone on the beach. It's funny here, on this island— how you can really *feel* the history sometimes. Maybe it's the color of the sky or the volume of the cicadas or something about dusk settling over the marsh. Or maybe it's just my own changing mood. Tonight, under the red moon, the ghosts of Blackwoods are everywhere, riding the turtles into the sea and dancing in their finest clothes and trying to fight the flames as Rosecroft burns.

According to my mom, on March 11, 1993, Aunt Claudine woke up knowing she would die that day. No floor dropping out from under her. No surprises. She was living at the inn then—or the house that became the inn—which she'd inherited after her father's death, and which she'd willed to the Park Service. She asked her mother's friend Clovis Samms to drive her to Rosecroft one last time, even though it was in ruins, having burned down two months before. At noon, she returned to her bed, her feet already cold. The coldness spread up and throughout her body. Hours later, she was dead. The autopsy would uncover cancer, but if she had ever been diagnosed, Claudine never let on.

I think about the knowing. Of Claudine waking up knowing she would die—what it would be like to wake up in the morning and know the end was coming. Of Tillie Donaldson Blackwood thinking her whole life was ahead of her on her wedding day. Is it better to be prepared? To have to wait for it, knowing there's nothing you can do? Or is it better to have the world change in an instant—like mine did, like Claudine's did—without warning?

I fish the blue notebook out of my bag and write these things down, my eyes adjusting to the dark and the moonlight. I'm so

deep in thought that I don't notice Jeremiah Crew until he's standing over me.

"Captain."

I blink up at him. For a second, I think he's a ghost too.

He says, "Miss me?"

"No."

Yes. And it's not just my heart that starts pulsing faster. My
entire body begins throbbing at the sight of him.

"I'm pretty sure you did."

He hands me something and it takes me a second to recognize
it. My sweater.

"Thanks for marking the nest."

He sits down next to me. I drape the sweater over my knees
like a blanket even though I'm the opposite of cold.

"So," he says.

"So."

He runs his hand over the sand. Scoops some up. Scatters it.
Rubs his hands together to brush them off.

"Look," he says. "I'm sorry. Once a shit-heel, always a shit-heel
to some degree. You didn't have to tell me, but you did anyway. A
little after the fact, but you told me."

"You're right. I didn't have to tell you. It's my body. I decide
what happens to it. And you weren't mad when you thought I was
just some easy summer girl that you could hook up with."

"I never thought you were some easy summer girl. *Nothing* is
easy about you, Captain. But okay. And you're right. And I missed
you too."

"I didn't say I missed you."

"But you did."

I'm thinking of Wednesday and Terri and the warnings they've
given me about him. But then I think, *Maybe they don't know him*

like I know him. Which is why that part of me says, "I did." Because what do I have to lose?

I look at him and he looks at me and neither of us looks away. And I can see it in there. He still likes me. And I can't help it: I like him.

He says, "So I had some time to think, and here's what I came up with. You be honest with me; I'll be honest with you. I'm talking this is you; this is me. We got off to a pretty good start, so let's keep it going. Take it or leave it."

I dig my feet into the sand as I try to formulate thoughts and words and organize them sensibly, intelligently, articulately. I've never done this before—spilled my soul to a person I've just met. Even with Saz, back when we were ten, it took some time. *What if I can't do this? What if I've done all the spilling I can do?* I open my mouth and say the first thing that comes out.

"You and Wednesday. What was that, exactly? And do you still like her? And are you planning to hook up with her again this summer while you're also hanging out with me? Because I don't know that I'm that evolved. I'm actually certain I'm not that evolved. Not that I love you or need you to love me, but I'm pretty sure I can only sleep with someone who sleeps with one person at a time."

He laughs. "Wow. Way to embrace the honesty. So you're saying we're going to sleep together again?"

"I'm talking theoretically. Hypothetically."

"That's not how it sounded."

I hold up my hands like, *Who's to say?*

"I guess we'll just have to wait and see." He rubs his face. Looks out at the ocean, and I can see him arranging his own thoughts. "So Wednesday and I hung out for a couple weeks last summer. It was basically just sex, and every now and then we'd, like, go to

216

the beach or hang out around the Dip, which is mostly what she wanted to do. I'm not planning to hook up with her again, much less while hanging out with you. If I wanted to be with Wednesday, I'd be with her."

"I don't want to find out that you're, like, comparing us in any way, and I'm some sort of consolation prize."

"You could never be a consolation prize, Captain. You're like that giant purple carnival bear, as big as a fucking SUV, that costs a bazillion tickets. The one you knock yourself out trying to win by playing Whac-A-Mole and Shoot-the-Duck and whatever else you have to do so that you can bring it home. Also, I'm not really a guy who sleeps with more than one girl at a time. And besides, you do know we're on an island." He gives me this half grin. "So what scares you most? With us?"

I give this a little thought. "That you'll be really into me one day and the next day you won't be, and I won't see it coming. Because apparently feelings can change overnight. Maybe it's me. Maybe I'm too much. Or maybe I'm not enough." All the things I've been thinking since my dad told me he was leaving.

"You're enough. Trust me. You're more than enough." He laughs a little, but I can also tell he means it.

"Not that you have to like me forever, but I just don't think I could survive another *Now you see the floor, now you don't*."

"That won't happen."

"How do you know?"

"Because I'm the guy who shows up. When the dad leaves, when the mom falls apart. And when I have feelings, they don't change overnight." I open my mouth to ask about Wednesday and he says, "I said *when* I have feelings." Which tells me maybe I am different in some way.

I take a breath. Let it out. "So what scares you most?"

217

"You."

Our eyes lock, his and mine, and it's the single most erotic moment of my short life. There's all this heat, but more than that. Something like love.

"And me," he says. "I scare the shit out of me. I have this way of sabotaging the good things in my life, because for a long time when anything good happened, I didn't think I deserved it. So I fucked it up, most of the time on purpose. I know enough to know I don't have to, but that doesn't mean I won't. As you can probably tell." His voice is soft and raw.

I think about this. "So I have trust issues because people leave me, and you fuck good things up on purpose because at least that way you won't get hurt."

"Pretty much."

"Perfect."

"At least we know what we're in for." He bumps my arm with his and I bump his back. Somewhere inside me, the wall crumbles a little.

I say, "For the record, I think you're a giant purple carnival bear too; otherwise I never would have done anything with you. I mean, what kind of girl do you think I am?"

"The likes of which I've never seen."

He smiles.

I smile.

"So does this mean you want me to be your girlfriend?"

"Is that what I said?"

"Pretty much. I mean, sure, if you want me to be."

"I want you to be."

"I want to be."

He leans over and kisses me. He wraps his arm around me and I nestle into him and it feels good there.

I say, "Maybe it's better not to talk about what happens when we leave here." I wave at the island.

"Whatever you want, Captain."

We sit there and for some reason I'm thinking *only* about what happens when we leave.

He looks up at the sky. "It's a full moon. Which means a king tide. Which means good treasure hunting."

I picture pirate galleons and gold coins and trunks of jewels—mountains of sparkling, glittering stars. I picture Miah and me sailing the seas in a pirate ship, scattering gold everywhere to everyone. Suddenly the world seems possible. I tell myself, *You can do this. Just be careful.*

"We should go tomorrow. I'll bring mud boots for you."

"Why do I need mud boots?"

"You'll see. What size are those feet of yours?"

"Nine."

He whistles.

"What? That's, like, average size."

"Nothing about you is average, Captain. Even your giant feet."

I'm home before midnight, and my mom is still awake, working in the little office. I stand in the doorway for a moment and watch her, the tilt of her head as she reads something, the way she leans into her laptop as she types, the way she hums to herself now and then, as if she's listening to a song I can't hear.

Suddenly I'm filled with all this love. I walk up and, without a word, wrap my arms around her. Mom drops the papers she's reading and hugs me back, and we stay like this for a long time.

DAY 11

The next afternoon, Miah and I rattle and bump past Rosecroft in the truck, down a dirt path through the scrub. On the dash, the shells and alligator bones and other island relics flash in the reflection of the windshield, disappearing and reappearing as we drive in and out of the tree cover. He is singing, completely off key, as I hold on to the fisherman's cap so that it doesn't blow away.

As he sings, I think about second chances and being human. About having no clue whether or not something's going to work out. I used to believe I knew all there was to know about myself and everyone around me. My world in order. Everything in its place. And now I'm riding in a truck with a boy I've just met—a boy I've had sex with—who is taking me somewhere I've never been.

The truck bumps to a stop on the edge of the marsh. Miah reaches behind the seat and pulls out a pair of rain boots, dark green and crusted with mud. "You're in luck."

"You don't have anything cuter? Like in a red polka dot?"

"Get out of the truck."

I perch on the running board in my bare feet and pull on one boot and then the other. There's water in the left one but I'm not taking it off again. Instead I stand in front of him—sundress, fisherman's cap, mud boots, left foot squishing in an inch of standing water—and squint up at him like, *Ta-da*.

He says, "You're officially an islander, Claude Henry. You're one of us now." In that moment, they're the loveliest words he could ever say, as if all my life I've been waiting for them. He's shoeless, of course, and wearing the super-short military shorts.

"You do know you look like a giant dork in those." I nod to the shorts.

"I actually prefer wild-animal-wrangling, shark-teeth-collecting, freedom-dispensing warrior. Why don't you touch them, Captain? Go ahead—you know you want to. They're the softest things on earth." He kisses me. "Next to your lips."

I kiss him back and then we're basically making out against the truck. His arm goes around me, and he's pulling me in, and I'm pressed up against him.

"Ready?" he says into my ear, and at first I think he means, *Are you ready to have sex again? Here, with me, in this truck?*

"Ready." *Yes I am.*

But then he's slinging the camera over his shoulder and we're off, and I'm following him down this path, which opens onto a vista of sky and water. We go tromping across the sand, packed flat and hard, not soft and white like Little Blackwood Beach and the dunes. The marsh water cuts in and out, and we wade through the shallows, hopping over the deeper sections. He extends a hand and I take it. When we come to water the size of a small river, he stands there.

"I don't like the look of the creek."

"That's a creek?"

"The tide's still coming in, which means we're going to have to swim when we come back." He frowns at my sundress.

"You're not the only badass here."

He goes first, and the water only comes up to his knees. He waves to me and extends his hand, and I go in, dress plastering to me like a second skin, and wade through sludge. I push in front of him and claw my way up onto the shore, into the marsh grass.

He's up after me, and we're already muddy and wet. He leads the way, through the reeds and onto the beach, what there is of it. All at once, the sand turns to mud, thick and dark and suctiony. My boots make a *thwup-thwup* sound as I walk. It's a balancing act, trying to go across it without sinking, and I feel it pulling me down, down, down. Whenever I get stuck, Miah takes my arm and wrestles me out.

"Pluff mud," he says. "Some people call it marsh mud. That grass growing out of it is spartina."

"I know so much about nature now."

This makes him laugh. He pulls off his shirt, and at first I think he's going to just keep going and shed his shorts too. I go kind of cold and hot all at once because I really want him to strip down, and I'm imagining yanking off my dress and standing there in only mud boots, my underwear, and five inches of bug spray. But then he holds the shirt out to me. "You're freckling. I mean even more so than usual."

"Thanks." I pull it on and knot it at the waist, and I can smell him on me—fresh and earthy, like a breeze. *This is my boyfriend's shirt,* I think. *This is my boyfriend.*

He sinks into the mud and I sink, and then we're both stuck and we go pushing forward, like we're moving through quicksand.

Shells and rocks are scattered across the sand and mud as far as the eye can see, as if this is all that's left of the world. They stretch out into the ocean, into the horizon. I walk looking down, not sure what to pick up and what to leave. Miah is collecting things. *This is a shark tooth. This is a fossilized shell. This is a prehistoric tooth*

222

of some sort. This is part of an alligator. This is an armadillo bone.
They all look the same to me and I don't know how he tells them
apart. It's like he speaks the language of the marsh and I'm on the
outside. Except that right now I'm not on the outside because he's
translating every bit of it for me in a way that makes me feel a part
of this island and a part of him.

He bends over, drawing a circle in the sand. "There's a shark
tooth in there."

I study the sand as if it's the most important piece of earth on,
well, earth. I bend over and pick up the smallest black triangle. I
hold my palm open for him to see.

"You're a natural." And the way he says it makes it sound like
he's talking about more than shark teeth. He leans in and kisses
me, tongue finding mine. I drink him in, the warmth of him, the
smell of him, the taste of him.

"I can't wait to be naked with you again," he says.

And then we're kissing like two wild animals, and just as we're
tugging at each other's clothes and getting ready to throw each
other down in this mud and spartina and marsh, a horn blares
from somewhere. I look up and it's the ferry passing by. Grady
waves at us from the deck, wearing a big fat smirk, and I think
what we must look like, groping each other, my hair standing on
end.

Miah and I break apart and move down the beach, him drawing circles, me picking out the shark teeth, until I have a fistful of
them. He pulls one out and holds it up. "Millions of years ago, this
fell to the bottom of the ocean floor in just the right place and was
covered in sand. And here we are, just you and me, after millions
of years, finding it."

I shake the teeth in my hand and think about how they're like
little broken fragments of something. Like little broken hearts.

"Where do you think love goes when people stop loving you? Do you think there's, like, a junkyard where all the lost and discarded love is collected?" I open my palm and arrange the teeth in the shape of a heart.

"Where love goes to die?"

"Yeah, or waits to be recycled."

"Recycled love. Now, that's something to think about. I don't know. Maybe it's even stronger because it's forged from all these different types of love, all the parts that survived."

"Maybe," I say. I think this over as he draws another circle and I pick up another tooth. I add it to the heart I've made and then I close my palm and shake all the teeth again, mixing up the pieces. I'm picturing all the different facets of love: understanding, sex, security, romance, hurt, trust, vulnerability. All the different pieces that make up romantic love and nonromantic love—like the love I have for Saz and my other friends, and the love I have for my mom. And, even though I don't want to, for my dad.

I say, "I used to think the fact that my parents were happy—or seemed to be happy—made me invincible, like I could walk into any room in the world and everyone would be my friend because I didn't know love could change or disappear. I mean, I had friends whose parents were divorced, but knowing that from the outside is different from feeling it."

"Maybe it wasn't about them being happy with each other. Maybe it was about them knowing how to love you that gave you superpowers. My parents couldn't stand each other, and when they were together, there wasn't a lot of room for us kids. If they were ever in the same room, I'd turn around and walk the fuck out because it was always going to end in a TV remote or worse getting thrown at you."

"Seriously?"

"Oh yeah."

"I've never even heard my parents argue. My friend Saz says that's weird."

"Maybe there's a world where parents don't yell at each other but they talk things out when they fight. I don't know. I don't think I saw my dad as an actual, like, person until about a year ago. He was just this invisible force that fucked up my mom's life and mine." He stares out at the horizon, as if he sees something— a memory, maybe. "But if he hadn't done that, I might not be here walking on this beach with you." He turns those eyes on me and I can see them coming back into focus.

"I wouldn't be here either. If my parents hadn't split up."

Would I trade walking on this beach with Jeremiah Crew if it meant my parents could still be together? Would I trade who I am right now, in this moment, sun shining on me, shark teeth in my hand?

He draws another circle and together we stare down at the sand. I bend over. Pick up the tooth. Hold it up.

I say, "I just wish they could have stayed together and I'd still somehow be here."

"If they hadn't split, you'd probably be a different Claude."

"Probably."

"What was she like? Pre-island Claude?"

"A big dreamer, wanting to go out and see the world and live a big life somewhere. I was, I don't know, restless but comfortable, maybe not in my own skin so much as at home, in school. I thought I knew exactly who I was. But I was also pretty naïve. You could say I have a much deeper understanding of how the world works now." I smile up at him. "My writing teacher told me I needed to feel more to make readers feel. And I used to wish something would happen to me to make my writing more interesting."

As nothing as these things sound, they're the hardest things I've ever said to anyone. *This is me,* I think. *Take it or leave it.*

"So are you writing now?"

For some reason, this makes me go quiet, maybe from some sense of guilt that I should be writing more than I am. Or maybe it's because I've been scribbling things down lately with no real purpose or goal, and I'm not sure I can call that writing.

I say, "Not really."

He raises the camera and aims it at the crabs scurrying past our feet. "My photos are a way of telling stories but without the pressure of all those words. I used to think of them as a way to capture everything that's good. Everything my life wasn't. But now I take pictures of all of it: the sad, the disturbing, the ugly. It's kind of why I collect bones. They tell a story. Usually a tragic story, because, you know, they're bones, but to me there's beauty in that."

"There's beauty in every story. And there's a story in everything."

"Like these teeth."

He draws a circle in the sand. I pick up a tooth and hand it to him and I think about what Wednesday said about never getting to know the real Jeremiah Crew. *Maybe I am different.*

He says, "Or maybe I've just been on this island too long." And he shoots me a grin that I feel all the way in my toes. I look away, directly at the sun, because it isn't nearly as blinding.

"So what was Pre-island Miah like?"

"You wouldn't have liked him. Bad boy. Angry at the world. Honestly, it's like a really reckless, really unhappy person who lived a long time ago. This is the only me I know." He shrugs, and it's honest. "That doesn't mean I don't wonder who I'd be or what all this would be like if my dad had stayed or been a different person. But it could be that no matter what happened, no matter what he did or who he was, I'd still have ended up the guy you see before you. I just know I've gone through some shit and it's made me, well, me."

As we walk, little crabs are scurrying everywhere. He says, "Listen." We stand still and you can hear them scuttling around in the reeds—the faintest music. The island already seems like a relic frozen in some other era. And right now, in this moment, I feel time stop. Suddenly I can see every shadow, every color. I can hear every sound. I look around me, and for maybe the first time in my life, I'm in the here and now. Not the past or the future, but here.

I straighten, half sunk in the mud, palm filled with shark teeth and shells and sand, and watch Jeremiah Crew walking away from me, head down, scanning the beach. He bends over, scoops up a piece of sea glass, keeps walking. And in that moment I'm filled with something like love for this boy who knows so many of my secrets. Who is teaching me to find shark teeth. Who brought me mud boots. Who is showing me his island. This barefoot boy, made of sun and light, who's one with the mud and sand and marsh. Collecting treasure. Finding beauty in the littlest things. Wounded like me, but not looking back. In the moment. Looking forward. Marveling at what's in front of him. At home in his own skin. At home wherever he is.

I think, *I could live here. I could be happy here. Right here with him. I could stay here forever.*

The creek that was a pond is now a river. The air is hotter and wetter. The bugs are circling. Miah stands in front of me, scanning the horizon. Water as far as the eye can see.

I say, "Are there alligators in there?"

"Not small ones."

227

"What the hell is that supposed to mean?"

"It means come on, Captain."

He helps me down off the bank, into the water, and I let out a scream because I'm slipping and sliding, and then we're both laughing our heads off, and my arms are around his neck and he's holding his camera above his head and he's carrying me, and my dress is hiked up around my waist, and he pulls it down and smooths it over my knees.

Then he kisses me and I feel safe here, in his arms like this, as if nothing bad will happen in the world ever again. I want to stay right here for the rest of the summer, maybe the rest of my life. But then he's setting me down on the opposite bank, and I'm soaking wet and muddy, and he slaps a mosquito on my arm and peels it off me.

I look up from the bite, which is already a bright red welt, and his eyes are on mine. "What?"

And then he takes my face in his hands, brushes the hair off my forehead, and kisses me again.

DAY 11

(PART TWO)

Mom and I walk arm in arm to the inn. I wear black because it makes me feel sophisticated. Red lips. Ballet flats. Enormous sunglasses perched on my head. I leave off the fisherman's hat. We've gone fifteen steps and my skin and hair are already damp from the heat and I have two new mosquito bites on my arm because I wanted to smell like Miss Dior and not bug spray.

I look up at the inn, which looks fresh and clean in spite of its age, and for some reason I think of the Secret Drawer Society. I ask my mom if she's heard of it.

"Addy and I used to dare each other to sneak in there and leave notes for the people we were crushing on. God, those notes are probably still in there, unless they've started cleaning them out."

I'm thinking about what I would write as we reach the steps of the inn, and I look up and see Miah before he sees me. He's waiting on the porch, straddling the railing, and when he turns his face toward us, I catch my breath. He's wearing this suit jacket the color of the ocean, and a light blue shirt. He is so beautiful it hurts my heart, and I want to be close to him.

Mom looks at Miah, at me. "From now on, I'm chaperoning the two of you."

"Mom." I think, *Oh my God, please don't know we had sex.*

"The three of us are going to have such a fun time this summer."

229

In that moment, Miah sees me and his face lights up. He meets us on the top step.

"Captain."

"I almost didn't recognize you with shoes."

"They're like prisons for the feet."

Beside me, my mom clears her throat.

"Jeremiah."

"Mrs. Henry."

"Call me Lauren." She doesn't correct him about the last name. "So tell me about yourself. How long are you here? What is it you do when you're not on the island? And what are your intentions with my daughter?" She pretend-frowns.

"Ignore her, please," I say to him.

He says, "The next three weeks. Try not to get in trouble. And I have no idea."

This makes her smile. "Okay, then. Interrogation over." To me she says, "Don't worry. I'm going to go talk to that nice couple from Cleveland. See you at dinner."

After she walks away, I say, "Are you eating with us?"

"I can't. I thought I was. Hence the prisons for the feet. But Bram's having an Outward Bound emergency. After I help save some stranded trail clearers, I'll come get you and we can walk on the beach. There's a meteor shower tonight and it should be pretty incredible, as long as the moon doesn't get in the way."

There are voices and the bang of a door, and suddenly all these guests and staff are milling around and converging on us. I wave to Jared and Wednesday but in my mind I'm going, *Don't come over, don't come over.* Wednesday looks past me at Miah and then turns away. I try not to focus on the way her hair shines in the early-evening light.

"You left your phone in my truck." Miah hands it to me and

says, "I brought you something else." It's a clear container with a black lid. Filled with treasure.

I open the lid and shake the contents back and forth, examining the shark teeth and shells and other pieces of things I can't identify. I pull out the prehistoric tooth he found. "But that's yours."

"We found it together."

For the first time, I feel this kind of weird formality with him. Maybe it's because we're dressed as if we're going to prom and he's not barefoot and my mom is somewhere nearby, but I don't know what to say.

The ringing of a bell makes me jump. Miah is on his feet, the ones imprisoned in shoes, and says again, "I'll be here afterward to get you." And he kisses me on the cheek, lingering there for a second. In my ear he says, "You are spectacular, Claudine Llewelyn Henry."

After dinner, we drive to the dunes and spread out the blanket, and we're the only living souls around. We lie down, side by side, under the largest moon I've ever seen. Miah says, "We may not get anything. But who knows? The brightest meteors can sometimes shine through, if we're lucky."

I'm feeling that same weird formality, even though I'm the only one dressed up. His suit jacket is gone, the pants have been replaced by shorts, and he's barefoot again.

The night feels muted, as if it's waiting, and we stay quiet, lying there, not touching. I want to lean over and kiss him or take his hand or feel his skin. I reach out to touch the gold of his arm, at the spot just below the rolled-up sleeve. My fingers are as light as a breeze. He looks down at them and then up at me.

"Captain."

"Crew." And then I laugh. "Captain. Crew. Get it?"

He stares at me for a good long minute and then he's laughing too. "Goofball."

Suddenly a single trail of light blazes above us, and the sky comes alive with streaks of light and color. We immediately go silent, staring upward. The meteors are like fireworks without the noise, and I imagine the sounds they would make if they could—a kind of bright, spiraling symphony.

"I thought we weren't supposed to see them," I whisper.

"We weren't."

We fall silent again, watching. *They're doing it just for us,* I think. *Our own private concert.*

At some point, a long time later, I tell him, "My dad says that it's a rare person you can be silent with. Companionable silence, that's what he calls it. He says most people talk too much about nothing." I can feel Miah's eyes on me. "He says there's a difference between not talking when you're there together and not talking when one of you is there and one of you is there but far away." My voice drifts off and now I'm thinking about my dad when I don't want to be thinking about my dad. At all.

I look at Miah and his eyes return to the symphony overhead. "Captain, not talking with you when both of us are here, under this sky, is better than talking with anyone else about anything."

By midnight, the clouds have moved in. We drive through the dark to Rosecroft, which is shrouded in fog. The moon is blurry and out of reach but the sky is bright from the glow. When we get to the ruins, Miah parks the truck but leaves the engine running.

I say, "I would hate to disappear without writing my story first." I'm thinking of Tillie Blackwood but I'm also thinking of myself, the way I disappeared from Ohio and who I used to be, out of my life and into my parents' secret.

"That's why stories are important, Captain. Maybe you can write about these people someday."

"Maybe." And for the first time in a while, I feel it, the old itch to work on my novel, or maybe write something new. Not just scenes and thoughts and feelings, but something whole, start to finish, about where I come from and where I'm going and the fact that I was here.

Miah fiddles with the radio and suddenly there's music: "Joy to the World" by Three Dog Night. He turns it up and gets out of the truck, leaving the doors open. The song sweeps out, surrounding us here, surrounding the ruins, charging the air. And then he starts dancing, and the boy can move—something I already know. I start to move too and the music fills me until I am the music and the music is me.

The two of us dance through the ruins, under the fog, under this weird glowing moon. I half expect Rosecroft to dissolve in front of our eyes, beneath our feet, absorbed by the mist.

He's playing air guitar and I'm playing drums, and now his flashlight is a microphone and we are singing into it even though I don't really know the words.

We leap and shake, and we *are* the earth tremors. I am freer than I've ever been, and in this moment it's the greatest song I've ever heard. And then Miah sweeps me into him and against him and we sway together. I wrap my arms around his neck and kiss him, and we are all this possibility and almostness and maybe.

Afterward we sit on the tailgate of the truck, legs swinging, music playing low. The fog has lifted and the moon is back.

I say, "What about you?"

"What about me, Captain?"

"Don't you want to write your story?"

"You mean besides leaving behind a criminal record?"

"I'm serious. What about your photographs?"

"I don't know. I've never really thought about it. I mean really thought about it. I've spent most of my life trying not to dream too big."

The moonlight on his face casts him in shadow, and for a second I feel like I'm seeing into him.

Before I can ask why he never let himself dream big, he says, "But when I'm with you, everything is quiet; everything just seems right, like my skin fits. And I don't mean just when I'm *with you* with you."

He delivers this last line in a sexy way, but the look on his face is hard to describe. It's a mix of sadness and light. My own face must look similar because I'm thinking about the girl I used to be in Mary Grove, Ohio, who sometimes felt wrong in her own skin.

Everything just seems right.

Yes it does, I think, and I look down at my skin, which—at least on this night—fits perfectly.

DAY 11

_____

(PART THREE)

The inn is still and dark. We sail by it on the way back from the ruins, and the thing I know is that I'm not going home yet because the night is magical and so are we. Without a word, we drive to Miah's house.

We pull up out front, truck engine idling.

He says, "I can take you home."

"Or I could come inside."

He cocks his head, studying my face. He's wearing this smile that's more like the ghost of a smile, as if it's only an echo. He's reading me. And he can. So I let him. I don't look away. I don't fidget. I look right back at him. An electric current passes between us, charging the air and the night and the moon.

Finally he says, "I like your idea better." Very soft. As if talking too loud will chase it away.

Inside, the house feels different from the other times I've been here. Or maybe it's that I feel different. He hands me a soda, and I don't even notice that I have it in my hand at first because my heart is beating out of my chest, so loud I'm sure he can hear it.

He sits on the couch and I say, "I want to see your room." And I feel brave and bold and perfect in my own skin.

He gets up and takes my hand and leads me through the living room and into this room with wooden beams across the ceiling and windows along one wall that look out over the backyard and beyond that the water.

He turns on a light, which casts a sliver like a crescent moon across the floor.

"Is there music?"

"There can be."

"You choose it."

While he sorts through a stack of vinyl, I take in the photos on the wall—more black-and-white shots of the live oaks, the horses, the dunes, various animal bones. "These are beautiful," I say, to him, to myself. "Even the bones."

One photo in particular keeps drawing my eye. A close-up of an open palm, and inside it three white, heart-shaped objects that look like shells. I stand looking at it, and there's something sad and lovely that paralyzes me. It's the same way I feel when I read Zelda Fitzgerald's letters or anything by Ray Bradbury.

He says, "Deer vertebrae."

"Making something lovely out of something not so lovely." I'm filled with this itching, gnawing feeling in my chest, a kind of envy, because no matter where he goes or what he's doing, he seems to know exactly who he is. And it's more than that—he knows how to look at things in a way I don't.

"When Bram gave me the camera, he said, 'Why don't you put all that anger to good use? Look for stories. Try being an observer rather than a participant in life, and get yourself some empathy.'"

"Did it work?"

"Very funny. Why, yes, Captain, yes it did."

I lean in to look at the framed photos on the built-in bookshelf. A woman with his same smile. A twentysomething guy in familiar-looking army-green shorts—an older, stockier version of Miah. Two girls, one redhead, one brunette, arms linked and laughing. Two younger girls, one with curly brown hair, the other blond, making faces at the camera. And this is his family. It's so strange to think of him having people out in the world who know him and love him. I wonder what Off-Island Miah is like. Is he different from the one I know?

I'm imagining this other Jeremiah Crew, one I barely recognize, when the music—raw and whiskey-laced—fills the room.

He walks over to me. Takes my hand and twines his fingers through mine. We're swaying a little to the music, and I'm looking into his eyes and thinking how amazing it is that you can live for eighteen years without knowing someone, and then they can come along and, like that, know you better than anyone. And you can't imagine what you ever did before they knew you and saw you and heard you and talked to you about all the things they've been through and all the things that matter to them.

"We don't have to do anything, Captain."

"I know. But I want to. You don't have to promise me anything. You don't have to love me."

"I can't promise I won't."

"I could break your heart."

"I know."

"Or you might break mine."

"So we should probably just shake hands right now, agree it was nice meeting each other, and say goodbye."

"Or we could see what happens."

Our eyes lock and I feel naked already. But it isn't terrifying. It's lovely. As if this is the closest I will ever come to having someone see me for me. The me I really am and all that that me encompasses. The things I like about myself and the things I don't.

He says, "As you may remember, I've got protection."

I lean in and kiss him. He kisses me and it's soft like a whisper. And there is the sensation of falling, as if I'm not in control of my heart or head or body, which means I actually don't have any protection, and I feel these alarm bells go off because the more I like this person, the more chance there is he can hurt me.

Stop it, Claudine. Because I can't be here and not here at the same time. I have to choose one.

I kiss him harder, and his mouth answers mine, and then his hands are on my face and my hands are on his back, and now I'm unbuttoning the sky-blue shirt. And I tell myself: *There is only Miah and me and this room and these hands and the two of us. We are the only ones here.*

At some point, my brain switches off and my body takes over, but unlike my first time, I'm here. No mental narration, just completely and totally one hundred percent on-the-bed here. The song that's playing is "Tennessee Whiskey." And I'm glad it's not some stupid song I'll be embarrassed to remember one day. It's perfect, actually. Just like we are in this moment.

It's this feeling of my heart being safe for the first time in a long time. And I know enough to know this isn't always how it will be, but this is how it feels right now with Miah as we fall onto the bed and undress each other until we are just skin against skin everywhere.

At no point do I leave my body, the way I always thought I would. I'm not watching us from above the bed or from the bookshelf or the rocking chair by the window or from outside the window looking in. I am on that bed with him. I don't wonder if my body is a disappointment. I don't worry about where to put this arm or this leg. I just move with him, and at first it's just us moving together but separately. He's touching me, and the room starts to spin with light. All these fireflies of light swirling and sparkling around me. When I touch him, he groans in my ear and pulls away.

I watch as he reaches for the condom. He hesitates and I know

he's not going to do anything until I say, "Okay." So I say, "Okay."
And I watch as he rolls it on the same way he did the first time.

And then he's back and kissing me. And a moment later I feel
the tip of him, and even though this isn't the first time, it feels like
the first time. Maybe the way the first time should have felt.

He is going slowly, watching my face, reading my face. I run my
hands over his back and arms, which are taut from the way he's
holding himself up and over me, and I want more of him. I want
all of him.

But first he leans down and kisses me, and I kiss him harder
and more urgently to let him know it's okay. It's yes. It's now. My
body is wanting his. And I am burning up, head to toe, little fires
everywhere.

Then I can feel him. All of him. And it hurts a little, but that's
more the surprise again of having another body *in your body,* the
getting used to something new.

But it's funny how fast my body adapts. It's like, *Oh, hello there.
Why haven't we done it like this sooner?*

And I'm into it. And he's into it. And he's literally *in* it, as in my
vagina. (*Vagina,* really? I mean, *penis?* Like, why are these words
so completely unsexy?) And then, oh my God, I laugh out loud at
this. And he pulls back and looks at me and goes, "Uh. Captain?"

And I say, "I mean, *vagina? Penis?* Could they have come up
with less sexy words?"

And then he's laughing too, and he kisses my forehead and
mumbles something into my neck like, "God, that brain of yours."
And then the laughter falls away onto the sheets, into the mattress,
and we are done talking. There's only music and the sound of our
breathing.

It takes us a moment, but then we hit this rhythm, and for a couple of minutes it's not like a second first time. I know he feels it too because of the way he's looking at me, and then the way he's kissing me, and then the way he stops worrying about hurting me and is just moving with me and not holding back, and I tell myself not to hold back either. Which for me means letting go of this summer and my parents and Saz and everything familiar, including my virginity. The way he's touching me tells me that he's remembering what I said about sex not being just about him.

He touches me here . . .

And here . . .

And here . . .

And moves inside me, his eyes locked with mine.

And then—

There is a moment where I actually do let go. It's more like a letting go and a taking total control at the same time. I feel infinite. Free. It's this perfect, beautiful moment, my body going heavy and light all at once. I hold on to it until I feel it melt away into the sheets and up toward the beamed ceiling and out through the windows, where it disappears into the ocean beyond.

His bed is up against the window, and from my pillow I can look up and out at the sky and the stars. He's sleeping, his breath steady and even. I lie there watching him. The way his eyelids flutter. The way his bare chest rises and falls. The way his hand rests on my leg, keeping me close to him.

"I could love you," I whisper. "I might already love you. I just thought I should warn you." And then I close my eyes and drift away for a while before I have to go.

DAYS 12–14

It's the middle of summer and I am thinking about sex *a lot*. When and where we can have it next, when and how I can sneak away with Miah. I walk down Main Road or along the beach and I feel taller and sexier, like this new Claude who feels completely at home in her own skin. I'm Captain Marvel and Black Widow and Domino and all my favorite superheroes rolled into one. I'm a wild-animal-wrangling, shark-teeth-collecting, freedom-dispensing warrior.

We do it everywhere—the truck, the beach, the carriage house at Rosecroft. I sneak into Miah's house, into his bed, and we find each other in the dark. We whisper under the sheets until we kick them off, along with pillows and blankets and anything else that has the misfortune of being on the bed with us.

Every muscle hurts from the unaccustomed activity, and I feel excited and hungry and something else. Happy. I am so busy that I don't go to the general store, not even to check messages.

The next two days are full of adventures.

We walk for miles in the mud on the marsh looking for treasure.

We follow the turtle tracks from the ocean and mark the nests.

We drive to Blackbeard Point and dig for pirate booty.

He takes me to what he calls the Love Is Love Tree, which is a live oak and a palm that have grown together, their trunks merged and intertwined into one.

At the beach by the island museum, we stand in the rain and watch a family of manatees. There are four of them. Gentle, snuffling creatures. Rolling and bobbing. Miah stands behind me and wraps his arms around me, and in the woods just beyond the museum, he shows me a cottage—part laboratory, part photography studio—that belonged to one of the Blackwoods. The windows are broken and the trees are reaching in, but other than that it looks untouched, as if they might come back any minute.

He says, "If we could stay here forever, I'd make this our studio. For you to write in and me to develop pictures."

Through it all, we talk about everything.

He learns:

I once had imaginary friends named Ribbony and Dental Floss.

I used to play this game where I told myself my parents were getting divorced and I had to choose who to live with. I always chose my mom.

In fourth grade I called Jessica Leith stupid to her face, and I never forgot how horrible I felt when she started crying.

I hate my freckles and once tried to wash them off with fingernail-polish remover.

I'm afraid Saz and I will never be friends like we once were.

I worry that Mr. Russo is right and I will never be able to write anything deep or true.

I secretly wonder if I'm unlovable and that's why my dad left us.

I learn:

He was eleven the first time he drank whiskey, and he used to hide alcohol in the crawl space under the house because that's where his dad hid his.

When he first got to the island, he stole a boat from the inn but crashed it on the jetties of the north end and had to walk fifteen miles back to the house he lives in now. That was the moment everything changed for him and he decided to let the island in.

He has a lot of friends, but no one best friend, and no one really knows him.

Something heartbreaking happened to him a couple of years ago, but he's not ready to talk about it.

His favorite color is blue like the sky, or green like the trees.

His middle name is Shepherd. For approximately three minutes in ninth grade, he tried going by Shep.

His favorite song is "Joy to the World" by Three Dog Night, not just because his name is in the lyrics, but because it captures the feeling of what it's like for him living on this island.

If he could live anywhere other than here, it would be somewhere out west, a place where the land is open and the people are broad-minded and easygoing and they leave you alone when you want them to.

The photo he's proudest of taking is the one of the heart-shaped deer vertebrae. He likes the simplicity of it. He likes that he didn't have to try hard to capture a feeling, like he does sometimes with other photos. He likes that it's honest.

Not all boys are the same. The way I touched Shane or Matteo or even Wyatt is different from the way I touch Miah because they are different people. It's like I had to think about it more with Shane and the others. Through a lot of trial and error, I had to learn the things they liked and the things they didn't. But touching Miah is more instinctive, as if my body and my hands and my mouth knew his from the beginning.

Most of all, he learns me—as in all of me—and I learn him. And in this moment, right here on this island, right now, we fit.

THE THINGS I LEARN ABOUT MYSELF

I love:

- The way he kisses me just behind the ear and at the curve of my throat where neck meets collarbone.
- The way he hums into my skin, making it vibrate.
- The way his hands are rough, gentle, strong, soft, light as a breeze.
- The way he explores me, as if he's creating a map of all my erogenous zones—the places that make me laugh and smile and sigh.
- The way his breath feels on my hip bone, on my inner thigh.
- The way he looks at me just before he kisses me, like I'm all there is in the world.
- The way I fit into him afterward, head on chest, shoulder under his arm, leg over his.
- The way I feel strong and beautiful. The way I know my body like I never have before. The way this body of mine feels desirable, powerful, invincible, and free. Completely and utterly free.

DAY 15

Another box arrives from my dad. The moment I open it, I can smell it—home—and I'm hit with a wave of homesickness, the kind that lodges in your throat so that you can't swallow or breathe.

> Dear Clew,
>
> Counting the days till I see you. Until then, here are some of your favorite Mary Grove-isms: thumbprint cookies from Joy Ann, nonpareils from Taggart's Chocolates, the disgusting sour balls from Veach's Candy, and the latest issue of the paper, because I know you and your mom like to read the Everyday People column, and this is a good one.
>
> See you soon.
>
> > Love,
> > Dad

I dig through the green-and-red reindeer tissue paper that lines the box. I pop a nonpareil in my mouth and browse through the *Mary Grove Tribune*. My mom and I used to read Everyday People to my dad like we were doing some sort of stage show. "I need to set that to music," he'd said one time. "Maybe an opera." And for the next week, the three of us sang our favorite lines to each other in our loudest operatic voices. For a minute I can hear us. I sing a few lines of the column and then start reading the article he's flagged with a Jane Austen Band-Aid he must have found in my bathroom cabinet.

I laugh out loud, and for a minute I picture my dad reading this same article, about an elderly widow who made a giant American flag out of dryer lint. He would have been sitting on the screened porch, drinking coffee out of his favorite Sex Pistols mug, the one I got him on Father's Day when I was nine. The only mug he's used since then. I can see his face, the way he must have smiled at the paper because he wouldn't have been able to help himself. The way he must have jogged into the house, one finger holding the page, to search for the weirdest thing to mark it with.

I imagine him after that, driving all over town to collect my favorite things, even if it meant not getting to eat all the thumbprint cookies himself. And then home again to box it all up, arranging everything in Christmas tissue paper. Writing me a card and having no clue what to say because he knows I'm mad at him, and I'm with my mom, who's also mad at him. But writing it anyway and sending it all anyway because for whatever reason he wants me to have these things.

And suddenly I can't swallow because there is a lump in my throat that has grown to the size of a baseball. The pain is so sharp that my eyes instantly tear, and I blink and blink and blink until the newspaper in my hand blurs away.

It takes me eight minutes to run to the beach, and I'm there at ten a.m. exactly. Miah's not here yet, so I wade into the water and watch for him.

Ten-twenty.

I strip down to my bikini and lie on the sand, which is so hot it burns my back. Every few minutes I sit up to look for him.

Ten-thirty.

We are supposed to have an adventure. He was the one who suggested it. He said last night, "I'll meet you on the beach at ten a.m." Right before he picked me up, my legs around his waist, and kissed me.

Eleven.

I flip over onto my stomach, even though this is too much sun exposure for my poor freckled Midwestern skin. I pop a thumb-print cookie in my mouth and savor it because I want to make them last. I rest my chin on my hands and keep my eyes on the path through the dunes.

Eleven-thirty.

I walk into the water to cool off. My skin stings from the sand and the sun. A wave rushes in and something brushes the top of my foot, but it's only a shell. I pick it up and throw it back into the ocean. *Goodbye, insecurities,* I think as I watch it fly. It disappears, and I imagine it sailing away into the deepest depths of the ocean.

I bend down, pick up another shell. *Goodbye, worry.* I toss it in. I find another and another. *Goodbye, disappearing floors. Goodbye, heartbreak. Goodbye, fear.*

By noon I've filled the ocean with all the things I've been carrying around since I left Ohio—maybe even before that—and Miah still hasn't come.

At home, there's no note, nothing to say why he didn't show. I slather myself in sunscreen, pack a bag with water and snacks, headphones, pen, notebook, phone, and head back out into the day. Before I leave, I stick a note to the door telling him that I waited for him and where I've gone.

I end up at the general store. When I walk in, Terri says, "I haven't seen you in a few days. Someone got too much sun."

"I've been busy." I don't say with who. I try to look as preoccupied as possible so she won't ask me. I spread my things out and take a seat, scooting one of the other chairs close enough so that I can prop my feet on it.

There are four voice messages from Saz. Three left over the past three days, all about sex. The last one, from this morning, just: Hey. Call me when you can.

My first thought is, *Oh no.* I play it again and again, my stomach turning over each time. Saz usually uses up every minute of available message, and if it cuts her off, she calls back to leave another. More than that, though, there's this color to her voice—a dreary gray, a dull brown, the way it sounded when her grandmother died. I try her back, but it doesn't even ring. I tell her voice mail, "This is me calling you. I love you more than kissing and foreplay and sex itself."

I set the phone down, faceup, ringer off, and try to write, try to focus. Terri is reading a book, and the only customer who comes in is a middle-aged man who buys ice cream and a soda.

After he leaves, I say, "Hey, Terri?" Her nose is back in *The Thorn Birds.* "What do you think is an acceptable excuse for someone who stands you up?"

She tears her eyes from the page, but I can see the effort it takes. "Depends on what you were supposed to be doing and who he was."

"Say he's your boyfriend and you were supposed to have an adventure."

"Do I know this person?"

"It doesn't matter." The last thing I'm in the mood for is another lecture on Jeremiah Crew.

She frowns because of course she knows who I'm talking about. "Hold on." She marks her place with her finger and starts flipping through the book until she finds what she's looking for. "I would say, 'There are no ambitions noble enough to justify breaking someone's heart.'" She waves it at me. "Colleen McCullough."

"That's a wise book."

"It is."

I write this quote in my notebook and circle it a hundred times. I replay our last conversation again and again, looking for plumes of smoke, earth tremors, something I did wrong or he did wrong, some clue as to why he didn't show up. If I had his phone number, I could text him or call him, but he hasn't given it to me and he doesn't have mine because he gave it back.

He could be with another girl, someone from Jacksonville. Someone I don't even know about who has a lot more experience and is easier and loves nature and has long, flowing hair and skin that doesn't burn in the sun.

I tell myself: *Calm down. Be rational. Be Thinking Claude, not Emotional Claude. Why do you always have to assume the worst?*

He could be dead somewhere. I should be worried, not angry, because what if something horrible has happened to him? He could have been attacked by wild hogs or drowned in the marsh or eaten by a gator. I picture every scenario, including the look on his face as he's swallowed whole and then spit back out onto the ground, nothing but bones for someone to take photos of or turn into a mobile.

I feel so, so stupid.

Because he made me trust him and tell him all my things, when he probably never really cared to begin with and was always going to stand me up as soon as something better came along. This is what I get for letting myself stop thinking for, like, a *second* about all the things he could do to my heart. And now he's left and taken the floor with him, along with all the things I've told him *and* my virginity. *This is what you get for caring.*

But when I get home to Addy's and my note is still attached to the door and there's no sign that he was ever there, I know what this is. This is Miah fucking things up because he's happy.

DAY 16

At ten the next morning, Jeremiah Crew shows up on my front porch—bare feet, swim trunks, *The Endless Summer* T-shirt—like nothing ever happened. He bangs on the door and I come outside, and from what I can see, he appears to be intact from head to toe, no bruises, scars, or missing limbs.

"Oh, good," I say. "You're alive."

"I said I'd meet you at ten." He cracks a smile, trying to make things light, trying to be my best friend. The dents at the corners of his mouth are flashing at me, attempting to seduce me into forgiveness.

"Ten *yesterday*. At the beach. Where I waited."

"Shit, is it today already?" He pretends to look for his phone, even though he never carries one.

"I thought you might be dead or off with another girl. I mean, as far as I know, there are hundreds of them."

"That's why I like you, Captain: you've got an incredible imagination." He leans against the doorframe—so casual but not casual. I catch a whiff of him and he smells like the ocean.

I stand as rigid as one of the columns on this porch, not about to bend toward him even a little. "I'm being serious. I don't even have your phone number."

"Even if you did, you wouldn't have been able to call me."

"That's not the point."

251

"So I'll give it to you."

"I don't want it."

He straightens, abandoning the doorframe. "Okay, so you're basically saying, what? You can't trust me? Or is it that you can't trust anyone?"

"Don't turn this around on me. Where were you?"

"I had something I had to take care of. Come on, let's go. We could both use an adventure." And he turns around, expecting me to follow him.

"Was it work-related?"

He pauses on the steps, one hand on the railing, squinting up at me. "No."

"Are Shirley and Bram okay?"

"Yes."

I wait for more but he doesn't offer it.

"So that's it?"

I can see him trying to decide what to say to me, just how much to tell me, and after all I've shared with him and confided in him, this burns me up, as in I can feel my ears and face catching fire. He opens his mouth and what I hear is, *I've changed my mind about you. I just don't like you anymore.* What he actually says is, "Something came up. I couldn't be here. But I'm here now." His voice goes completely Southern, the way it does when he doesn't want to get too serious. But there's an edge to it. He's here, but not here.

"If something came up, you could have found me or left a note or told someone to find me. You know what, not that it matters. I mean, you're free to do whatever you want. It's just rude to make someone wait around for you."

"So let's go now."

I could tell him I have plans, try to make him jealous, but instead I'm honest: "I don't want to." And I go back inside and shut the door.

I stand against it, face and ears hot with anger and something else—the sting of betrayal, but not quite that strong. Disappointment, maybe. I feel let down. He's letting me down by not telling me the truth about where he was. I wait for a good minute or two before looking out the window, and by that time he's gone.

The museum sits on the water on the southwestern side of the island, a simple white building that was once used as an icehouse for Rosecroft. I can tell Mom is surprised to see me, but all she says is, "I'm glad you're here."

I step inside and suddenly I've gone hurtling back in time. The building itself is old, with worn, cracked walls made of tabby, a concrete mixture of lime and crushed oyster shells. The air is musty, as if the windows haven't been opened in a hundred years, or however long this place has stood here. My mom locks the door behind us because the museum is only open on Fridays and Tuesdays or by appointment.

The glass cases hold mostly animal bones, an old tortoise shell, arrowheads of all sizes, and china and silver engraved with a *B* for Blackwood, among other things belonging to the family—a Bible, a guest book opened to a page covered in signatures, candlesticks, several pieces of jewelry. Framed photos and paintings of the more famous island residents line the walls, going all the way back to the Native Americans.

I follow Mom into the musty back room, which is smaller than the general store and stacked floor to ceiling with books and boxes and old peach crates. In that moment, I suddenly see what she's been doing the past two weeks: the labeled file boxes, the papers in piles, marked by names and eras. It's like all of the island—its years and years, its people—is right here. And this is one of the things that amaze me about my mom. She is bringing order to the history of this place, finding universal stories in the scraps. She has done this in fourteen days in the midst of her greatest heartbreak.

She says, "Before I got here, these papers were just sitting out on display, where anyone could pick them up and take them home. No one had ever bothered organizing them before now. Still no word from Tillie, though, and I've pretty much laid eyes on everything. I'm worried Claudine might have destroyed whatever existed, because otherwise it's so strange. Like, who leaves nothing behind?"

I recognize the tone in her voice and the expression on her face. When a project catches hold of her, she is flushed and dusty and her eyes shine like quarters, and you can almost hear the crackling and popping of her brain, even when she's doing something completely unrelated, like eating dinner or watching TV. When she's deep in a project, a part of her is always in it, no matter what.

"You're in the throes," I say. Because that's the way she's always described it—like falling in love with someone for the first time. You're swept away and it's all you can think of, and you feel it everywhere, not just in your mind.

She holds up her hands like, *I have no choice.* She says, "I'm in the throes."

I want to be in the throes too. I want a project like this that will fill every inch of me and float me around like I'm a helium balloon.

She shows me her filing system and then drops onto the chair behind the old wooden desk by the window. I sprawl on the floor, filing and organizing the papers by date. Every now and then I stop to read some of the words there. Descriptions of parties or hunting trips or dinners. Illnesses. Arguments. Love affairs. Children born and lost. The big and the small, the significant and the mundane. Pieces of lives.

There is pain and love and ache here. All forgotten now. I think of the heartbreak of my dad and the ache I'm feeling over Miah right now. Life is an accumulation of aches. They fill you up and take your breath away and you think you'll never breathe again, but before you know it, you are just words on paper, gone quiet and asleep until someone finds those words and reads them.

For a while I lose myself in the history. Then Mom and I take turns telling each other some of the things we come across, and I'm suddenly transported back to Ohio, back to other projects I've helped her with over the years.

She tells me:

According to a letter from Tillie's husband, the two of them would set up a table on the beach, where they would play cards and then drink under the live oak trees.

They took midnight sailing trips to the surrounding islands.

They dressed in their finest and drank champagne and danced on lawns like Daisy Buchanan and Jay Gatsby.

For the first time I'm seeing Tillie in moving, vivid color, and I don't know why this is surprising, because of course she was a living, breathing person once.

Mom tells me:

On the north end of the island, Shirley's great-grandmother Clovis became the first female root doctor, and people—including Tillie—would come from as far away as Savannah and Charleston to see her.

I tell her:

Clovis's daughter Beatrice collected stories, creating the first oral history of the island. She set out one day from her house on the north end, carrying a walking stick and a knife, and told her family she would be back when she'd spoken to every person who had a story to tell.

Clovis's other daughter, Aurora, became the lighthouse keeper after her father and brothers were lost at sea.

She tells me:

Claudine returned to the island from Miss Porter's School for Girls when she was nineteen. She never left again. She married the son of the Rosecroft landscaper, a man named Tom Buccaneer.

After Tom was killed in a plane crash, Claudine armed herself with a pistol and started patrolling the beaches, watching for poachers, prepared to protect her home at all cost.

She tells me:

Rosecroft was supposedly burned by one of those poachers. The family saw the flames from the inn, but by the time they reached the mansion—the hub of Blackwood life on the island—it was gone.

I tell her there are other rumors about the fire, mainly that Claudine herself burned Rosecroft down two months before she died so that it would die with her, ensuring that no one else could ever live there.

All these words and stories. My mom calls them the color of a human life: those little moments that are so uniquely ours. I think, *Claudine—just like all of us—was writing her story as she went.*

I stop thinking about Jeremiah Crew and where he is now. I lose myself in this other world. I begin to recognize names I'd never heard before today. I begin to piece together this person's life and that person's life. I learn about the separation of blacks and whites on the island, the Geechee at the north end, the Blackwoods at the south. Clovis Samms was the first to cross that invisible boundary line.

And then I come across a letter about twenty-two-year-old

Samuel Blackwood Jr. and his marriage to nineteen-year-old Tillie Donaldson of Indianapolis, along with a newspaper clipping. Following a whirlwind courtship and a honeymoon to New York City, Samuel and Tillie were planning to head to their winter home, "an island off the coast of Georgia, abounding in natural beauty."

I feel a pang in my heart for young Tillie, who believed her whole life was ahead of her, only to have the floor drop out beneath her feet.

I ask my mom, "How did Tillie meet her husband?"

"I believe he was friends with her older brother and came to visit one holiday break from college."

"You know, I used to be fascinated by Aunt Claudine and the fact that she stayed here her whole life. All because the floor disappeared. Or was pulled out from under her. But that disappearing floor didn't seem to stop her. She wrote and collected family history and married the man she loved and protected and guarded the home she loved. It's Tillie I want to know more about."

"Me too. I think part of it's not knowing why she died. And part of it's not being able to get to know her because she didn't leave us any clues."

"Have you heard the ghost stories?"

She is on her knees now, hands in a file box. She stops sorting and looks at me. "No."

I recount the real story of Tillie—the one Miah told me. How she died of a broken heart due to losing her baby and her brother and her mom. Then I tell her how Jeremiah Crew and I got locked in the basement of Rosecroft.

Mom sits listening, and when I'm done, she says, "Well, that's something, at least, that we know about her."

And I can feel the slightest bit of helium filling me and lifting me off the floor.

She says, "You know, that happened to me a long time ago. Getting locked in the basement of Rosecroft. Unfortunately, I was by myself and not with a cute boy."

She tells me then about the first time she came to visit Aunt Claudine, back when the house still had a ceiling and floors and all its walls were intact. While the grown-ups did boring grown-up things, my mom wandered off alone and found herself in the basement. She says it was used as storage then too, and she picked through old books and clothing until she heard her mom calling her. That was when she tried the door—the same one she'd come in, the one that led up to the hallway—and it was locked. She said she banged on the door and shouted her head off, and eventually she hoisted herself out a window. When she was back inside the house, she asked why they hadn't let her out, and they said they'd never heard her, and besides, the door was unlocked.

"So I tried it myself and it opened. Just like that." She sits back on her heels.

"Do you think it was Tillie?"

"Maybe. I'm not sure I believe in ghosts, but I do think we're all made up of energy, and it makes sense we would leave some of that behind, especially in the case of someone who died so tragically. I always think of it as leaving an imprint."

I look around me, not just at this room but at the island outside the windows, and wonder if I'll leave an imprint after I'm gone from here.

For four hours we talk and read, and at some point I look up at my mom, at the way her hair is falling over the page of the book she's thumbing through, at the way she blows it out of her face now and then, not bothering to brush it aside with her hands, which are too busy with papers.

"Mom?" I say.

She looks up. "Yes?"

"Thanks for introducing me to this side of the family."

She smiles, and suddenly she looks like the mom I've always known my whole life, the one who chased nightmares away and had the answer to every question, no matter what I wanted to know.

"More than words," she says, which is shorthand for *I love you more than words*.

"More than words," I say.

DAY 16

(PART TWO)

A black truck sits in the road outside Addy's house. I walk past it, up the path, my mind still back at the museum with my mom and Tillie and Claudine. Miah is waiting for me on the porch steps. I'm surprised and not surprised, glad but irritated to see him. He sits like an old man, hunched over in the sun. The moment he sees me, he changes into Miah again, up on his feet, stretching, smiling down at me.

I say, "What are you doing here?"

"I've got a surprise for you."

I look past him at the truck.

"It's important, Captain."

And his smile wavers, like he can barely hold on to it. Every part of me—well, almost every part—wants to tell him no, but there's something in his voice and that wavering smile, and more than that, there's me not wanting to be the person who worries for the rest of her life that the boy she's seeing is having sex with another girl or being swallowed by an alligator or who just generally doesn't let herself believe anything ever again.

For all these reasons I say, "Okay."

We head north on Main Road. The truck is bouncing and shaking over the ruts created by the rain and the July heat. I can hear my teeth chattering from the impact, but he is being quiet. The kind of quiet where he is far away. I look at him to make sure he's still there, one hand on the wheel, the other on his leg.

I don't talk and neither does he, and this isn't companionable silence. This is me being so deep in my head that I can't get out. This is him being somewhere else completely. I stare out the window and concentrate on the trees.

A few minutes later he pulls the truck over on the narrow, grassy shoulder of Main Road, leaving just enough space for another vehicle to pass. He gets out, walks around to my side, and leans in the window.

"Why are we stopping?"

"Can't I just make out with you?" He's grinning at me, but not really at me because he's still somewhere else, like he's phoning it in.

"You can, but why are we stopping?" Because I know he's up to something.

"It's time for you to learn to ride a bike."

"Here?" I stare at the road stretching out ahead.

"Here."

"But I'm wearing a dress. And flip-flops. I can't learn to ride a bike in a dress and flip-flops. And, I don't know, it might rain." I squint up at the sky, which is nothing but blue and sun. "And I don't think I'm cut out to ride a bike. And really, it's fine. I mean, if I never learn to ride one, I'll be okay." This is true, but I'm also feeling cut off from him and irritated and like, *Why am I even here?*

All the while, he's rummaging around in the truck bed. He comes back with a bright red helmet and says, "Captain, you're going to learn to ride this bike so that tonight at low tide, we can ride on the beach under the stars." He hands me the helmet.

And then he opens my door, and I'm standing on the side of

Main Road in my sundress and flip-flops, and he's ducking behind a giant oak tree and wheeling out this old blue bicycle.

"Isn't there a better place to learn? The road is too rough and someone could come along."

He says, "It's not rough anymore."

And I look past him, and that's when I see that the road is completely flat and even.

"I raked out the washboard so you could have a level surface to learn on."

It must have taken him hours. And maybe some part of him is still here and not far away after all, which is why I strap on the helmet and walk over to the bike and throw a leg over the seat and stand there waiting. I don't want to look like an idiot. I don't want to fall or break myself in two, and I don't want to let him down. But he came out here and flattened the road so that I could learn to ride on it, which might be the nicest thing anyone has ever done for me, so the least I can do is try.

He moves to the front of the bike so he's facing me.

I say, "What if I can't do it?"

"Oh, I'm pretty sure you can do anything you set your extremely stubborn mind to."

"I'm not stubborn."

He laughs, and it sounds more like him than anything I've heard him say so far today. Then he places one hand on the seat and the other on the left handlebar. "Okay, a few things to remember. Pedal hard. Pedal fast. And keep your chin up and eyes forward. The bike's going to go where your eyes go. The trick is to pedal. The faster you go, the easier it is. And don't overthink it."

"Easy for you to say."

"On three. One . . . two . . ."

"Wait. Kiss me."

262

He moves closer, bracing the bike with his legs. Then he puts his hands on either side of my face and pulls me to him. And kisses me long and deep, as if I'm a soldier going off to war. I drink it in because his hands on my face and his mouth on mine make me feel like he's actually here after all, and even more than that, they make me feel like I'm here too.

He counts down again, and on *three* we take off, me pedaling and him pushing. I'm pedaling as fast as I can, and the bike is wobbling, and just when I think I'm going to go over, he steadies it.

"I'll be right beside you until you get so good at it you're ready to fly down the beach."

We go like this for a while—me pedaling fast, him pushing. The bike wobbling, him holding on, my feet hitting the ground. Over and over again. Nothing on earth but Miah and me and this bike. Every time, I hit the brake too hard and nearly fly over the handlebars.

"Go easy on the brake. Worse comes to worst, you're going to fall. But if you do, screw it. You'll be fine."

"I don't want to fall."

"But you might. The sooner you accept that fact, the better, Captain."

"This is some bullshit life lesson, isn't it?"

"I'm just here to teach you how to ride a motherfuckin' bike." He wears an easy grin, like, *Everything's good, I'm just messing around.* But there's a sudden edge to his voice that I've never heard before.

"Whoa."

"What?"

"That." I point at him. "That tone. What's up with you?"

"Nothing."

"Bullshit. It's not like you to blow me off and then pretend

263

nothing happened and then be all, *Everything's great, everything's fine.*"

"Maybe you just don't know me very well." And it feels almost like he's testing me.

"Maybe if you'd tell me what's going on with you, I'd know you better."

"Listen, I'm good, Captain. I'm fucking great. I'll be even greater if you learn how to ride this bike."

I narrow my eyes at him, just to let him know that I don't buy any of it, not for a second.

"Now come on. Let's do this."

"Fine," I say. "But we are not done talking."

I take off, mostly to get away from him. He runs beside me. "Pedal hard, pedal fast." I pedal harder and faster so that he can't keep up. The last thing I hear him yell is, "Chin up. Eyes forward."

And then it goes quiet. I'm pedaling and pedaling, and in a few seconds I realize he's no longer there. For one instant, I take it in—the air on my face, the wild, exhilarating rush of sailing past the world. *I am completely and utterly free.* I want to keep going. I want to go faster and faster until I go soaring off into the sky like in *E.T.* I want to fly above the earth and the clouds and the sun.

Suddenly the pedals are spinning too fast and furious for my feet. I brake too hard and nearly go over, a dust cloud billowing around me. But I steady myself, digging my feet into the road, coughing up a lung, and when I turn around, I see him sprinting toward me.

He nearly tackles me, and we're laughing and I'm jumping up and down, only I get tangled in the bike, and then we both go toppling over into the dirt of the road. We lie there catching our breath, and the trees and sky are our ceiling.

We blink up into the blue. I tell myself to let the silence be. To let him talk when he wants to. If he wants to.

I quiet my heart and my pulse. I quiet my brain, which is saying, *He's changed his mind. That's what yesterday was about. You don't really know him. You'll never know him, no matter how naked you both are. This is what you get when you let yourself care too much. Even if he says the thing you dread most—"I don't like you any-more; I never liked you or loved you because you are unlovable"— you are going to be okay.*

I tell myself to live right now in that blue and to stop bracing myself for the worst. I lie perfectly still until the blue surrounds me, until it moves through my veins and holds me there, part of it.

From the ground he says, "My mom had a panic attack in a grocery store last week. My sister called the inn yesterday to say she's been in bed since it happened. She hasn't gone to work or eaten, and Kenzie's trying to look after everything. I had no idea."

"Is she okay? Your mom?"

"She will be, to the extent that she's ever okay. The first episode I remember, I was six, only I didn't know what it was. I thought she was playing a game. . . ." His voice trails off. "So that's where I was yesterday. I had to go to Jacksonville to take care of it." There's more that he isn't saying. I can hear it under his words.

I lie back and say, very still, very quiet, "I can only imagine what that was like, and I'm so sorry it happened. But it's not okay to get edgy with me or take it out on me or make me feel like some kind of inconvenience. And it's not okay to ghost me. The first thing I'll think is that it's something I did or that you've changed your mind or that you're fucking things up because this is good, you and me, and I'd rather just know what the real story is. You be honest with me; I'll be honest with you. I'm talking this is you; this is me. Take it or leave it."

He holds my gaze for a second. "Shit." He turns his eyes back to the sky. "Okay." He sighs. And I can see him thinking and struggling and trying to figure out what to say. Finally he goes, "So I'm used to it. It happens. It's been happening all my life and I'm there, I show up, I handle it. But I'm supposed to have eight weeks this summer here on this island. Just me. Eight weeks. That's all. Two months for me to be here and do the work I need to do without having to go take care of everyone."

"What about your brother? He's older. Can't he help?"

"Was older."

"What?"

"My brother *was* older."

Before I can ask what happened, if this is the heartbreak he's alluded to that he's not ready to talk about, he says, "It's the first summer I haven't ferried home every weekend. I'm getting ready to go away for a year, and they need to get used to me being gone. But how can I go away when my mom needs me? The thing is, she's sick but not sick enough to *not* know what she's doing. 'So now that you have this fancy life, you're just going to turn your back on us? Do you want to tell your ten-year-old sister that you don't care about her enough to stay here and look after her, or are you going to leave just like your dad? Who do you think put up with you all those years you were causing trouble? Of course you want to be there with all those rich people instead of here where I raised you.'" He exhales as if he's been holding his breath. "This is going to sound stupid, Captain, but I just want to be eighteen. Free to fuck up and make my own decisions and not be an adult all the time. It's like, what if I go away and something happens, something worse, and I'm not there? Or what if I stay in Jacksonville and nothing happens? Either way it's shitty."

I picture what this life would look like for him. No island. No

266

adventures. No Jeremiah Crew lit up by the sun, only Jeremiah Crew working and worrying and withering away indoors.

"It's your life too."

"But it isn't. It never has been. It's always been someone else's."

I say, "My dad broke my mom's heart. And sometimes all I want to do is give up college and stay with her and make sure no one ever hurts her again. But she's the adult. She's the mom. I have to go do what I'm supposed to do."

"But the difference is, she lets you be free to worry about you. You don't have to feel selfish if you want to go off and live your life. It's what you get to do. I can't even look my sisters in the eye knowing I'm going to leave them, much less my mom. The day before I came to the island this summer, my sister Channy gave me a present wrapped in a paper grocery bag. It was her favorite stuffed animal, the one she's had since she was a baby. The one she sleeps with every night. She said, 'I'm giving you BeeBo so you won't have to go away.'"

I don't know what to say, so I reach for his hand, threading my fingers through his. We lie there for a long time, the blue filling us both.

After a few minutes, I turn to look at him. "So what are you doing in the fall? The real answer."

"Joining the rodeo circuit, becoming a full-fledged cowboy."

"Is this before or after NASA and the CIA?"

"Somewhere in between."

I feel this rankle of frustration over the fact that he's still deflecting. I want to ask where he's really going and what he's really doing, but instead I stay here, on this ground, staring up at this sky, in this moment.

At some point he says, "I know you technically met Shirley, but I want you to meet Bram, too. We should go have dinner with them, like she said. Let them tell you all about what a shit-heel I was when they first met me."

He's letting me in. This is a big deal, but something tells me not to make it a big deal, as if he might change his mind and take back the invitation.

"I'd love that," I say, light and breezy. "Jeremiah Crew, thank you for teaching me to ride a bike." Even though there is so much more I want to say.

"Claudine Henry. Thank you."

"For what?"

I sit up and look down at him, lying there.

His eyes meet mine.

"For you."

DAY 17

I ride the old black bike to the general store, where there's a sign tacked to the front door written in a lopsided scribble: *Gone to mainland. Back soon.* I jiggle the doorknob, but it's locked. I peer in the window, and the chairs are upside down on the tables and there's no Terri behind the counter.

I sit for a while on the step, trying to get service. I hold the phone up this way and that. I try calling Saz anyway, and when it doesn't go through, I write her a text:

I know you asked me to call you and I'm trying. I hope you're okay and that everyone is alive and well, most of all you, Sazzy.

I read it over and then add:

What are you and Yvonne planning to do about college? Isn't she going to Prescott in Arizona? Do you talk about it or not talk about it? Do the two of you ever just want to stay in Mary Grove so you don't have to leave each other?

There's nowhere for the text to go, and I try everything. I see an old nail in the wood of the door and pry it out. I've never picked a lock before, but I jiggle the nail around in the keyhole and hope it will work. It doesn't budge, and so I stand on one leg, on the other leg, phone outstretched to the sky. I set the phone on the ground and do a handstand and my skirt balloons over my head so that the world is a black-and-yellow swirl of leaves and flowers. I think, *What would the world be like if these were the only colors?*

Suddenly there's a loud, long whistle and I go toppling over onto the ground. Grady strides past, giving me the eye. "Nice undies." He laughs.

I dust off my skirt, fit the fisherman's cap back onto my head, pick up my things.

"What're you up to, Claudette?"

And for a second I'm like, *Why is he calling me that?* But then I remember that it's the name I gave him.

I almost make up something now, wild and outlandish, but instead I tell him, "Trying to get a phone signal."

"You know if you need service, you can come by the Dip."

"I thought this was the only place you could get service."

"Sometimes, if we're lucky, we can reach the outside world over there."

There's something in the way he looks at me, kind of sideways and heavy-lidded, and the way he says it—*come by the Dip*—all guttery but smooth.

"No thanks," I say.

"Your loss."

I hop on the bike and wobble away from him.

I hear him call after me, "Or maybe it's mine."

On my way home, I pass a group of campers scattered off the trail in the thick of the trees. I almost stop to ask if they're lost, but then I see that they're collecting debris and dead limbs, victims of some recent hurricane, and piling them on the side of the road. One of them glances up at me and then bends back over and keeps working.

I start to move on when I hear a shout. I look upward and it's Miah, shirtless and perched high up in one of the live oaks, at home there as Tarzan, holding on with one hand as he points something out to the campers, who must not be campers after all but Outward Bound kids. He yanks at a dead limb, lodged in the branches of the tree, and I watch the way the muscles of his arms and his shoulders tense. In a second the limb gives way and goes falling toward the earth.

I can't help but stand, feet planted on the ground on either side of the bike, and watch him, the way he's completely lost in the work. He looks peaceful and happy. So happy that I don't call out to him, because I don't want to disturb him or bring him out of it. I want him to stay right where he is.

I eat an early dinner at Addy's so that I can meet Miah for a sunset dune walk, which means we wander the canyons and hollows of this other world between the dunes. When the path narrows, I fall behind him, watching the way the gold of the dying sun catches his hair and skin and holds it.

I'm pretending we're actually in another world when he says, "I want to spend the night with you. The entire night, start to finish. You in my bed. I want to wake up next to you and see what that hair looks like in the morning. And I have other questions, like are those real freckles or do you paint them on? And how loud *do* you snore?"

"First of all, the freckles are real. You should know by now that they don't come off. Two, I don't snore. Three, my mom will never go for it."

"So I'll stay with you."

"I don't think she'd like that, either."

"Why don't you invite me over and we'll see what happens from there?"

DAY 18

The first and only party I've ever thrown was in seventh grade. Saz and I spent days making the decorations and invitations and creating a Twister-size board game that combined Seven Minutes in the Closet and Spin the Bottle and Never Have I Ever all in one, guaranteeing we would get to, at the very least, second base. We invited everyone in our class and spent the entire night watching my crush (Zachary Dunn) and her crush (Harriet Loos) making out in a corner.

I find Jared in the kitchen at the inn, at the sink, washing and drying dishes.

"I'm having people over tomorrow night and I want you to come."

"Just tell me what time. I can bring drinks."

"My mom'll be there, so I'm not exactly sure how much drinking there's going to be."

"Sodas, then, and maybe I can liberate some dessert."

Wednesday appears, dumping more dirty plates into the sink. " 'People' as in Jared, me, you, and Miah?"

"And Emory."

I catch a whiff of something—weed, maybe. And then I feel this little rush of air on my skin as Grady goes walking past. "I can't wait," he says.

"Great." Even though I wasn't planning to invite him. "And Grady, apparently."

Wednesday looks at Jared. "He'd be hotter if he didn't try so hard."

Jared says to me, "We'll be there."

Just after six, my mom finds me as I forage in the kitchen, taking inventory of what snacks we have and whether I need to order anything from the mainland for the party. She starts helping, holding up a bag of chips. I nod. She holds up almonds. I shake my head. We do this for a while, a perfectly orchestrated dance we've done since I was little.

She clears her throat. "So. Jeremiah."

"Jeremiah. Sometimes known as Miah. But never as J.Crew."

"Good to know. You're seeing him a lot."

"You told me not to mope around the house."

"I don't think I used the word *mope,* but it's good to see you getting out of the window seat."

I open a soda. Pour her some. Drink out of the can. Wait for what she's going to say next.

"It's been a long time since we had the talk."

And there it is. "I remember it. We're all good here." Fifth grade. My mom came to my room and sat down on my bed and answered every question I had about sex. The next day she gave me a copy of *Our Bodies, Ourselves,* and I learned to masturbate. I did it almost every day for all of fifth grade, like this miraculous secret hobby that only I knew about. I used my hand, my electric toothbrush, my stuffed animals, anything I could rub up against. My stuffed animals developed crooked necks from all the rubbing.

She says now, "I'm not going to ask, but you know I'm here for you. And please just tell me you're being safe."

"If anything was happening, I'm being safe. I'm not stupid."

"I know that."

And she's gone as short with me as I'm being with her.

"Sorry."

"I'm sorry too."

I sit next to her and we drink our sodas, the Llewelyn women. Same way of sitting, same way of bouncing one foot as if we're listening to music. Still alike, even with all this space between us.

"Do you want to tell me about him?"

"No."

"How old is he?"

"My age."

"He looks older."

"He's not."

"Is he going to college?"

"I think he's taking a gap year. He came here to work with Outward Bound because he wants to help people." I don't mention that it was originally that or juvie. "He's a really talented photographer. He takes photos where there isn't much beauty and makes them beautiful."

I've clearly made him sound like a mother's dream, because my mom, who could earn her living as a psychic due to her ability to see through people—especially me—goes, "Wow. Sounds serious."

"It is and it isn't. It's only for the summer."

"I remember my first time," she says.

"Oh God."

"His name was Ryan and he was a year older, and I thought he was the most amazing thing ever. I was going into my senior year, and he went off to college in Texas and said he wanted me to still be his girlfriend. I think he only called me, like, twice after he left. He was always too busy, and later I found out he'd come home to see his parents but hadn't told me. I was devastated. He tried to win me back over the summer, but by that point I was done."

"Do you wish you'd waited for someone else?" I ask, thinking about my dad, about the life that might have been.

"No. At the time, he was everything. But that's a very personal decision. I haven't been with a lot of men, Claude, but I've been lucky that they were good men."

She falls quiet and I know she's waiting for me to say something.

"I'm not talking about him with you." But I wish I could say, *I think I love this boy. But I don't want to love this boy because I'm going to have to say goodbye in two weeks and I'll probably never see him again. So I'm trying not to love him. I'm trying to just hook up with him and have fun with him and not get too attached. That's how I'm supposed to do it, right? That's how Alannis does it, and she's been dating since she was twelve.*

"You don't have to, as long as you know you can always talk to me."

We stare down at our bouncing feet.

She says, "Addy's coming to see us."

"When?"

"Sunday."

I don't know what makes me ask, "Dad isn't coming, is he?"

"No."

"Good."

DAY 19

I sit on the living room floor playing Jenga with Jared, Wednesday, Emory, and Grady. His white hair falls in his eyes and he's wearing three skull rings on his left hand. His fingers are long and thin and make me think of a spider.

Emory says, "I was fifteen the first time. I thought it was mind-blowing. But I look back now, experienced man of nineteen that I am—"

Wednesday coughs loudly in his direction as she sits forward, tapping on the blocks, light enough so that she doesn't knock over the tower.

Emory bumps her arm and she pulls her hands back, away from the tower, which wobbles but doesn't fall. She play-slaps him on the shoulder. "Asshole."

He laughs. "As I was saying. I look back now and I'm like, *Yeah, it was actually a disaster.* Neither of us knew what the hell we were doing."

Miah walks in from the bathroom and settles himself next to me. "What'd I miss?"

Wednesday says, "How You Lost It. Specifically when and, if you feel like offering it up, who." She smiles at Miah, at me, and my whole body goes rigid because of course she's doing this on purpose. She says, "I was seventeen. His name was Nicholas. I waited as long as I could. My sisters are saving themselves for marriage, and I'm pretty sure my family assumes I am too. I can't talk to any of them about it because I'd probably be cast out or something."

I go, "Is that why you cast yourself out first? Before they could?"

She freezes, fingers on a block. "Maybe." One of the blocks gives, and she pushes it out and places it on top, then sits back. "What about you?" She looks at Miah.

"What about me?" He leans back, studying the tower through one eye and then the other. He tickles my foot.

"How old were you the first time?" Wednesday looks back and forth between us. I have this sudden urge to get up and run for the bathroom because I don't want to hear about all the girls before me.

He says, "A gentleman doesn't kiss and tell," and his voice is polite but cool.

She stares at him and he stares back, and neither one is blinking.

"I do." Grady sits up, reaches in. Pulls out a block and drops it on top as if he doesn't care whether the whole thing crashes down. "I was thirteen. I think her name was Bridget. Maybe Brittany."

Jared shakes his head. "Dude. A little respect."

Grady just blinks at him. "What?"

"Either you're really good at pretending to be a douchebag or you really are a douchebag."

Emory says to Grady, "Strictly girls?"

Grady grabs a handful of chips. "Mostly girls. I actually have a girlfriend." This makes us all go quiet. "She lives on the mainland. We've been off and on for, like, five years."

Wednesday says, "Does she ever come here?"

"She's in Savannah. I'll see her during the school year." And that's when we learn that Grady goes to SCAD, the Savannah

College of Art and Design, and majors in sculpture and performing arts, which goes to show that you can't always judge a book by its cover.

I'm in the kitchen with Jared, getting more drinks, and from there I can see the rest of them playing Twister. I try not to look as Miah and Wednesday cross legs and arms and body parts, try not to think about them using these same positions for other activities.

Jared glances into the living room, then back at me. "Don't tell them, but I've only slept with one person. Last year. I was twenty."

"I won't. I actually think that's pretty cool."

"It was never going to be anything, but it was okay. I mean, it was sex. She wanted to. I wanted to. We knew what it was going to be. We kind of agreed what it was going to be. But I think the next time I do it, I want to be in love."

I watch through the door as Wednesday collapses in a heap, nearly bringing Emory down with her. Miah is practically in a handstand, which makes me think of handstands on the beach, which makes me think of naked midnight swimming under the moon.

I say, "Love complicates things. People tell you that all the time, but it's true."

"I'd rather have complicated than nothing." He adds ice to a cup and hands it to me. "So." He gives me a look. "We don't see you much lately."

"We've been having adventures."

"That's cool. I'm glad he found you, because he's a good guy and you make him happy."

"I'm glad I found him, too."

He helps me pour. A shout from the other room. Laughter.

278

He says, "You shouldn't worry. About Wednesday, I mean. It's different with you."

"Thanks." But as I say it, I wonder, *What does it matter if it's different with me? It's not like I have a future with this boy.*

Like he reads my mind, Jared says, "He's leaving soon, isn't he?"

"Yeah." *In thirteen days.*

"What are you guys gonna do?"

"I don't know. We haven't really talked about it. We're just concentrating on right now."

"I hope you work it out. It's funny. We're like this weird little family here. Like the Island of Misfit Toys."

More laughter as Miah and Emory topple over at the same time. Wednesday is snapping pictures with her phone while Grady does a victory lap around the coffee table.

"Yeah, I guess it is." And I'm glad to be part of it.

Everyone leaves around midnight, and Miah's the last one out. At the front door he says, a little louder than necessary, "Good night, Captain." He aims his voice toward my mom's room.

"Good night, Miah," I say, even though my mom went to bed twenty minutes ago.

He kisses me and walks out into the night and I shut the door hard behind him, just in case she's listening. I take my time turning off lights, pouring myself a glass of water. My bedtime routine. I collect my notebook from the window seat. Brush my teeth. Wash my face. Give Dandelion some treats. Make my way to my room, shutting the door with a click.

A tap at the window, and Miah is on the other side. I push it open and he says, "I'm being eaten alive out here."

*　*　*

I'm on top of him in my bed, and he's laughing. I lean in and kiss him, and when I pull away, there's this look on his face. It's hard to read, but it's like this mix of happiness and something else—love, maybe.

I say, "Why didn't you play How You Lost It?"

"Because I'm not twelve." He kisses me again, and that look is still there.

"I wish you hadn't slept with her. It would be a lot easier to be her friend."

"I wish I hadn't slept with her either."

"So how many have there been? Girls, I mean?" And as I ask it, my heart is racing, and I want to say, *Don't tell me. Please don't tell me.*

"Why?"

"I guess I just want to know where I rank."

"First, I don't rank. There's no list, if that's what you're thinking. Second, there's not much of a list. When I'm not on a deserted island, I'm pretty much a full-time caregiver to a grown woman and four younger siblings."

"Sorry."

"It's okay. Do you want to tell me where I rank?"

"You're the only boy I've slept with."

"But not the only one you've fooled around with."

"That seems like a long time ago. Like another person."

And it does. Shane Waller and Matteo Dimas and Wyatt Jones seem like boys who happened to someone else.

I say, "Have you ever heard of the Viennese oyster?"

*　*　*

Five minutes later, we're going through *The Joy of Sex,* studying the police drawings and reading misogynistic passages to each other in a whisper. He delivers his with the drollness of Mr. Hernandez, my tenth-grade Spanish teacher, and I bury my face in the pillow to muffle my laughter.

"Man, this book really is horrible," he says. "But the positions are . . . interesting." He holds one up. I shake my head.

"There are better ones." I take the book from him.

We settle on the *flanquette,* which is like Twister, only without the board. The book doesn't give us much to go on, and right away he gets a foot to the nose, to the eye, to the chin, and I get a cramp in my calf, which means we have to take time out while I hop up and down, wrapped in the sheet because there is no way I'm flapping around in front of him with my boobs hanging out.

The cramp eventually goes away. We compose ourselves. I climb back onto the bed and we try again. This time he gets another foot to the face before I end up falling off the bed with a loud thud. We freeze, me on the floor, and listen. I say, "I think we need something a little quieter."

I lie back down and he closes the book, sliding it under the bed, out of our sight. "Maybe this is a good time to tell you about the research I've been doing." His voice is almost a whisper.

"What kind of research?"

"Sexual research."

"Like porn?"

"I'm talking actual educational articles, like 'How to Give Your Woman Pleasure' and 'How to Make Sure You're Taking Care of Your Lady.' I figure you can never learn enough when it comes to satisfying your girlfriend."

"When did you do this research?"

"The last time I was off-island."

"So did you learn anything?"

"Not a damn thing." He reaches for my phone. "May I? For illustrative purposes?" I nod. He props himself up on an elbow. The glow of the screen lights his face as he pretends to read. "Actually, that's not true. There are eighty thousand nerve endings in the clitoris."

"Okay. I did not know that."

"Also: 'She may not appreciate direct contact.' One said: 'Use her body as your guide.'" He lies there, pretending to scroll through the phone. "Useless, useless, useless." He stops scrolling and then fakes throwing my phone across the room. He leans over and kisses me. "I want the lights on to see every bit of you."

I take his hand and place it between my legs, positioning his fingers exactly like I'd position mine.

"If you want to know how to give your woman pleasure," I say, "just ask."

A little later, he does the same, guiding my hand, showing me when and where and how to touch him.

Afterward we lie on our sides, facing each other, and I ask him, "What does sex feel like for you?"

He takes my hand, presses our palms together, finger to finger. "Jesus, Captain, your hands are big for a girl."

"Answer the question."

He twines his fingers through mine. "I don't know. I used to say that nobody does me better than I do, but then you came along. I guess it's kind of like this pressure, good pressure, on every square inch of my body that builds and builds, until finally it gathers all in one spot and it feels as if I'll explode into smithereens. And when I do, it's like I've been carrying sixty thousand pounds—like

282

what's-his-name, Atlas—only instead of carrying the world, I can lift it up over my head and start winging it around until I launch it into another solar system. It's sunrise, sunset, and the perfect tide combined into one." He lets go of my hand and traces my curves with his fingers. "What's it feel like for you?"

"You know that night we drove with the lights off and we saw a million lightning bugs? It's like if you could catch every single one of them and put them in a jar, and as they're all lighting up at once, you open the lid and set them free."

He whistles. "Is it too late to change my answer?"

"Yes."

"You should put that in a book someday, Captain."

"Maybe I will."

"I'll know you're talking about me."

"Or maybe that's just how it feels with everyone."

"Yeah, I don't think so."

We kiss for a while, my hands in his hair, his skin against mine. I concentrate on the warmth and the heat, forgetting about my mom down the hall.

After a moment he whispers, "One of those articles did offer some interesting advice."

"What's that?"

He says in my ear, "Don't forget about the rest of her body."

A little later again, I lean over to the bedside table, dig in the drawer. I hand him a thumbprint cookie from the bag I've stashed there.

"What's this?"

"A taste of Mary Grove, Ohio."

He pops it in his mouth and closes his eyes.

"They're from a little bakery downtown. The Joy Ann Cake Shop. The best bakery on earth. Inside it smells like sugar and birthdays and every happy occasion."

I tell him about the family who owns it, about the squirrel that stands outside the door every day to get a peanut butter cookie, about the secret morning ritual my dad and I have had for the past six years.

He said, "That's one amazing cookie."

I hand him another and eat one myself, and then I shut the drawer. I fit myself back into him, my head on his chest, and we lie there. I feel the rise and fall of his breathing and the way his hair tickles my cheek.

I say, "It's like lightning bugs, but it's also like writing. There's this feeling you get when you write a really good, true sentence or paragraph or scene, and it makes you feel invincible, as if you can do anything. It feels like a superpower, and in that moment no one can touch you. You're the best there is. That's how you make me feel, Jeremiah Crew. Like I'm the best there is."

He strokes my hair. He strokes my back, his fingers tracing circles down my spine. He says, "You are."

DAY 20

Bram and Shirley Bailey live on the northern tip of the island. As we head north on Main Road, we pass a sign that says WILDERNESS AREA. RESIDENTIAL PERMIT ONLY. NO TRESPASSING. Miah keeps driving. As wild as the forest is down by Addy's and the inn, the forest here is wilder. Palms and live oaks mix with pine trees, and whole portions of the road disappear under the sprawling green of the undergrowth.

We pass the one-room Baptist church; the crumbling hotel that once belonged to Clovis Samms; and something called the Shell Ring, which is four thousand years old and made up of Native American ceremonial mounds that were formed over time by the nearby marsh. Miah says you can still find pre-Columbian tools and bits of pottery if you dig.

The Baileys live in an area called Belle Hammock, in a stout red house with wide windows and a wide porch and a tin roof that shines in the late-afternoon sun. A school bus is parked in the backyard, sprouting up out of the earth like the plants and flowers that grow alongside it.

Bram is a stocky man in his fifties with salt-and-pepper hair, weathered brown skin, and a wry face, like he's just been told a joke. Even though his mouth is barely twitching, his eyes are smiling, and I like him immediately.

Shirley opens her arms and envelops me in a hug and says over my head to Miah, "It's about time you brought her up here."

We sit on the screened porch and eat oysters, which we suck down with a lemon sauce, and Shirley tells us stories about the island. "He says you're a Blackwood." She nods at Miah.

"Distantly. One of the poor ones. I was named for my great-great-aunt Claudine."

"I knew her when I was a little girl. I thought she was a queen because she carried herself like one, those dogs following her wherever she went. She always had a pistol on her belt, and some said it was the one from long ago, the one that her mama used to kill herself."

"Do you know what really happened?"

"To Tillie?" Bram throws more oysters on our plates and passes me the sauce.

"In true Southern form, no one talked about it after," Shirley says. "But most likely a kind of postpartum depression made worse because she lost her baby. People didn't call it that, though. They said, 'Oh, poor Tillie. Did you hear? That poor young woman died of a broken heart.'" Shirley smiles at me. "You would have liked her. She was good people. Vibrant people. Kind people. Hilariously fun and funny people. Alive people. She was so alive." She shakes her head. "My great-grandmother Clovis was maybe her best friend. She took it hard when Tillie died."

"Your great-grandmother was the root doctor."

"For fifty-two years. She died at age one hundred."

I ask her then about her ancestors—Clovis and Aurora, the lighthouse keeper, and Beatrice, the storyteller and collector.

Shirley gets up from the table and walks into the living room, where she stands in front of the bookcase, hands on hips, clearly searching for something. Bram says, "Bottom shelf, three from the end." He winks at us.

She bends over, pulls something from the shelf, and comes walking back with a photo album. "This man," she says, nodding at Bram. "He always knows where everything is."

"It's a good thing, too," he says to her. Then, to us: "This woman would lose her own nose if it weren't on her face." But I can hear the love behind the words.

Shirley sits and opens the photo album and then slides it over to me. She taps a hazy black-and-white picture of a woman in white, who looks as if she can barely sit still for the camera. "That's Clovis. The only photo we have of her."

I stare at Clovis and she stares back at me, and I think of all the stories she must have lived and collected—long before Beatrice could record them—and taken with her when she died.

The talk turns to their work with Outward Bound. They had been involved with the organization for sixteen years when they met Miah.

"You never saw such a pain in the ass as this one here," Bram says, waving his glass at Miah. "That first time he was here, Shirley threatened to quit every day."

Miah looks at me. "Told you." He points to himself. "Shit-heel."

Shirley shakes her head. "But we could see the good in there behind the hurt. There's usually good hiding in people somewhere if you look hard enough."

Miah says, "No one bothered looking for it before you all."

And I can suddenly see him at thirteen, the boy who had to take care of everyone whether he wanted to or not. Believing he could never have a life of his own because other people's lives were more important. I reach for his hand and he takes mine without breaking away from the conversation, as if it's the most natural thing in the world.

They want to know about me then—where I'm going to college in the fall, what I'm studying, what kind of work my mom does. They don't ask about my dad, and I'm not sure if Miah's told them why I'm here on the island.

Over dessert the conversation turns to Outward Bound again.

I say, "Do you leave at the end of the summer, or are you staying through the year?"

And Shirley says, "We head to Montana soon with this one." And at first I think she means Bram, but she's looking at Miah. "It's his first year as a guide."

I look at Miah. He glances down at his plate.

"That's amazing," I say, and the pie is stuck in my throat. I drink. Swallow. But the lump is still there.

In the truck afterward, we don't talk about Outward Bound. It's as if he knows not to bring it up and I'm definitely not bringing it up, so we pretend it's not a thing between us. I tell myself I didn't learn anything I didn't already know. In less than two weeks he's leaving the island. Period. That hasn't changed.

He says, "You're quiet over there, Captain."

"Sorry."

"Bram and Shirley loved you."

"I loved them, too."

And I think: *Love complicates everything. It makes you hurt and it makes you doubt and it makes you wish you didn't love. It makes you want to be watchful so that nothing bad or surprising ever happens. It makes you never want to love anyone again because they'll only hurt you too.*

"Do you want to ask me about Montana?"

"Not really."

It's one thing to joke about NASA and the CIA; it's another to know the truth, because the truth means having to picture him across the country doing what he's meant to do. While I'm in New York making new friends and meeting other boys. And Miah's in Montana making new friends and meeting other girls. And let's not forget Saz in Chicago making new friends too. And my dad in Ohio, and my mom somewhere other than Ohio, and everyone separate everywhere.

Suddenly all the things I've been not thinking about are right here. The drawbridge comes up. The gate comes down. I sit in my fortress, looking out. I can see him but he can't see me.

"Okay." He slows, stops, turns the truck around, and now we're heading north again.

"Where are we going?"

"There you are, Captain. I thought you'd left."

"I'm here."

"Then come with me."

"Where are we going?"

"I want to show you something."

Past Bram and Shirley's, the lighthouse sits at the very northern tip of the island, red and weathered, as if it's been there from the beginning of time. This is where Clovis's daughter Aurora Samms took over for her father and brothers after they died at sea. The foundation of her house is still there, a large square of stone and brick, no more than an outline in the grass.

We get out of the truck and Miah has a blanket, and the wind tries to pick us up and carry us away. "That was Aurora's house," he shouts as we run past the foundation.

"Where did it go? Did it burn down too?"

"Aurora was the last one to live in it. She died sometime in the 1970s, and the Park Service just let it fall down."

We race through the wind, holding on to our clothes, to ourselves, to the lighthouse itself. He jimmies the door, which is warped from the wind and the weather, and finally it swings open. Inside, there is a smell of damp, of a hundred years of rainstorms and hurricanes, but it's quiet and still. We step in and the light is dim. He closes the door on the wind, which beats against it, trying to get in. I half expect him to keep us in the dark, to prove that we can adjust our eyes, but he has a flashlight because Miah is always prepared.

The stairs curve upward from the entryway, and Miah starts to climb. I follow him, twisting up and up. We pass little rectangular windows, which rattle in their casings and look out over the black of the ocean. This is the darkest part of the island, and I try to imagine this young woman, Aurora, living here by herself, tending to the light.

"How much farther?" My voice comes out cross and grumpy, the voice of a child, but this isn't how I'm actually feeling. My voice should sound confused and far away.

Miah says, "All the way to the top."

I look down below and the spiral of the staircase is like a seashell. It narrows the higher we climb, until, two hundred stories later, it finally dead-ends into a wooden floor, worn and scuffed and threadbare in places. The room is perfectly round and all windows. In the center is the light itself, sitting like an enormous blind eye, black and silent.

Miah hands me the flashlight and spreads out the blanket. "Come here, Captain."

I don't want to come there because I want to stay here, in the fortress. I don't want him to think I've fallen in love with him and that I'm going to miss him. I want him to think I'm three hundred percent cool and fine and *Whatever happens, happens.* This is what I promised him, after all.

He turns off the flashlight. The windows rattle, and on the other side of them the wind howls, but in here we're safe. He lies down, hands behind his head, and waits for me.

So I sit at first. And then I lie back, and the ceiling is painted in stars.

"Look," I say.

"Aurora painted them. That's what Shirley says. To keep her company on dark nights when she was the only one here."

I find the Big Dipper and the Northern Cross and Orion's belt, tracing them with my eyes.

In a minute he says, "What's on your mind, Captain?"

Somehow it's easier to answer him like this, in the dark, staring up at the constellations.

"You're going to Montana."

"You don't like Montana?"

"I've never been. But you're going there. And I'm going to New York. And Saz is going to Chicago. And I'm not sure why we're doing this when it can't be anything."

"And by *this* you mean us?"

I keep my eyes on the stars. "Yes. I mean, I know we agreed that it's just for fun and it's just for the summer, and I'm good with that. Honestly. But I also feel like, *What's the point?* I mean, what's the point of any of this if it's just going to end?" And I don't know if I mean Miah and me or Saz and me or my parents' marriage or love in general.

"See, I think it is something. Just because I'm going to Montana doesn't mean it isn't something right now."

"I get that. It's just that I promised you I wouldn't be crushed when you left, but maybe I'm going to miss you a little."

"Wow. A little?"

"Maybe."

He reaches through the darkness and takes my hand. "I have a feeling I'm going to miss you a lot." And he kisses the back of my hand and then places our hands, laced together, on his chest.

I look at him in the dark, and my eyes have adjusted enough to see that he's looking at me.

"You're a pretty good boyfriend, you know that?"

"I try."

"Keep in mind that I haven't actually had a real boyfriend, so I don't have a lot to compare you to."

"Keep in mind that I live on an island, so I don't get a lot of practice."

We lie there, listening to the wind and the rattling.

I say, "I think it's better not to talk about the end of summer." The same way Saz and I promised not to talk about college until it was time to go, as if somehow the not talking would protect us.

And it's better not to think about it.

"Whatever you say, Captain."

And this makes me feel better and worse because of course I'm thinking about it.

In a minute he goes, "Do you feel it?"

"What?" Up here, at the top of this old, old tower, I brace myself for the wind, thunder, a coming storm.

"The floor."

I close my eyes and concentrate until, through the blanket, I can feel the wood beneath my hands, my legs, my back, my head.

"I feel it."

Without a word I move closer to him so that I'm against him, right where I fit, and he pulls me in so my head is on his chest and his arm is around me. "I got you," he says, so low I almost miss it. "I can be your floor."

My heart grabs on to this even as I tell myself, *This moment is enough. Right now is enough. We don't need to be anything more than now.*

DAYS 21–22

To get ready for Addy's visit, Mom and I change the sheets in both bedrooms and run the vacuum and clean the bathrooms. We give Miah a grocery list, and three and a half hours later he drops off four brown bags. I watch through the window as he moseys backward down the path toward his truck, grinning at me the whole way.

I say to my mom, "I can stay with him while Addy's here."

"Nice try, but no. Someone can sleep on the sofa in the office." Which means me.

"But you two have a lot to catch up on. If Saz was coming, we'd be up all night."

"Addy and I are old. We'll be going to bed by ten."

The general store is open again. I leave my bike outside, next to the door, under the sign that says ICE, ICE CREAM, BEVERAGES & MORE! As I walk in, Terri looks up from her book (*Valley of the Dolls*) and says, "I heard Addy Birch is coming in today," because the island is small and everyone knows everything.

I ask her about her time off-island, and she tells me about her sister's new grandbaby and the movie she saw starring that boy from *Rocketman*. I buy an ice cream sandwich and say I need to call my friend.

I throw my bag down on the table, and before Terri can go back to her book, Saz answers the phone. "The hell?"

"Sorry. The store's been closed since Wednesday and it's literally the only place I can get service. Are you okay?" I unpeel the wrapper from the ice cream and take a bite, enjoying the cold as it moves down my throat.

"I need to tell you something."

"You're getting married."

"It's about your dad."

"My dad?" My ice cream starts dripping onto the table. For some reason it takes me a second to realize she's talking about my dad, as in *my dad,* Neil Henry. This is how little I've been thinking about him lately.

"My parents were out at the White Lion—you know, that bar over on the west side? I guess they saw him there with someone."

It takes me a minute because I'm trying to imagine my dad at a bar. "Someone?"

"A woman. I don't know who it was. She had brown hair. They didn't recognize her."

"What were they doing?"

"Just having a drink. My mom said when your dad saw them, he left, like, a minute later. The woman stayed, so maybe it was someone he was just talking to, someone he met while he was sitting there. I mean, right? That was probably it."

"If that was it, why are you telling me?"

"Because in case there was more to it, I thought you should know. I'd want to know."

"Would you?" My voice goes loud and sharp.

"Yes. And I'd want to hear it from you."

I want to hang up on her. Actually, I want this conversation to never have happened because until this moment it's been a good day, bright and warm but not too warm, and Addy's coming and there's the promise of seeing Miah later. But I don't hang up on her because this is Saz and she's my best friend and she means me no harm and she loves me more than Etsy and Jolly Ranchers and Byron, her favorite brother. So in this dry, small voice I thank her and tell her I have to go because Addy's almost here and that I love her too. Not that I love her more than this and that and that, because my brain has gone blank and silent, but I love her just the same.

Addy arrives on the afternoon ferry. Mom and I meet her, and she hugs my mom first and then me and then my mom again. Addy Birch is trim and elegant, with gray hair shorter than mine and dancing blue eyes. From the second she steps off the ferry, dressed in white linen pants and a flowing kimono top, she looks like the Addy I've known since I was a little girl—timeless, ageless—and I get a lump in my throat. *Home.*

My mom has been close with Addy all her life. She was there for her when Danny drowned in the rip current. She was there for her after Addy divorced her husband, Ray. That was when Addy came here to this island house—the one she'd inherited from her mother—to catch her breath, as she called it. It was always Addy and Mom, Mom and Addy, just like Saz and me.

We go to dinner at the inn and no one mentions my dad. I take the image of him at a bar talking to a strange woman and shove it as far down inside me as I can. Way deep down where no one will see it, where you would need mining gear to find it.

Addy talks about the man she just started dating—an attorney from Columbus—and she talks about her work as a landscape ar-

chitect, which takes her up and down the East Coast and sometimes to California.

Addy has never made me feel smaller than. I've always felt like
she was my friend too. But as good as it is to see her, it also feels
wrong. Like she shouldn't be here. Like even though we're staying in her house, living in her universe, she's bringing the outside
world into this one, where it doesn't belong.

I am busy with Addy and my mom at the museum and he is busy
clearing trails with the Outward Bounders. I sit on the floor, sorting through files, and think of him, replaying our adventures in my
mind. I go over them and over them so that I don't lose a single
detail, but I can already feel the edges starting to blur as we get
closer to leaving.

I tell myself that Saz's parents only thought they saw my dad.
That the person they actually saw was a man with curly hair and a
scruffy beard who just looked like Neil Henry.

I say, "I'll be right back," and then I get up and go into the
room with the displays, where I dig through my bag until I find
the blue notebook, which is beginning to fill up. I go outside into
the afternoon and sit on the step. I flip to the middle of the book
and find the blank pages. I smooth them open, running my hand
across the paper as if I can feel the blankness and the words to
come.

After dinner, back at Addy's house, back in the office, I leave the
window open, the same way Saz and I have always left ours open
for each other. For a long time I sit there, night air warming my

face, gazing out into the buzzing, humming dark. *The window is open and I'm here waiting. Please come.* Even though we haven't planned it, I'm hoping Miah will show up.

I slap at a mosquito on my leg. At another by my ear. I close the window, except for a crack, and curl up on the sofa, restless under the sheet. I finish the thumbprint cookies and write until my eyes grow heavy and I can't keep them open. I lay my head on the pillow and at some point nod off. Around midnight, I feel the pull-out couch sink a little, and Miah is there. I open my eyes and he has turned off all the lights but one.

"Took you long enough," I say. "I was being devoured by bugs."

"I think we both know I'm worth the wait." He gives me this exaggerated wink and I roll my eyes.

He takes the pen out of my hand, and as he reaches for the lamp, I say, "Wait." Instead of telling him about my conversation with Saz yesterday or my time with Addy, I show him the notebook. "You asked me if I was writing. I am. At least, I'm writing things down but I don't know what they are yet. Maybe they're nothing, or maybe they'll be something more one day."

His eyes are on me and he is listening, really listening. He says, in this soft, soft voice, "I hope I get to read them."

DAYS 23-24

Early the next morning, Mom, Addy, and I walk to the beach. We stop to pick up shells and watch the shrimp boats anchored off the shore, and I can hear the lilt in my mom's voice, like music. When she laughs, the lines around her eyes crinkle, and I remember something I read once about the difference between a fake smile and a real one, and how you can always tell a real one by the lines around the eyes.

Addy and my mom tell old family stories, the ones I like to hear, about when they were growing up in Georgia. I join in now and then, but these stories belong to them, and gradually I fall behind to give them some room, even though it's just the three of us on this beach, under this broad blue sky. I watch my mom's blond head and Addy's gray one. They link arms and for a minute they look like sisters, gliding over the sand like swans. Addy says something and my mom starts to laugh again. She laughs so hard she bends at the waist and holds on to her knees, and when she straightens up, she wipes at her eyes and she is still laughing. For some reason the sight of this makes my own eyes go wet, and I concentrate on picking up shells.

And then they're waiting for me to catch up, and Addy asks me about college and am I excited and do I know who my roommate is going to be. I answer her questions, but I want to tell her to live in the moment. *Let's not think about college.* I don't want to think about college, even though it's the thing I've thought about for so long. Most of all I don't want to think about what happens to Miah and me when we leave.

I bend down to pick up a shark tooth, and she says, "You know, Danny collected those. He kept jarfuls in his room. He loved this island. For a long time it was hard to come back here after he died."

"Did you ever think of selling the house?"

"All the time. But there's something about this place. . . ." She trails off. "It took him away, but it can heal you. We've had our share of tragedy in this family, but generations of us have found solace here. That's why I'll always think of this island as ours. It belongs to us in ways you can't see or describe."

"The island has this way of giving you what you need." I say it almost without thinking, as if Miah's words had been waiting *right there* for the perfect opportunity to come out.

"That's right." She looks at me in a way that tells me she gets it or she's heard it before.

She hooks her arms through mine and my mom's, and the three of us walk like this for a while. My mom says, "Claude met a boy."

Addy quirks an eyebrow at me. "A good one, I hope."

Mom goes, "His name's Jeremiah Crew, and he works on the island."

"I know Jeremiah," Addy says, and it's hard to tell if this is a good or a bad thing.

I bend down to pick up another shark tooth, hoping they won't see how red I've gone. The tooth is the best one I've found so far. As large as a quarter, smooth and black. I'm thinking about how I can't wait to show it to Miah when my mind goes to Danny. I hand Addy the shark tooth.

"You should have this."

She blinks over and over, and I'm afraid she's going to cry, but instead she takes the tooth and slips it into her pocket and gives it a pat.

"Thank you," she says. "He would have loved it."

That night, while Mom and Addy are opening a bottle of wine, I slip out with Miah. We drive down to the ferry dock. He grabs a bucket and two fishing poles from the back of the truck and we go walking out on the pier, where we catch and release, catch and release, as the night settles around us. Across the water, at the end of the world, I can see the glow of the mainland.

When we're done fishing, we sit on the bench at the edge of the dock and look up at the stars, taking our time, delaying going back.

"We should go," I say, even though I don't want to.

"I know."

We sit for a while longer, and then I get up and he gets up, and my hand is in his and we're climbing into the truck again.

When we get back to the house, the living room lights are on and I can see my mom and Addy through the front window, right where I left them. Under those stars, up against the side of the house, Miah kisses me. I stand on tiptoe so I can be almost as tall as he is, so I can kiss him as hard as he's kissing me.

I want you I want you I want you, I think. *Now now now.*

The next day, the late-afternoon thunderstorm leaves the air cooler and less suffocating, and Addy offers to cook dinner. Afterward the three of us sit on the porch, Dandelion watching through the window, and eat ice cream while I tell them the ghost stories I've heard since I've been here.

"There's also a lady in white," Addy says. "Over at the carriage house by Rosecroft. I saw her once when I was little. She was just hovering at the upstairs window. Watching me." She stands, ice cream cone in hand, and demonstrates, staring blankly at me, then my mom.

"Who was she?"

"I don't know." She sits again, takes a bite of her cone. "No one's ever been able to figure it out. But if you ask me, it's Tillie. Some ghosts stay still and some move around. Tillie is one of the moving variety. She supposedly protects Rosecroft, and that includes the grounds and all its buildings."

I tell her about Tillie taking Miah's bracelet, and then I mention the Secret Drawer Society, about how Mom said they would write notes and leave them there.

Addy groans. She and my mom exchange this look, and suddenly I can see them at my age, even younger. Addy says, "Every summer I would fall in love with someone, and every summer before I went home, I would write them a letter telling them everything I was too chicken to say in person. When Ray and I divorced, I came here for a while, to get my bearings." She glances at my mom. "And I wrote him a few letters too." She laughs and then pops the last bite of ice cream cone into her mouth. "What about you?" She turns her gaze on me. "Getting any writing done while you're here?"

"A little. Nothing earth-shattering. But a little."

Addy says, "The writing can save you."

My mom winks at me and I say, "So I hear."

I don't want to talk about my writing, so I tell them I'm going inside to get a drink. In the kitchen, Dandelion threads through my legs, and I stoop down to pet him. In a minute I hear the screen door slam.

"So how are you really doing?" Addy stands above me, hands on hips.

"Oh, you know."

"I know." She squats down beside me and rubs Dandelion under the chin. "I'm sorry about your parents, sweetheart. Your mom is one of the greatest women on this planet and my very best friend. She's more my sister than my own sisters. Something like this—I don't know. I can't imagine it, even though I've been through it. But she loves that man. I'll never understand it."

And it's hard to know what she doesn't understand—why my mom loves my dad, or why this separation is happening at all. But in that moment it feels like a curtain is lifting and I'm seeing my mom behind it, completely exposed, and all I want to do is look away but I can't because now I've seen it.

I say, "She's always got it together, at least on the outside. I think the work helps. It's good that she's busy."

"As long as she's not hiding. She can do that, you know. That's why I came here. To make sure she's not hiding too much. I want her to know she's got me, always. And of course she has you. I need you to keep an eye on her for me until I can come back, especially now that people know."

"People know?"

"About the separation, about the fact that your mom is on an island off Georgia indefinitely, about the girlfriend." She mutters this last thing so that I almost don't hear it. Only I do hear it. *The girlfriend.*

And in that moment the floor disappears again. I look down, searching for it, and even though it's technically there, I know it's

303

gone. I don't have to ask, *What girlfriend?* because I know. It goes beyond Saz's parents seeing my dad in a bar with a woman. The way my stomach has just turned over tells me. The cold, cold chill in my bones tells me. The too-fast beating of my heart tells me.

I don't want you to think there's anyone else. It's important that you know that.

But there is someone else. Which means not only did he drop the floor out from under me, but he also lied about it.

"The fact that she works with him is such a fucking cliché."

"I know." Because it's easier than saying, *I didn't know. I didn't really know any of this. I didn't even know she existed till just now.* I don't want to hear this. Whatever this is. I want to forget I've heard any of it. I want to reach inside my ears and grab the words and fling them at her.

"Your mom is being a real trouper, but it's hard for her. And I know it's hard for you, too."

I somehow say, "It is."

If it's true that my mom knew about this, that she kept it secret and chose not to tell me, then she lied too. And because it's her, this is so much worse than my dad.

Addy puts an arm around my shoulder and squeezes me. I can smell her perfume and her shampoo. I can see the mole on the side of her neck, just behind her ear. I think of how long I've known her, all my life, and that I've known her perfume and her shampoo and the mole behind her ear just as long. But right now they seem like things that add up to nothing.

What I hear is, *Everyone knew but you. We all think you're so stupid for not being able to see that this was happening with your own father.*

What she really says is, "You let me know what I can do for you. I'm not just here for your mom."

"Thank you." And suddenly I have to go, because if I don't, I will start crying, and I won't stop until I have melted into an enormous puddle on the floor. I say, "I'll keep an eye on her."

Then I tell Addy I need the bathroom, and I go in and shut the door and throw up my entire dinner. Afterward I sit on the closed toilet for a period of time that could be minutes or hours. And then I rinse my mouth out and reapply lipstick and smooth my hair until I look just like me again.

Back on the porch, my mom and Addy sit drinking lemonade and chatting in light, cheerful voices. Seeing Addy always does my mom good, and my mom needs this right now.

My mom looks up as I sit down next to her, and her face is happier than I've seen it in a while.

"Are you okay?" she says.

"Fine." I smile. I'm good at smiling because I can hide too. I say, "Just thirsty." I drink. My hand doesn't shake.

She loves him, and he doesn't deserve her. He doesn't deserve either of us.

I want to lean into my mom and have her put her arm around me, have her shield me from everything. I want Addy out of our house, which is her house. I want us out of her house. I want to go back home, but not to Ohio home, because my dad lives there and it isn't my home anymore. I want some unseen home where I will be safe and my mom and I will be happy and I won't ever have to think about my dad again.

DAY 24

(PART TWO)

I am sitting on the bed, staring into space as if it's a movie screen, faces flashing across it. There are three women who work directly with my father. Michelle, Fiona, and Pamela, the executive assistant. I've known all of them for years. They've come to the house for dinner. They came to my parents' twentieth-anniversary party. They came to my graduation. Hovering like ghosts in the shadows. Like Tillie in the carriage-house window. Watching from the wings. Waiting. All of them have brown hair.

I'm not sure where to go, but I need to get out of the house. I tell my mom I'm supposed to meet Miah. I hug Addy and say I'll see her later, even though I don't plan to come home until they're asleep or until she leaves the island.

I walk out.

I can barely feel my legs.

But I somehow manage to walk.

No more floor.

The words play in my head like a skipping record.

No more floor.

No more floor.

No more floor.

This is the second time in my life that the floor has disappeared from under me, and now I realize that you can never count on the floor because it's a movable, changeable thing that anyone can take away at any moment. Same with the ground. Same with love.

I follow the drive to the sandy lane that circles in front of the inn. I walk the loop three times, and then I go back to the house and grab my bicycle and fly down Main Road.

I go past the horses that are grazing like it's just another dusky evening. Knock on the door of the bright blue shotgun shack. Wait for him to appear. I'm not sure what I'll do if he doesn't. I don't know where else to go. I wait and I wait, but he doesn't answer.

I ride to the general store, as fast as my legs will take me. I push myself and the bike as hard as I can, trying to go faster, even though there's nowhere to go because this is an island.

When I get to the store, I ditch the bike and run for the door. I pound on it, over and over until my fist hurts, even though—big surprise—it isn't open because it's late and Terri's long gone. I dig out my phone, but of course there's no service.

Back on the bicycle, I fly toward the Dip, hitting every bump in the road, holding on for dear life so that I don't go soaring over the handlebars. I hear the music before I see the house, and then there are lights and people, and I drop the bike and go running.

Around ten p.m., I'm in the yard playing some sort of beanbag-toss drinking game. Miah is nowhere to be found, and so it's

Wednesday and me against Jared and Emory, and I'm downing beer after beer and enjoying the way the alcohol and the music are drowning out the noise in my head. I tell myself there is nothing in the world but this island and this beanbag toss and these people, my friends.

When we've used up our turns, Jared and I sit and watch the others play.

He says, "My friend Rashid was the best at this game."

"He was the one who died?"

"Yeah."

I study his face, which is usually wide open and easy. Right now he's hard to read, as if a veil has dropped over his eyes.

Finally I say, "What happened to him?"

It takes him a few moments to respond. Then he tells me that Rashid killed himself three years ago in August. But this is all he says about the death. Instead Jared tells me about Rashid's short, brilliant life, and about the strength it takes to be the one left behind. *Like Aunt Claudine,* I think, *following the death of her mother.*

Jared says, "Has Miah taken you to the old airfield yet?"

"I don't think so."

"We should go before you leave, maybe pack a lunch. There's not much to see there, but for some reason I like it. I'm pretty sure you'd like it too."

I stop thinking about one of the worst things that can happen to a person—suicide, your best friend gone forever, and all the upside-down that comes with it—and start thinking about a boy named Rashid who made the most of every second he was here and a boy named Jared who is choosing to live as fully as possible.

*   *   *

At some point, I go inside in search of the bathroom. I close the door and lean into the mirror and examine my face, not as a whole, but each feature—mouth, nose, eyes, eyebrows, freckles, forehead, chin. I stand back and look at all of me. I smile. The girl smiles back. I stick out my tongue. She sticks out her tongue. I scrunch up my face. She scrunches up her face. But it's like Addy's shampoo, perfume, mole—they're just details that mean nothing.

I come out of the bathroom and crash right into Grady, so hard we almost fall over. "Watch it," he says, rescuing his drink before it spills everywhere.

"Sorry."

He studies me in a way that makes me go down a checklist of my mouth, nose, eyes, eyebrows, and the rest, as if I've forgotten to put something back in place.

I say, "So you're going to SCAD." Because I need the spotlight on him, not me.

"That's the plan."

"With your girlfriend."

"Not with her. But yeah, she'll be there too."

"How can you do that? You're with her, you're not with her. What is that?"

"It's what works. Not just for me. For her, too."

"So do you sleep with other people during the summer?"

"Why?"

"Just curious."

"Are you asking for you or just generally?"

"Generally."

"Uh, then I say that's nothing you need to worry about."

"Does she know you sleep with other people?"

"Again, you don't need to worry about it. Although you seem to be worrying about it. A lot."

"I'm not worried," I say. I stare at him without blinking. I'm thinking about honesty and how it doesn't matter how much you open up and put yourself out there—people are still going to lie. "Do you have any of your art here?"

"Not really. One or two things, maybe."

"Can I see it?"

And I'm not sure who's talking—me, who's had too much to drink and is walking around with no floor, or the girl in the mirror, whose features are all in place, just like always. What I do know is that a slightly ominous burning feeling is growing in my stomach, which means I'm about to do something I'll regret.

Grady says, "Sure."

His room is upstairs, at the end of the hallway, facing the marsh. It's just a room, not some love den filled with pinups and bongs, like I expected.

I sit on the bed. "So show me." It feels as if I'm daring him. *Show me. Show me the kind of guy you are. Show me that I'm here.*

He leaves the door open. "What are you doing?"

"Waiting for you to show me your art." I try to say it as breezy as a summer's day. And I know I should get up and walk out, but there is this terrible, hollow ache inside me and I need it to go away. I need to fill it with something so that there isn't any room for the ache or all the thoughts that come with it.

He closes the door. My heart is beating too fast and my face is flushing hot and red and a little voice inside me is going, *What are you doing, Claudine? Back away. Turn away. Run away.*

310

He walks over to me and holds out his hand. I give him mine and he pulls me to my feet, and then that hand is on my face, tracing the line of my jaw, and his forehead is against mine, and his eyes are on my mouth, and I stand like a statue, stiff and un-moving. But I don't pull away because suddenly I want his mouth on mine, to chase away the thoughts that are creeping back into my head. Maybe that's what I've wanted since I crashed into him downstairs.

And then—without asking—he kisses me. And there's the sur-prise of a new and different mouth from the one I'm used to. I make myself kiss him back even as part of me is going, *Stop this. Walk away.* Both his hands are now on my face, just like in a book or a film, and even as I'm thinking this is a move he knows well and uses all the time, and even as the voice in me is starting to shout, *STOP THIS RIGHT NOW,* I keep kissing him.

I kiss him harder and he kisses me harder. His teeth bang against mine, and instead of stopping I keep going. Harder and harder.

I kiss him until I feel his hand on the skin of my back, under-neath my shirt, and then I pull away as if my brain has suddenly come back to me, along with all my common sense, along with me, actual Claude, who—floor or no floor—doesn't want to kiss Grady.

"I can't do this. Jesus."

"You could a second ago," he says.

"I changed my mind. Sorry."

He's smiling at me, but it's not a friendly smile. Anger hides at the corners. He says, "I don't fucking get you."

"You don't have to."

As I head toward the door, he steps in front of me.

311

"I'm pretty sure you came up here to lead me on. And you started all this, and now you're walking out. Which is frustrating, if you know what I mean. You're lucky I'm a nice guy."

"So lucky. Please move." It's as if every part of me is holding its breath, even my heart, which is no longer beating fast or maybe at all.

When he doesn't move, I say, "I may have come up here and I may have started this, which—believe me—is not one of my proudest life choices, but when I ask you to move, you should move."

I want to wait for him to get out of the way because I shouldn't have to be the one to walk around him. But I also know that I need to get out of here, the faster the better, and in one piece.

He doesn't stop me as I walk around him, as I push out of his room, down the hallway, past Wednesday, down the stairs, out the door, off the porch, into the yard, past Jared, who calls after me, and Emory and the others. I forget about the bicycle and run as fast as I can.

DAY 24

_____

(PART THREE)

The blue shotgun shack is lit up now. In a second, the door opens and it's him. Standing in bare feet, no shirt, grinning at me. I don't say anything. I half expect to start crying until I've flooded his house and this entire island. But instead I launch myself at him. Kiss him hard. Catching him off guard. He wraps his arms around me and lifts me over the threshold and into the house, and now I'm against the wall in the kitchen and I can't kiss him hard enough. I tug at his shorts, as in I practically rip them off him, and that's when he pulls back. Lays his hand on mine.

"Hey. What is this?"

"I want you."

"Yeah, we've established that. What's going on?"

"Nothing. Can't I just want you?"

"Fair enough."

I kiss him again and he starts kissing me back, and there it is—his wonderful mouth, the mouth I know, the one I'm supposed to be kissing. And then he wraps an arm around me and kind of carries me upright to his bedroom, where we fall onto the bed and I can't get him close enough. I'm swept up in him and the heat of us, and at the same time Grady's mouth is there. I need to forget the way it felt on mine. To forget everything Addy said about my dad. I need it out of me, back on the mainland, maybe as far as the moon.

It's like my life depends on the sex I'm about to have.

The rest of his clothes are coming off, and mine are coming off, and we're naked, but not naked enough, and I just don't want to think about anything other than us and my body and what I'm feeling. Because if I stop, Grady is there and my dad is there, and I have to think about my mom and me, the two of us, homeless and cast out except for the house Addy's letting us live in. I don't want another before and after. Before my dad left us. After my dad found this other woman. No more befores and afters. For once I just want to be Claude Now.

Suddenly I realize there's no condom.

I say, "Aren't you forgetting something?"

"Shit. Hold on."

Afterward I lie there staring up at the ceiling, and Grady is still there and my dad is still there and the sex hasn't chased them away. And then something else is there. The reality that Miah is leaving, that I'm leaving. And the reality of what I've done. The stabbing in my chest turns to an emptiness, and then a tightness, as if the breath is going out of me.

I go far, far away. He thinks I'm lying there, but I'm actually not in this room, not on this island, not even on this earth. I'm somewhere beyond it, looking out through my eyes, which are acting like computer screens, transmitting to me in space. And this is what happens when you are protecting yourself from caring too much. Because inevitably people will hurt you, and it's better to cushion the fall. This way you still fall, but not as far, and maybe it won't hurt as much when you hit the ground.

Miah says, "Hey. Captain."

I kind of come to, and it's clear he's been saying something that I haven't heard.

He rolls over onto his side, one arm draped across me. "Where are you?"

"Here."

"No you're not. What's going on?"

"Nothing." *Everything.* Instead of making me feel closer, the sex has made me further away, not just from him but from everyone.

"Yeah, no. Don't do that."

He reaches for my arm but I move it away.

I say, "Maybe I just want to have fun without thinking so much all the time."

"Great, me too, but not when you're acting weird."

"I'm not acting weird."

"Bullshit."

"Don't be a dick."

"You don't be a dick."

"You're the dick who almost didn't wear a condom."

"Yeah, well, you were there too, Captain. And I hope you know that wasn't on purpose. You're going to run into guys who tell you they can't get off wearing a condom, and they'll try to convince you to forget protection. They'll be all, *Let's be in the moment, let's not worry—*"

"Why are you talking about other guys?"

"I just want to prepare you for when I'm not around."

"Thanks, but I'm not stupid. And I'm not going to sleep with anyone who tries that with me." And now I'm seething. We're still naked, and he's already thinking about when we're not together anymore.

"Sorry. With four younger sisters, you get used to being the protector."

"I don't want to talk about other guys I'm going to sleep with, not with you, not right now."

"I get it. And just so you know, I don't really want to talk about that either."

We go quiet for a minute. Then he says, "So who're you mad at? Your dad?" He sits up a little and he's looking at me, and all I want is to get away, but then he goes, "Hey. Come on. It's me."

And he touches my face and lifts my chin and won't let me look away. And the way he touches me is so sweet and gentle that I pull back so he can't reach me. But I tell him. I tell him because I have to.

It comes out broken, little shattered pieces of glass, too sharp to pick up, too many to put back together. I tell him about my dad and his girlfriend. And then I tell him about Grady.

He sits listening. So quiet. So still.

"Say something."

"I don't know what to say."

His voice is like an empty room, one that's been vacated abruptly and completely.

"Please say something." There is a weight on my chest that is making it hard to breathe, so heavy and fast-spreading that it's suffocating me. In this moment, I suddenly feel as if the functioning of my organs—lungs, heart—is dependent on him speaking.

"I think it's better if I don't."

"Miah, I'm sorry. I didn't know what I was doing. I came to find you and you weren't here. . . ."

He turns to look at me, and the emptiness is in his eyes too. When he speaks, his voice is controlled and quiet. So quiet. "Are you really throwing this on me like it's my fault? I'm not here, so you might as well get it on with the next guy you find?"

"No, of course not. Look, I didn't mean it, and I don't know why I did it. It's like I was there but I wasn't there. I know that doesn't make any sense, and it doesn't make it okay, but that's how it felt."

"You can't use sex or kissing or anything to erase shit. Jesus, Claude."

He never calls me Claude, and then I can feel them—the tears burning the backs of my eyelids. Before I can stop it, one leaks out and down my cheek.

"If it makes you feel any better, it only made me feel worse."

"No, it doesn't make me feel any better. But hey, I get it. Life can be shitty, and that stuff with your dad, that's just fucked up. But I didn't do that, Captain. That wasn't me." He sits there calmly. So calmly. His voice is even and measured and completely devoid of emotion, and I've done this to him.

He gets up, and for a second I think he's going to hug me. But then he pulls on his shorts, slips on his shirt, and walks out of the room. I wait *one*, *two*, *three* seconds, and then I throw on my clothes and follow him. Without looking at me, he opens the front door.

"Where are you going?" I ask.

"I'm driving you home."

The drive to Addy's seems like it takes three years. As we pull up, as he stops the truck, as we sit there with the engine idling, which tells me he's not walking me to the door, I say, "I'm sorry."

I've never in my life wanted to go back in time to fix something like I want to right now. *If only I hadn't gone to the Dip. If only I hadn't crashed into Grady. If only I hadn't gone up to his room.* I run through it all over and over again, like reliving it will somehow change the outcome.

"I'm sorry," I say again.

"Me too."

Half an hour later, on the pull-out sofa, I lie back, head on the pillow. I am alone in my head and alone with myself, the most dangerous place I could be.

He's got every right to be hurt and angry. You'd be hurt and angry too. You know you were wrong and you hate that you were wrong, but that doesn't change anything. You need to say you're sorry and keep saying you're sorry and stop being so afraid of being you.

I dig the blue notebook out of my dresser and write every last, horrible thought.

DAY 25

The next morning, we walk Addy to the dock so she can meet the ferry. Miah carries her overstuffed luggage like it's weightless, and when we get to the pier, Grady is sitting there with Emory and a couple of the local guys. His eyes go to me and then to Miah. He stands. "I'll take it from here."

"That's okay," Miah says. "I got it."

He strides past him, sweeps the bag up as if it doesn't weigh eighty-five pounds, and swings it onto the ferry. Addy offers him a tip but he holds up his hands and backs away. "Not necessary," he tells her, flashing that grin.

"See you later," he says to me. Not *See you in an hour* or *See you later tonight,* just *See you later.* I watch as he walks past Grady again, as Grady calls something out to him that I can't hear, as Miah keeps right on going without a word, Grady watching him the whole way.

"What was that about?" Mom is next to me.

"You know. Men." I say it lightly, but I'm looking at her face for signs that she agrees because she knows about my dad and this other woman, whoever she is.

"Men," she echoes.

"Men," says Addy. "I wish I didn't love them so goddamn much."

The captain strolls by and Grady follows. I look away so he

can't catch my eye. Suddenly there are other guests there with luggage, boarding the ferry, taking their seats. Archie, the island dog, goes ambling along with them, tail wagging lazily in all this heat.

Addy's arms are around my mom and then me. "You take good care of her," she says in my ear. "And let her take care of you."

"I will."

"And be careful with that heart of yours. There's been enough heartbreak in this family for a while." And I don't know if she's making a general statement or one specifically targeted at Miah, but I want to go, *You should warn people about me, not the other way around.*

And then she's hugging my mom again, and when she lets go, I see the tears in Mom's eyes, and I have to look away from this, too.

We wave as Addy boards the ferry and takes her seat, and we wave again as the ferry goes sailing off. Mom stands there longer than I do, hand in the air, smile on her face. When Addy's out of sight, Mom turns to me. "It's hard to see her go."

I don't say anything, but I throw my arms around her. "I'm glad it's just us again."

She studies my face, but I'm not giving anything away. I go blank and smiling, the dutiful daughter, the one whose heart is still intact. "I was thinking I could help you at the museum today if you want."

She's still studying my face, still trying to read me, but finally she says, "I'd like that."

Mom and I spend the rest of the day together at the museum, sifting through and organizing Claudine's papers, and I don't say anything about my dad.

We walk home together and I don't say anything.

We eat dinner together and I don't say anything.

We sit on the porch of the inn and watch the lightning bugs flickering in the trees and across the grass. And I don't say anything. She's already been through enough and now it's my job to protect her and buy her honeysuckle perfume and tell her she's beautiful and make sure she has a floor—as flimsy as it is—to walk on.

The screen door slams and I look up. Wednesday waves at me like, *Come here.* I look away. I hear footsteps, and of course she's walking over. She frowns down at me. "I need to talk to you, Mainlander."

"I'm busy."

"Claude." This is from Mom.

"Fine."

I get up, feet dragging, and follow Wednesday across the porch, inside the inn to the library, which is empty.

She says, "Did Grady hurt you?"

"No."

"Tell me the truth."

"No. I was stupid. It was my fault." *I hurt me. Not Grady. Not Miah. Me.*

"Did something happen?"

"No."

"Claude?"

And maybe because she's using my real name for once, I say, "It started to, but I stopped it."

"You know he's a total dirtbag."

"I know."

She sighs. "Does Miah know?"

"I told him."

"Why?"

"I had to."

"Shit." She shakes her head, and the braids swing back and forth like pendulums. "So look, when I was sixteen, I started putting myself in a box because I figured it would keep me from getting hurt. I took care of that box like it was my freaking home. At first, the box was good. Small, compact, everything safe inside it. I kept it neat and tidy. I painted it. Painted who I wanted to be. I didn't let myself be seen or heard. I made my sexuality small and quiet instead of big and bright. But I started not being able to breathe, so that's when I pushed open the box flaps, one by one. The last was running away from Alabama to live the life I wanted to live. And saying to someone other than myself, *This is me. I want to be a singer. I want to change the world with my music. I want to fall in love and get my heart broken. I'm pansexual. I seem tough, but I'm not. At least not always.* So yeah. Here I am. Out of the box. And sometimes it sucks. But at least I can breathe."

After a long moment, I say, "Okay."

"Okay?"

"Yeah."

"That's all I wanted to say."

And then she walks away. A second later, I go to the doorway and call after her, "Hey, Wednesday?"

She's by the stairs leading down to the dining room, one hand on the railing. She looks back at me. "Mainlander?"

"Thank you."

My bicycle is waiting on the porch of Addy's house. Mom and I climb the steps and I look around at the woods and the inn and the road, but there's no sign of anyone.

Mom says, "Where did that come from?"

"I don't know."

Inside, we curl up on the couch, Dandelion between us, and watch a movie, Wednesday's words swimming in my head. *Do I put my-self in a box? Is that what I've been doing?* I chew on my fingers, lost in thought.

The minute Jean Seberg comes onto the screen, my mom looks at me. "Now I recognize that haircut."

Her voice pulls me out of my own head. I watch Jean Seberg's bright face. "She looked effortless, and that's what I want to be."

"She does, and this film made her an icon, but she had an un-happy life." My mom's voice is soft. We are reading the subtitles. "She died at forty of suicide. She was missing for ten days before they found her body in the back seat of her car, three blocks from her Paris apartment."

This hits me harder than it should. On-screen, Jean Seberg smiles and laughs and strides down the street, and some part of me still wants to be her, or at least this pretend version of her. "If I could dig a hole and hide in it, I would," her character is saying.

I think, *You never know what someone's hiding. We all hide ourselves when we need to.*

"Is everything okay with Jeremiah?"

The question surprises me, but I keep my eyes glued to the screen. "I did something really stupid and really hurtful that I wish I could take back, but I can't."

"Do you want to talk about it?"

"No. I feel bad enough. I just want it to go away, like somehow build a time machine and go back to yesterday and change everything so that it never happened." I wait for her to say, *Maybe you should try harder. Be a nicer, less complicated, less fucked-up person. Maybe you shouldn't lock yourself away behind that wall you've built.* All the things I tell myself.

Instead she says, "Oh God, we really are alike."

I look at her.

"I'm just saying I have, from time to time throughout my life, been known to do stupid things that I wish I could take back and make right."

"You're perfect."

"I'm not. No one is, thank God. Otherwise what a boring world this would be. There are so many things I wish I'd done differently at the time, including with your dad. But we can only pay attention, hope we learn something, try not to fuck up again—at least not in the same exact way—and keep going forward, knowing that we're absolutely going to fuck up. A lot." My mom rarely swears, and I raise my eyebrows. She smiles. "Sorry. The important thing is to do your best, always, to not be too hard on yourself when you don't, and to let go of regrets. You have to trust me on this because I'm a lot older than you and I know things."

I run my hand over my hair, smoothing it around the ears, around the forehead. "I get that I'm going to fuck up a lot, no matter what I do. And I get that I shouldn't be too hard on myself. But right now I don't want Miah to be some sort of life lesson. I want him to be more than that."

"Then talk to him—even if he doesn't want to hear it—until you've said what you need to say."

DAY 25

(PART TWO)

It's eleven o'clock and I am pedaling through the night to Miah's house. I'm not sure what I'm going to say to him, but I just know I need to tell him how I feel.

So my dad has a girlfriend.

The words run round and round in my mind. I say them out loud, hoping this will stop the endless loop, and they escape into the air where I can see them, right in front of me, just out of reach. I want to take them back, but I can't take them back because they're true.

My dad has a girlfriend.

It's not that I thought my parents were getting back together. I don't actually know if I thought that or not. But this makes it clear that's not going to happen and my mom and I were in the way.

And these words are also true. *We were in the way.*

I find him outside on the porch, under the moon, shorts, black shirt, bare feet. He stands, arms folded across his chest, looking up at the stars. I prop the bike against a tree and wade through the grass and the cactus spurs. I climb the steps and now I'm next to him.

"Hey," I say, a little out of breath.

"Hey." His eyes don't leave the sky.

I think of all the things I want to say to him, and then I don't say anything. I follow his gaze upward and it's like a blanket of the deepest, darkest blue, covered in a million tiny pinpricks of light.

He says without looking at me, "What do you want, Captain?"

"I want to tell you I'm sorry. I want to apologize a thousand times and tell you why I think I did what I did, not that there's any excuse. I want to tell you how scared I am that I just fucked this up, when it's the best thing that's happened to me for a long time. *You're* the best thing that's happened to me for a long time. I want this Grady thing to not exist, but it does exist and that's my fault and I want you to know that I know it's my fault, no one else's. I want to tell you how much I hate my dad right now and how confused I am and how lost I feel, but how I know that doesn't make it better. I want to be here with you, even if I do all the talking and you never speak to me again. I want to have the chance to tell you how I feel and what you mean to me. Like, you'll never know how much you mean to me. I want to tell you that I don't want this to be the end of us, right here, right now. I want to ask you to forgive me."

My throat has gone lumpy and my eyes have gone wet. Miah is looking at me now, not the sky. For a moment, he just stands there. But then he says, "Let's get out of here."

Before he can change his mind, I am up and in the truck. I wait, listening to my breath. I sound like I've just run a marathon. I focus on breathing in, out. Steady. Calm. I wait, and he doesn't get in, and he really has changed his mind. But then a *thud* as something is dropped into the back of the truck, and then the door swings open and he's climbing in.

* * *

We drive in silence, bouncing down Main Road. I have no idea where he's taking me. I'm trying to think of the right words to say, but there are too many things to say, so we're both just sitting there. We turn toward the beach on a wide, overgrown trail I don't recognize. Every time I think I know this island, he takes me down some road like this, somewhere I've never been.

We don't talk and there's no music except for the cicadas, which seem louder than normal. Trees blur past and we move through the dark, no headlights, fireflies lighting our way. I half expect us to drive until we hit the ocean, but at some point he slows the truck, and then we're stopped.

He gets out and I get out, and we still haven't spoken. He grabs something from the bed of the truck—a bag—and I follow him under the tree canopy for what seems like a mile. We cross the inner dunes, the ones closest to the woods, and before we get as far as the beach, he turns into the little valley between the inner and outer dunes. Here, sheltered from the wind, he stops, drops the bag, and hands me a pack of matches.

"What's this for?"

"It goes with this." He holds up a bottle of lighter fluid.

"It's a little hot out for a bonfire, isn't it?"

But too late: he's gathering driftwood and stacking it in the basin of the dunes. He douses it with lighter fluid and then he nods at me. I strike the match and drop it onto the wood. I watch as it catches hold and the fire grows, snapping, crackling, flames dancing in the night.

He digs through his backpack and comes up with a notebook, which he hands to me. "Write down every shitty thing you're too scared to say out loud. Write anything that's keeping you from you. Write anything that's keeping you from me."

"Why?"

"So we can burn them up."

I don't mention the day I spent on the beach waiting for him, tossing shells and worries into the ocean. I'm too busy thinking there isn't enough paper in that notebook or even on this island to write down everything that scares me or every bad thought that's filling my mind.

He writes *Grady* on a sheet of paper, then rips it out and holds it over the fire. I watch as the paper starts to smoke and burn, dissolving away, one letter at a time.

He writes, *I miss my brother,* rips it out, drops it on the fire.

He writes, *I want to live my own life, not someone else's.*

And *I just want to be eighteen.*

I write, *I hate my dad.*

I miss Saz.

Grady means nothing.

I'm sorry, Miah.

I will never trust anyone again.

For the next twenty minutes, we take turns writing things down and tossing them into the fire. I empty myself onto the paper until there's nothing left.

When we're finished, we sit on the sand. He smells like sunshine and fresh sheets, and I don't know whether to touch him or not because it feels like I don't have that right anymore. I sit with my hands in my lap and try to figure out what more I want to say to him.

And then he says, "I know what it's like to be in a rough place."

I look at him, and he's looking at the fire. "That doesn't mean I should have done what I did."

"No, it doesn't." He makes this frustrated groaning sound and shakes his head at the ground. He closes his eyes. Opens them.

"Shit." He sighs. "But I get it. Sometimes you do things just to make it worse. Back when I was thirteen and life was at its absolute shittiest, I wanted something to numb the pain and I found it. It worked for a little while, but the problem is, you want more, you need more, and before you know it, you can't feel anything." He stares down at his hands. "But you know what I finally figured out?" He looks up at the fire again. "You have to feel it. You have to feel it even if you think it's going to kill you."

"I'm sorry. About Grady. So sorry."

"I know. We don't have endless time here, and I still want to hang out with you too. Like, really want to hang out with you."

"But?" I brace myself because I know what's coming.

"But it hurts. And I think I'm supposed to forgive you, because if I want to spend any time with you before we leave this island, I'm going to need to. And I want to do that, but we've been pretty honest with each other, and I'd be lying if I said . . . I mean, as much as you worried about Wednesday? I don't know. The thing is, you got in there, Captain. You got way the hell in there." And he's talking about his heart, or maybe all of him.

"So what does that mean?"

"It means we need to be bigger than what happened with Grady. We're bigger than Grady." He looks at me then. "Well, I know I am." Our eyes lock and the corners of his mouth turn up, and suddenly the dimples are there. Different, but there. "But I still feel shitty."

"I'm sorry," I say again.

"I know." Like that, the dimples disappear. His eyes move back to the fire.

There are a million things I want to say to him, but I don't say any of them because I know they won't help. So eventually I say, "Tell me about your brother. If you want to."

It takes him a minute to answer.

"I never really felt like I got to know him, because by the time I was old enough, he was gone to basic training, Ranger School, his first tour, then another. He was tough, but funny. Whenever he came home, he'd wear those dumb-ass shorts, the ones you love so much. He'd say that after all that gear in the desert, wearing them was like 'cradling your junk with a pillow of angels.' It's stupid, but when I put on those shorts, it makes me feel like he's still here. Like it's just him and me having adventures."

"I don't think it's stupid."

"Before Bram and Shirley, he was maybe the only person in my life who never let me down. But that doesn't mean I was always a good brother to him."

"What was his name?"

"Flynn."

"I'm sorry about Flynn."

"Yeah, me too." He looks at me then. "Here's something else I've figured out, Captain. At some point, you have to start trusting that there's a floor again. What's the worst that can happen? Okay, so it disappears. You've already survived one disappearing floor, and you're still here, walking around. So you can survive others. Yeah, you can put yourself on twenty-four-hour watch, never take your eyes off it, but that's not going to keep bad things from happening. Because life is going to do what life's going to do. The thing you can count on is that at some point something bad *will* happen. Which makes things like blood moons and treasure hunting and you even more important." He takes my hand. "I'm sorry about your dad."

"At least he's still here. And I get that. I try to remember that. I just pretty much feel like the last to know, like everyone saw it coming but me." With my free hand, I pick up the notebook, write

I feel so stupid, and hold it out until the flames catch it and swallow it and turn it to dust.

We sit like this for a long time, watching the fire die down. I concentrate on the feel of his hand in mine—fingers, skin, warmth. No matter what happens to Miah and me, I want to always remember the feel of his hand.

I say, "I've been thinking about it and you should dream big. You need to dream big. Whatever that means. Montana. Outward Bound. The rodeo circuit. The moon. You deserve to live your own life, Jeremiah Crew."

I meet his eyes, and there is this look on his face that's hard to describe. It's as if I can suddenly see him as a little boy, before all the loss and heartache, before he had to grow up too fast and become an adult and take care of everyone.

He reaches for me and pulls me close.

At some point we lie back. He closes his eyes. I close mine.

"I got you," he says.

I lie there for a long time, feeling his arm around me. Telling myself it's okay. *Right now it's okay, I'm okay, and he's here.* Telling myself this is enough.

He's got me.

He's got me.

He's got me.

"I got you, too," I whisper.

DAY 26

The next morning I find my mom in the kitchen. We move around the space, pouring ourselves coffee and cereal, cutting up fruit, spooning yogurt into a bowl, and not talking. I don't say anything. I don't mean to say anything. Ever. Then she looks at me and asks, "Is everything okay?" And I start to cry.

In a second, her arms are around me and I'm crying into her shoulder. I stay there for a moment, holding on to her, and then I make myself pull away.

I say, "I need to talk to you."

By the expression on her face, I can tell she's bracing herself. She probably thinks I'm pregnant.

"Is this a window-seat talk or a walk-and-talk?"

"Neither. It's a monsters-in-the-woods talk."

This is code for *Let's sit on the bed and build a pillow fort to keep the monsters away.* It was what we did when I was seven and terrified of the trees surrounding our house. I was convinced something dark and menacing lived there, and my mom would sit with me at night and explain that there weren't monsters in the woods, but if there were—which there weren't—in order to get to me they would have to first unlock the front door, and if they could somehow do that, they would have to get past the dog and then my dad and her. So many lines of defense.

We leave the coffee and food on the kitchen counter and go into her room. Once we're barricaded and sitting cross-legged, knee to knee, face to face, I tell her about my conversation with Addy. As I talk, I start crying again—tears over my dad's girlfriend, tears over my entire roller coaster of a life.

She wraps her arms around me and holds me, and even though it doesn't change anything, it's enough. I let it be enough.

She says, "First, I'm sorry you found out that way. I love Addy, but it wasn't her place to say anything. That said, she didn't know that you didn't know, and I should have told you. That's on me. Your dad and I are trying to maneuver this situation the best way we can, but neither of us knows what the hell we're doing. Second, this isn't your fault. Let's make that clear right now."

"I know." But I'm not sure I do. And then there's this overwhelming urge to crawl up into her lap like I'm a little girl again and have things be simple and easy, with monsters in the woods the only thing to fear.

"What did Addy say exactly?"

"Just that he has a girlfriend and she works with him."

I wait for her to tell me this isn't true after all, but her face confirms it.

"You knew." I'm still hoping by some miracle she'll say, *No, I didn't, I had no idea.* Not that I want to be the one to break it to her, but I need her to not lie to me, not even by omission.

"I've known for a little while."

My stomach drops. "You should have told me."

"I know." She doesn't make excuses.

"It's just another secret."

"I know and I'm sorry."

"I hate him."

333

"Relationships are complicated, honey. It takes two to make one and two to break one. They aren't black-and-white. And I know all of this seems sudden to you, like love can just go away or change in the blink of an eye. But at least in the case of your dad and me, I'm realizing it was a progression of little fractures. Even if I didn't exactly understand that at the time."

"I still hate him."

"I get it. I kind of hate him too. But I also know your dad better than anyone knows him, and he gets in his own way. He always has. It's like that book you love, the wallflower book."

"The Perks of Being a Wallflower."

"That line about how we accept the love we think we deserve? That's your dad."

"So who is she?"

"Michelle."

"Is it serious?"

"I think so. He said something about moving in with her, so we're talking about selling the house, me getting my own place. Whether that happens or not, this does not mean he loves you any less. Your dad loves you more than he loves anyone, including himself."

"Okay."

I can hear myself. I sound like Robot Claude, but I feel like a tornado or like something cornered and scared and angry. *Is all this what you meant, Mr. Russo? Do you think now I'll be able to write something real and true that will make people feel?*

"Claude."

"Yes."

"I'm your mother. I've known you all your life. And you need to talk to me, no matter what. I'm saying this as a person who can also hide when she wants to."

"Okay."

"That includes talking about anything. Your dad. The house. Saz. College. Sex."

"I really don't want to talk to you about sex."

"Fair enough. You know, my own mother has never said that word to me. Maybe that's why I want to make sure you can talk to me, but I get it. Just tell me once that you're being safe, because I'm a mom and moms need to know that."

"I'm being safe."

"And you're okay?" She means about the sex and Miah, not about everything else.

"I'm okay."

She sighs. She tilts her head toward mine and my forehead meets hers. We sit like this for a minute. Then she sits back. I sit back. I picture my house, which will soon be someone else's house, and my green room, which will no longer be my green room but someone else's green room.

She says, "I'm glad to see you cry. I've been worried about you. If the tears don't come out as tears, they're going to come out some other way. And hey, it's okay to still be a child to your parents. No matter how grown-up you get. It's okay to let me be the mom. Actually, it's good for me, too. Especially right now. So let me be the mom."

That afternoon the two of us, Lauren and Claude, Claude and Lauren, walk outside into the day. The sun and the heat envelop us, as if to say, *You're okay.*

Mom stares up at the sky. " 'All is well. All will be well. All manner of things will be well.' " My mom and dad don't do organized religion, but this is something she likes to quote from the Quakers. Then she looks at me, eyebrows arched. "Let's play hooky."

"We should take bikes and ride to Rosecroft."

Her eyebrows shoot up into her hairline. "When did you learn to ride a bike?"

But I'm already straddling the bicycle—bare legs, bare feet, bare head because I've forgotten my fisherman's cap—and sailing down the lane.

We ride side by side down Main Road, the sun on our faces, hair blowing. At Rosecroft, the two of us pick our way through the grass and the brick until we get to a broad staircase at the back of the house, the one closest to the marsh. I go first and she follows me, up the stairs to the second floor. Most of the floor is gone, but at the top of the stairs is a single room, broad and airy, blue sky for ceiling, and smelling faintly of flowers.

We walk in and I catch my breath.

The closet door sits open, and she shows me the bullet hole. I fit my finger inside it, the way she said she did when she was young, and wonder if Claudine ever did the same. Did she come in here or close off the room? Is this where she slept? Or did she stay as far from here as she could? I think of her in this grand old house, roaming its halls, sitting alone in these giant rooms, walking down the stairs—as I'm doing now—to the main floor, only the ghost of Tillie to keep her company.

Standing there, I'm suddenly filled with all this love for Tillie, this beautiful and sad young woman who died too soon. And in that moment it hits me. This is why Claudine stayed here all those years. She didn't want to leave her mom.

* * *

Back outside, on the ground, we walk the length of the house, up one side and down the other—Mom describing the way the place once looked, room by room. The blue wicker furniture on the north veranda. The big wooden swing. The golden oak doors with black iron hinges. The square entrance hall. The brass container used for outgoing mail. The card room, where the guest book was kept. The archway into the great hall with its fireplace, the Blackwood motto chiseled into the mantel: VIVIS SPERANDUM. WHERE THERE IS LIFE THERE IS HOPE. The large red sofa where Claudine took her naps, the one nobody dared sit on because it was hers and hers alone. On and on.

By the time the sun starts to set, we've put the house back together again, rebuilding the ruins.

I sit in my bed rereading *Zelda* for the five hundredth time. Fitzgerald is in Hollywood trying to be a screenwriter, while Zelda is at Highland Hospital in North Carolina being treated for her schizophrenia. He is having a wild and flagrant affair with a gossip columnist named Sheilah Graham, who will later write a book about it, while Zelda is locked up in a mountain sanitarium, where she will literally burn to death.

Fuck you, Scott Fitzgerald.

I lay the book down and fall back, head on my pillow, and wait for Miah to come.

We lie on top of the sheets, clothes on, facing each other. At first there's the feeling again of not knowing whether I should touch him. He is Miah but not Miah, or maybe it's me. Maybe too much has happened—my dad, Grady—for us to be like we were before Addy came to the island. I say this to him now.

"Well, what are we going to do about it, Captain?"

"I don't know."

He takes my hand and places it over his heart. "Let's start here." And then he kisses me. I kiss him. This goes on for a minute, maybe two.

We break apart.

He says, "You know, we don't have to do anything. Sometimes your head's just not in that space, and that's okay."

"Do you still want to?"

"Pretty much always. Yeah."

"I mean with me."

"So do I. As in I pretty much always want to with you."

I kiss him. He kisses me. I rest my hand on his heart again and I can feel the beating of it, slightly faster than normal, but steady, so steady.

DAY 27

We are up before sunrise, riding bicycles to the beach. We leave them by the footpath, the one that will take us over the dunes and onto the sand. I carry my bag and he carries his camera. As we come over the last dune, I see it. The sky is a palette of soft blues and pinks and gold. The water has captured all these colors and holds them there so that everything, ocean and sky, is bathed in the same dazzling light. The universe feels new and washed clean.

When I mention this to Miah, he says, "Shirley calls it *dayclean,* when the world kind of starts over."

Like us, I think.

I breathe in the air, which is cool and light. By midmorning it will be as heavy as a wet blanket, but for now it feels good on my skin.

I say, "I have to write." But the truth is, I'm already writing. My mind is reeling with all the images and words and scenes that are in it. I need to get them out of me and onto the page.

I wander for a minute until I find it, the perfect place to sit with the perfect view of the sunrise and the boy who is wandering the beach, this way and that, taking pictures.

Every now and then I look up to make sure he's still there. I watch him as he wades into the water, as he kneels in the sand to get the angle he wants, as he covers the camera screen with his hand to check the photos he's taking. He turns to look at me, as if he can feel me watching.

He laughs. "I see you, Captain."

I write, *I see you, Captain*. I wish I could draw him with words and put him down on paper the way he looks right now, as if he's part of the sunrise.

At some point—a click. I glance up, and there is Miah, lying on the ground, a few feet away, camera pointing at me. I'm so deep in me that it takes me a moment. *There you are,* I think. *I'm glad you're here.*

Sometime later—who knows how long—he is standing in front of me, shirtless. "Come for a swim with me."

"I can't. I'm in it." Even though I want to do both, stay and go.

"When do I get to read it?"

"Probably never."

He laughs. "Okay," he says. "Stay there." And I know he means, *Stay in it.* He spins around and takes off running. The sky beyond him is blue and bright. *When did the sun get here?* As he runs, he tries to shuck off his shorts and nearly falls over. *Click.* I'm taking word pictures as he goes. *Click.* As he hollers, "Nothing to see here!" *Click.* As he's running full speed again into the water. *Click. Click. Click.*

DAY 27

***

(PART TWO)

I sit at the general store, in one of the four chairs set up in a corner, and chew at a hangnail. The place is empty except for Terri behind the counter.

At noon exactly, my dad calls.

"Dad."

"Hey, kiddo."

I have no idea what I'm going to say or whether I'm going to mention the other woman, at least by name. I need to hear what he has to say first.

"I talked to your mother. Kiddo, I'm so sorry." Not *Clew*. She is now *your mother* and I am apparently *kiddo*. "I'm sorry you found out this way and I'm sorry I told you not to talk about it and I'm sorry that I've let you down."

My heart is pounding in my ears. If I can just get things back to normal, everything will be okay. My house will still be my house. My parents will still be my parents. Maybe my dad will not have fallen in love with Michelle from work and that will go back to normal too.

He says, "I wish I could be there."

"Do you?"

"Yes—"

"Did you want to leave us before you did?"

"Clew . . ." And suddenly I'm Clew again. *Oh no*, I think. *You*

341

can't just throw that nickname out there like that, whenever you want to. Take it away, give it back. Take it away, give it back.

"Did you?"

"It's complicated."

"You met someone and you're leaving Mom. That doesn't sound very complicated."

The line goes completely quiet.

"You told me there was no one else. You literally said, 'It's important that you know that.' Why would you say it if it was a lie?"

"I'm sorry."

It's my turn to go quiet.

"Clew? Are you still there?"

"You know if you marry her, you'll have to be a family again, right? You do realize that?"

The line goes silent again.

I give him plenty of time to respond. When he doesn't, I say, "So I guess it really was us, wasn't it? It's not that you didn't want a family. You just didn't want our family."

"It's not like that. I never should have said that. I just didn't know how to say it, and so I said it wrong."

"Is it true you and Mom are selling the house?"

"We're thinking about it. Nothing's definite."

"Is that why you've been sending care packages? To get my stuff out of there?"

"I sent you those things because I thought you might want them."

"Well, I don't care what you do with the rest of it. Light a match and burn it all to the ground if you want." As I say it, I immediately want to take it back. My things are not to blame here. They shouldn't be the victims.

And suddenly I'm adding it all up—kicking us out, selling

342

the house. He probably knew he'd do this all along. That's why I couldn't find his Nirvana shirt. It was already at her place, folded in some drawer or sitting on some closet shelf. And this woman will be using my mother's things and my parents' things and *our* things, and living our life, only in some new and improved version that doesn't include my mom or me.

Before I can say anything else, he says, "I know I'm going to see you soon and we can talk more then, but there are some things I need you to know right now. First, I don't want you to ever doubt how I feel about you. While I haven't always been the dad you might create on paper, I love you very much. Second, I won't always meet your expectations in the future, but it won't be for lack of trying."

As he talks, I start to pinch the flesh of my arm. But then I just let it go.

"It takes a while to get to know your parents. You're lucky enough to have a really special mother. I'm not sure that even you can fully appreciate the truth in that, but you'll discover it as you get older. I'm not quite as special—you know that and I know that—but I hope the years ahead will also show you just how much I care about you and how important you are to me, no matter how much I fuck things up."

And even though I'm used to hearing my dad swear, I don't want him to do this—tell me he loves me and be all sensitive and real. I want to hate him. I sit there trying to hate him.

"I don't want to see her. Michelle." I can barely say her name.

"You don't have to. Not right now."

I don't want to see her ever.

I say nothing. He waits.

Finally he lets out this sad little sigh. "We can talk more when you get home. We'll go to the bakery and buy their entire stock of

343

thumbprint cookies. We'll buy as many as it takes. We'll buy the whole fucking bakery."

"We can't just go to Joy Ann like normal, like all of this didn't happen. Like all of this isn't happening. Things like you and me and Joy Ann died when you sent us away."

"They don't have to, Clew. Not even when you're in college. Not even when you're in California being a famous writer." Then he says, "I love you more than Beethoven and the Joy Ann Cake Shop and my Nirvana shirt you're always stealing. I love you more than anything."

And now he's taking the thing I do with Saz and using it to try to win me over, and this is the last straw. I hang up without telling him I love him too.

I find Miah outside his house, shirtless, bent over a pile of bones and a bucket of bleach water that makes my eyes sting from the smell. Music blasts from this ancient-looking radio and at first he doesn't see me.

I stand watching him and he looks lost and happy in the work, the way he was that day with the Outward Bounders, only this time I need to bring him out of it.

"Doesn't that ever feel morbid? All these bones?" It comes out angry, like I'm accusing him of something. I reach over and turn the music down.

He's dunking each one in the bucket. "Think of it as that junk-yard you're always talking about, where love goes to die. Think of these as survivors. The things that remain. Like the love that lives to see another day."

I say, "What happens to us in a week?"

He stands, shaking the hair out of his eyes. "What do you mean?"

"What happens to us?"

"I don't know."

"Have you even thought about it?"

"Yeah, I've thought about it. Of course I've thought about it. I'm not just like, 'Wham, bam, thank you, ma'am. Thanks for a great summer.'"

"Be serious."

"I am. I don't know what happens with us, Captain. I don't even know what happens with me. Maybe I'm going, maybe I'm staying. Maybe five years from now I'll be here in this exact same spot, ferrying back and forth between my mom's house and here, bleaching the bones and thinking about the girl I knew one summer. Back when we were Claude and Miah. Wild-animal-wrangling, shark-tooth-collecting, freedom-dispensing warriors."

"Don't make a joke. Not right now."

"Sorry." He sits down on the top step of the porch, wet hands dangling off his knees. "Captain, we're two people who didn't expect to meet each other but did, probably years before we were supposed to."

"I've never met anyone like you."

"I've never met anyone like you, either. I won't again because I'm pretty sure there aren't a lot of Claude Henrys running around in this world. But we can't borrow trouble."

"So what do we do with that?"

"I don't know. I can't imagine saying goodbye to you, and I can't imagine a version of us where we call and text each other like we're everyone else."

"Then what's the point of all this?"

I want it to be four weeks ago, with the summer stretched out before us. But it isn't, and I suddenly have to go away from him, because I can't just stand here and pretend to be in the moment when in my head it's already time for him to leave and I'm watching him sail away from this island and me forever.

He says, "Come sit by me. . . ."

"I have to go."

"Don't run away."

"I can't stay, because if I stay, I'll lose it, and I don't want to lose it. I want you to remember me like this." I smile and then point to my smile like, *Ta-da*. "So I'm not running away from you; I'm running away from you leaving and me leaving. Just for a little while. Just long enough to catch my breath."

And before he can say anything else or try to stop me, I run.

The beach is empty except for the gulls and the sandpipers. I walk across the sand, straight into the water. The wind is trying to push me back onto the shore, but I push against it, deeper and deeper until the drop-off happens and I go under suddenly, all at once, arms extending up toward the surface on their own, without any direction from me, reaching for air.

I force my body down, down, down, imagining what it would be like to live here in this other world. The anger burns so big and deep inside me that I'm surprised I don't sink from the weight of it. Anger at my dad, my mom, Michelle, Saz, Yvonne, Grady, everyone, even Miah.

I hold my breath until my lungs are empty and I go lightheaded and my body pulls me to the surface. The world tilts as I suck in air, and I think of the female loggerheads and how it must feel to be unable to stand, crawling up on shore, collapsing there, disoriented and lost.

I tell myself, *Feel this. Feel every last terrible, uncomfortable, overwhelming part of it. You have to feel it to get to the other side.*

I drag myself out of the water and drop onto the sand. I lie there and stare up at the sky and think about my cousin Danny. I think about all the things he will miss, all the things he will never get to see or experience. But there are other things he'll never know—pain and secrets and the way it feels when your heart breaks in two.

I walk back to the general store, and now I am thinking about my parents. My dad telling me he loves me. My mom needing to be a mom. And then I picture saying goodbye to Miah next week. All of this is the reason I call Saz again to tell her I love her.

She answers right away. She says, "I love you too."

"More than shark teeth and loggerhead turtles and blood moons."

"More than pizza without pineapple and sleepovers and Yvonne. More than anything or anyone."

I say, "What happens to your room after you go to school?"

"Nothing. My parents are keeping it the exact same for when I come home. Remember how when Mara's sister went off to college, her parents immediately turned it into an exercise room? My mom was like, 'I'll go to the Municipool in a bikini before I do that to yours.'"

I take a breath. Let it out. "My parents are selling our house. Which means my green room will be someone else's green room, until they paint it some other color, and my house will be someone else's house, and they will move in and change it completely."

And I don't know which is worse—for a room to be turned into something different or for it to not be your room at all anymore, ever.

"You know, you're not the same Claude Henry who lived on Capri Lane in a green room with a canopy bed. Besides, you'll always have a home with me, Hen."

For one long second, I can't speak. Then, somehow, I manage to say, "I miss you, Sazzy."

"I miss you too."

"I wish you were here."

"You know I am, right? There? Even though you can't see me."

And maybe she is and maybe she isn't, and maybe I do know it and maybe I don't. The point is, it's what you say to your best friend when you don't know what else to say, and all you want to do is be there for them and make the bad things go away.

Which is why I say, "I know."

DAY 28

I ride my bike to Rosecroft. Except for two wild horses on the edge of the trees, the place is deserted. I go up the steps and past the NO TRESPASSING sign until I'm standing in the ruins. I pick my way through, room by room, carefully stepping over bricks and debris until I am in the heart.

I stand there and I see it—not Claudine's house, but mine.

Over here is the living room, and the window—the one closest to the front door—I left unlocked for Saz, like the ones she left open for me at her house down the street, in case we couldn't sleep.

And here, in front of this same window, is where we placed our Christmas tree so that you could see it from the street because there's nothing like going up the walk on a cold winter night and seeing those lights. The piano sat across from it, against that wall there, opposite the sofa. I hated practicing, but for years I took lessons with Ms. Gernhoffer, who would get so frustrated with me that her wig would be crooked by the time I was done. My dad played the piano best of all of us, and Bradbury would just howl and howl. "Jingle Bells" was Bradbury's favorite. We hung our stockings by the fireplace here in the basement family room.

Over here is the porch, which looks out over the creek. My dad screened it in so that the dog and the cat could enjoy it too. The five of us—Mom, Dad, Claude, Bradbury, Dandelion—used to sit out here after dinner and listen to the woods.

These height markers in the kitchen doorway, that was something my mom did—measured everyone who came to the house, even the adults, even the pets. My bathroom was this one, in the upstairs hall. If you look closely, you can still see the dent in the tub from where I threw my hairbrush at it the first day of middle school, when my hair just wouldn't cooperate.

This was my mom's office, with the floor-to-ceiling bookcases my dad built one weekend after we first moved in so that every one of her research books would have a home. This is the chair I would sit in while she worked, reading and helping her when I could, and learning to find the story in everything. This is where I first started writing stories, back when I was ten.

My parents' room was this one at the end of the hall, looking out over the creek. This is where my mom and I had the talk about Santa Claus and, later, the talk about sex. This is where Dandelion used to sit on my dad's dresser every morning, knocking all his things off one by one until Dad got up to feed *the goddamn cat*.

And this big green room with the slanted walls was mine. It was filled with music and space for dancing. My books lined this wall. My closet was here, but most of the clothes lived on the floor. The canopy bed was over there. The posters were here and here and here. My desk—the one where I first started writing my bad, overly long novel—was in front of this window. And this window was the one where I stood while I watched Wyatt Jones and his friends toilet-paper my yard before my dad interrupted them. . . .

I sit on the green of the grass, the green of my floor, until I can see every last detail.

* * *

An hour later I am on the steps, leaning back against one of the columns. Through my shirt, the brick feels rough and cool. I pull out my pen and notebook and write.

I lose track of time. No counting days or minutes. No worrying about how much time has passed or how much is left in the day. I fill up pages with thoughts and scenes and pieces of me. I write until my hand cramps, and then I close my eyes and rest my head on the cool, rough brick.

When I open my eyes again, it's sunset. The sky is pink and gold and orange. I sit watching as it grows brighter and then darker as the sun begins to fade. I write *twenty-eighth sunset* because that's how many I've seen here. And then I pack up my things and head home.

That night I leave the window open and fall asleep to the hum of the cicadas. Sometime around midnight Miah slips into my room, into my bed. I feel his skin and his chest and his breath on my neck as he pulls me into him.

"Here's what I know," he says. "I'm right here. We're right here. I can't tell you what the point of this is except that I'm so fucking happy I met you, and I can't tell you what's going to happen tomorrow or next week or next summer or five years from now. But I do know that right now, in this moment, on this island, I'm where I'm supposed to be, and that's with you."

DAYS 29–30

I wish there was a way to freeze time. Like if this was a Ray Bradbury story and we were each given five chances in our lives to stop time for as long as we wanted so that we could live in a certain moment indefinitely.

On days 29 and 30, this is what I wish for. The ability to breathe because he is here and I am here and no one is leaving.

THE ISLAND

THREE

DAY 31

The day before he leaves, it rains. My mom stands in the living room, papers spread across the floor like tiles. She scans the pages, glasses on the end of her nose. Every now and then she moves the papers around, stands back, scans them again. Dandelion walks in, sits on one of the stacks, and starts washing his face. She picks him up and sets him on the couch.

"What are these?"

"Letters written immediately following Tillie's death. Apparently there was an inquest before the police officially concluded it was suicide."

"Was her husband a suspect?"

"For, like, a second, but never seriously, no. His devotion to her was widely known. And the coroner's report"—she taps one of the papers with her foot—"was pretty conclusive that she killed herself."

We stand side by side, staring down at the papers. Pieces of a life. I want to sit on the floor right now and read all of them. I want to help my mom put them in order so that we can get the clearest picture of Tillie before and after, so that we can solve the mystery of *why* once and for all.

But Miah is waiting. My heart does this little tug.

I say, "I'm going to Miah's."

"Okay." She is distracted, and I can see that she's deep in it, taking the puzzle apart and putting it back together as she stands here.

"He leaves tomorrow and I may be back late."

She gathers her hair, ties it in a ponytail, and frowns at me. The glasses are green and I remember when she got them, on a road trip with my dad and me, at a drugstore in Memphis.

"How late is late?"

"The morning?"

"Claude."

"Mom. You'll know where I am, and if you want to come get me and bring me back here, you can. But this is important to me."

"What exactly am I supposed to say here? If I tell you no, I'm standing in the way of you and this boy and you may resent me forever or at least for a long, long time. If I say yes, I'm the world's most negligent mother, someone my own mother would disown in a heartbeat, if she only knew."

"How about 'I get it'? How about 'I don't love it, but I get it, because I remember what it was like to be eighteen and in love, and you are a semi-responsible adult who will soon go to college and I will long for the day you asked my permission to spend the night with a trustworthy boy who doesn't drink and who makes art out of bones'?"

"He makes art out of bones?"

"Animal, not human, and maybe I should have left that out." She settles onto the arm of the couch and studies me. "You told me when we got here to let you know what I needed. I need this," I say. "Please."

She sighs. "Are you really in love?"

"I think so."

We look at each other for a long time. And then she says, "Go."

* * *

Miah and I drive down Main Road, and neither of us is saying anything because we don't have to. The weather says it all. Dreary. Wet. Gray. No matter how much he talks about living in the moment, I know he's feeling it like I am—our time here has run out. I'm telling myself it's all going to be fine.

Halfway to Rosecroft, he pulls off on the side of the road at a break in the trees and a path that leads into the forest. He digs through the glove compartment and then the center console until he comes up with a ring of keys, shining gold and silver against the bleakness of the day.

He climbs out of the truck and comes around to my side, opens my door. We walk together, hand in hand, fingers entwined, over the damp leaves under the live oaks.

"Where are we going?"

"You'll see."

Several yards later, we arrive at an arched and rusted gate with an old-fashioned lock and a NO TRESPASSING sign. He tries one key after another until he finds the right one.

I say, "What is this place?" The rain is pouring, relentless and resolute, as if it will always fall like this for the rest of our lives. Taking off my fisherman's cap, I just give in to it, and within seconds I am drenched, head to toe.

"Behavior Cemetery." He pushes open the gate.

And then I see the graves: flat gray rectangles all in a line, rugged markers that jut up out of the earth, plain headstones covered in moss, carved angels with hands outstretched or folded in prayer.

Miah says to the cemetery and the trees and the sky, "We ask permission of the dead to enter."

Then we're inside, the rain falling in a steady, tapping chorus.

Some of the graves are covered in flowers, books, dishes, cups, oil lamps.

"There's a belief that the spirits of the dead stick around, and the only way to keep them from bothering the living is to give them a kind of offering, things that belonged to them when they were alive." His voice is hushed, as if the dead might hear him. "The lamps are to light their way through the unknown."

We walk each row, reading the epitaphs, words of love and loss, the names and dates, and sweet, sad lines from Rudyard Kipling and J. M. Barrie and Oscar Wilde.

THIS IS A BRIEF LIFE, BUT IN ITS BREVITY IT OFFERS US SOME SPLENDID MOMENTS, SOME MEANINGFUL ADVENTURES.

SECOND STAR TO THE RIGHT AND STRAIGHT ON TILL MORNING.

TO LIVE IS THE RAREST THING IN THE WORLD. MOST PEOPLE EXIST, THAT IS ALL.

At the end of a row, beside her mother, is Claudine Blackwood. SHE REFUSED TO BE BORED CHIEFLY BECAUSE SHE WASN'T BORING. It's Zelda Fitzgerald.

"I love Zelda too," I say.

There are names I recognize and names I don't.

I say, "There are so many stories here that no one outside this island will ever know."

"All the more reason to write them down."

We make our way into the African American section of the cemetery, past Clovis and Aurora and Beatrice Samms, their graves covered in flowers. A lantern rests on Clovis's headstone, the light burning bright in the gloom of the day.

"Who's in charge of the lantern?"

"Technically, Clovis's family, but the Park Service keeps an eye on it too. And I check in on it now and then. Make sure it doesn't go out."

At the far end of the graveyard is a crumbling stone wall, shoulder height, curved like a half-moon. We climb up on it, and Miah tells me the stories of our adventures so that I'm reliving them from his point of view. He tells me about how he felt the first time I found a shark tooth on my own. He tells me how he'll always think of me whenever he sees a firefly light up. He tells me about our night at the ruins and how it forever changed the way he sees them. He talks about us getting stuck in the pluff mud and how there's no one else on earth he'd rather be stuck with.

His tone is light but I don't feel light.

I say, "What are we doing?"

"Sitting here on this really awesome wall."

"Be serious. Do you leave tomorrow and that's it, I never see you again?"

"Maybe?"

"I don't want to leave."

"I don't want to leave either." He takes my hand and rubs the top of it with his thumb.

"So what if we don't leave? What if we stay right here?"

"In the cemetery?"

"In the cemetery. On the island. We keep it going—this. You come see me in New York. I go see you in Montana." I want him to fight for me, fight for us.

He rubs his jaw. "Okay. You blow off college. I'll blow off Outward Bound."

"This isn't a joke."

"I'm not joking."

And for a minute I let myself pretend it could happen, Miah and me. Us. Living here in his bright blue house under this bright blue sky, having adventures and never once worrying about disappearing floors because instead there will be sand and grass and an ocean to wade in.

He sighs. "Or."

"Don't say *or*."

"Okay." There are raindrops on his hair and face and lashes. "Captain, you've got places to go in this world. Stories to write. Adventures to have. Would I rather have those adventures with you? Abso-fuckin'-lutely. But I don't know how that works."

"You could come to New York with me. There are all these great schools there with photography programs. And all these places to photograph. I mean, it's an island too. Just a different sort of island." But even as I say it, I know he will never go to New York.

"Captain. Have you met me? I'd be miserable there."

And something in it sounds so final.

"So that's it?"

"I hope not. But we have right now. And the rest of today. And tonight. And tomorrow. Those are the things I know."

He smiles, and it's sad but happy.

I give him a sad, happy smile in return.

And then he kisses me, but it's too late. I can feel it in my heart—a little death.

"We should go," he says. "But first. Stand there." He points at one end of the wall, and then he hops down and goes running, barefoot, to the other end.

I am telling myself not to cry. *Don't cry. Don't you do it.* I jump to the ground and stand by the wall.

In a second, I hear him. "You there, Captain?" It's a whisper, coming through the crack by my ear, plain as day. I turn to look at him and he waves.

"Yes," I whisper into the wall.

"What are you most afraid of?"

I almost say, *Missing you. Never seeing you again.* But instead I answer, "Not writing my own story. Not figuring out who I should be. What are you most afraid of?"

"Still you."

We go to his house to dry out. I take a three-minute shower because this is time I'm wasting when we could be together. He gives me a shirt of his and a pair of shorts, and I walk around feeling swallowed up by Jeremiah Crew. I am barefoot and I smell like him.

While he showers, I examine the photos on the walls like I'm at a museum. I study each individual shot. The bones, the ruins, the skeletons of things.

From the bathroom, there is the sound of singing. "Joy to the World," his favorite song.

In his bed, I am still wearing his shirt but the shorts are on the floor. Miah is naked. Outside the window, the rain is falling. I run my fingers across his skin. "If you could change one thing about your body, what would it be?"

"Oh, Jesus, Captain. I don't know. My left big toe."

"I'd get rid of my freckles."

"I like your freckles." He starts tracing the ones on my stomach. "They make me think of summer and long days and sunshine and blood moons."

"I look like I have the measles." And I know I shouldn't be doing this—pointing out the things I don't like about myself—but I'm trying to be light and cheery and free and not think about the time that's passing too quickly. I'm trying not to miss him already because he's still right here.

I stop touching him and raise my arms in the air like I'm conducting a symphony. He takes one of them, examining it as if it's the most fascinating thing in the world, looking at each individual freckle up close. He runs his fingers across my skin. He plants a kiss on my elbow. He rotates my arm a little to the right, to the left, and then kisses the inside of my wrist. The back of my hand is next, followed by my shoulder and my palm.

"What are you doing?"

"I'm kissing all your freckles." He kisses my knee. "Or maybe all of you." He kisses my other knee. "I don't think I've ever kissed you here." And then he kisses my belly button. "Or here." He kisses my ear. On and on, taking his time.

I know without kissing him all over that he has a heart-shaped freckle on his left shoulder and a scar under his chin. I know that the arm hair that is gold in most light turns reddish in the sun. I know that his right big toe is slightly longer than his left big toe and that there is another scar on his left knee.

As he makes his way up my other arm to my shoulder, to my ear, I worry about all this close-up scrutiny of my body in the daylight. The freckles, the little too much flesh here, the not enough flesh there, every bump and flaw. But it's like his photos, real and honest and lovely, and no one has ever done this before. So I let him kiss me. And I stop worrying because it's just Miah and me, and there's no hiding anymore, not even if I wanted to.

"I've never kissed you here," he says. "Or here."

I could just stay. I could live on this island with Jeremiah Crew.

"Or here." He kisses my forehead, and whatever happens with us, I know there will be at least one person in the world who has seen all of me.

As we lie there afterward, he wraps his arms around me, my head on his chest. He says, "I want to spend all day with you tomorrow."

"Me too."

"There are a lot of things we haven't done yet, Captain. I want to take you up north to hunt for oysters. And we need to go camping out at Blue Hollow and canoeing through the marsh."

And I need to keep loving you. And to have you love me. And I need to sleep in your arms because that's when I sleep best, no waking up and lying there for hours. Just peaceful, happy sleep.

"I guess we'll have to come back," I say.

"I guess we will."

I'm determined to stay awake the entire night so that I don't lose a minute. When I feel him fading, I say, "I'm floating."

His voice is dreamy as he says, "I love you too." And he is drifting, drifting.

I want to nudge him awake, to have him repeat it so I can be sure I heard him right. I want to shout, *You actually said it first, even though you don't think you did. You love me, Jeremiah Crew.*

But instead I lie there, feeling him breathe next to me, low and even. He shifts and pulls me closer and I stare up toward the ceiling and let myself live in those four little words.

DAY 32

When I wake up, his side of the bed is empty. I lie there, not wanting to get up, because once I get up, the day will officially start and the countdown to his leaving will begin. Maybe if I just lie here all day, somehow I will freeze time.

"Morning, Captain." He stands in the doorway, already dressed. Black shorts, sky-blue shirt. He says, "This day is a regular shit show." His walkie-talkie buzzes and he glances at it, shakes his head. "Everyone needs something, the way they always need something when they know I have to be somewhere else." He leans over me, kissing me. "Like here with you in this bed."

I try to pull him down onto the bed with me, but he breaks away, groaning a little.

I say, "So what does that mean?"

"That means I have a couple hours of things I have to do, but then I'm all yours."

He smiles.

I smile.

And part of me wonders if maybe he's pretending to be busy to protect himself, because he knows he has to leave and it's better to just get it over with. And part of me wonders if it might be easier to never see him again. I can tell myself I made him up and the summer wasn't real, and go back to Ohio and see Saz and my dad and all my friends, and then go off to college like nothing ever happened.

Except that he happened and we happened, and I just want one more day with him. An entire day, start to finish, with no *This is the end* but instead *I'll see you again someday.*

But no, he's not making it up, because now he is on the walkie-talkie, pacing off down the hall, speaking to some unseen person. I sit up, swing my feet onto the floor, and reach for my clothes.

We are going to meet after lunch and head to the beach. He drops me at the general store, where I buy a new notebook because mine is almost filled. This one is large and fat, with a green cover the color of spartina. I walk home in the sunlight.

Back at Addy's, I find my mom in the kitchen, book in hand, drinking coffee. Her hair is piled up on her head in a messy bun, and she is wearing her BADASS AUTHOR shirt, the one I bought her last Christmas.

"I'm home."

"You're home." She sets down the book. "Everything okay?"

"Yes." I can feel the wall, and I don't want there to be a wall. I hug her and she hugs me back like she can feel it too. Together we knock it down, and then we pull apart because this is the thing about hugs—they have to end sometime even when you don't want them to. I pour juice into two glasses, grab two bowls from the cabinet, open the cereal boxes. She hands me a cup of coffee. Then she nods at the window seat and the package sitting there.

"Is that from him?"

"Yes."

"I told him to stop sending me my things."

"So don't open it." She smiles. "But if I know your dad, that's an apology."

I pick up our bowls and our glasses and our mugs—a balancing act—and take them to the table. I sit with my back to the window seat. My mom sits across from me.

We eat for a moment in silence and then I say, "What was he like when you met him?"

Her hand freezes in midair. She sets her mug down and stares up at the ceiling.

"Complicated. Funny. A little full of himself, but in an endearing way. He believed he could do anything. He wore black because he was going through an artist phase and he felt older than everyone else, and he was this musical genius. I was a little in awe of him." She doesn't ask why I want to know.

"After he graduated from Juilliard, why didn't you stay in New York? Why didn't he try to make it as a musician?"

"Your dad never felt at home there, at the school or in the city. Music has always just come to him, but I don't think the structure of a program like that worked for him."

"But he still could have done something with it."

"It's not easy to make a living as an artist."

I say, "You do it."

"And I feel extremely grateful and also a bit like, *God, I hope they don't find out what a fraud I am.*"

"Do you think you'd still be together if he hadn't given up music?"

"I don't know. I want you to promise me something, though. That you will go out into the world and fulfill all your Claudeness."

"I promise."

We sit, picking up our cereal spoons at the exact same moment, picking up our coffee mugs at the exact same moment, perfectly synchronized.

"Stop it," I say.

"You stop it."

And now we're laughing. And now we're both making the winding-down noise, like a sigh, which gets us started again.

"Mom? I'm going to miss you."

"I'm going to miss you. Something awful. But I'll be coming to New York to see you. I may even bring Dandelion. And it'll be Thanksgiving before you know it. In the meantime I'm going to be cheering you on as you go out and write your life, and I'll be busy being so incredibly proud of who you are."

"What are you going to do?"

"After I take you to New York and drop you at your residence hall and hug you goodbye? Probably eat a pound of Oreos and cry into Dandelion's fur."

"And what are you going to do after that?"

"I don't know." She looks past me, out the window. "Probably stay here for a while. Your aunt Katie wants to come down. And"—she shrugs—"I like it. It feels good. There's work to be done."

"The island has a way of giving you what you need. Like the sunrise. When the world starts over. Miah's friend Shirley calls it *dayclean*."

"*Dayclean.*" She smiles her best Mom smile. "That's lovely."

I say, "I love you more than bike riding and Rosecroft at dusk and words. I love you more than words."

"I love you more than words too." She sits back, both hands around the mug, sunlight catching the gold in her hair. "You know, you get that from him—I love you more than."

"No I don't. Saz and I made it up when we were little."

"You and Saz may have made it your own, but you got it from your dad."

* * *

367

A knock on the door, and it's Jared. He hands me a note with an apologetic smile, and immediately my heart sinks. *This is it. Miah's goodbye.* I almost hand the paper back to Jared, but instead I open it.

> *Captain, putting out fires everywhere. (Not actual ones, thank God.)*
>
> *I'm taking a later boat so we can have some time.*
> *I'll meet you at Addy's tonight at 5 p.m.*
>
> > *Love,*
> > *Miah*

Jared and I bike to the old airfield for a picnic lunch. A horse and her foal graze nearby. Afterward we lie in the grass and watch them. My eyes are heavy from the heat and the meal.

He goes, "Claude?"

I turn my head and he's looking at me, hand shading his eyes.

"Yeah?" I raise my own hand to my eyes so I can see him.

"What does it feel like to be in love?"

I stretch my arms over my head and turn my eyes and face skyward. I take my time answering because I'm not sure how to answer. It's more emotion than words, and I've never really thought about how to describe it. I think of the fear and doubt and worry that come with all this *feeling*. The questioning and the opening up about every little thing until you feel like a frog on a dissection table, completely exposed. The caring too much, or maybe just enough, and the scariness that comes with that. The fact that there is one person on this earth who has the ability to hurt you more than any other because that's how much you love them. The having to trust that they won't and that maybe, just maybe, they mean what they say and that, at least for a while, they can be your floor.

Finally I say, "When it's with the right person, you feel invincible and seen and at home, no matter where you are in the world."

He sighs. "I'd like to feel invincible."

Afterward we bike back to the inn and he sneaks me into the Blackwood Suite, where the Secret Drawer Society letters live. The room is airy and bright, and the desk takes up one entire wall. It looks as if it's sleeping, a great hulking giant. Two suitcases sit by the dresser. Clothes hang in the closet.

"Someone's staying in here?"

Jared says, "It's okay. I asked permission."

I'm not sure if I believe him, but it's too late—he's reaching his hand deep inside the giant's mouth, the recesses of the desk drawer, and pulling out a fistful of letters. He hands them to me and together we read.

Father to son, mother to daughter, husband to wife, sister to brother, friend to friend. Words of wisdom and longing and love. Apologies, poems, a marriage proposal, an epitaph. Sometimes the notes are anonymous. Some are just a sentence or two; others are pages long.

I say, "What's the oldest letter you've read?"

"Uh . . . 1994, I think."

"Is that as far back as they go?"

"We clean them out now and then to make room for new ones. There are boxes of them up in the attic here."

"So there could be some in there from the Blackwoods."

"There are for sure some Blackwood letters in there. One of the Blackwoods actually started the SDS."

"Claudine?"

"Her mother."

And he points to the wall above the desk, where a simple gold frame hangs. Inside the frame is a note, the size of a postcard, written in black ink on light blue paper, edges yellowed. The handwriting is neat and elegant and perfectly slanted, as if it's bowing.

> *Dear Friend,*
>   *Welcome to the Secret Drawer Society. You're invited to leave letters, notes, souvenirs. Write it down, whatever it is. Your words matter. Tuck them in here, where they will be kept safe.*
>   *Sincerely yours,*
>   *Tillie Donaldson Blackwood*
>   *September 23, 1933*

Five years before she died, and the year that Claudine was born.

I feel a chill go through me, and then something more—a kind of lightning warmth. As far as I know, this right here is the only piece of Tillie correspondence that remains. A lovely, romantic legacy from a vibrant, alive woman. I pull out my phone and take a photo of the letter.

Before we leave, I add one of my own.

Dear Claude, write your own story. Love, me.

Back at Addy's, I sit on the window seat and pick up the package, which is heavier than it looks. I give it a good shake and it rattles. Whatever is in here will never be enough apology, but I open it anyway.

Inside is a mound of Christmas tissue paper, silver and blue with snowflakes. On top, a postcard. *Welcome to Ohio, worst of the Midwest,* it says over a photo of the giant blue arch over I-70 that welcomes you to the state. Underneath the arch stretches a flat, endless highway. *We have fields! Corn! Pigs! Meth! And more fields!*

I flip it over. On the back, my dad has written:

> Dear Clew,
>
>   I'm thinking you can't find this on the island and you're probably really craving it by now. If you can eat up all of them before you leave, I'll be beyond impressed. Awed, even. Bring the survivors (if there are any) home, and I promise to make them for you. I love you.
>
> > Love,
> > Your dad, such as he is.
> > For better or worse, like
> > it or not. The dad you're
> > stuck with, who doesn't
> > deserve you, but will
> > always love you, no
> > matter what.

I set the card aside and dig through the tissue, and suddenly I'm blinking and blinking as hard as I can because I will not cry. *I will not cry.* I will not forgive him and I will not cry.

Five minutes later, I'm wiping my face with a washcloth and staring at my red, puffy eyes in the bathroom mirror. I go back into the dining room, back to the window seat, where I've lined up the contents of the package, one by one. Twelve boxes of Kraft macaroni and cheese.

* * *

It's five o'clock when Miah drives up to Addy's in his truck. I hear him coming and run to meet him on the porch.

He says, "I'm sorry, Captain. Someone broke into the Park Service office, two of the Outward Bound campers are lost, Bram and Shirley need me to close up their house, and my sister called."

"Is your mom okay?"

"I don't know yet."

He rests his forehead against mine and whispers, "Let's just run away."

"Yes," I say. "Let's do it."

He closes his eyes and I close mine.

After a moment, he pulls away and lets out this long sigh. "I'm going to charter off at nine-forty-five tonight. That gives us a little more time."

He gives me a sad smile, and he's trying his best to make it seem bright and normal, and then there's this instant when the smile vanishes and he's looking *into* me, so deep I can feel it.

He says, "I've got a few more things to do and then I'll come find you."

Suddenly it washes over me—this sinking feeling. I try to shove it aside. I tell myself it's just sadness over him leaving and the fact that our time on the island is at an end. But it's more than that. I feel this flash of panic because something in me is saying, *This is it. This is your goodbye.*

"What is it, Captain?"

He's smiling again but his eyes are worried. I can tell he thinks it's true, that he'll come find me.

"Nothing," I say. Because I have this need to chase away the worry, to look into his eyes right now and see only me.

Then he kisses me, and it's just kissing. Nothing more. But somehow it means the most of all.

DAY 32

(PART TWO)

I'm sitting at dinner and trying to focus on the conversation, but my eyes are on the door, watching for Miah. I've told myself I was being dramatic earlier. Of course he's going to come find me. Then I have this vision of him appearing, just like he promised, and me not seeing him, and him leaving, no chance to say goodbye.

I say to my mom, "I'll be right back. Bathroom." I slip out of the dining room and past the bathroom to the wide double doors that lead onto the front lawn, which is empty. I wait for a minute. Two minutes. And then I slink back to the table and sit down.

Mom glances at me but doesn't say anything.

Jared brings in dessert and tells me he's going off-island tomorrow for a few days to visit friends. He says, "You have to let me know when you're back."

And I say, "I'm not sure I'll be back anytime soon. But if you're here, then maybe I'll come see you."

"Well, you're always welcome here on the Island of Misfit Toys. You're one of us now." Wednesday walks past and I wave. She waves back.

I say, "I'm honored to be one of you."

And then Jared throws his arms around me and hugs me so hard I can't breathe. "I'm glad I met you," he whispers in my ear.

"I'm glad I met you, too."

He walks away and I sit a little straighter, blinking away the tears that have sprung up for some reason. I push the dessert around on my plate and set down my fork.

My mom is talking and the other guests are talking, but they are like background music. It's 9:21 and his charter leaves at 9:45.

Nine-twenty-two.

Nine-twenty-three.

Nine-twenty-four.

At 9:25, I don't say anything to my mom or the people at our table. I just get up and walk out. This time I go upstairs to the main floor and out the front door.

Outside it's dark and the rain is falling, just a sprinkling now, and the stars are emerging like flowers, hesitant but hopeful, and the cicadas are humming and it is summer everywhere.

I stand on the porch and watch for his truck. Tonight there will be headlights because the lightning bugs, like the stars, have gone momentarily dim from the rain. I will see the truck before I hear it, if he's coming from the south.

Nine-twenty-eight.

I splash down the front steps, the little dips and hollows in the old wood collecting puddles. I stand at the bottom, in the drive, the rain wetting my skin and my hair and my dress. I look south and north because he could be coming from anywhere.

Nine-thirty-one.

I tell myself he's running late as always. He's probably packing feverishly and trying to close up the little blue house and Bram and Shirley's house. He's probably putting out a fire or helping the Outward Bound campers who aren't lost anymore but found because of him. He's probably loading the boat before he comes to tell me goodbye.

Nine-thirty-five.

I will meet him at the boat. I take off my shoes and run down the drive, underneath the live oaks that are out of some ancient fairyland, toward the water. I run down the path littered with shells, barely feeling the way their sharp little edges jab into the soles of my feet, and I am looking for headlights as I go. I don't stop running until I'm at the dock.

Which is empty.

I stand for a long time, staring out over the water, black and endless except for the glow of lights in the far distance. And this, I know, is the mainland. It might as well be light-years away.

I wait for a boat to appear.

I wait for Miah to come.

I wait.

I wait.

Suddenly, I don't feel the rain on my skin or my hair or my clothes because the only thing I feel is the ache in my heart. An ache like I've never felt before. It's both terrible and beautiful. And it fills me. It fills me.

We were supposed to have more time.

We're always supposed to have more time.

I sink onto the bench, which is damp and which leaves me damper. At some point the rain stops completely. I look up and the stars overhead are a carpet of light. There's this feeling I have here. Miah's a part of it. But he's not all of it. It's the summers of childhood when I was eight, ten, twelve. And those kinds of beautiful moments where everything is full of love and light and possibility.

I rest one hand on the wood of the seat and my fingers bump into something cool and smooth. I look down. A shark tooth. The largest one I've ever seen. And there, drawn around it, a circle.

* * *

I turn back up the path and walk toward the inn, shark tooth in my pocket. Through the trees, the porch lights shine like beacons, like lanterns illuminating the way to the world beyond. I go up the steps, feet splashing in the little dips in the wood. I slip on my shoes, brush the hair off my face, but otherwise I don't bother. This is me, take it or leave it—wet and rumpled and missing Miah.

"Claude?" Mom's voice calls out to me from the end of the porch. She is perched on the edge of the swing, as if she's been watching for me. I walk over and sit down beside her, a lump in my throat as large as the ocean.

"Everything okay?" she says. And she knows. I can see it in her face.

"It will be." But my heart doesn't believe it.

She takes my hand, and the swing rocks back and forth, back and forth, as we listen to the rain.

At 9:53, I feel it. The island is emptier because he's no longer on it.

I don't want to go home yet, so I head to the beach, not caring if I run into alligators or snakes or wild hogs. Under the trees, over the dunes, onto the sand, until I'm beneath the moon and all this sky. I'm too restless to sit. I drop my bag and kick off my shoes and walk. The tide rolls in like thunder and I'm the only one here.

I walk for at least a mile. I'm trying not to look at the lights in the distance, the ones that are the neighboring islands. Because beyond those islands is the mainland, and on that mainland is Jeremiah Crew, who didn't say goodbye.

The old me would have told myself he didn't care, that I didn't mean to him what he meant to me, and that's why he left without seeing me even though he told me he would come.

But I know it isn't true.

He didn't come because—what was it he said the day he was bleaching the bones? *I can't imagine saying goodbye to you.*

The waves thunder in. The waves thunder out.

I move to the soft sand high above the tide line. And then, for some reason, I start thinking about my parents. Maybe there's no one answer to why they had to end. And there's no one answer to how to make love last. My parents were two people who loved each other for a long time. Until they didn't. But that doesn't change the fact that they once loved each other and that they'll always love me.

I am so busy thinking about this that I almost miss it—the markings of a path leading to the ocean. I tell myself it's probably a ghost crab or a raccoon. I bend over, studying the path, which is almost like a single tire track, deeper ridges on the outside, fainter ridges on the inside.

My heart starts hammering away, and I scramble to find the start of the trail, which is from a nest up against the dunes. *Please don't let the path end.* For some reason, it can't.

I follow it down, down, down, until it disappears into the water. And maybe the tracks ended before the tide rolled in, or maybe the hatchling made it all the way. I tell myself it made it all the way.

I scan the ocean, as far as I can see, searching for any sign of this brave survivor even though I know it's long gone by now, and the thought of it out there in the world makes me want to cry. *Good for you,* I think. *I hope you make it as far as Africa.*

And then I gaze out at the distant glow on the horizon that is the mainland and think about Jeremiah Crew, who is also out there somewhere. I may never see him again, and the thought of never seeing him again is a cold, sharp knife. But maybe he was right. Maybe it doesn't matter where I go or what I do or who I know— I'll always have Claude and Miah, Miah and Claude, forever.

I say, "Jeremiah Crew, I hope you're on your way to the airport. I hope you get on that plane to Montana and don't look back."

I walk until I find my pile of things and then I drop onto the sand and dig in my bag and pull out two notebooks, one blue and one green. I open the battered cover of the blue one and flip through the pages, reading by the moonlight every word I've written since I've been here. Every thought, good and bad, every ache, every longing, every adventure.

Hemingway once said, "All you have to do is write one true sentence. Write the truest sentence that you know." So I don't think about Mr. Russo telling me I don't feel deeply enough, and I don't think about whether or not it's going to be any good. I open the blank green notebook—the color of spartina—and start to write.

You were my first. Not just sex, although that was part of it, but the first to look past everything else into me.

Some of the names and places have been changed, but the story is true. It's all here because one day this will be the past, and I don't want to forget what I went through, what I thought, what I felt, who I was. I don't want to forget you.

But most of all, I don't want to forget me.

DAY 35

I ride my bicycle down Main Road, under the green, green canopy of trees. I feel the sun on my face and the wind in my hair. The day is bright. I am bright.

I roll to a stop and I can see his house from where I am. I want to sit on his front step and wait for him to come back and take me on adventures. Take me treasure hunting. Take me for a walk on the beach under the moon. Kiss me in the rain in a cemetery by a whispering wall.

I don't think, I just hit play, and suddenly this song is blasting in my ears—his favorite song, the one that will always belong to him, and to the two of us dancing through the ruins, under the fog. And he is there, smile half-cocked, staring down at me like I'm a miracle. *You,* I hear him say, *are spectacular, Claudine Llewelyn Henry.*

Him. Me.

Me. Him.

Us. Intertwined. Hands on my face, in my hair, trailing down my back, his fingers—soft as a cloud—on my skin, where no boy had gone before. But it's more than this. It's muddy feet and locked basements and blood moons and all the things we said to each other when no one else was listening.

I think of all the reasons I love him.

Like the jolt of his touch. Which is a kind of lightning. An electric current. Not enough to kill you, but enough to leave you wired and hungry and alive.

Like the fact that he smells like tomorrow, if tomorrow had a smell.

Like a shirt you've worn in just enough.

A sunset over a cornfield, the kind that turns everything gold and warm.

Sheets just out of the dryer.

Fresh snow.

He is all of these things and home.

The song ends and the quiet is filled with the steady, shimmering hum of cicadas, as if the air itself is singing. The sun beats down, heavy on my skin. The ferry will be here in an hour and I need to get back to the house. But for a moment I am rooted to this sandy path, staring past the horses, tails flickering, that graze in the grass, and the great sweeping arms of the live oaks, dripping with Spanish moss. At the blue rocking chairs and the various bones and skulls—bleached a hard, bright white—gathered in one corner of the porch. His house is quiet, no signs of life. His truck is parked out front, dusty from our last beach trip.

I wave away a bug. Touch the back of my neck where my hair has grown out a little. It's still short. I think I like it this way. The freckles on my face and shoulders have multiplied since the beginning of summer, but I don't mind them as much as I used to. I feel taller. Older. Good and right in my own skin. But still like myself. Claude Before and After.

Here we laughed. Here we fought. Here we loved and dreamed. Here is where the fire started. Here is where the first brick fell. Here is where the floor disappeared. Here is where I built a new one underneath my feet.

And here is where I began.

The last thing he said to me: *I've got a few more things to do and then I'll come find you.* I tell myself if I stand here long enough, he might appear. And then I almost see him, walking toward me down the path. Bare feet. Shirt untucked. Face lit up at the sight of me. Ready for our next adventure.

ACKNOWLEDGMENTS

At the end of my senior year of high school, days after I turned eighteen, my dad came into my bedroom and told me that he and my mom were splitting up. All my life, it had been the three of us—Mom, Dad, me. My parents were everything. And suddenly, my world turned upside down. I couldn't get my bearings. It was as if the floor beneath me had disappeared. I wasn't allowed to say anything about the separation to anyone, which made it even more painful. Five days after graduation, my mom and I moved away from my Indiana hometown—leaving behind my childhood home, my dad, my dog, my best friend, and the boy I liked—to the mountains of North Carolina. It was a summer of lasts and firsts, and all these years later, that time of my life is still a very emotional place to visit.

Breathless is the book I never thought I'd write. It is, in many ways, even more personal for me than *All the Bright Places*. It's the book I needed when I was sixteen, seventeen, eighteen. But it's not a story I could write without the support and encouragement of a great many people.

Seven years ago, my literary agent, Kerry Sparks, took a chance on me, believed in me, and changed my life forever—both personally and professionally—in ways glittering and unimaginable. She is electric sunshine, brilliant and amazing, mama bear supreme when she needs to be, super-savvy editor, dear, hilarious friend, and my absolute hero on this earth. Thank you to Kerry and to everyone at Levine Greenberg Rostan Literary Agency for all you are and all you do.

Knopf's Melanie Nolan is one of the very best editors I've ever had the privilege of working with. From that first lunch, where we bonded over *Little Darlings* and I knew she just *got it,* to our cowboy-boot shopping spree to every astute, insightful, aha-inducing note, and the way in which she has so giftedly offered guidance, while at the same time cultivating and nurturing my creative freedom, our collaboration has been invaluable. I am honored to work with her.

I have the most wonderful home at Penguin Random House, and the most wonderful publishing family. Deepest, heartfelt, unceasing thanks to Barbara Marcus, Felicia Frazier, Judith Haut, Jillian Vandall, Dominique Cimina, Morgan Maple, Arely Guzmán, Pam White, Jocelyn Lange, Lauren Morgan, John Adamo, Elizabeth Ward, Kelly McGauley, Jenn Inzetta, Alison Impey, Adrienne Waintraub, Emily DuVal, Megan Mitchell, Jake Eldred, Kate Keating, Noreen Herits, Gillian Levinson, Karen Sherman, Artie Bennett, and everyone else there who has helped bring this book into the world. You are eternally some of my brightest places. Also immense gratitude for artist Tito Merello, whose exquisite painting of Claude and Miah brought them to life on the cover.

My fabulous UK editor, Ben Horslen, and the entire Penguin Random House UK family are also the brightest of places. I send them one million thank-yous and my undying appreciation for this, our third literary journey together. Thank-yous and undying appreciation as well to Sylvie Rabineau and Lauren Szurgot of WME for their faith and enthusiasm in my books and me. With them in my corner, I feel like I can conquer the world—and I want to be both of them when I grow up.

I have enormous love and thanks for the generous, welcoming folks of Sapelo Island, especially Chris and Barbara Bailey, as well as the folks of the Outer Banks and Cumberland Island. (Jared Hilliard, I'm fortunate to not only call you my friend but to include you in this story!) I had the privilege of sharing some memorable summer evenings of dinner and wine with fellow bibliophile and friend Lisa

Langshaw, who died before I could finish this one, but whose effervescent soul lives on in Addy.

My delightful, what-would-I-do-without-her assistant, Briana Bailey (all mentions of wild hogs are for you!). And my terrific social media assistants, Mackenzie and Lila Vanacore, whose expertise and inspired ideas fill me with awe on a daily basis. Special shout-out to Kenzie for letting me share her profound words, mixing them with my own, for Wednesday's last speech to Claude, the one about breaking free of boxes.

My very first reader, Justin Conway (more on him in a moment), who is also a dynamite editor. And my earliest young readers, Briana Bailey, Annalise von Sprecken, Mackenzie and Lila, Katie-May Taylor, and Gabriel Duval. As well as Kerry Kletter, who is not only one of the best editors I know, she's also one of the very best writers. (Seriously, please do yourselves a favor and go buy all of her books right now!) Speaking of excellent writers who are dear friends, Angelo Surmelis and Ronni Davis are a very important part of my floor. They hold me up and make me laugh and love me, freckles and all.

Thank you to The Lovelies for making it lovely, and Lisa Brucker, Grecia Reyes, Krista Ramirez, Beth Jennings White, Megan White, Jennifer Koerner, Shari Franklin, Logan Franklin, Karen and Jon Preble, and Janet Geddis (whose Avid Bookshop is THE BEST) for your friendship. Thank you, Alex, Hilda, and Terrie (not to mention Sloane!), for looking after the furry ones while we're away.

Big appreciation to the actual Wednesday for supporting CLIC Sargent and letting me use your name. (Fingers crossed you like fictitious you!)

Thank you, Paula Mazur and Mitchell Kaplan, for believing in my books and me, and for all of your beautiful, sensitive understanding and genius.

The homefolks, back in Indiana—Elizabeth Bailey, one of my cherished second moms, for being there for my eighteen-year-old self when I needed to talk to someone. Thank you for protecting my secret all these years. Jim Resh and his staff at the Wayne County Convention & Tourism Bureau, for being tireless champions of my books and me. Joe Kraemer, for being my brother and best friend and partner in crime and general bad influence (but in the most good way). Saz is for you and Laura Lonigro, gone too soon but forever young in our hearts and so, so missed and loved. I raise a glass to you both from the steps of the Dayton Art Institute. *Our* art institute.

Thank you to my family for their unwavering love, humor, and support, including cousin–daughter–kindred spirit Annalise von Sprecken, sister-cousin Lisa von Sprecken, brother-cousin Derek Duval, my adoring and adored aunts, Lynn Duval Clark and Doris Knapp, my favorite niece, Grace Payne, and favorite sister-in-law, Jennifer Payne, and my uncle Bill Niven, beloved surrogate father, protector, friend, and cat whisperer. Thank you beyond words to my spectacular Ansley for getting me, heart and soul, for hamming it up on Instagram Live with me, and for spontaneous dance parties (Harry Styles and the Jonas Brothers forever!). And to my marvelous Ashton for being always the gentleman, teaching me things with great patience, and reminding me—frequently—to calm down. All the snugs and love in the world for you both.

I don't know what it would be like to write without cats walking across my keyboard or running away with office supplies or making sure I'm awake at three, four, or five a.m. Thankfully, I'm fortunate enough to have five very interactive literary kitties—Her Highness, Queen Lulu, of the computer keyboard and the early-morning awakenings; dear, perpetually befuddled, purr-factory Rumi; grateful, courageous Scout (with her giant polydactyl feet); the ever-maddening Linus "Shitbag" Niven Conway (whom I often wrote this book in spite of); and wide-eyed Luna, our "sweetly dim" (but oddly willful), bicoastal rescue fluff, who travels better than we do and is destined for movie stardom (consider this the start of my campaign for Luna as Dandelion in the movie version).

As I mentioned, this book is a personal one. Neither Claude nor I would be here without my parents, Penelope Niven and Jack Fain McJunkin Jr., who taught me I could be or do anything, who told me never to limit myself or my imagination, who gave me unconditional love, and who saw to it that, no matter what, I was encouraged and enabled to fulfill all my "Jenniferness." I have been missing my funny, gruff, marathon-running, cookie-stealing, gourmet-chef-in-his-spare-time dad for eighteen years, and my exceptional, sparkling, heart-calming, book-writing, soul-twin of a mom (best friend, mentor, Penny and Jennifer, Jennifer and Penny, the Niven women) for six, but I am surrounded by and filled with their extraordinary love. And every word I write comes from them.

This book is personal in another way. In 2018, I traveled to a remote Georgia island, laptop in hand, the idea for *Breathless* forming in my head. My first day there, I met my now-husband, Justin Conway—the real-life Jeremiah Crew—who swept me off my feet and into his truck. I'd gone there in search of this book and instead found a golden, bare-foot, age-appropriate flesh-and-blood version of the character I'd been envisioning for a year or more. This man who, on our first day together, learned my secrets and told me his. Who taught me to find shark teeth. Who brought me mud boots. Who showed me his island. Who carried me through a creek that became a river. Who drove me through the night by the light of the fireflies. *Him. Me. Me. Him. Us. Intertwined.* This book is for him. For our *muddy feet and locked basements and blood moons and all the things we said to each other when no one else was listening.* We just *knew* that first day. Six months later, we were married, and we've been continuing to write our love story every day since.

Last but not least, I need to thank my readers. Dear lovelies: none of this would be possible without you. I never lose sight of that, and I never will. I love you more than I can ever say.

Now.

Close the book.

But first—remember to open yourself up to love and possibility, to almostness and maybe.

Use your voice.

Let others in.

Choose your future. Choose your body. Choose yourself.

And go out there and write your life.

The story of a girl who learns to live
from a boy who wants to die.

Now a major Netflix movie starring Elle Fanning and Justice Smith.

'The next *The Fault in Our Stars* – this is it'
Guardian

Discover what it means to be seen
for who you truly are . . .

HOLDING
UP THE
UNIVERSE

New York Times
bestselling author of
ALL THE
BRIGHT PLACES

Jennifer Niven

'Gorgeously written and oh-so-deeply felt'
Nicola Yoon, author of *Everything, Everything*